LOVELY TORMENTOR

"Whose room is it?" Rosamund asked as Henry pushed the door shut with his foot.

Taking her in his arms, he leaned her back against the door, pressing against her. "This is the bridal chamber," he whispered before he kissed her fully on the lips.

Rosamund's gasp of surprise was silenced by his mouth.

He chuckled when he asked, "Do you suppose the devil will take my soul for sullying the marriage bed?" Then, without giving her time to reply, he swept her off her feet and bore her to the black-shadowed bed.

They fell together on a soft mound of feathers, rumpling velvet covers beneath them. The weight of his body drove the breath from her. Henry pinned her beneath him, feeling her strain to meet the iron-hard strength of his arousal.

"Now you see how hot I am for you—so hot I'm like to burst. Let's have an end to play. 'Tis you who are the wicked one to keep me so long unsatisfied. What answer you to that, lovely tormentor?"

THE ROSE OF RAVENSCRAG

PATRICIA PHILLIPS

LEISURE BOOKS **NEW YORK CITY**

A LEISURE BOOK®

February 1996

Published by

Dorchester Publishing Co., Inc.
276 Fifth Avenue
New York, NY 10001

Printed in the United States of America.

For my mother, Lily, who was also a North Country woman.

PART I

PART I

Chapter One

1459

Dusk fell early in December. A chill wind had risen, stirring dead leaves clinging to the beech limbs across the green. Rosamund stood on the sheep-bitten turf to watch the misty sunset. Orange and rose bled across the western sky; the distant hills were haloed in gold. Tomorrow would be a fine day.

"This is for you, Rosie." Shyly Steven held out his hand, opening his huge fist to reveal a sparkling blue-and-silver ribbon.

Rosamund gasped in surprise as she eagerly accepted the gift. " 'Tis very fine," she said, smoothing the satin surface. Her work-roughened fingers snagged the delicate fabric.

"For your hair," Steven said, clumsily patting the thick, nut-brown braid hanging down her back. A deep blush suffused his fair skin. He ducked his head, hiding his embarrassment beneath a shock of corn-colored hair.

His discomfort was apparent and Rosamund was anxious to escape. "Thank you. It's kind of you Steven. I'll wear it tomorrow to the goose fair. I must go. It's getting dark."

Still keeping his face averted, Steven said gruffly, "I want all the other lads to remember whose sweetheart you are."

"Good night, Steven." Rosamund patted his muscular arm, which was hard as rock beneath his homespun sleeve.

They turned away from each other at the same time, the blacksmith's son heading for the glowing forge, Rosamund for the cottage at the end of the village street. The farther Rosamund walked from Steven, the lighter her steps grew. Her reaction puzzled her as she put the ribbon inside the purse hanging from her waist. Why didn't she want to linger with Steven? He considered himself her sweetheart; he had spoken for her at the harvest festival. He would even have married her that day had she been willing. Fortunately the priest would not allow such a hasty union, thereby granting Rosamund the blessed space of time to grow accustomed to the idea. Most wenches were eager to marry. By Whitton standards, brawny Steven was an excellent catch. More than one wench had set her cap at him, but he only had eyes for beautiful Rosamund. He had become so besotted with her that his father had threatened to march him down to End Cottage to do the job if he did not speak for her soon.

Rosamund supposed even to have had a marriage proposal was flattering. The blacksmith's son was strong and pleasant to look at with his fair skin and thick, yellow hair. Someday he would inherit the forge and the means to provide a good income for his family. Then why did she hesitate to set the date? Steven had poured out his love for her, his bright blue eyes filled with tears. Surprised, Rosamund had listened fascinated as he revealed his love, even though she did not share his emotions. He had said that she was prettier than a spring lamb, fairer than a hawthorn flower. He had declared that he loved her more than life itself.

Steven's was the most heartfelt declaration of affection she had ever received. And she feared it might also be the only one. Since that crisp, autumn day, Steven had been stinting with his compliments, as if, once said, the words had no need of repeating.

" 'Ere you are, you good-for-nothin' wench. Out till dark with that rutting blacksmith's lad. Get inside and help your mam."

Hodge, her mother's young husband, was waiting for her at the cottage door, his heavy face set in a pugnacious scowl. Sidestepping him, Rosamund slipped under his outstretched arm and went inside the smoky cottage.

Rosamund's mother, Joan, was tending to two fretful infants

before the hearth, while scrawny seven-year-old Mary stirred a cauldron of stew hanging over the flames. Theirs was one of the few cottages without the old-fashioned central hearth. Joan was proud of her hooded fireplace, though the chimney drew so badly that their cottage was almost as smoky as those of their neighbors.

Pushing her scraggly, gray-tinged hair off her brow, Joan smiled. "There you be, chuck. We wondered where you got to." Her mother's thickened speech revealed the large quantity of ale she had already drunk. "Been out setting the date with Steven?" she asked as Rosamund came to the hearth to warm her hands. Nudging her daughter, Joan added with a bawdy leer, "A right fine one 'e be, girl. What're you waitin' for? They says you can allus tell the size of a man's cock by the size of 'is thumbs, and with them great hamhocks of fists—" Wheezing with laughter, Joan leaned over to lift her puny baby from its cradle.

"That's something I've not given much thought to, Ma."

"Well, then, can't be my daughter, can ye? Must be some changeling fairy child." Joan chuckled as she opened her bodice to suckle her daughter.

"I only met Steven when I was coming back from Gillot's. We was making plans for morning." Rosamund picked up the grubby toddler who scrabbled at her skirts. Without being asked, she began to spoon thick gruel into Tom's ever open mouth. "Gillot and her brother's comin' by at first light. The geese are that fat this year, Ma. We'll do right well at the fair."

"Thank the Blessed Mother for that. We need every groat we can get our 'ands on since—" Joan's voice wavered and her eyes filled with tears. The great tragedy of their days was no longer discussed, but it hovered like a gloomy presence in the background. "Great lords soon forget a girl once her looks fade. Remember that, Rosie, if you got ideas of following in me footsteps." Joan flicked the baby's cheek, trying to encourage it to nurse. "Times is hard these days."

"Maybe if Hodge shifted himself to find work," Rosamund

11

said, though Joan quickly shushed her, glancing toward the closed door to make sure they were still alone.

"You know 'e tries 'ard. Not much thatchin' to be 'ad this time of year."

Rosamund abandoned the subject. As usual Joan was going to defend her shiftless husband. Rosamund wondered why her mother clung to Hodge. He was the first man Joan had ever bothered to take before the priest; thus only her last two children were legitimate. Did she endure him because it was a feather in her cap to have snared a young husband at her age? No matter that Hodge lived off Joan's labors as a washerwoman, enjoying the hospitality of her bed, hearth, and board without contributing a farthing to the household.

Great lords. Rosamund's mouth curled as she considered her mother's words. Joan had always claimed Rosamund's father was a nobleman. It was so hard to imagine any nobleman fancying the raddled woman who leaned against the hearthstone, her grimy face bemused with drink. Yet folks said that, in days gone by, the golden-haired tanner's daughter had never wanted for suitors.

Rosamund shifted position on the wooden cricket, finding the drowsy toddler in her arms growing heavy. If the rumors were true, poverty and drink had stolen her mother's beauty. Could it really be true that Rosamund was the daughter of a nobleman? The young woman had always dismissed the tale as one of her mother's fantasies. Secretly, though, she wanted it to be true. In the past her hopes had been bolstered by two unexplained events. Every quarter day a reeve in a fur-trimmed cloak had brought a bag of coins to their cottage, and an anonymous benefactor had also paid for Rosamund to be schooled by the Sisters at Thorpe. For some unknown reason both benefactions stopped suddenly. The Sisters had sent Rosamund home to Whitton when her tuition at the convent fell into arrears. It was the loss of that income that had become the tragedy of their lives, the dark presence forever hovering in the background.

The door slammed, forcing Rosamund's thoughts back to

the present and the unwelcome sight of Hodge. The noise startled the infant, who began to wail, and Hodge snarled for the
baby girl to be quiet. Neither Rosamund nor her mother
thought it prudent to point out Hodge was the cause of the
disturbance.

Shoving young Mary away from the cauldron over the fire,
Hodge pulled the dipper out of the pot and blew on the stew,
spraying droplets of hot brown liquid.

" 'Ere, she be nodding off. Look lively," he snarled
through a mouthful of stew.

Joan's head was lolling against her chest and Rosamund
sprang forward to rescue the baby before it slid to the rushes.
After Rosamund had quietened Annie, she put the infant down
in the cradle beside the hearth.

Hodge watched Rosamund's movements, leering as his
lecherous gaze shifted from her full breasts to her trim waist
and curving hips. His brown piggy eyes burned with lust. A
chill sped along Rosamund's spine as she interpreted his
thoughts.

"Sit down. I'll get your supper," Rosamund said, aware
that food would create only a temporary distraction for Hodge.

Obediently Hodge sat beside the hearth, extending his blunt
hands to the blaze. Rosamund kept a wary eye on him while
she filled his deep wooden bowl with stew. Scorning the spoon
Rosamund handed to him, Hodge slurped stew from the bowl
like an animal. Rosamund marveled at his ability to down the
bubbling liquid without burning himself. She ladled out a
smaller bowl for Mary, who shyly thanked her sister before
wisely retreating to the corner to eat in peace.

Rosamund had also filled a bowl for her mother. Though
she shook Joan's soft shoulders and shouted down her ear, she
could not rouse her mother from her drunken stupor. Joan had
slid down the hearthstone until she finally sprawled on the
rushes. Rosamund drew a blanket over her mother's snoring
form, putting the sleeping Thomas next to Joan under the
cover. The same ritual was occurring almost nightly. Rosamund was becoming so resigned to the ritual that she no longer

felt the sinking dread in the pit of her stomach, nor did she cling to the vain hope that Joan would stay sober one night.

"She's not going to be much use to me tonight," Hodge said, smacking his thick lips as he eyed Rosamund speculatively. "Now, a sweet young piece like you would do me a treat."

When he grabbed her skirts, Rosamund smashed away his hand. "Her being asleep never stopped you afore," she snapped, unpleasantly reminded of the disgusting sights and sounds she had witnessed in their cottage.

"A man gets tired of suet pudding. Sometimes he fancies something with a bit more life to it."

Hodge ran his wet red tongue over his lips in anticipation and the sight made Rosamund shudder. Without warning he suddenly came up off the bench and grabbed her arms.

"Let me go!" Rosamund shrieked, kicking and punching him.

Mary shot forward to help her sister. The little girl pummeled Hodge's thick legs with her puny fists, shouting in anger.

"Get the hell away," he bellowed, his rough voice waking the baby, who began to scream.

"Go tend Annie!" Rosamund shouted to Mary above the racket, sending the child out of Hodge's range as he kicked and swung at her.

Hodge wrestled Rosamund about the room, the acrid stench of stale sweat wafting from his clothing. Finally, losing patience, Hodge slammed Rosamund against the wall, rattling her teeth. He pressed his noisome body against hers, pinning her helplessly against the wattle and daub.

"Enough of that, you bitch," he growled. "Reckon I've a sight more claim on you than yon blacksmith's lad, me being your stepdad and all."

"Don't you dare touch me," Rosamund said through gritted teeth, fighting to break his grasp.

"Why, is yon blacksmith's lad going to give me a thick ear?"

"He'll string your balls round your neck," Rosamund said as she carefully positioned her knee beneath her skirts.

Hodge guffawed at her suggestion. "Oh, I'm shaking with fright! What about that noble father of yourn? Joan says he'll cut me throat if I lay a hand on you. Never seed him round here. Must be an owd bugger by now."

Suddenly Hodge screamed in pain. His eyes bulged. Rosamund had smashed her knee into his groin. His hands fell from her arms. Then Hodge crumpled onto the rushes, his legs drawn up, his face flushing crimson. Swearing vilely, he began to retch before bolting outside to vomit in pain and shock.

"Hush, chicken. He's past hurting us tonight," Rosamund said when she saw Mary still sobbing in fear. She held Mary's hot, tear-streaked face against her breast. Although Rosamund felt great satisfaction, she knew her family would have to pay for her resistance. Still, that reckoning lay comfortingly in the future; life in Whitton had taught her to live solidly in the present. "Go to sleep, love. It'll be all right."

Mary sniffled loudly and hugged Rosamund tight. Obediently she scrambled under the covers on the straw pallet they shared. A few minutes later she was asleep.

Rosamund clasped her hands together to keep them from shaking. Hodge had never come closer to raping her. She forced herself to be calm as she pulled off her gown and hung it on a nail beside the shutters. Even though Hodge was still outside, habit made her draw closed the ragged curtain which afforded her only privacy.

The door opened and Rosamund stiffened. To her relief Hodge ignored her, going instead to the hearth, where he burrowed into the pallet he shared with Joan.

Assured he was settled for the night, Rosamund began to relax. Stretching beneath the homespun blanket, she wriggled around on the straw-filled pallet to find a comfortable position. At the convent she had slept on a real bed. The wood frame had had ropes slung across it to hold a mattress of feathers. How luxurious that bed had felt. Rosamund sighed at the memory. Maybe, after she married Steven, they could have a real bed with a down mattress.

Beside her Mary whimpered in her sleep and Rosamund placed a protective arm about the girl's skinny body. When Rosamund married Steven she would take little Mary to live with them.

The prospect of leaving the smoky cottage with its unpleasant memories was comforting. Though it was Rosamund's home, life there had not been happy. The two years she had spent at Thorpe had taught her that not all the world lived like the Whitton villagers. There, gentle voices, heavenly music and singing had surrounded her. And though Rosamund had not enjoyed the convent's strict lifestyle, she regretted the loss of that genteel and peaceful world. At Thorpe she had not been beaten, nor had she had to live with brawls or drunken carousing, rough-bellowed speech, or the stench of middens. Yet, in all honesty she had to admit there had not been much laughter, gaiety, or color either inside those gray walls.

Even in Whitton some lives were not as violent as those spent inside End Cottage. Rosamund's household would be influenced by Thorpe, not by her mother's household. Rosamund sighed. Life there could be colorless and very matter-of-fact. Whitton girls were not overly concerned with romantic love. She accepted that romance was reserved for dreams. If a peasant girl was lucky, she could marry a good man with a steady income, like Steven. The unlucky girls settled for a variation of Rosamund's stepfather. But she wanted to be in love. She wanted her heart to race and flutter at the sight of her beloved. Never had she felt any heady emotion for Steven. He was a good honest worker who said he loved her—no more than that.

Rosamund snuggled deeper under the covers. Then, as if she were opening a secret treasure chest, she began to remember her cherished dream life. At local fairs over the past few years, she had noticed a handsome stranger. Nay, not just noticed him. His appearance had riveted her. Oh, how her heart and her breath tangled when she glimpsed him in the crowd.

He was tall and broad-shouldered; his lithe athletic body was usually clad in Lincoln green. An idealized vision of his handsome face floated mistily before her. She saw a firm, generous mouth, a square, determined chin with a cleft, finely chiseled cheekbones, and an intelligent brow. Oh, he was like a god! No man who could compare with him had ever lived in Whitton.

The handsome stranger had been accompanied by a party of huntsmen clad in russet and green, though his own garments were of velvet. Rosamund could recall the way his dark hair curled above his embroidered collar, the crisp waves gleaming in the sun. Once he had turned around to watch her. When their eyes had met he had smiled at her, displaying even white teeth in his tan face. Most people of her acquaintance had discolored teeth and gaps in their gums. That man's appearance was so unlike what she was used to, she almost believed he had come from another world. Rosamund had long ago decided he was a great nobleman in disguise, possibly even a prince. On the other hand, he could be a romantic outlaw, like the legendary Robin of Sherwood.

When he smiled at her, Rosamund's heart fluttered so wildly she thought she would faint. She had not heard him speak. One of the other men called him Harry. Prince Harry, as she liked to think of him, figured prominently in her dreams. In one of her most satisfying fantasies, Rosamund imagined Harry riding up to the End Cottage to ask for her hand in marriage. Then she would ride away to his castle, mounted before him on a sleek milk-white charger. All the village would stand outside their huts gaping in awe at the magnificent spectacle.

Rosamund was well aware her fantasy was farfetched. Still, she enjoyed it. Such happiness did not come in real life, not to peasant girls. Despite her mother's favorite tale, Rosamund knew noblemen, or even finely dressed huntsmen, did not court girls from Whitton village. If such men had any discourse at all with a peasant girl, it was to casually lie with her behind a hedge. That was the truth. The comforting, yet ex-

17

citing, journeys she took with her dream lover were an escape. However much Rosamund dreamed of being loved by a handsome stranger, she was aware her reality lay in a future with Steven. Marriage to the local blacksmith was the best she could hope for. And if she had any sense, she would set a date for the wedding before he settled for someone else.

Long before dawn, Rosamund was awake and staring up at the rafters, where scuttling mice dislodged scraps of thatch that dropped on her face. The cottage was gloomy, lit only by the glow of the fire, which had been banked for the night. The mingled odors inside the shuttered room were so unpleasant that Rosamund wrinkled her nose and tried not to breathe too deeply.

She should get up and replace the baby's rags, clean Thomas, who had probably soiled himself in the night, and empty the slop pail. Those chores alone would vastly improve the fetid atmosphere. She generally began her mornings in such a manner, but not that day. She was going to the fair. Long before the others roused, she would be traveling the highway toward Appleton.

Energized by her plans for the day, Rosamund slid out from under the bedcovers and shivered in the cold room. Her breath formed a steamy cloud while she hastily pulled on a clean gown saved for that special occasion. She scooped her thick brown hair in a bunch and tied it with her new ribbon. She loved the ribbon merely because it was pretty, not because Steven have given it to her. That admission made her feel sad, because she longed to love and cherish in return. However hard she tried, she was emotionally unmoved by the young blacksmith, despite his declaration of love for her.

Rosamund gasped as she splashed her face with icy water from the pail. Then she vigorously toweled her skin dry with a coarse towel. There was only half a loaf of stale bread to eat; so she left it for the others. She had a few secret coins hidden under a loose board. The treasure would buy her a hot meat pasty or a sweetmeat at Appleton Fair.

Two dark mounds stirred before the glowing hearth as

Hodge and Joan snored and muttered in their sleep. Rosamund crossed the room stealthily and raised the door latch. The dark morning was frigid and she caught her breath, pulling her cloak tight around her. Quickly she shut the door, fearful of awakening Hodge. There was no bellow of rage following her and she knew she had escaped. Let Hodge beg or borrow his breakfast for a change, the way she usually had to. Hodge was more likely to steal a neighbor's eggs for his meal.

The steady clop of hooves came out of the thinning darkness. Geese cackled and a dog barked. Rosamund could see Gillot and Matt's cart. She stepped onto the beaten track as the horse slowed, snorting and tossing its shaggy head, its breath forming great smoking clouds.

"Hop aboard," Matt said, grinning down at Rosamund. His hood was pulled down about his face against the cold.

Willing hands helped haul Rosamund up to the wagon seat. She squeezed into place between Matt's hard body and Gillot's soft one. The old farm cart was loaded high with wooden crates of cackling fowl. Six of the geese, the speckled ducks, and a basket of eggs belonged to Rosamund. She had seen to their loading the evening before. The other fowl she had helped Gillot tend on the common. Two milk cows were tethered to the rear of the cart next to a sturdy donkey laden with panniers of goods for sale. Primitive carved animals, toy bows and arrows, goose quill pens, and pots of healing salve made from goose grease and primroses filled the bottom of the baskets. On top of those items were the knitted wool caps and mittens, baby dresses and embroidered shifts over which Rosamund and Gillot had labored diligently. The Christmas fair was the major district event of the dark winter season. Money earned at Appleton Fair helped many families through the long Yorkshire winter.

"Reckon we'll 'ave a tidy sum come evening," Gillot said, pleased by the thought. "How's you going to keep yours hid from Hodge?"

Rosamund shrugged. During the hours she had stitched and dreamed beside the hearth, she had given little thought to Hodge's demands for her earnings. To outwit him she could buy gifts for everyone. And she would eat to her heart's content. She could secretly pocket a few coins and give some to Joan. What was left she supposed she would have to turn over to Hodge.

"It's a shame—that's what it is—that lazy bastard taking what you make and 'im not turning a tap all year," Matt grumbled, clicking the plodding horse to quicken its pace.

"When you's married to Steven you won't need to sell things at the fair to get by," Gillot said, patting her friend's arm. "You'll be well away with him. They shoe the gentry's beasts now, so I've heard. When's you two getting married?"

"We haven't decided."

"Don't wait too long. 'Appen 'e might change 'is mind."

"That's what I'm waiting for. Then Rosie can marry me," Matt said, giving Rosamund a playful nudge. "I've already set me cap at her."

"Rosie wouldn't 'ave you on a wager, me lad," his sister said scornfully. "Our Rosie deserves better'n a farm hovel, her being nobility an' all."

Matt snorted in derision; then they all laughed. Rosamund's uncertain parentage had always been a topic of discussion. While not actually taken seriously, Joan's claim was not wholly dismissed either. Many villagers insisted Joan Havelock had come close to being set up by a great noble. Of course, the fact the great man never visited Joan, or had even acknowledged his supposed daughter, was a definite drawback to the romantic tale. But daily life in Whitton was so deadly dull, legends were an important part of village lore.

Darkness thinned and the first greenish glimmer of dawn showed in the east. Rosamund snuggled for warmth against her friends, her wool cloak drawn tight. The December air was sharp and frosty. As the day slowly lightened, she noticed frost gleaming on the rutted road and spangling spiderwebs adorning the hedgegrows.

Soon the voices of other fair goers could be heard as the trio caught up with the straggling crowd. The moos and baas of slaughter animals drifted to Rosamund and her friends over the hawthorn hedges while drovers shouted and whistled to their dogs. There was a steady clop of hooves and rumble of wagons coming out of the gloom ahead. The closer Rosamund and the others came to the fairground, the larger the crowd grew. Groups of cloaked figures heavily laden with baskets and bundles plodded along ahead, cloaks drawn tight, shoulders hunched against the cold.

"This way be too crowded," Matt grumbled, having to slow their pace to a crawl. "We'll not get to the fair before noon. Reckon we'd 'ave been better taking the top road."

"The top road—don't be daft," Gillot cried, tossing her head so that her hood slipped back to reveal a tangle of carroty locks framing her round face. "This cart'll never make it up the hill. Too much weight."

"Might 'elp some if you two was to get off and walk," Matt said, already turning Dobbin's head toward the approaching crossroads.

"Oh, come on. It's time we stretched our legs," Rosamund said.

Matt flashed her a grateful grin. He stopped the cart so Rosamund and his sister could slide down from the seat. The women discovered their limbs were stiff from sitting hunched in such close quarters on the hard wooden seat. Cold air rapidly penetrated Rosamund's threadbare cloak and she began to walk briskly along the narrow road, trying to stay warm. Gillot raced after her and they waved good-bye to Matt as he clopped away.

Some fair goers ahead were singing country rounds and the two women hurried to catch up with them. A sudden shout of warning made the travelers scatter to the sides of the road as a fast-moving party of horsemen appeared behind them. Almost forced into the ditch by the lightly armored men, Rosamund and Gillot stared in wonder at the horse's fine trappings. The soldiers must be headed for Appleton Fair. Though she craned her neck, hoping for a glimpse of the man in the Lincoln-green doublet, Rosamund was disappointed to find he

21

was not riding among the finely dressed party.

When they saw the young women, several passing riders whistled under their breath and the nearest soldier slowed his pace so he could lean from the saddle to talk to them.

"What's your name, sweetheart?" he asked Rosamund.

Without flinching she met his bold gaze. "None of your business, lad." She tossed her head disdainfully, bouncing her thick bunch of gleaming hair.

The man pulled back in surprise at her sharp reply. Slouching in the saddle, he gazed his fill of her creamy complexion and flashing, dark-lashed eyes. Slowly his gaze roved from her well-filled bodice, down to her trim waist, and over her curving hips. Finally he came back to her arresting, high-cheekboned face. Staring yearningly at her full, lush lips, which were as ripe as cherries, he couldn't keep his thoughts off his blunt Yorkshire face.

"Likely you be a princess hereabouts," he said at last. "The most beautiful in all the realm."

"Aye, likely I am," Rosamund said, tossing her head again and that time the movement brought some bright hair free from its confining ribbon. Not wanting to speak further with the man, Rosamund strode ahead, though he kept shouting to her to stop.

Gillot gasped as she finally caught up with her friend. They both pretended not to hear either the man's shouts or his comrades' comments and laughter. The hooves thumped behind them at a more leisurely pace. Then a man's voice bearing the definite ring of authority commanded them to stop.

Rosamund turned to find a cloaked figure on a black stallion rapidly bearing down on her. The great horse pawed the ground and its nostrils flared as the man reined in. Only a nobleman would possess such a spirited beast. Swallowing uneasily, Rosamund wondered what a richly dressed nobleman wanted with her—apart from the obvious. And if that were the case, how was she to resist his advances. The other peasants had stopped a small distance away, eagerly taking in the scene, their haste to reach the fair temporarily forgotten. None of them would come to Rosamund's aid if the man decided to take what she withheld.

Raising her gaze to his, and trying to ignore the nervous fluttering in her stomach, Rosamund faced the stranger boldly. "What do you want with me, sir?"

"Is there an apothecary or a wisewoman hereabouts?"

Shrewd dark eyes met hers. The man's beaked nose gave him a stern, predatory look; deep lines seamed his weathered face and his hard mouth was set in an embittered line.

"Aye, but they'll all be headed for the fair."

"What fair is that?"

"Appleton Fair."

The man leaned down and his mouth relaxed, his gaze softening as he looked more closely at her. Rosamund was surprised at his intake of breath and the gleam of recognition in his eyes. To her knowledge she had never seen the man before.

"Do you need a potion for yourself?" she asked curiously.

"Not I. My daughter. I'd hoped for something to cure her ills. How far to this fair?"

"Just over the hill. You can't miss all the tents and booths in the meadow beside the river."

"Appleton," the man said, studying Rosamund intently until she looked away. "That's near Whitton, is it not?"

"Yes, Whitton's where we're from—Gillot and me."

"Ah." He nodded and asked in a softer voice, "And what's your name, sweeting?"

"Rosamund, sir." She swallowed her unease. Did she imagine his gasp or the shock in his dark eyes before he swiftly hid the emotion beneath hooded lids?

"Thank you, pretty Rosamund, for all your help."

Abruptly the man straightend up and signaled his men to move forward. The party of horsemen surged along the lane, the force of their passage fluttering Rosamund's cloak.

Gillot squeezed her arm, her fingers digging in as she squealed in excitement. "Oh, Lord spare us! I thought he'd ravish you, Rosie, the way he was looking at you so close."

Rosamund smiled as she let out a sigh of relief. "Me too.

Did you ever see such a fine beast?''

"Which one: the man or the horse?''

"The horse, of course.''

"I thought he was splendid too. Did you see his gauntlets all embroidered in gold? And I swear his horse's trappings were gold. Oh, Rosie, maybe he's a prince and he'll give you a chest of gold for your help. That does happen,'' Gillot added indignantly as Rosamund cast a skeptical look at her.

"In a pig's eye. The only thing noblemen give girls like us is a bun in the oven, then a swift boot out the door for our pains.''

Gillot shook her head. "Oh, Rosamund, you haven't a romantic thought in your head.''

"It's just that life's taught me not to expect too much. Then I won't be disappointed.''

"What about that man in the green doublet you dream about?''

"Dreams and reality are two different things.''

They were mingling with the crowd spilling over the meadows. The muddy fields were rutted by farm carts and horses' hooves. As they walked, Rosamund smiled to herself. Gillot had always considered her to be a rock in the face of any calamity. She never revealed to her friend that, despite her brave face, she was frequently quaking inside. Gillot relied on Rosamund and she could not disillusion her friend. Like most village girls Gillot firmly believed in fairies and magic potions.

The Sisters at the convent had quickly dissuaded Rosamund from such fancies, branding them peasant superstition. Their enlightened teachings had showed her that all good came from God, all evil from the devil. Though Rosamund had little quarrel with their simplistic doctrine, the Bible stories the nuns told appeared to rely just as heavily on magic as any village fable. Only the religious name for that kind of magic was a miracle. Wisely Rosamund had kept her observations to herself, aware that had she voiced them she would have been made to atone for her sinful thoughts.

Just as the Sisters had worked to rid Rosamund of her childhood belief in magic, so had life with Hodge and Joan erased much of the romance she had formerly attached to the love between a man and woman. It was no wonder she sometimes felt far older than her years.

Rosamund thrust away her gloomy thoughts. At the fair, she intended to be wildly impractical. She had come to have fun. Like Gillot she would marvel at magic tricks, clap for the dancers and jugglers, maybe even have her fortune told. For those few brief hours she resolved to believe in all the fantasy and romance she otherwise eschewed.

The sheer noise of the fairground made Rosamund's head spin. Crowds of people milled about, all clad in their best clothing. Some people she recognized from the surrounding villages, but most were strangers. Brightly garbed musicians strolled amongst the crowd, while jugglers and tumblers gave impromptu performances wherever they thought a few coins might be forthcoming.

On the rows of wooden stalls were displayed all manner of enticing goods. Rosamund constantly had to fight the temptation to buy some bit of finery for herself. That would have to wait until she had purchased her gifts. If anything remained she could be frivolous.

The tantalizing aroma of tasty food was just too much temptation to overcome on an empty stomach. By noon Rosamund had already consumed two hot meat pasties, a spicy gingerbread angel, a slab of sweet, rose-scented paste, and two painted marchpane fruits. Though Gillot kept begging her to share her twisted honey sweet, Rosamund declined, knowing her stomach had indulged enough for one morning.

At noon Matt handed Rosamund a cup of ale and a hunk of bread and cheese with a handful of candied medlars for dessert. She ate her meal huddled over a glowing brazier behind their stall. At first the day's frosty chill had been eclipsed by the sheer excitement of the fair, but as the morning wore on, Rosamund was grateful for the chance to thaw her frozen fingers.

That year people seemed to have more money to spend than

in previous years. Though there were still many who merely looked, a respectable dent had been made in their merchandise. Rosamund patted the purse at her waist, just to make sure the money was still there. She was rewarded by the comforting clink of coins. All day she had been alert for cutpurses. Some were so skilled their victims were unaware a robbery had taken place until much later.

Appleton Fair was a two-day event. If Rosamund and her friends had enough left to sell they would return the next day. With housewives mindful of the upcoming Christmas festival, the fat, cackling geese were a popular item. They had only three ducks remaining and a half basket of eggs. Rosamund was pleased by her good fortune. Contentedly she stretched her hands to the blaze, enjoying the unaccustomed feeling of goodwill.

The noisy colorful crowd milled around the stall. Acrobats performed in the dirt before her, but with extreme willpower she kept a tight hold on her purse strings, though she felt the performers deserved a few coins for their skills. When Matt suggested he would handle the stall while the women looked about the fair, Gillot begged Rosamund to go with her to the fortune-teller's tent on the riverbank.

Inside the fortune-teller's musty tent the odor of sweat and garlic filled the air. The woman wore a gypsy's scarlet kerchief knotted about her gray hair and large gold rings glinted in her ears. Her shabby gown, with its gaudy tiers of purple and red, had knots of tarnished gilt ribbon dangling from the sleeves. Impatiently the woman waved her clawlike hand, motioning for the girls to sit on the bench beside a black cloth covered table.

A swarthy youth lounging against the tent pole swiftly assessed the attributes of their latest female customers. Smiling at Rosamund, he laughingly commented in some foreign tongue before the fortune-teller slapped at him and shooed him outside.

Rosamund was glad the man was gone. She had no need of magical skills to interpret his thoughts. Confidently she held out her hand for the old woman's reading. Gillot had already handed over their coins and the gypsy bit them before putting the money in her purse. Glittering black eyes met Rosamund's as the fortune-teller took her hand and studied her palm in the murky light.

"Ah, you'll have much luck in life . . . more good fortune than anyone I've seen . . . luck, riches aplenty . . . and pain."

Gillot squeaked in shocked surprise at her friend's fortune, but Rosamund said, "Everyone has some pain."

"Ah, trying to best me at my own game, are you, sly one?" the gypsy said. " 'Tis a quality that'll stand you in good stead. But be not too clever for your own good. Here I see a finely dressed man, very handsome and rich. It is through him your destiny will be fulfilled." The fortune-teller leaned forward, her dark eyes fixed on Rosamund's face. "You've already met he who's to shape your future. But I warn you: Your coming together will be full of obstacles."

Rosamund's heart thudded uncomfortably. The only rich man she had met was the man she'd encountered on the road that morning. Though she would not have called him handsome, he was not ill-favored. She pulled her hand from the woman's claw, shuddering. Suddenly she regretted having gone there. A man like that could have but one interest in her.

"Oh, Rosie! How exciting!" Gillot cried, her hazel eyes aglow. "Oh, come. Do mine." She thrust her plump hand under the gypsy's nose. Though the woman still watched Rosamund, she took Gillot's hand.

"Remember, girl. Fate can't be changed, however much you try." Her dark eyes hooded, she leaned forward. "Be on your guard against danger. There's much ahead. And always watch your back."

Their eyes met and Rosamund saw compassion there. The expression alone generated a great wave of unease. She did not want to hear another word; she had already heard more than enough.

As if the gypsy read Rosamund's mind, she turned her

whole attention on Gillot. "Now, my pretty, I see many fat children and a loving husband in your future. What more could a girl want?"

"Tell me when, oh, when!" Gillot said excitedly.

"You already know the lad, but you have to wait. Death has a hand in shaping your future. Besides, men are slow to know what they need rather than what they hanker for."

A young couple stepped inside the tent and the gypsy stood to greet them. But before Rosamund and Gillot could leave, the old woman grasped the edge of Rosamund's cloak and, her voice barely audible, said, "And you, girlie—you'll stand close to the Crown before you're done."

The gypsy's last startling prediction came as such a surprise Rosamund would have questioned her further had she been willing. But, despite Rosamund's presence, the gypsy began to read the young couple's palms. Finally Gillot pulled Rosamund outside into the weak December sunshine. Once they were out of the tent, Rosamund's mood lightened, as if a weight had been lifted from her shoulders.

"Riches and a handsome man—oh, Rosie, how lucky you are."

"Don't believe a word of it, Gillot. It's only a fairy tale." Her own words filled her with courage. She straightened her shoulders and took a deep breath of cold air, filled with the aroma of spice and burnt sugar. "Besides, how am I ever going to stand close to the Crown?"

Though her voice was full of bravado, she could not quell a growing unease whenever she thought about the startling prediction. Was her fate linked with that of the rich man she had met on the Appleton road?

"Maybe that man we saw this morning has something to do with your future," Gillot said. "How could the gypsy have known about him? You could be getting a chest of gold from him after all, Rosie. What can it all mean?"

"Nothing, silly goose. Fortune-tellers only say what they think you want to hear."

The Rose of Ravenscrag

"Then why'd she say I'd have a husband and children and not say that to you?"

"Maybe she thought I'd rather have riches and a lover. Remember what I keep telling you about magic."

Gillot pouted. "Those nuns don't know everything, Rosie."

"Let's just have fun. Don't spoil things by worrying over something that'll never happen."

As they walked back to their stall, Rosamund was aware of the admiring glances she got from passing men. The bolder ones even caught at her sleeve, trying to make her stop to talk to them.

Gillot could hardly wait to tell her brother about Rosamund's magnificent fortune. To Rosamund's dismay, Matt was greatly impressed. He said he knew Rosamund's destiny was not to live out her life in Whitton. Had he dismissed the tale as nonsense she would have felt far happier. Ever mindful of the fortune-teller's warning of danger, Gillot bought her friend a plaited corn token, putting it on a ribbon about Rosamund's neck to keep her from harm.

As the chilly afternoon wore on, Rosamund watched the passing throng for the man in the green doublet. To her disappointment there was no sign of him. This was the first fair in years he had not attended. Had he gone from the district or been wounded in a far-off battle? Her heart plunged at the thought. No, nothing so dire had befallen him. After all he was her dream hero and therefore immune to ill fortune.

Rosamund had no lack of admirers, some well dressed, others village lads. She readily exchanged banter with them, enjoying their compliments, but her head and heart remained firmly in place. The village lads gave her gifts of ribbons or flowers in exchange for some attention. Those lads declined to flirt with her, though their gifts were bold. They were ever mindful of Steven's prior claim. Their restraint suited Rosamund well, though she resented becoming the blacksmith's chattel even before the banns had been called.

The December afternoon drew in; heavy clouds banked the sky and the wind blew sharp from the north. By four the wan sun had finally slipped from view behind the building gray cloud.

Many stall holders were packing up their wares and preparing to go home. Peddlers, fortune-tellers, and jugglers were still going strong, the approaching night having little effect on their livelihood. By night Appleton Fair took on a more sinister appearance, and that subtle change sent many respectable people home at dusk. Some fair goers and stall holders pitched camp at the edge of the fairgrounds. Because Gillot and Matt's invalid mother depended on them, they would return to Whitton and come back in the morning.

Noisy, painted women were already emerging from the shadows along the riverbank, calling out to passing men, advertising their charms in graphic ways. Where the willows swept low to the water they found cover for their trade. Rosamund stared in fascination yet at the same time she was repelled by the rouged and gaudily dressed whores. The village priest said those women would burn in the fires of hell for their sins. Yet some in the village said the priest waxed holy out of guilt because he wasn't beyond patronizing the local whores himself.

Though Rosamund was tired, she was not eager to go home to End Cottage. When she got back she knew there would be a scene with Hodge. He would be furious to find she had squandered his ale money on gifts for the others. She had bought a length of wool for a new winter gown for Joan. There was linsey to make clothes for the children, along with some sweetmeats and a ribbon for Mary's hair. Hodge would probably not begrudge the money spent on the ham and cheese in the bottom of her basket. He would insist on the lion's share of those luxuries. Had he known, he would definitely begrudge her the coins she had hidden about her person, intending to share some of the money with her mother. Not entirely selfless, Rosamund had bought herself a violet girdle embroidered with green leaves. It was the loveliest silk girdle she had ever seen and she intended to wear it every Sunday to Mass. She suspected the girdle had been stolen. The peddler had been most anxious to sell the garment, accepting a lower price than it was worth in order to make the sale. Still, the girdle was hers, paid for with her hard-earned money.

The journey home seemed endless. The cart rattled along the rutted roads, an icy wind finding every chink in Rosamund's wool clothing. She kept thinking about the fortune-teller's prediction and she drifted asleep still puzzling over her proximity to the Crown.

A glint of light still showed through the shutters at End Cottage when the cart stopped outside. Matt had shaken Rosamund awake down the road so she could prepare her basket and distribute her wealth. At the last minute, she took several coins out of hiding and put them back in her purse, hoping they would blunt Hodge's anger.

Chapter Two

"You thievin' little bitch! Where's the rest of it?" Hodge grabbed at Rosamund's hair and swung her about.

Tears stung her eyes and she thought her hair would come out by the roots. "I spent the rest. We're to go back tomorrow. I'll get more money then."

"There'd better be more to show for it than this, or you'll be sorry," Hodge snarled, his fleshy lower lip thrust forward. Then his wet red lips slackened into a hungry leer. "You could make up for it, girl," he said, his grip relaxing until she pulled free. " 'Appen you know how."

Rosamund gave no reply. She merely stared sullenly at him, waiting for the painful chastisement to stop.

Joan sat placidly with the children before the hearth, viewing the scene with a slack-mouthed smile. She had already been heavily at the ale jug. Joan had thanked her daughter for the unexpected gifts, surprised by her thoughtfulness. Though Joan loved Rosamund in her fashion, she didn't like the tension the girl caused between Hodge and her. The sooner Rosie were married, the better, as far as Joan was concerned.

"She done 'er best, Hodge. Let be. She brung us this fine ham and the cheese is a rare treat," Joan said, finally gathering her wits in an effort to soothe Hodge's temper. "Come on now. Eat your supper, love, and let the girl be."

Hodge considered the tempting offer. "Right. I could use a bite to eat. Reckon I'll let you go this time."

The family called a truce as they sat down to eat their supper. The ham was a rare treat, pink, juicy, and bursting with flavor; the pungent yellow cheese was a delicious side dish.

A small pot of mustard was kept for such special occasions. Rosamund spread it sparingly on chunks of bread and put thin slices of ham and cheese between them for the children. Mary's eyes shone with delight at the luxury. Her sweetmeat of almond and rosewater paste was a delicious conclusion to the feast.

When everyone had eaten his fill Rosamund put what was left in a wood chest out of the reach of the rats. She was aware Hodge watched her movements as she readied the children for bed. The baby was already asleep at her mother's breast, so Rosamund covered Joan and Annie with a blanket. Then she mended the fire and cleared away the used utensils.

"That were a right good meal, girl," Hodge said grudgingly.

Rosamund smiled in surprise. That remark was the only kindness she could remember him saying to her.

"There's eggs to gather," Hodge said when Rosamund appeared to have finished for the night. "Our Joan was out washing most of the day, so she didn't get 'em."

Rosamund exercised great restraint not to remind her stepfather that he could have collected the eggs himself. It was cold and pitch-dark outside, but she was not afraid of the dark. She pulled on her cloak and took the lantern with the stub of candle still burning inside.

"Heh, taking me light," Hodge said as Rosamund moved to the door.

"The fire gives enough light. I won't be long."

The girl gasped as the cold wind slapped her in the face when she rounded the corner. Her mouth set in determination, she wrapped her cloak tight and left the shelter of the building, heading for the ramshackle henhouse. The birds had not been laying lately and she was surprised that Hodge expected eggs.

Rosamund opened the coop door, which swang crazily on a broken hinge. When she shone the lantern inside, moving the light across the straw-filled nests, she was surprised to see three speckled eggs. Rosamund put the eggs in her basket;

then setting down the lantern, she made the warped door fast behind her.

As she stepped away from the henhouse Rosamund cried out in shock as she collided with a hard object. To her horror she discovered she had walked into Hodge's outstretched arms. He chuckled in glee at his cleverness in capturing her. When she tried to pull back he held her tight.

"No need to be afeared. It's only me."

"That's why I'm afraid. Let me go."

"Not so fast." He chuckled again, enjoying her fright.

At such close quarters Rosamund could smell strong ale on her stepfather's breath. He had probably downed another tankard to bolster his courage.

"Now's the time to settle yer debts, Rosie. I said I'd forgive you if you was nice to me."

When he pressed his slack, wet mouth against hers, bile came to her throat. Rosamund shoved Hodge hard, rocking him back on his heels. But he did not let go.

"It's cold out here. Let's go inside." Rosamund tried to push past him.

"Naw, lass, not so fast. I'm that hot fer you. 'Ere, feel this."

He pressed Rosamund's palm against his swollen crotch, where she felt the hardness leap beneath her touch. The unwanted intimate contact turned her stomach and she snatched her hand away. Distracted by lust, Hodge did nothing to stop her. Rosamund pushed as hard as she could and he fell backward.

Freed from her captor, Rosamund raced over the uneven ground, tripping over rocks and turning her ankle in grassy hollows. But she dared not stop. She must get as far from the cottage as possible. There was no safety there. Joan would be unconscious by then. With only young Mary to lend assistance Rosamund would have no chance of outwitting her stepfather.

Hodge's bellow of rage came out of the darkness, too close for comfort. Rosamund flung down the lantern since its bobbing light betrayed her movements. Without the light the night looked blacker than ever. She could still hear Hodge's heavy breathing behind her. No one came out of the nearby cottages to find out what the commotion was about, though glints of light still glimmered between shutters along the street. Rosamund doubted any of the villagers would help her. More likely they would join Hodge in the pursuit of his wayward step-daughter.

A sharp pain stabbed Rosamund's side and she knew she had to rest. Goody Clarke's orchard lay beside the road, Rosamund's best chance for escape lay there. After scaling the rock wall, she slipped down the other side and darted into the cover of trees. The apple orchard stretched nearly to the Pontefract Road. Belatedly Rosamund also remembered that Goody Clark kept a large mastiff to discourage thieves. Fortunately December trees were bare, giving the watchdog nothing to guard. If she were lucky the dog would be asleep in its kennel on that frosty winter night.

Rosamund crouched at the foot of a large tree where a shielding branch hung low to the ground. The bare trees offered little cover. She had to hope that, in his befuddled state, Hodge would find the orderly rows of trees confusing. She had heard him scramble over the wall, stumbling and cursing as he walked into trees. Hardly daring to breath, Rosamund lay still; wrapped in her dark cloak, she huddled against the tree trunk.

Hodge had started shouting her name as his temper grew short. In the distance a dog barked; the sound rumbled deeply through the night. Hodge fell silent upon hearing the watchdog. Rosamund's stomach lurched and heart pounded when she realized she might indeed have to contend with the threat of the dog. Preparing to fend off an onslaught of ripping teeth and muscular body, she waited with her cloak wrapped protectively about her face and arms.

Time passed. No slavering beast approached, nor were there any further sounds from Hodge. Gradually Rosamund relaxed and uncoiled her aching legs beneath her heavy wool skirt.

She closed her eyes as she waited, and soon she was using the rough tree bark as a pillow.

Sir Ismay de Gere stretched his slippered feet to the blaze, glad of the welcoming fire. The low-ceilinged inn room was plain, but the bed was clean and there were fresh rushes on the floor. What was more, the place had palatable food and decent wine. He had been pleasantly surprised to find that the thatched Drover's Arms offered more than the sour ale, hard bread, and flea-infested straw he had expected.

A yawn escaped, then another. He had resolved to stay awake until the servingwoman delivered her final report for the night about his daughter's condition. But sitting there before the blazing hearth was making his resolve hard to keep.

His mind kept straying to that morning when he had seen the wench on the highway. His heart still soared when he pictured her beautiful face. He would have known that face anywhere. True, she also had a look of her mother about her, but that other likeness could not be mistaken. Thick, glossy nut-brown hair, big, dark-lashed hazel eyes flecked with green and gold, perfect complexion, and fine bone structure—the wench was the spitting image of Lady Rosamund Langley, who in her day was a renowned beauty. And while Sir Ismay's mother's chest had been flat and her long limbs excessively slender, the peasant girl, Joan, had done her part to improve upon the original.

Each time he thought about the wench, Sir Ismay smiled. What a waste to hide such a woman in Whitton. The place hadn't changed in 20 years. Had she been at court, the wench would have been the toast of kings and princes. As it was, she would likely marry some crude swineherd and birth a passel of runny-nosed brats. Unless. . . . Sir Ismay stroked his chin. Mayhap he would take a hand in shaping her future. There had been a time when he had plans for the girl. . . .

He was so deep in thought he did not at first hear the tap on the door. When the woman rapped harder, he sat up and gruffly bade her enter. The servingwoman curtsied to him, envying him his blazing hearth.

"Well, woman, any news?" Sir Ismay snapped, not bothering to look at the woman's tired face. Had he done so, he would not have asked the question. Her flesh sagged with weariness and defeat dulled her dark eyes.

"If you mean good news, master, the answer's no."

"And bad news?"

"We've got that aplenty."

Startled by her reply, he jumped to his feet. "Well, tell me. Don't keep me guessing."

"My lady's fever burns hotter than August. The wisewoman's potions won't budge it. I've sponged till me arms ache. The room's cold as a tomb, yet she's still afire."

"I'll come. Is the wisewoman still here?"

Having had little time or interest to consider the wisewoman's whereabouts, the servingwoman shrugged. "Don't matter. She said she can't do no more for her."

Sir Ismay reached for his furred bedgown and struggled into the quilted sleeves, pulling the garment closed as he strode toward the door. His seamed face was exceedingly grim.

Down the narrow passage they went, feeling their way along the paneled wall. The light from a sconce at the far end cast giant shadows over the ceiling as they hurried toward the sick room. There were several men-at-arms guarding Sir Ismay's door and they snapped to attention when they saw their lord. Usually Sir Ismay would have had a pleasant greeting for them, but that night his mind was on the news of his daughter's worsening condition. Her decline could not be happening! It was vital that she got better . . . and soon.

He thrust open the door of the room at the end of the passage. The cold air engulfed him as he entered. Two weeping women jumped to their feet and, backing away, dropped a swift curtsy before leaving the room.

When Sir Ismay looked down at the young woman lying on the narrow bed, his heart sank. Her sharp face was the color of wax, paler than the homespun pillow on which she lay. Yet her cheeks blazed red with heat. He put his hand to her forehead and drew back, alarmed by the fire in her flesh.

"Sweeting," he whispered, making his gruff voice gentle as he knelt beside the bed, aware of the rushes spiking his knees. "Can you hear me, sweet?"

The girl moaned and turned toward him, muttering something unintelligible. It was a few minutes before he realized she spoke in French. He could make little sense out of her words. Delirious, he conceded grimly. Delirious, burning with fever, possibly even dying!

That chilling thought rocked him back on his heels. No, she could not die! He wouldn't let that happen! Not his only daughter. And please, God, not when he had brought her from France for the marriage that would help cement his rocky position in the warlike north. The alliance would bring him needed support, many skilled fighting men, wealth, and a son-in-law most men only dreamed about. Powerful Henry of Ravenscrag was the answer to his prayers: A mighty Northern lord of vast influence, he was allied to the Percies, the uncrowned kings of the north. Sir Ismay couldn't let all that slip away.

The lord picked up a sodden cloth lying on the table beside the bed and he pressed it on his daughter's fevered brow. Then he snarled at the servingwoman to bring fresh water. Obediently she left the room.

How old he felt. He was aware of a deep weariness in his heart and limbs. Cold reality punctured his ambition, which felt like a deflated pig's bladder. He knew that without the marriage between Henry and his daughter he would slowly lose his hold over all he cherished. Without the pampered girl, there would be no alliance with Ravenscrag, no hope for the future. Ismay De Gere laid his head on the coverlet and prayed to God not to take his daughter from him. Never familiar with the workings of the Lord, he hoped the heartfelt fervor of his prayers made up for his past lapses.

Could God be so cruel as to punish Sir Ismay when everything lay just within his reach? He had finally brought the girl—who'd been carefully nurtured in France until the proper time—home to England only to have her fall ill. Ravenscrag

was primed to accept Sir Ismay's heiress without question,
aware of the wisdom of allying himself to the old house of
De Gere. He had not even quibbled over the haste with which
the nuptials had been arranged. The wedding preparations continued even at that moment, designed to be part of the castle's
famous Christmas revels. A special dispensation had been
granted Ravenscrag during the Penetential Advent season. The
wedding must take place.

Finally Sir Ismay sighed and raised his head, toying with
the idea of possibly dressing his daughter in her wedding finery and hastening the ceremony. She need only rally for a day.
Yet Henry of Ravenscrag was no fool, Sir Ismay acknowledged gloomily. He wanted to do nothing to make Ravenscrag
examine the situation more carefully. Ravenscrag might then
discover the fiefdom his bride would inherit was burdened
with debt. And he was bound to demand the wedding night
with her. It was his due. There was no way Sir Ismay could
pass off the sickly girl who thrashed and sweated in the flickering candlelight as a shy, convent-reared bride. No power on
earth could disguise the truth. She was sick unto death.

A sudden ominous thought made Sir Ismay step back from
the bed. What if the girl had brought plague with her across
the Channel? Of course, none of her women ailed beyond the
usual seasickness. At first he had thought she suffered from
the same affliction, merely as a result of a choppy crossing.
Would that it had been so. Only on closer scrutiny did he
notice her unusual pallor and the sticklike thinness of her
limbs. When he had heard her cough, his heart sank and he
realized that the twin spots blazing on her cheeks were not the
sign of bursting health, but the troubling stains of serious illness.

The servingwoman returned and he stood aside whilst she
wrung out the cloth in icy water and laid it on the girl's brow.

Was it wishful thinking or did the girl seem at ease? Had
her flailing stopped? Again Sir Ismay's hopes began to mount.
He had never expected such a swift answer to his prayers.
Mayhap the fever had broken.

"She seems eased," he said gruffly, but the woman only shrugged. "Let me know if there's any change, regardless of the hour."

"Yes, master. Are we still to travel tomorrow?"

"God willing."

Cheered by his daughter's apparent turn for the better, Sir Ismay found a kind word for the yawning guards outside his door. When he entered his bedchamber the room seemed brighter and more welcoming. All might proceed as planned after all. Mayhap the girl had survived the crisis and was on the other side. Muttering a prayer for her deliverance, he threw aside his bedrobe and climbed into bed. There was no need to wake Tim to attend him. The lad had already prepared his master for bed. Sir Ismay was not helpless like some nobles of whom he had heard tell who could not even turn back their own bedcovers. Sir Ismay had always prided himself on his self-reliance.

Soon, however, that self-reliance was to be put to a severe test. In the middle of the night, when the inn lay quiet, all guests sleeping peacefully in their beds, there came a sharp rap on his door. Since he was sleeping lightly, despite the comfortable bed and his own weariness, Sir Ismay was awake at once.

"Come in," he said, aware that whoever disturbed him must have just reason. He dealt severely with fools.

Hartley, his trusted captain, stepped inside the room, the weary servingwoman in tow. "Sorry to wake you, my lord, but Sarah has news for thee."

Sir Ismay's heart plunged like a stone. "News," he said, reaching for his bedgown as he pushed back the covers.

"Aye, my lord. It seems the lass . . . is gone," Hartley said in a calm and reverent voice.

"Gone?" Sir Ismay asked, repeating the word like an idiot.

"Oh, master, there were nowt I could do for 'er. She just slipped away," the weeping woman said. "I come as soon as I was sure."

The captain and the servant stood respectfully silent while their master grappled with the awful truth. Sir Ismay was aware

40

of the crackling fire and the thump of his own heart. It even seemed he could hear his own blood pumping in his veins. A wave of mingled shock, pain, and thwarted ambition washed over him. Suddenly finding his legs grown weak, he reached for a chair. Hartley quickly thrust the bench beneath his master, even taking the liberty of patting his shoulder in comfort.

"Who else knows?" Sir Ismay asked after a long silence.

"No one besides us, my lord."

"Keep it that way. I've got to think . . . what to do now."

"Aye, lord." Hartley stood dutifully silent and he pinched the woman's soft arm when she started to speak. "Shall we leave you alone?"

Sir Ismay nodded, then as an afterthought, he added, "Keep her under guard until further orders. And tell no one about this. Do you understand?"

"You can trust me—us," Hartley said, fixing the whimpering woman with a stern look. "We'll wait for your orders."

Sir Ismay hardly noticed when they left. For a long time he sat, his head in his hands. He went back and forth over the devastating news. There was no hope of her rallying, no chance to hoodwink Ravenscrag. All was lost: Sir Ismay's family name, his estate, his castle—all were on a final descent into a morass of shame and debt.

Sir Ismay clenched his fist and glared up at the ceiling, railing at God for dealing him such a cruel blow. "You took away my daughter! What good was she to you, God—a puny, whey-faced girl like that? Did you snatch my only daughter away just to spite me?"

His head in his hands, he quailed slightly as he reviewed his outcry, then cast away the fear. The threat of divine punishment no longer scared him. God had already dealt a death-blow. Like a house of cards the house of De Gere would fall because its very existence had hinged on the marriage between Sir Ismay's heiress and the mighty Ravenscrag.

The fire sputtered and again Sir Ismay became aware of blood thundering in his temples as he sat there trying to adjust to the hateful mantle of failure. Hadn't God punished him

41

Patricia Phillips

enough by denying him sons? All the male babes his wife had
given birth to had died within hours of their deliveries. One
child alone had survived—that girl, his firstborn. . . .

Sir Ismay's head snapped up. That statement was not strictly
true. His firstborn had been conceived in a dew-wet ditch one
fine spring morning. He had glimpsed heaven in the plump
arms of the tanner's daughter, whose curving body was afire
with passion. That episode stayed in his memory, forever be-
jeweled with dew and washed by soft golden light. The tanner's daughter had been the love of his youth—that was before
he had gone to France and his senses were dulled by death
and battle. Life had moved on. Gone were his youth and the
shapely tanner's daughter with the golden hair. Yet there ex-
isted a lasting memento from that magical time.

Sitting bolt upright, Sir Ismay felt a little of the De Gere
pride returning. Weakness and despair had made him grovel
to a god who had rarely walked by his side. Resilience and
self-reliance had been the hallmarks of the nobleman's life.
Once again those virtues would triumph.

He had hope, slender to be sure, but strong enough to make
his blood quicken and his heart thud with excitement. God had
not robbed him of his only child after all. There was still that
wench he had met on the Appleton Road.

Sir Ismay went to the door and beckoned to Hartley, who
was waiting in the shadows. The inn was quiet. The stillness
of the night would serve his purpose well.

"Tell the men to prepare for travel. I want the wagons ready
also, just as if nothing were amiss. You, woman, stay out
there." Sir Ismay motioned for one of his men to guard her.
"Hartley, you come inside with me. Do you know the Appleton Road?"

Hartley nodded, waiting for the new plan to unfold.

"This task is to be carried out in the utmost secrecy," Sir
Ismay said, his voice low. "Our very existence could depend
on it."

"Whatever you say, my lord."

"Sit down and listen well."

42

Chapter Three

Rosamund ran along the road before she finally slowed to a walk. When she had woken that morning she had been relieved to find herself unharmed and sitting in Goody Clarke's apple orchard. She smiled as she considered the small miracle that had allowed her to go through the night unscathed. Hodge must have given up his pursuit in fear of the watchdog. She knew she would have the devil to pay for eluding him. If only Joan would take her side, things would not seem as hopeless. But Joan preferred to hide behind a tankard of Whitton brew rather than believe her daughter.

Overhead the sky was still black. In December the sun did not shine until late in the morning, if at all. The road was empty. Rosamund did not know if Matt and Gillot had already gone by on their way to the fair or if it was too early for them. If the later was true, they would eventually pass her on the road. Already in the distance she could hear voices. A group of peddlers came onto the road out of the nearby woods. Once again the silence of the winter morn enveloped her as the peddlers disappeared around the bend.

For the next few miles Rosamund walked in silence, her ears straining for the comforting clop of Dobbin's hooves and the creak of the farm cart. It looked as if she might have to walk all the way to Appleton Fair. When the sound of hoof-beats came behind Rosamund in the darkness, she moved to the edge of the road to let a mounted party pass. Though light had begun to glimmer in the sky, she was wary of being ridden down in the gloom. As the horsemen drew closer, the thud of many hooves warned her that a sizable party approached.

Rosamund glanced back along the road and, her eyes already accustomed to the murky light, saw that the soldiers were bearing down on her.

"Ho, there. You, girl, stop."

Rosamund started to run, but realizing the futility of her actions, she stopped. Her heart thumped in fear. Now what? She was acutely aware of the loneliness of that stretch of road, and there was no place to run or hide since the banks of the sunken road were a tangle of thorn and bramble. To add to Rosamund's distress, the peddlers were too far ahead to come to her aid.

The lead rider, a captain, maneuvered his mount about to bar the girl's way. Two other men joined him, one man holding a lantern so that the flickering light shone on her face. After conferring amongst themselves, their leader asked if she was Rosamund from Whitton village.

"Yes," she said.

"Bound for Appleton Fair?" the captain said.

Rosamund nodded, growing more wary. The man had a Yorkshire accent, which meant he was probably from the area, though she had never seen those riders at the fair. The leader swung from his saddle and stepped purposely toward her. As Rosamund backed away from him, her feet slid into the ditch at the edge of the road, where she stood ankle deep in cold water.

"No need to be afraid of me, wench. I mean you no harm," the captain said, grinning. He took her hands and heaved her back on the road. "You're to come with us."

"No."

"You've no choice," he snarled, his humor souring. "My master sent me to fetch you."

"Who is your master and what does he want with me?"

"That's not for me to say. Now come on. Time's wasting. Come quietly or otherwise—it's all the same to me."

"No!" Rosamund cried again.

Finally losing patience, the leader grabbed the girl's arms and another man came to his assistance. They soon had her off her feet and slung across a saddlebow like a sack of flour. Shouting and fighting to sit upright, Rosamund made her captor's life a misery until he yanked her up before him, swiftly binding her arms against her sides. He warned her that if she didn't shut her mouth he would gag her as well.

As Rosamund bounced in the saddle through the lightening December morn, she tried to calm her fears sufficiently to concoct a plan for her escape. At first she even pleaded with some passing peasants to rescue her. But then the man cracked her across the mouth to remind her of the wisdom of silence. For a while, Rosamund hoped that she would pass Matt and Gillot on the road. She abandoned that idea, however, as the riders changed direction at the crossroads and headed for Hutton. At Hutton village cross the riders turned to the right until they entered a cobbled innyard, where several loaded wagons stood ready for a journey.

With pounding heart, Rosamund sat bound astride the horse, resenting the soldier's large hand clamped bruisingly over her mouth. She had heard tales of women kidnapped and taken to stews in the city, where they were enslaved in a life of prostitution. Horrible pictures of such a fate flitted across her mind as she waited for the men to finish debating amongst themselves about what to do next. She took comfort in the fact that the men did not look like criminals. Their horses' trappings and their own liveries were rich; so she assumed them to be in the employ of a great lord. Even the insignia on an unfurled banner looked familiar: a leopard rampant. She looked at the glittering gold thread as the banner sluggishly unfurled in the light wind. Then her heart lurched as she realized why the insignia seemed familiar. The rich man she had seen the day before on the Appleton Road had had the same gold insignia embroidered on his saddlecloth!

She made the connection with a sinking heart. She needed no longer question what business these soldiers' master had with her. She needed only to recall the admiration in his face to guess. Though when she recalled his expression, she remembered one of pleasure without lust. Abruptly Rosamund's musings were interrupted as she was dragged from the saddle and untied.

"Now, you, keep yer trap shut and I'll let you walk like a free woman," the captain said.

Though she wanted to hit him, Rosamund wisely cooperated, aware of the soldier's superior strength. Besides, she knew he was following his master's orders. With her head held high, Rosamund followed the men inside the inn. The captain walked in front of her, with a man on either side of her and one bringing up the rear. The other soldiers stayed talking and drinking ale in the gloomy innyard as the winter morning light finally broke through the clouds and a wan sun struggled into view.

Up several flights of stairs and along a narrow passage, she was marched before they stopped in front of a closed door. Their master's bedchamber, no doubt, Rosamund concluded. Her assumption proved correct when the door swung open to reveal a chamber filled with a huge bed. Rosamund stepped inside the candlelit room, trying not to show her fear. Just as she expected, the man she had met on the road stood at the window. He was dressed for travel, his dark cloak slung across a bench. When he turned to greet her, his smile was welcoming.

"Here she is, my lord, the girl named Rosamund," the captain said.

"Yes, she's the right one, Hartley."

The captain sighed with relief. "There weren't that many wenches abroad this early; so it weren't too hard to find her," he said, making light of his task. However, despite the cold day, he wiped sweat from his brow. He alone amongst the soldiers knew how important their quest had been.

"Thank you, Hartley. You can leave us alone now."

"Right, my lord. I'll be outside if you need me."

Rosamund waited as the captain shut the door behind him. She could hear his heavy tread retreating down the passage as she formulated what she was going to say to his lordship.

"You look worried, wench. I assure you there's no need. I

know being taken prisoner was frightening and I apologize for the need to alarm you. There was no other way I could get you here before we left. I'd intended to ask your mother's permission, but you'd already left for the fair.''

His explanation sounded sincere and Rosamund relaxed slightly. Her anger dissipated somewhat. But despite his soothing voice and ingratiating smile, she doubted he could give her a good excuse for capturing her, however hard he tried.

"Tell me why you brought me here," Rosamund said.

"Not for the purpose you suspect. Now, are you disappointed, wench?"

"I'm no loose woman. I'm virtuous," she declared angrily, trying to muster her courage.

"That's admirable and much to your benefit." He stepped closer and Rosamund took a step backward. He smiled in amusement at her defensive move. "I have no designs on your virtue. Not that I'm a monk—far from it. But in this instance you're safe. Do you know who I am?"

When Rosamund shook her head, he said "I am Sir Ismay De Gere, Lord of Langley Hutton."

"What does the Lord of Langley Hutton want with me? I'm just a washerwoman's daughter."

"Nay, you're far more important than that." He held a candle aloft to better see her face. "Rosamund. I've a daughter named Rosamund also, named for her grandmother, Rosamund of Langley."

The girl's face brightened at the mention of that revered lady. "The benefactress of Thorpe. The Sisters told me I was named for a great lady."

Sir Ismay nodded and he took her thick braid in his hand and fingered her smooth hair.

"You still haven't said why you brought me here," Rosamund said sharply, drawing away from his caress.

After some thought Sir Ismay asked, "How would you like to be maid to my daughter?" Then he went to the window and, keeping his back to her, added, "You'll want for nothing. Life in a castle—what do you say?"

Rosamund's thoughts were in a whirl. So excited did his unexpected offer make her that she had to clasp her hands to keep them from trembling. She had never even dreamed about such good fortune. To be able to live in a grand castle with lords and ladies, to wear fine clothes and eat rich food . . . and best of all, to be free of Hodge! No more ale-sodden nights at End Cottage, no more drudgery. Even her obligation to Steven would be over. A maid to Sir Ismay's daughter would never marry a village blacksmith. But could Rosamund trust the nobleman to keep his word?

"You are asking me to be your daughter's maid?" she asked, anxious to pin him down to her exact duties. "To wait on her, bathe her, care for her clothes?"

"You would be more like a companion. Would you like that?"

"Yes, if that's all you'd expect of me."

Sir Ismay's mouth twitched. "Still guarding your virtue? If it will set your mind at ease, I'll make an oath on these holy relics that I have no intention of bedding you."

His honesty was a surprise. Rosamund blinked in amazement as he took a gold reliquary from inside his doublet and held it out by its glinting chain.

"I swear I'll never seek to bed you—Holy Mother, that would be incest," he added to himself. "I give my word, if you agree to serve me, no harm shall come to you. In fact, you'll have more riches than you've ever dreamed about."

His choice of words made Rosamund gasp. They were an echo of the fortune-teller's promise. Had the gypsy meant that, instead of being beholden to some rich man, Rosamund's fortune would come as the companion of his daughter? Hope soared in the girl's breast at the idea.

"Tell me your decision. We've not the luxury of time. We leave within the hour. Your family will be paid. A purse of gold would greatly sweeten your leavetaking."

Rosamund's eyes shone. A purse of gold! That would be the riches promised. "Do you swear to that also?"

Sir Ismay chuckled at her audacity in questioning his word,

but he put his hand on the reliquary and duly swore his oath.

The clouds slowly lifted from Rosamund's heart and she shivered in joyful anticipation of her bright future. No longer tormented by her stepfather or beholden to a man she did not love, she would be free to lead her own life. She'd never been inside a castle; so she could not even imagine its splendor.

"Rosamund," Sir Ismay said, his voice tense, "I'm waiting for your answer."

"Give the gold to my mother, or Hodge will drink it away. If you say it's only for her and the children, he is too much of a coward to go against your word."

"Done. You're wise as well as beautiful. Rest assured, Joan will have the money. That's the least I owe her. Now, come. We've no time to waste. I'll send a woman to help you dress for the journey."

After Sir Ismay strode from the room, Rosamund clasped her hands in excitement and looked down into the innyard. This was like a dream! Sir Ismay had even known her mother's name, which was exceedingly strange. Then she clapped her hand across her mouth. Of course! Sir Ismay De Gere must be the mysterious nobleman about whom the villagers spoke. He must be her father! Hadn't he muttered something about incest being a barrier to their coupling? She gasped and spun about in delight. At last, she belonged. She was no longer some fatherless offspring of the village washerwoman.

The door clicked open and Rosamund spun about. A servingwoman came inside the room, a bundle of garments in her arms. The woman stopped, her eyes rounding in shock as she looked her up and down.

"Oh, lady," she gasped at last, belatedly dropping to her knees. She kissed the hem of Rosamund's gown. "All the saints be praised. You be recovered! 'Tis a miracle! And I swear, lady, you're far lovelier than before. The picture of health. Oh, the Blessed Mother be praised."

Rosamund was startled by the woman's reaction. But when Rosamund asked her to explain, the woman kept talking about the sea and the sickness it brought, never allowing the girl to get in a word. When the conversation became more baffling, Rosamund finally gave up trying to talk to the woman.

Being dressed by another made Rosamund feel awkward. And the garments were so fine she would have liked to slow the task to admire them. Yet the woman urged her to speed. A fine linen chemise was topped by a wool petticoat, then a gown embroidered around the hem in sparkling blue flowers. The fabric gleamed so, Rosamund believed there might have been gold threads woven amidst the fibers. And if she, a mere servant, was to be gowned so richly, what manner of splendor did the nobles wear?

Once Rosamund was dressed, the servingwoman urged her from the room and hustled her downstairs. Sir Ismay's party was gathered about the inn door awaiting her arrival. Several pale-faced women huddled in their cloaks, standing apart from the soldiers. At the sight of Rosamund dressed and ready for travel, they too gasped in wonder. They gathered around her, chattering in a strange tongue, curtsying and laughing, their eyes shining with tears of joy.

Their behavior also was very strange. Did all rich people behave so oddly? she wondered. Rosamund smiled at the women, but could not understand a word they said to her. Not knowing how to communicate with them, she held out her hands in friendship. To her amazement, they seized her hands and covered them with kisses.

Sir Ismay pushed forward and angrily shooed the women aside. They appeared put out by his actions, protesting his gruff impatience as they tried to dodge behind him and come back to Rosamund's side. The women were brusquely ordered aboard their wagon, and when they still proved reluctant to go, several soldiers marched them to it. They sulkily obeyed.

The wagon pulled away from the rest and the women leaned out of the back, calling good-bye to Rosamund and waving their kerchiefs in farewell. She waved back and their delighted laughter showed her they were pleased by her gesture.

Scowling, Sir Ismay watched the wagon, accompanied by four outriders, pull out of the innyard. Not until the vehicle was safely down the highway did his mood lighten.

"Prattling Frenchwomen—I can't abide them," he said to those closest to him. Then he beckoned to Rosamund to stand at his side.

His statement answered Rosamund's question as to why she had not understood a word the women said. The girl smiled at Sir Ismay, aware she was looking her best in the fine clothing. She saw as much in Sir Ismay's face, because he caught his breath in surprise when he looked at her.

"Can you ride?" he asked in an undertone.

Rosamund nodded, though she knew riding cart horses would probably not prepare her for riding with the nobility. "I've ridden before, though nothing fine, my lord."

"Mayhap you should ride in the litter. We'll try you in the saddle later."

"Where's your daughter?"

He turned away from her eager question. "Resting," he said gruffly. "You'll meet her when it's time".

What a strange arrangement this was. It seemed logical that the girl's maid would need to attend her. "Are those Frenchwomen also her maids?"

"They were. They're on their way home to France. And good riddance to them."

Several soldiers respectfully helped Rosamund aboard a curtained litter. They too failed to answer her questions about their destination. They would not even say how long they expected to be on the road. The steps were folded up and the curtains pulled across. Indignantly, Rosamund swished the leather curtain aside on their jangling hooks.

"It's too stuffy in her. Why must I keep the curtains closed? Am I to stay out of sight because there's danger ahead?"

Sir Ismay rode close to the litter. He scowled as he said, "Aye, there's much danger. Do as you're told. Be quiet and rest. We've a long journey ahead of us."

Annoyed by his abrupt manner, Rosamund knew she must hold her tongue. After all, Sir Ismay was lord of the manor. She thumped back against the upholstered bed of the litter.

The red silk pillows and coverlets were very grand. There was also a sleek cover of brown fur and she plunged her fingers into its silky softness.

Rosamund decided that Sir Ismay's daughter must be traveling in her own litter, though when she looked between the leather curtains she saw only men and wagons. The riders had formed an orderly troop, keeping the litter in the center of the body of men. Sir Ismay rode directly ahead; she could see the twitching tale of his black stallion.

After a few minutes, one of the wagons pulled away from the others, turning instead toward the road leading south to Whitton. Rosamund wondered why that particular wagon was not going with them, yet she knew better than to ask questions. Either the soldiers did not know their destination, or they were under orders not to discuss it with her. Either way she was met with a wall of silence.

Sir Ismay's party had been on the road for several hours before a stableboy made a grisly discovery at the inn. He ran to the innkeeper, babbling about a dead woman. A woman's body had been found stuffed in a water butt behind the stables. The woman had been strangled. Several of the inn's servants recalled having seen the woman buying potions from the local wisewoman to cure her mistress's ills. No one had seen her since.

On the third day of the journey, Rosamund cast all caution aside and demanded to speak with Sir Ismay. Her former reticence about questioning her betters had evaporated. She was bored and tired of being cooped up inside the uncomfortable litter, which rocked and swayed like a ship at sea. Each night they stopped at an inn where she was given a fine room and servants to wait on her. To her surprise, they too insisted on addressing her as a lady. Also to her surprise, the women already knew her name.

After sourly hearing her complaints, Sir Ismay agreed to let her ride for a while the next day. "I suppose enough time's passed by now," he muttered almost to himself, wearily rubbing a hand across his brow. "Now eat something, wench. We must go to bed early. Tomorrow's to be the last leg of our journey. We leave at dawn."

"Will we be at Langley Hutton?" Rosamund asked between bites of spiced meat and bread. They sat companiably at the table, the others keeping a respectful distance. Servers came to replenish their cups and platters.

"No, Langley Hutton's in the other direction. That's where we came from before Whitton."

"Well, where am I to meet your daughter? I thought she traveled with us."

Sir Ismay turned his bloodshot gaze on her. "You're mighty free with your questions."

"I'm tired of all the secrecy. Why must everything be a secret? Surely it's not too much to want to know where we're going and when I'll see my mistress."

Sir Ismay continued to eat for a few minutes, saying nothing. Finally, with his mouth full, he muttered, "When I want you to know, I'll tell you."

Her eyes flashing, Rosamund banged down her ale tankard. "You were so kind to me when you wanted me to come with you. Now you've turned sour and hostile."

"Yes, well, there's little you can do about it, is there, wench?"

Rosamund could not overlook the thinly veiled hostility in his voice. "What do you mean by that?"

Sir Ismay ran his hand over his brow, cursing under his breath. "All right, you confounded curious wench. We reach Ravenscrag in the East Riding tomorrow if we make good time. 'Tis where we'll spend Christmas."

"And there I'll meet your Rosamund?"

"My daughter will be there." He stared down into the ale in his cup. "Take my advice and don't ask so many questions. From now on try to act sweet, devout—and for God's sake, be quiet."

Rosamund had begun to dislike the man. His mood fluctuated from day to day. Where was all the praise for her looks and her virtue? Had those compliments been uttered merely to win her confidence? She was beginning to suspect there was far more to Sir Ismay's generous offer of employment than met the eye.

"I am devout. If by quiet you mean docile as a sheep, you've chosen the wrong woman."

"I'm beginning to find that out."

"And I'm beginning to smell something foul about this arrangement. If it proves not to my liking, I'll take me back to Whitton."

"Oh, will you?" His lip curled sarcastically. "Walking across Yorkshire in winter will prove quite a feat."

"I can walk if need be." Rosamund tossed her head defiantly, meeting his gaze without flinching. "You don't own me, my lord."

"Now that's where you're wrong." He seized her wrist, his fingers biting in cruelly. "I own you body and soul. Have no illusion about that. You will do as you are told, now and in the future."

"You never intended me to be your daughter's maid." Rosamund gasped in shock. "This was a sham from the start."

"Oh, hush, you wretched wench. Keep your voice down." Sir Ismay glanced about the room in agitation, afraid they would be overheard. "I suppose this is as good a time as any—though God knows I don't relish this discussion. You've been a vast disappointment to me."

"The feeling's mutual."

His lip curled at the undisguised scorn in her voice. Abruptly thrusting aside his trencher, Sir Ismay said, "Come with me." He signaled to Hartley to accompany them.

A fire blazed brightly in Sir Ismay's bedchamber. Though the room was warm, Rosamund felt a chill of impending doom pass over her. Her unease mounted as Hartley bolted the door, then looked under the bed and behind the draperies, making sure they would not be overheard. Finally, Hartley joined his master before the hearth.

Sir Ismay stood scowling, his back to the fire. He felt as if he were about to beg the wench's cooperation and the feeling was alien to his De Gere pride.

Rosamund looked up at the two men towering above her, where she was seated on a wooden bench like a naughty child awaiting punishment. When she started to rise, however, she was thrust back on the bench.

"Now listen well to what I have to say. What you hear tonight is never to be repeated," Sir Ismay said.

"Why won't you answer my questions?" Rosamund asked.

"What more do you need you know?" he cried in exasperation. "I've already told you we're to spend Christmas at Ravenscrag."

"Am I to be your daughter's maid? Where is she? And if I am not to serve her, what are you going to do with me?"

There was a long pause during which Sir Ismay cleared his throat, clearly uncomfortable with the girl's direct questions. "No, you are not to be a maid. I only suggested that to get you to come with us without a fuss. It was the best I could do at such short notice."

Rosamund stifled a gasp of alarm. Fear curled through her stomach as she hesitantly asked, "Why did you want me to come with you?"

"Not as a maid. You'll never be anyone's maid. After all, you are a De Gere. We bow to no one."

"Then it's true—you are my father!" Her heart pounded since she had finally voiced what she had long suspected.

"Yes, it's true. You were an indiscretion of my youth. God be praised."

"Why have you waited so long to claim me?"

"Because until now I'd no need of you. Rosamund, I'm in desperate need of a daughter."

"Any daughter?"

Shamefaced, he looked down. "Aye, even a washerwoman's get will do. Besides that, you're the spitting image of my Rosamund. Nay, you're fairer by far, and healthy. You're what I wished her to be instead of such a frail and puny wench." He sighed heavily, weighed down by the portent of his words.

Lowering his voice, he said hoarsely, "This Christmas, Rosamund was to wed a great lord. 'Twas to her wedding feast we traveled."

"Was?" Rosamund said uneasily.

"Aye, she took sick and died at Hutton. You will take her place."

"Me! To marry someone I don't even know. To pretend to be somebody I'm not. No, I can't do that." Rising to her feet, Rosamund backed toward the door.

"You'll do as you are told. You have no choice," Sir Ismay said.

"That's where you're wrong. I had a life before we met. I'll get me back to Whitton and you can keep your generous proposal, my lord."

"No." Sir Ismay shook his head. "Not possible. You have nothing there—except a headstone!"

Rosamund held her hand tight across her mouth to stifle the scream of protest. "You intend to kill me?"

"Nay, there's no need for that. The fair maid of Whitton is already dead. Felled by some strange malady. You were buried at my expense. God forgive me for the deceit."

Hartley yanked Rosamund away from the door, propelling her back to the hearth. "Stop yowling," he growled, shaking her in his anger. "That wench is dead. You're to marry a great lord. You should be grateful to Sir Ismay for the gift."

"That's enough. I'll handle her." Sir Ismay shook off the grief that had momentarily bowed his head. He reached out to take the girl's hand. "Come, Rosamund, daughter. Greet your father like a dutiful wench. I promise you can ask for no greater riches in the world than to become the bride of Ravenscrag."

"Why is it so important for your daughter to marry this man?"

"Because we've signed a pact allying our armies. Without him, the house of De Gere will fall. I've long hoped for this alliance and nothing, not even the grave, will take it from me."

"Aren't you afraid I'll tell him the truth?"

"I don't recommend it, unless you fancy living your life under guard. It won't be hard to convince everyone your illness affected your mind. I don't think you'd like to spend the rest of your days locked up as a madwoman. No, I thought not."

Rosamund recoiled from his threat, a chill going over her at the idea of perpetual imprisonment. The wagon traveling to Whitton must have carried the other Rosamund to her grave. It was chilling to picture her own headstone in the churchyard. Had her passing been mourned? Steven surely would be distraught, and poor little Mary. A tear slid from Rosamund's eye as she considered her family. Joan would miss her until the next few tankards of brew were drained. Hodge would regret the loss of her body and the money she earned. As Sir Ismay said, life for Rosamund in Whitton did not exist.

"You buried your daughter in my place?" Rosamund asked.

"Aye, and it makes me heartsick to know my own blood lies beneath a peasant headstone." Sir Ismay groaned angrily, his face grim as he considered the indignity. "My daughter died of a fever. She'd been so ill since she arrived. That's why the Frenchwomen were moonstruck over your miraculous recovery. I couldn't let them dally long enough to discover you couldn't speak French. At Ravenscrag no one will be any the wiser. No one there's seen you since ... she ... left for a French convent. Speaking of which, can you read and write?"

"Some."

"Good. I'd hate to think I wasted my money sending you to Thorpe."

"You couldn't have known about this then."

"No, not that you'd prove so useful to me. I think at that time it was merely a generous gesture. I had some notion to marry you to a man in my household. That was before the family fortunes were dissipated fighting the King's wars. Then you became a luxury I could no longer afford."

"The nuns sent me back to Whitton," Rosamund said accusingly. "No one told me why. It was hard living in Whitton after my time at Thorpe."

"Yes, well, I'm growing weary of this discussion. Just remember: When we reach Ravenscrag, try to act according to your station. Remember what the nuns taught you, how they disported themselves. Forget you ever knew a washerwoman. And remember, if you think to have vengeance by telling what you know, I'll have you declared insane."

His warning hung oppressively in the air, making the small room suffocating. He was the man she had long hoped to meet—her noble father. Any soft thoughts she may have cherished about a father's love had been quickly dashed. Their relationship was merely business. Still, she could not mourn the loss of that which she had never known.

Rosamund went to the window, peering through a chink in the shutters to the dark village beyond. Would someone there help her get back to Whitton? Yet what would she do once she got home? The superstitious villagers would be terrified by her appearance. The Rosie they knew was buried in the churchyard. She would be an apparition returned from the dead.

With a sigh of defeat, she turned from the window to find Sir Ismay watching her, a sympathetic smile on his hard mouth.

"Not thinking about escape, surely," he said, as if he had read her mind. "Not advisable, Rosamund. You have nowhere to go. We need each other, like it or not."

She knew he was right. The only future she had lay in the hands of the Lord of Langley Hutton.

"So, my loving father, you intend to cheat this man who is to marry your daughter."

"Don't forget, righteous one: You are my daughter also. And your name is Rosamund. I doubt Ravenscrag will consider himself cheated when he sees you, and when you bear him an heir. You'll be far more welcome in his bed than that other poor stick of a wench, God rest her soul. Now, get you to sleep, and remember at all times, you are Lady Rosamund De Gere."

Chapter Four

It was dark by the time they entered the great stone fortress of Ravenscrag. Sputtering torches lit the cobbled inner bailey. The yellow torchlight revealed many blurred figures milling around the new arrivals; horse and human breath steamed great clouds in the icy night air.

Rosamund was quickly hustled indoors out of the biting cold. A dozen maids scurried about her, guiding her up winding stairs to her warm tower room. Sir Ismay had sent an advance rider to warn the household that Lady Rosamund was in a delicate state of health and must be guarded against taking a chill.

The first glimmers of dawn crept murkily through a narrow opening high in the stone wall. Gradually the deepening finger of light entered the unglazed window until it shone across Rosamund's face. When she opened her eyes, she did not know where she was at first. Then with an excited pitch of her stomach, she remembered. She was inside the mighty fortress of Ravenscrag. And soon she would be the castle's mistress. The idea of such unexpected good fortune filled her with delight.

She stretched in her warm sea of down, thick coverlets heaped atop, soft, sinking pallet below. Rosamund had been so weary the night before she had barely been able to keep her eyes open whilst she was readied for bed. Everything had been a blur of smoking torches and chattering women, swiftly followed by the blissful comfort of the huge bed to cushion her aching limbs. Riding cart horses had not prepared her for hours in the saddle, but she had stubbornly refused to give in and ride inside the litter. Rosamund was convinced that Sir Ismay had known how much had she suffered and that he had taken perverse delight in her torment.

She glanced about the unfamiliar room. The gray stone walls were adorned with colorful hangings depicting what she supposed to be biblical scenes. The high oak bed, where she lay, had curtains of blue velvet edged with gold and the embroidered blue coverlet beneath her clasped hands bore the crest of a sharp-beaked bird perched on a crag.

An unexpected noise caught Rosamund's attention and she saw a servingwoman arranging clothing in a wooden chest in the corner. When the servant noticed that Rosamund was awake, she came to the bedside and curtsied.

"Good morning, my lady. My name's Kate and I'm here to wait on you."

Rosamund murmured a greeting, uncomfortable to assume the position of lady. She knew if she were to continue the charade she must soon accustom herself to the position. She slid out of her down cocoon and went to the crackling hearth. Totally unprepared for a sudden flurry of curtsying women, she panicked inwardly before she forced herself to act accustomed to the attention.

From that moment on her time was not her own. Though being waited on made Rosamund feel like royalty, she did not know how to address the servants. They seemed quite content that she keep quiet as they bathed and massaged her. They commented on Rosamund's unblemished skin in such an impersonal manner that she felt as if she was an object instead of a person. Her hair was washed, dried, and perfumed with oil of roses. The women braided her hair with strands of pearls, then fastened it to the back of her head with a bone pin. Cosmetics were artfully applied to bring a glow to Rosamund's pale face.

Next the women laced Rosamund into a rich gown of spangled ivory and gold damask edged with cream fur. A short veil attached to a circular padded headdress was fastened atop her head. Everything was blurry as she peered through the veil, as if she was looking through water. But when she pulled back the veil, the women clucked in disapproval and quickly put it back in place, saying, "No, my lady, it's expected." The narrow satin shoes were slipped over her white silken hose.

When at last Rosamund was pronounced ready, she was whisked outside. As they moved along, Rosamund was surrounded by the women who clucked in pleasure over their handiwork and assured her she was a vision. Downstairs and around corners they led her, as she walked, the wavering shadows seemed water shrouded through the thin veil.

They stepped into the courtyard, where two pages holding lighted torches waited for them. All around towered the massive stone keep, its forbidding walls shutting out the sky.

Rosamund shivered as the north wind came singing biting cold around the corner of the buildings. It was a relief when they quickly entered the buildings over the courtyard and hurried down a gloomy stone corridor, where the torches cast giant wavering shadows.

It was not until they were inside a huge, hammer-beamed hall that seemed even darker than the gloomy outdoors that Rosamund realized she was probably about to meet her future husband. The very idea gave her chills, robbing her of any pleasure she had felt at the prospect of becoming mistress of the huge castle. Her stomach churned in apprehension as the procession crossed the hall at a solemn, measured pace. Gradually her eyes grew accustomed to the murky indoor light and she could see many people watching from the shadows.

Abruptly the procession halted and Rosamund nearly ran into the large woman who led the way. Over the women's heads she saw a plume atop a velvet hat, then heard Sir Ismay's unmistakable gruff tones.

"Ah, here she is at last, my lovely Rosamund."

Though she forced a smile, Rosamund squirmed inwardly, ashamed of the charade. Beneath her veil, her lips were set as she accepted Sir Ismay's beringed hand. Trying to step regally, she matched his pace as they crossed the expanse of herb-sweetened rushes, heading for the far end of the hall, where a whole tree trunk was blazing in an enormous stone hearth.

A glaring flood of light bathed the dais containing the lord's table. Its unexpected brilliance made her blink. A blurred figure came toward her, blocking the light. Rosamund blinked back unexpected tears. It was foolish to cry. Life inside the castle was already more luxurious than she could have imagined. She need only play along with Sir Ismay's scheme and it would be hers forever. Yet what of the stranger she must accept as her husband? Would he beat her? Would he demand unnatural sexual acts? Would he be a monster?

A rushing sound began in Rosamund's ears, warning her that she was close to fainting. When she stumbled and swayed, Sir Ismay quickly reached out to take her weight against his hard shoulder.

"Does the wench still ail?" someone in the background asked.

"Nay, she's just tired. 'Tis a long ride to Ravenscrag and she's not recovered from the crossing. You must forgive my Rosamund for not being herself, Lord Henry," Sir Ismay said in smoothly ingratiating tones.

As Sir Ismay pretended to pat Rosamund's arm, he gave her a surreptitious pinch. There was an expression of warning on his face. He followed the reminder with a gentle push as he urged her to kneel on the bottom step of the dais.

Rosamund did as she was bidden, aware a man had stepped toward her. Strong legs in shimmering blue tights stopped before her; then a pair of warm hands gently raised her bowed head as the man motioned her to rise. Through the blur of her organza veils, Rosamund looked at his dark blue velvet doublet. The jewels on his garments alone must be worth a king's ransom! A broad expanse of velvet-encased shoulders tapered to a narrow waist; his slim hips were encircled by a gold chain. Rosamund blinked, forcing herself upright as the rushing sound again filled her ears. She had the scant consolation of discovering the Lord of Ravenscrag was not some raddled old knight in his dotage. Yet when she considered the fact, she wondered if such a man might be preferable; a young virile husband would demand his right nightly. Taking a deep breath, Rosamund finally forced herself to look at the Lord of Ravenscrag as he lifted her veils.

"Welcome to Ravenscrag, Lady Rosamund. You're grown up indeed. You're not the skinny child I remembered, but a great beauty."

Rosamund blinked, hardly able to believe what she saw. The roaring in her ears grew deafening. Blinking away tears, she was dazzled by the myriad points of light reflecting off Henry's doublet. A handsome, lean-jawed man gazed down at her; his firm, generous mouth curved in a quizzical smile at her shocked surprise. Thick dark lashes surrounded his deep blue eyes and raven-dark hair curled about his collar. Rosamund was faint with shock. She was sure she was looking at him far bolder than was considered proper, but she had to know if the man was a figment of her imagination.

No, he was real! She gulped back a choking sensation in her throat and her knees began to tremble. The dreaded Lord of Ravenscrag was no stranger! Before her stood the man in the Lincoln-green doublet about whom she had dreamed long into the winter night. Her heart leapt with joy. As he politely pressed her hand to his mouth, some of her euphoria dissolved. His firm, inviting lips, which she had longed to press passionately against her own, were politely indifferent.

Sobered and brought back to earth from that heady realm by a good dose of reality, Rosamund chided herself for her foolishness. He had not shared those romantic adventures. Yet at the same time she was disappointed. It was as if a fairy godmother had cast a magical spell over Ravenscrag Castle to grant Rosamund her heart's desire. Yet one vital ingredient had been overlooked: The object of her romantic passion felt no emotion for her.

Lord Henry had already stepped back and turned his attention to Sir Ismay. Rosamund felt as if a door had been shut in her face. Wounded without cause, she swallowed, remembering the look of pleasure that had crossed his face when he had lifted her veil. He had not been wholly indifferent. It remained for her to turn fantasy into reality.

Henry's resonant voice penetrated the rushing in Rosamund's ears, filling her head with his words. She measured the quality of his voice, finding, though his speech was cultured as befitted his rank, his accent still betrayed his North Country raising. Though his words were inconsequential inquiries about their journey, he might have been reciting fine poetry for all the pleasure Rosamund got from listening to him.

Many hands grasped her sleeves, impatiently urging her about. Her veil was dropped back in place as her attendants tried to move her from the dais. Rosamund would not budge, convinced her groom would ask her to share his table.

Aware the party waited, Lord Henry glanced up. Thinking Rosamund politely awaited his dismissal, he smiled and inclined his dark head.

"You may return to your room to rest, Lady Rosamund. Tonight we're having a masked revel, but you won't be disturbed. That's why I had your room prepared in the south tower, far from the noise."

"Thank you, my lord," she whispered, her voice choking in her throat. That was not what she was waiting for him to say. She was going to ask him why she had not been invited to the Christmas revel, but he had already turned his back on her.

Her attendants grasped her arms so firmly she had to move with them as they marched her away. As she left she heard Henry ask, "Will you ride the boundaries with me, Sir Ismay? Better dress warmly. It looks as if we're in for a cold spell."

"Certainly . . . Henry . . . if I may call you that?"

"Aye, I insist on it. And shall I call you Father?"

There followed a burst of laughter; cups clinked as the men drank more ale to toast their new alliance.

Rosamund could no longer hear what was being said because she and her retinue were near the carved screen at the rear of the hall. She smarted with annoyance. She had not been asked if she would like a tour of the estate or even a tour of the castle. After their greeting, her future husband had shown no further interest in her.

Picking up the pace so that her attendants had to hurry to keep up with her, Rosamund retraced her steps. Far from a colorful adventure, life for her promised to be as dull as ditch water. She supposed she had Sir Ismay to thank for the convenient role of invalid that had been thrust upon her.

The hours passed. No one came to inquire about Rosamund's health. And though she hoped Henry would come to visit her, he did not. That night's entertainment was only for the wedding guests and not for the bride. Rosamund felt abandoned and dispirited. No longer even Rosie of Whitton, she had become Rosamund, anemic, ethereal bride of a man who cared naught for her, invalid daughter of a second noble who used her to further his own ambitions. She could destroy Sir Ismay's scheme with a few well-chosen words, but in doing so, she would also destroy her own hope of happiness.

But her plight was not all bad. She had been given as husband the man of her dreams. She vowed to make Henry of Ravenscrag love her.

Glumly Rosamund watched mounds of holly being carried over the courtyard. Folded red festival cloths borne by servants followed, and pages carried boughs of pine and fir decorated with ribbons. They were preparing the great hall for the feast. Oh, why had they not seen fit to invite her to the revel? Sir Ismay was probably afraid she would give herself away before she was wed; so he had made the most of her delicate health to buy himself time.

Determined to go down to at least see the decorations, Rosamund was dismayed to find armed guards outside her room. She was urged back inside none too gently by Sir Ismay's men and told to rest in preparation for the next day's religious ceremony.

Rosamund leaned against her door and fought back tears.

Soon muffled voices beyond the door and heavy steps told her she had visitors. Maybe her bold foray had been reported and her lord had sent for her to come join them after all.

Sir Ismay, with Hartley at his heels, walked inside the room. The captain stood at the door to make sure Sir Ismay and Rosamund were not overheard by any of the castle spies.

"Am I to go downstairs?" Rosamund asked eagerly, hurrying to Sir Ismay.

"God forbid! I don't want anything going wrong—not yet. Stay put. Surely it's not too much of a penance. The room's warm and the bed's soft. It's better by far than what you're used to, wench. For your own good be not so bold and do as you're told." Sir Ismay grasped her shoulders. "Now, before we go farther, remember our future depends on you. You told me you are virtuous. Are you still virgin?"

Rosamund started in surprise at his unexpected question. Sir Ismay's eyes narrowed and a cruel expression tightened his face. As his fingers bit into her flesh, he growled, "Damn it, don't tell me you lied, you bitch!"

"I didn't lie. I am virtuous. I give you my word."

He glowered at her. "We need more than your word. We need proof. I've a mind to have you examined, but that would likely cause gossip and we can't afford that." Brows drawn together, he leaned close and hissed a warning. "There'd better be blood on the marriage sheets. Will you guarantee me that much?"

"Yes," she said clearly, shaking free of his grasp.

Some time after Sir Ismay had left, Rosamund again opened her door to discover the guards were gone! She could not believe her good fortune, but she lost no time in taking advantage of it. She was going to join the revels after all.

Down the twisting stairs she hurried, expecting to meet opposition at every bend. But no one stopped her. The stone walls were icy to the touch as she felt her way along the corridor. The corridor was gloomy, yet at the end of the passage a cresset sputtered.

Rosamund wished she could have disguised her identity in a servant's homespun; then she would have had more chance of going unrecognized. Any guest who had been in the hall when she was introduced to Henry of Ravenscrag would recognize the distinctive gown. Perhaps she could find some more suitable clothing in one of the unattended rooms.

Several doors opened off the corridor and she could hear voices from behind the closed doors. No sounds came from one door and she tentatively pushed it ajar. The room appeared to be empty but was far too fine for a servant's quarters. This was definitely the room of a guest. A huge bed was in the center of the firelit room. Best of all a heap of discarded garments tumbled over the bedcovers and spilled onto the rushes. Some wedding guest had conveniently emptied her trunks for Rosamund to choose from.

Aware she had not the luxury of time, Rosamund grabbed the first gown she came to. It was marigold velvet trimmed in fur. The gown was lovely but she was too hurried to spare much time in admiring it. The gown fit, though the bodice was tight. It could not be helped. Rosamund pulled a surcoat over the gown, unsure how to tie its intricately laced sides. A gilt mask was propped against a candlestick on the chest beside the bed. The disguise was perfect.

Rosamund was already at the door when she heard voices coming her way. There was barely time to duck back inside the room before a party of chattering women passed the door. The voices died away. Just as Rosamund headed out the door, one of the women broke away from the others and ran back along the corridor. Rosamund barely had time to hide behind a wall-hanging before the woman came inside the room. Hardly daring to breathe, Rosamund stood there, knowing the flickering firelight and the light of a single candle left the room in deep shadow. She watched as the woman rummaged through the clothing on the bed, then crawled about the rushes and looked under the bed, muttering curses beneath her breath as she failed to find what she sought. Finally she stood beside the bed looking baffled.

Rosamund realized the woman searched for the mask she clutched in her hand. She would have gladly given it to her had she been able, but any movement would betray her. She could not reach out and drop the mask to the rushes without revealing her hiding place.

Suddenly the woman cried out and clutched at her belly. Then she bolted along a passage leading from the room. Gagging sounds echoed along the stone wall. From the odor wafting her way, Rosamund knew the passage led to a privy. It seemed strange that the castle privy was indoors. Mayhap it was in case of seige. But Rosamund had no time to spare to wonder about that matter at present. She had to be off quickly. And just to make sure the woman stayed put until she could return the gown, Rosamund latched the wooden door, shutting off the passage.

Rosamund clutched her heavy velvet skirts and held the mask to her face with her free hand, before stepping out into the corridor. Two pages holding flaring torches startled her as they beckoned, offering to light her way. Though Rosamund protested, her voice was lost in the burst of sound echoing along the corridors from the great hall.

A party of would-be revelers eager to join the Christmas festivities crowded behind her, urging her forward. Rosamund was swept forward by the tipsy guests, who followed the pages into the castle's great hall. She had meant to slide inside the lighted room unnoticed, but it did not matter. She knew she could easily slip away. It would not hurt just to have a look at the decorated hall and maybe watch the dancers for a few minutes before she returned to her tower prison.

Once Rosamund saw the colorful scene unfolding before her, she had little desire to leave. She stared in wonder at the guests' splendid clothing. She had never seen anything so magnificent! Jewels were everywhere, adorning garments, sparkling on hands and necks. The dark smoky hall had been transformed. The room vibrated with color, music, and laughter. Minstrels hidden from view behind the fretwork of a gallery played a lively tune for dancing. The finely dressed guests formed circles and skipped hand in hand through the intricacies of the dance. Though their dance was a more refined version, their steps were similar to the village dances Rosamund had enjoyed on Mayday and Midsummer's Eve.

Humming as she watched, Rosamund tapped her feet in the rushes and longed to join the guests. Dressed as she was, with a mask in place, no one would recognize her. Just one dance then she would slip away.

The round ended abruptly amid much laughter and applause. Before anyone could catch his breath, the musicians struck up again for another dance. Fresh couples ran forward to take up the tune. All around the room, there seemed to be an unusual amount of hugging and kissing. Many beribboned kissing boughs dangled from the rafters, yet the guests seemed to need no such encouragement to be amorous.

The hall was warm; a huge tree trunk blazed in the hearth. The fire put out a cloud of heat that seemed to draw Rosamund forward, flushing her cheeks and melting all caution. Tables had been pushed back against the walls to make more room for dancing. Guests lolled, enjoying the delicacies freely offered.

Rosamund was startled when a man's hand slid about her waist. A husky voice in her ear invited her to join him in the dance. Her partner was dressed in stark black and silver; the combination gave him a rather sinister appearance.

"My name's Geoffrey. What's yours, sweetheart?" he asked, his hot, wine-laden breath fanning her cheek.

"Jane," Rosamund said quickly.

"Are you from Ravenscrag?" Geoffrey asked.

"No, I'm from far away," she said, laughing in delight at the exciting prospect of dancing.

"Me too. I'm Percy's man." Geoffrey had to shout to make himself heard above the din. "From up Northumberland way."

Rosamund nodded as Geoffrey seized her hand and joined the fast skipping circle. She had heard of the Percys, a powerful family living near the Scottish border whose power had made them the virtual kings of the North Country.

Rosamund and Geoffrey skipped about in a sinuous circle, bending this way and that. Several times her tipsy partner tried to kiss her cheek, but Rosamund easily twisted away from him. Emboldened by her anonymity, she playfully tapped his cheek, scolding him for his brazenness.

Geoffrey laughed, delighted by her actions. He considered it flirtatious play, a game at which he was most skilled. As they danced he breathed extravagant compliments in Rosamund's ear. When his hand crept too close to the swelling of her bodice, she deliberately removed his fingers, relieved to find he good-humoredly accepted her rebuff. Empowered by her success in handling the fair-haired nobleman, her confidence grew. Rosamund was thrilled by the realization that the cohort of the mighty Percys readily accepted her as a lady. One of the worst hurdles to becoming Rosamund De Gere had been overcome with surprising ease.

Bewailing the fact he must desert her, Geoffrey bowed as the two dancing circles overlapped and everyone changed partners. Rosamund blew him a kiss and he reciprocated with a dozen more.

Many of the guests had already dispensed with their masks, while others took them off and on as it suited them. Rosamund kept her own glittering mask firmly in place, checking its fastening as a new partner reached out to claim her. Behind the glittering disguise she felt anonymous, able to live a make-believe existence without fear of discovery. The freedom made her giddy and flirtatious, and she welcomed another richly dressed man on which to try out her charms.

The man who clasped her hand firmly wore emerald-and-green particolored velvet; his silver mask, complete with a curving beak, was shaped like a bird's head.

"It is my pleasure to find such a lovely partner," he said as he bowed over her hand. "It would be even more enjoyable if you'd take off your mask," he added, his long fingers already sliding beneath the mask's ribbon fastening.

"Oh, no, I cannot," Rosamund cried in alarm, startled by his unexpected move.

She was relieved when he shrugged and did not pursue the matter. There was something achingly familiar about the broad-shouldered man. While they waited for the chord to set the dancers back in motion, Rosamund studied his thick, glossy dark hair and his firm jaw below the sparkling mask. Her heart skipped a beat as she discovered she was standing beside the Lord of Ravenscrag.

"Cannot or will not?" he asked huskily as the circle slowly began to revolve.

"Both . . . Henry," she answered boldly, slipping her hand in his as she hugged his strong arm against her side.

"Not fair. Am I that easy to recognize?"

"You are to me."

"Then if that's the case, surely I must know you also, sweetheart."

She shook her head, laughing at the baffled expression betrayed by his firm mouth. Their lighthearted banter continued as they swept around the large room until gradually the dance grew too frenzied for speech. Their arms joined, they whirled about, skipping, running, leaping amid the bay-and-laurel-scented rushes crunching underfoot. Rosamund felt light-headed though she had drunk no wine; she was intoxicated with pleasure as Henry's protective arm held her fast. Her dream had come true and she wanted to pinch herself to make sure she was still awake.

When at last the dance ended, Henry refused to let her go. "Nay, pretty one, stay beside me," he urged as Rosamund stood trying to catch her breath. "You're too lovely to let slip away. Come." He drew her into the shadows, where they sat on a bench beside a table loaded with food. From a pewter jug he poured her a goblet of dark, sweet wine. Rosamund's mouth watered as she saw a plate of sugar-sparkled rice cakes. She had not eaten for hours and her stomach was growling in protest. Finally giving in to the temptation, she scooped up a handful of cakes, not stopping until she had devoured them all.

Henry clucked over her apparent gluttony. "Have you not eaten all day?" he asked in surprise.

"No, and I traveled far to attend your revel, my lord. Surely

71

you don't begrudge me a few cakes?''

"Nay, sweeting, I'd not begrudge you a thing. And I'd much rather you called me Henry instead of my lord."

As he spoke, he softly traced his fingers along her arm, sliding beneath her long, trailing sleeve to feel the pulse beating thunderously at her wrist.

"I'll call you Harry . . . Harry Ravenscrag."

Impatiently he pulled off his mask and tossed it amid the plates on the table, the better to drink from his goblet. "Come, sweeting, let me see your face. I confess the rest of you sets my pulses racing," he said softly, caressing her neck.

Rosamund swallowed, fighting to hold on to her wits. The evening was turning into one of her treasured fantasies wherein she sat beside Henry and enjoyed his undivided attention. She could not believe it was happening after his cold reception of her that afternoon. Even when other women beckoned to him and boldly invited him to partner them in a dance, he declined their offers, making the excuse he was tired and had drunk too much wine to keep his head clear for dancing.

"Here, let me help you," Henry said, his hand stealing again to the fastening of her mask.

"No. If you persist, I'll have to choose another partner," Rosamund said, drawing away from him.

Laughing at her protests, he said, "Not on your life. You are mine for the night. And 'tis true I have drunk too much wine, but not near enough to turn me into a fool. Must your name also stay a mystery?"

"It's Jane," she said, settling more comfortably on the bench so she could enjoy his lazy caresses, which set her senses jangling and sent waves of heat along her limbs.

"Jane . . . from where?"

"Oh, a long way off." He persisted in naming towns and districts and would not accept her answer until Rosamund finally said, "Far to the north, in Percy country. That's all I can tell you. You see, Harry, I'm not even supposed to be dancing."

"Aha, so you've given your old husband the slip?"

That seemed a suitable tale; so she nodded and smiled. Let him imagine what he would. Once the truth was revealed it would make matters all the more humorous. Rosamund found their flirtatious game growing more exciting by the minute. They had gradually moved closer on the bench until their garments brushed; the sweet scent of musk rose wafted from his velvet doublet. He began to feed her sweetmeats like a child, and as the game intensified, Rosamund kissed his fingers. Tension crackled between them. At the touch of her lips his expression changed and desire gleamed in his eyes. Knowledge of his heightened interest sent shivers of anticipation along Rosamund's spine.

Though he had betrayed his mounting passion to her, outwardly Henry maintained his composure, casually talking about his lands and his favorite beasts, asking in turn about her home. Warily Rosamund gave short answers that revealed nothing. When he brought her fingers to his lips, his cool indifference was gone. His lips lingered deliciously along the length of her fingers, the memory of his passion lasting long after his kiss was done.

"Ah, sweet Jane," he whispered, moving even closer so that his hard, muscular thigh burned through the marigold velvet gown. "I've never known a woman who turned my blood so hot at first meeting. If I don't soon hold you in my arms, I'll go mad with longing." His fiery breath stirred her hair against her brow as he asked, "Tell me, sweet, have you bewitched me to arouse me so?"

She merely smiled, not daring a reply, because her own blood had come close to boiling as he drew his mouth along her neck.

"Perhaps we should dance again," she gasped, fighting to control her jangling senses. A need for drastic action drove her to make that suggestion, though it was far from what she wanted to do.

"No, I want to be alone with you." The husky invitation behind his words made her pulse race.

"Alone—oh, Harry—for shame. Would you have me

thrashed?'' she protested playfully, studying him through the eye slits in her mask and wishing she could dispense with her disguise. Soon—it was not yet time.

He smiled at her mock protest, but he did not move away from her.

"No one would dare thrash you. Not while I've breath left in my body. In fact, I propose to steal you away from your doddering husband. What say you to that proposal, sweet Jane?''

While he spoke, his fingers traced the soft flesh above her fur-trimmed bodice before boldly stealing beneath the fur to stroke the tops of her breasts. Rosamund had to steel herself not to shiver in delight at his touch.

"That depends," she said breathlessly, moving slightly so that his fingers touched the deep cleft between her full breasts. He hesitated over pursuing the more intimate caress. When she made no objection, he slid his finger deep within that delectable valley.

"Would that my mouth could follow," he whispered ardently, trying to gauge the expression in her eyes, but finding the mask an effective shield. "Come, sweetest. Let's go where we won't be disturbed."

Rosamund ached for the return of his tantalizing caress. She longed to follow where he led, not being so naive as to misunderstand he invited her to his bedchamber. With a shiver of anticipation, Rosamund wondered what would be his reaction when at last she was unmasked as his future wife.

"For shame, Harry, making such wicked suggestions and you soon to become a bridegroom," she chided playfully.

His expression turned puzzled. "Bridegroom?" he said. "What has that to do with it? Men marry for power and heirs. It's hardly a love match. I owe the lady nothing."

"Then you don't care for your future wife?"

"I don't even know her. She's useful because of her father's position and she's also young enough to bear me an heir. Now, no more boring talk of wives. We're not speaking about duty, sweetest. We're talking about love and passion—all those wonderful feelings you arouse in me."

Surprised and displeased by his casual attitude toward their marriage, Rosamund drew away from him. In those few sentences, he had explained the reason he had showed her such indifference at their meeting. She was no more to him than a chattel. She longed to reveal her identity to him, if for nothing more than to dispel all his preconceived notions about wives being boring, colorless necessities of life. Sense kept her tongue in check, though she still could not resist asking, "Your future wife must be an ugly witch then?"

"Nay, surprisingly, she's most pleasant to look at. But I grant you, she'll be cold as ditch water. Raised in a French convent. By God, she'll likely pray each time I bed her." He laughed at the amusing thought.

How like a man! Somehow Rosamund had expected her dream lover to be different. Had she allowed it, his attitude could have disillusioned her about him. But she need only look at his handsome face and remember that he would soon be hers to shape and mold into a different man. The anticipation of that magic time made her shiver. That odious attitude must be typical of his class. It was an eye-opener. But she was confident she was up to the challenge. She would show him he could ache just as easily for a wife as a pretty sweetheart. And duty had not a thing to do with it.

"So you don't intend to be faithful to your wife?"

A look of sheer astonishment crossed his face. His expression was swiftly replaced by amusement. "You jest, sweetheart. Don't you know all men are unfaithful to their wives? We aren't a race of saints. And by God, I'd gladly do penance if you'll let me be unfaithful with you." His hand stole to her hair, where he fumbled again with the fastening of her mask.

"No!"

Rosamund was on her feet and headed for the swirling dancers. Swiftly Henry caught her and swung her about to face him. He imprisoned her against a stone pillar. Though it was difficult with the hard gilt mask hiding her upper face, he covered her mouth with his own. His kiss struck fire through

75

her veins and her legs went weak until she clung to him with shaking hands. Wonderful though his imagined kisses had been, they were no substitute for hot reality. Heat throbbed through his body as Rosamund realized the substance of muscle and sinew pressing against her was startlingly real. Beneath her hands she was aware of the thud of blood coursing through his veins. Had he not held her tightly, she would have swooned in delight.

In the background, a troupe of mummers sang a bawdy round while the guests laughed and clapped in time to the song.

"No. You won't let me make love to you?" Henry asked softly, drawing back.

"No, I won't let you take off my mask—yet," she whispered invitingly, her hands on his hard shoulders. His plush velvet doublet felt like silk beneath her fingers. Teasingly she allowed the tips of her fingers to trace the steel-hard tension of his jaw.

Her implied assent merely accelerated his passion. His eyes were hot with desire and Rosamund went weak with longing as she came closer to turning her cherished dreams into reality. That arousing man would soon be her husband. That night would be the first of many such blissful nights spent in his arms.

"Oh, sweetheart, tell me you want it too," he urged, drawing her close against him until she could feel the thud of his heart.

The soft sheen of his velvet doublet caressed her cheek as she rested her head against his shoulder, fighting to gather her wits, to keep calm and not give herself away too soon. Her fantasy world had become reality in such a heady way she still could not believe she was not just having another arousing dream.

Henry's heartbeat was music in her ears as Rosamund allowed him to take more of her weight against him. She reveled in the hot strength of his thighs burning against her own as if they would ignite the marigold velvet gown. His body was a furnace of muscle and sinew slowly consuming her being until she felt herself melting against him. Despite the pleasure, a small voice of conscience persisted, slightly marring her bliss. Would he be angry when he learned her identity? No, she told herself. He would be overjoyed to learn the masked woman who had captured his heart was his own wife.

The heat of his lips on hers made her heart thunder in excitement. As he traced his mouth along her sensitive nape, his tender kisses grew teasing.

Rosamund turned his hand palm out and pressed her lips there. "Oh, Harry Ravenscrag, I've wanted you since first I knew what loving meant," she said breathlessly, gazing into his shadowed face so close to her own.

"Dear God," he breathed raggedly, his gaze turning to molten fire at her intimate confession, "waste no more time, lest I forget where we are and bend you across a table." His passion mounted with every heartbeat. Tension coursed the length of his body, making him unyielding as iron.

"And you dare call me a temptress," she whispered, running her tongue over her full lips, drawing his attention to their lushness.

"Let us slip away while everyone's watching the mummers."

"What about my husband?"

"What about him?" He paused, considering the question. "Can he see us?"

Pretending to look around the hall for her nonexistent husband, Rosamund shook her head. "Mayhap he has fallen asleep."

"Then let us hurry before he wakes." Henry seized her hand and raced with her over the rushes littered with debris from the Christmas feast.

Those who noticed their lord's departure merely smiled indulgently, curious about the masked woman's identity.

The air in the passage was so cold it was like a reviving slap in the face. Rosamund shivered, wondering if what she did was wise. The thought fled from her mind as Henry pulled her against him, warming first her mouth, then her bare shoulders with his ardent kisses. Soon she was forced to push him away, lest she succumb there in the passage.

"Someone will see us," Rosamund protested feebly, trying to put distance between them though in the narrow passage she was still dangerously close to his disturbing body.

"Let them. Have you forgotten I'm lord here. Come this way, Jane."

"What if your intended sees us?" she could not help asking him as he took her hand.

He muttered an oath beneath his breath before snapping in annoyance, "Your concern for my future wife's feelings grows tedious."

It was warning enough. Rosamund teased him no further about his bride to be. She would have satisfaction enough when she took off her mask. The reminder that their enjoyable game would soon be over was sobering. She would have liked to have him make love to her before he knew her identity. Since she could not expect him to make love to her while she was wearing the mask, she needed a gloomy place where her identity could remain a mystery a little while longer.

"There's too much light here. Come where the shadows are deepest," she said, her voice shaking as once again she contemplated making her fantasies reality.

"Are you that modest, wench?" Henry asked in surprise, drawing her to an alcove. "Here both your passion and modesty can be satisfied at the same time."

A burst of drunken laughter nearby told them they were not alone. Henry cursed at the discovery.

"Come. I know of an empty room nearby."

"How can you be sure it's empty?"

He did not reply. He merely hurried Rosamund up a short flight of stairs and down a corridor where the chill of the dank stone cut to the bone. He fitted a key to a lock and thrust open a door to reveal a large room bathed in murky shadow with only silver moonbeams to light their way. The size of the great bed in the middle of the room told Rosamund the bedchamber belonged to an important guest.

"Whose room is this?" she asked as Henry pushed the door shut with his foot.

Taking her in his arms, he leaned her back against the door, pressing against her. "This is the bridal chamber," he whispered before he kissed her fully on the lips.

Rosamund's gasp of surprise was silenced by his mouth.

He chuckled when he asked, "Do you suppose the devil will take my soul for sullying the marriage bed?" Then without giving her time to reply, he swept her off her feet and bore her to the black-shadowed bed.

They fell together on a soft mound of feathers, rumpling the velvet covers beneath them. The weight of his body drove the breath from her. Henry pinned her beneath him, feeling her strain to meet the iron-hard strength of his arousal.

"Now you see how hot I am for you—so hot, I'm like to burst. Let's have an end to play. 'Tis you who are the wicked one, Jane, to keep me so long unsatisfied. What answer you to that, lovely tormentor?"

His hot tongue traced a pattern along her jaw and down her neck, stopping at the bare flesh swelling over her bodice. He pulled down the neck of her gown, releasing the twin globes of her full breasts. Though her flesh was merely a white blur in the gloom, Henry shuddered because his imagination well supplied what the darkness stole.

Rosamund's limbs turned to molten liquid when he took her nipples between his lips and drew them out, suckling her flesh, his hot tongue swirling around the hardness. She uttered cries of delight as she fastened her hands in his thick hair, imprisoning him there for her delight.

Finally Henry's mouth moved up, leaving a trail of kisses until he captured her mouth. To her surprise, Rosamund felt his tongue probing her lips apart, then shooting fiery hot inside her mouth. Heat flamed through her veins at the unexpected intimacy. When finally he lay on top of her, hip against hip, she was powerless to keep her thighs from straining to meet that iron-hard proof of his passion. Shuddering with desire,

Patricia Phillips

she pressed against him, aware of the furnace heat through his clothing and delighting in the knowledge that Henry of Ravenscrag shook with desire for her!

His hot tongue darted and flicked inside her mouth, simulating the act they delayed. She drew on his tongue, sucking it until he abruptly pulled away from her. His hands swept beneath her marigold skirts to stroke and caress her thighs. Automatically her legs spread at his touch as he gently sought that passion-sweet chamber between her legs, his fingers penetrating gently and making her gasp.

Rosamund fumbled clumsily with his unfamiliar clothing, trying to negotiate the fastenings of his doublet and shirt, eager to caress the hot, solid frame pulsing against her. Temporarily distracted from his own pleasure, Henry helped her until between them they unfastened his clothes. Rosamund marveled as she ran her hand over his hard, muscular chest, tangling her fingers gently in his abundant chest hair. She fondled his nipples, then took the dark bud in her mouth, sucking on his flesh the way he had done to her.

Henry gasped in delight at the unexpected sensation; then he clasped her head so tight it hurt. "Dear God, Jane, have done," he groaned at last. He thrust her hand down, pressing her fingers against the hard swelling inside his clothes.

Though she wanted to touch him and learn the secrets beneath his fine velvet clothing, Rosamund hesitated, modesty suddenly overtaking her. Gently and wonderingly she began to mold the fabric about the thrusting length. Tiring of her modest caresses, Henry impatiently released the throbbing seat of his passion, which leapt eagerly into her hands, assuming a life of its own. Prepared though she was for a man's arousal, Rosamund was still not prepared for the sheer strength and heat of him. Gently she caressed his soft velvet skin, tracing the knotted veins and spanning the thickness of that throbbing brand. His arousal excited her beyond measure.

"Do I please you, sweetheart?" he asked huskily, wondering at her silence.

She whispered that he pleased her immensely and fondled

80

him anew, caressing the silken heat with such tenderness he was forced to stay her hand.

"Stop, unless you'd have me spill too soon," he said through gritted teeth. "Come. Let me take you now," he whispered as he rolled her on to her back, his kisses burning with passion.

Rosamund nibbled his earlobe, aware she throbbed with love for him. "Oh, Harry, I swear I love you with all my heart," she whispered sincerely, pressing her mouth over his hard jaw and tasting the hotly arousing fragrance of his skin.

"Come. Love me now, sweet," he urged again, his hands on her breasts, fondling and cupping until her senses whirled.

The burning pressure between her legs made her open wider in an effort to take him inside, his passionate kisses and husky endearments driving her mad. Hot pain suddenly seared between her legs and tears filled her eyes as he drove home. The searing heat probed deeper than she had thought possible. An intoxicating wave of pleasure engulfed her body. Eagerly she slid her legs around his hips, clinging as he raised her up, driving even deeper inside her until her entire being was consumed with fire. His kisses no longer tantalized; his mouth was a furnace of desire that quickly consumed her startled yelp of pain. He pressed her deeper into the feather mattress until he completely possessed her, searing their bodies and souls into molten passion.

Rosamund was no longer aware of her surroundings. She knew only the heated lovemaking of this man who swept her into fire-sparked blackness. Her body was racked with shudders of ecstasy before she finally began to drift back through layers of soft black velvet, spared from a jarring reentry into consciousness by his tender mouth and caressing hands.

The unexpected explosion inside her body was slowly transformed into a wave of contentment. Rosamund held Henry tightly, as she gradually remembered who she was and with whom she lay. That blissful emotion he had aroused inside her came as a startling surprise. Though she had often imagined how it would feel to be loved by him, she had never dreamed their coming together would be so intense.

Gently he kissed away tears from her lashes while Rosamund clung against him. "Oh, how much I love you," she whispered, devastated by her depth of passion for him.

He kissed her tenderly, but he did not lie and say he loved her in return. Only later, as she slowly came back to earth, did that omission seep inside her brain. The truth stole a little of her joy. Feeling suddenly exposed, she reached amidst the tumbled covers for the mask he had pulled off her face. Henry was too quick for her. He threw it across the room.

"No, you can't hide from me any longer. I will see what you've kept hidden so long. Oh, Jane. Thank you, my lovely one. I can't recall when I've felt so much pleasure. Promise you'll come to me again and soon. I won't lose you now. Your husband's a fool to let you out of his sight."

His amused words, though she supposed them to be appropriate to the supposed situation, made her sad and robbed her of the last of her lingering pleasure. How matter-of-fact he had become, while she still lay devastated with emotion after her total surrender. She was still weak and otherworldly, while he was returned completely to the present. When he drew away from her, disappointed tears filled her eyes. What irony that, though he had made love to her so magnificently, she must accept the unpleasant fact he did not love her!

He fumbled on a nearby chest and in alarm she realized he struggled to light a candle. The hearth was cold; so he must be using a tinderbox. She awaited the lighted revelation of the truth, no longer feeling any delightful anticipation over his discovery.

Henry gave a triumphant cry as a flame errupted and he quickly touched it to the silver-branched candlestick on the chest.

"Let there be light," he jested, holding the candlestick aloft as he came toward the bed. "No longer will I be thwarted, Mistress Jane. At last I shall see your face. But first, let me look my fill on your arousing body."

He moved closer to the bed, the candle flames casting triple pools of light over Rosamund's legs, then moving slowly upward over her hips. So delicious were her full breasts, Henry was unable to keep from caressing them one last time. Gently he molded those full white orbs, finally able to admire the magnificent sight he had only seen in his imagination.

Rosamund noticed he had already rearranged his clothing; though his doublet and shirt hung unfastened, his codpiece was closed and he had tied his points to hold his tights in place. Finally the triple-yellow glare reluctantly moved off her breasts and he shone the candle over her dark banner of hair spread across the pillows. Purposely he delayed until the last to reveal the mystery she had hidden beneath her mask.

"From the top of your head to the tip of your toes, you are a lovely goddess, Jane. Where have you been hiding all my life?" he whispered, taking handfuls of her rich brown hair to his mouth to kiss its silkiness. "And now, my sweet, the final mystery is revealed," he cried with a flourish, holding the candlestick high.

Rosamund blinked as the light glared across her face. He stood in shadow beyond those yellow pools. The light hovered above the bed like a separate entity. Then she heard his swift intake of breath.

"Oh, dear, sweet Jesus, tell me it's not so," he groaned, standing there as if frozen to the spot. "You're not Jane . . . you're . . . you're. . . . "

"Rosamund," she whispered, licking tears from her lips. "Your future wife."

He swore in anger, the flames jumping about as he shot forward. "It can't be so! Why? Damnit, why? Tell me?"

He caught her by the hair and yanked her upright. Then he flung her discarded dress across her body to hide her nakedness. "Cover yourself, woman. Have you no shame?"

Appalled by his changed mood, Rosamund could only stare at him in disbelief. Where was the romantic lover who had so magnificently fulfilled her dreams?

"Why are you so angry with me?" she whispered at last, licking salt from her lips.

"Because you should have stayed virgin!" he cried in anger.

"But you are my husband. What difference does one day make?"

"And you lied to me! You deceived me into thinking that—" His voice shook with anger. He fought for the words. "You are my wife! Dear God, it's unheard of. A man seducing his own bride. That's rich, by God, if it's not." Seeing the humor in the situation, he began to laugh until he was forced to sit on the end of the bed, where he shook the frame with his bitter mirth.

"What difference tonight or tomorrow—and I meant what I said, husband."

He thrust aside her hands when she tried to caress him. "Why did you do this? What insanity possessed you?"

"It was you who invited me to your bed," she said sharply, scrubbing tears from her eyes.

"Only because I thought you were someone else," he said, glowering at her. "And I might add, you came right willingly."

"That's because I knew exactly who you were," she said, annoyed by his preposterous attack. "It shouldn't matter that my name's Rosamund and not Jane. We made such magnificent love together," she said, her eyes glittering at the memory of their grand passion. She hoped to jar his memory into forgiveness. She was alarmed to see her words merely seemed to inflame him.

"Had I known it was you, this would never have happened," he spat through gritted teeth, thundering his fist into the mattress. "I might have drunk too much wine, but I was quite capable of knowing what I did. You misrepresented yourself as some easy—"

"And you took pleasure in me."

He refused to answer. He sat for a long time, his head in his hands. Then at last he looked up and rubbed his face, finding the truth still hard to accept.

"Who else knows of your trickery?" he asked, standing up

and towering over her, his face dark with anger. He grasped her shoulder, giving her an impatient shake when she still would not answer. "Tell me. Who else knows of this deception?"

"No one but you," she whispered at last.

"Well, thank God for small mercies. Now, I have to think how best to proceed. You stupid wench. Did they not teach you more sense in that confounded convent?"

Rosamund could not reply. She merely sat sobbing quietly amid her shattered dreams. That she would be his wife should not have made any difference to him. They would be married on the morrow. A few hours could not matter. Again she reached for his hand, but he shook her off.

"I still meant what I said—about loving you," she said, hoping to please him with the truth.

Henry turned about and glowered down at her. "How can you love me? You don't even know me."

His cruel retort stole the last of her strength. Rosamund buried her face in her hands and wept bitterly. He did not try to comfort her. He merely sat still rubbing his face, trying to clear away the cobwebs of wine and desire.

Finally she felt his hands on her shoulders as he made her sit up. "Now, stop weeping. It's done and it can't be undone," he said gruffly, offering her meager comfort.

He sat looking at her until she finally turned her face to the wall. "Don't look at me," she said, trying to hide her tear-swollen face from him. "I'm ugly now."

He reached out to her and turned her about. "No, you're still lovely. And I wish to God you weren't. A man's wife is not supposed to arouse him like this."

Chapter Five

When the winter dawn broke over Ravenscrag Castle, Rosamund was still awake. She stared at the patch of sky visible through the narrow, unglazed window, watching as blackness gradually gave way to gun-metal gray. How she wished the past hours had been only a nightmare. But she knew what had taken place was no dream.

Each time she mentally replayed the hours spent in the smoky, brightly decorated hall, and later in that moonlit bedchamber, her heart sank. Yet curiously, at the same time, her pulse quickened at the treacherous memory of Henry's lovemaking. She touched her lips, which were still burning from his kisses. Then that small chill voice of reason reminded her there had been little love to it. The cruel reminder made hot tears fill her eyes and spill down her cheeks.

The truth was that Henry of Ravenscrag had used her like some loose woman, his passion changing to anger once he had discovered who she really was. What had she done that was so terrible? Was her handsome husband incapable of passion inside the marriage bed? she wondered uneasily as she recalled he had not anticipated any pleasure from his marriage. Were his emotions aroused only by clandestine liaisons?

Surely some of his anger was directed at himself for making passionate love to his wife instead of to an easy slut named Jane. The very thought had seemed to appall him, as if by so doing he had broken some ridiculous masculine rule excluding wives from all sensual pleasure.

Whatever his reasoning, he had both loved and desired her for a little while. That crumb of hope would sustain her. Henry's mind-set would be difficult to change because he must first admit shared passion with his wife was not only possible; it was much to be desired.

When Henry had brought her back to her room in the small hours of the morning, he had demanded to know where she had found her disguise. So that none should be the wiser about her escapade, a trusted servant retrieved her gown from the guest's bedchamber. And mindful of the poor woman still imprisoned in the privy, Henry told the servant to release the guest. When Henry finally bid Rosamund good night, his face had been grim. He offered her no kiss in parting, but then she had not really expected one.

Later, while Rosamund was still smarting under his black anger, her mood turned rebellious. Why was she being punished? At the time, tricking her betrothed into thinking he seduced some loose moraled chit had seemed innocent enough. Henry had not hesitated to rise to the bait—and most handsomely at that. The reminder made her smile—a sure sign her pain was dwindling. Perhaps his anger stemmed more from his own transgressions than from hers. By bedding her so readily, he had revealed to his bride his own immoral habits. That exposure, she was sure, would be a most humiliating experience for any man.

That explanation for what lay behind Henry's anger lightened Rosamund's spirits. It was likely that, when Henry reviewed the episode with a clear head, he would see the humor of it. Quickly she thrust aside the reminder of his bitter mirth last night, determined that nothing should mar her pleasure in his passionate lovemaking. Henry of Ravenscrag was everything she had imagined him to be when she had spun her nightly fantasies at End Cottage. Rosamund still found it hard to believe that the handsome man of her dreams would soon be her husband. In a way, her favorite fantasy, wherein he swept her aboard his charger and took her to his castle, had already come true. And though she had not actually arrived aboard his magic steed, she had come to his castle nonetheless.

A bump at the door alerted her. To Rosamund's surprise,

a serving woman didn't come into the room. Rather, Sir Ismay and his faithful shadow, Hartley, entered.

"Well, well, already awake and eager for the big day," Sir Ismay said, striding to the bed. "I trust you're well rested, Rosamund, my love. After all, this is to be the most important day of your life . . . and mine too."

Rosamund reached to the neck of her shift, making sure the garment was in place. Fortunately, Sir Ismay could not see the glowing imprints of Henry's ardent lips, which she was sure must mark her breasts.

"Why is that, Father?" she asked, her voice sounding small and tight in the stone-walled room.

Sir Ismay chuckled as he rested his hard hand on her brow, absently brushing aside glossy strands of hair. "Ah, feeling confident enough to jest, are we, daughter? Let's hope your confidence remains after the bedding. Remember, you gave me your word—your very life depends on it."

Her stomach pitched at the veiled threat behind his words. A wave of dread for what lay ahead swept over her. In the distraction of the previous night's romance she had forgotten that her wedding was to take place that day. In a few hours, she would be united for life with the powerful Lord of Ravenscrag, an important figure there in the North. She would be mistress of a castle, wife of a rich nobleman. So far life had left her unprepared to accept such responsibility. She must keep her eyes and ears open at all times so she would learn what was expected of her. And always she must take care not to give away her humble beginnings. Daunting though the prospect was, she knew, even had she been able, she would not change places with another. To have Henry was ample reward for any ordeal she must endure.

"Are you to examine the sheets just to prove I spoke the truth?" Rosamund asked, trying to keep her voice light as though in jest, while in truth her heart thudded uncomfortably as she awaited his answer.

"As God is my witness, wench," Sir Ismay said angrily,

"don't play me false, or you'll regret it for the rest of your days."

"I'm no fool," she said, her heart lying leaden in her chest.

"Nor I—and neither is his lordship. Remember that. Curb your loose tongue, lest you betray us. I'll send the women in to prepare you."

The two men turned in unison and strode to the door. Sir Ismay paused at the threshold, unable to resist a final glance at the woman with whom his destiny rested, if only to reassure himself the pawn with which he played so high a stake was worthy of the gamble. He caught his breath at her beauty. Her face was shrouded mistily in the half-light; her rich hair tumbled unbound on the pillow.

"Harry Ravenscrag won't be able to help himself," he muttered with satisfaction as he pulled the door behind him.

Later, Rosamund was led from her chamber, heavily veiled and magnificently gowned in yellow satin and brocade, to her waiting groom, who expressed no joy at the sight of her. His body language revealed his stern, unyielding mood as bride and groom knelt side by side before the altar, remote as strangers.

Ravenscrag Castle's vaulted chapel was hung with banners of blue, gold and crimson; black velvet kneelers embroidered in gold rested before each pew. The ends of the carved pews were decorated with evergreen boughs. The pungent scent of pine mingled with incense, and the close-packed bodies of the guests had been liberally doused with perfume. The chapel held no more than 20 of the most important guests. Tallow-laden heat from many blazing candles blended with the nose-tickling clouds of incense inside the small stone chapel.

Rosamund gulped for breath, feeling suffocated in the heavy atmosphere. She stood before the marble steps leading up to the altar, fighting to overcome a feeling of faintness as the nuptial Mass droned on. A half-dozen choirboys with voices as pure as those of angels sang an anthem with many verses. Afterward, the old priest resumed singing the prayers in his wavering falsetto, his knees creaking audibly each time he genuflected before the altar.

Everything about that day seemed unreal, almost as if Rosamund was watching a play not unlike the traveling mystery play she had enjoyed the previous Eastertide. Rosamund was tempted to pinch herself just to make sure she was not dreaming. But, no, the strength of Henry's hand gripping hers was real. And the cold ring he slipped on her finger was all the assurance she needed to know the marriage was really taking place.

Her groom lifted the veil so he could kiss her cheek. Rosamund looked into his eyes, trying to interpret his mood, but they were hooded and closed off. At his continuing formality, she caught her breath in pain. Was she never to be forgiven?

A flicker of fear began in her stomach as Rosamund stole a sideways glance at his set face. Why was he still so angry with her? Her life was controlled by two powerful men and she did not think either of them would be very forgiving of her various deceptions. Her husband could renounce her as unchaste. In that event, she knew Sir Ismay's vengeance would be swift. Perhaps she would get only a flogging in payment for destroying his plans, though she did not think he would consider letting her off so lightly. His duplicity would create a dangerous rift between the houses of Ravenscrag and De Gere. Why had she given in to her whim to see the dance before she had hidden a vial of blood about her person? How was she to save the day now?

The continuing heat from Henry's handclasp reminded her how sweet his caress had been and how swiftly his passion had changed to anger. He looked rich and very lordly in his lapis velvet doublet. Cloth of silver trimmed the garment and made his dark hair look blacker by comparison. He was cleanly shaved; his hair had been freshly barbered for the ceremony. As Rosamund looked closely at him, she was surprised to see lines set about his mouth, making him appear far older than she remembered. The many cups of wine he had drunk the night before must have afflicted him. He moved his head little and kept his jaw tight, as if his head ached.

The Mass finally wound to a close. All eyes were upon the bride as she walked slowly over the rush-strewn floor, her hand on her husband's arm as she matched his measured gait, their slow pace befitting the solemn occasion. A crowd of well-wishers thronged the walkway beyond the chapel. The boisterous guests had not been amongst those 20 privileged souls admitted to the ceremony, but their waiting had not gone unrewarded. Servants had liberally plied them with burgundy. Laughing men pounded the groom on the shoulder, offering congratulations laced with bawdy advice for the upcoming bedding. The ladies, only slightly more delicate in their approach, singled out the bride for their attentions. The bridal pair separated wordlessly, each escorted by a crowd of revelers of their own sex who led them to the great hall, where a wedding feast was spread.

That noon the lofty room was bright with the decorations from the previous night's feast. The red tablecloths had been turned clean side up. At the bridal pair's approach, a fanfare was blown. The hundreds of guests rang the rafters with their cheers as Rosamund and Henry mounted the steps leading to the lord's table.

The noise was deafening. Tension had already made Rosamund's head throb. How she longed to escape to the quiet darkness of her chamber, yet she realized she could never again enjoy such anonymity. Prepared or not, she was the lady of the castle! It was a shocking discovery. How would she manage the great household with no training in the art? How would she command these servants, who in reality were probably several stations above her? She knew nothing about provisioning so many people, nor how to care for linens.

"Come, wife. Sit beside me."

Through the clamor Rosamund heard Henry's voice and the chill behind the words encased her heart in ice. He had not forgiven her. Maybe he would never forgive her. Tears welled up in her eyes and she stumbled on the steps. Henry, thinking her overtired, caught her arm to guide her to her seat. A ser-

vant had pulled out a chair for her. Only slightly shorter than
the lord's great carved chair, the lady's chair was cushioned
in velvet and emblazoned on the back with the Ravenscrag
arms.

It was a relief to be able to sit. Rosamund's knees shook
with nervousness; all morning she had been afraid she would
faint. When Rosamund looked sideways at her handsome husband, his profile appeared as unyielding as the big black bird
on his crest. The yellow candlelight made his glossy black
hair gleam like a raven's feathers. Above his set mouth his
nose appeared somewhat beaked, creating an even more striking resemblance to his coat of arms.

Then suddenly Henry laughed, and his face was transformed. A flutter of hope stirred in Rosamund's breast when
she saw his humor changed. Yet to her disappointment, she
discovered his good humor was reserved for the brightly
dressed troupe of mummers who tumbled the length of the
hall. Several small dogs with red ruffs round their necks
twisted and leapt beside the mummers. The dogs jumped high
in the air to land on their masters' shoulders before bouncing
back to the rushes, almost as if they had springs on their paws.

"Oh, aren't they clever, husband?" Rosamund laughed, delighted by the entertainment. At her words the smile faded
from Henry's face; she did not imagine the change.

"Will you give us a toast, Sir Ismay?" Henry said, turning
from his wife to her father.

Sir Ismay fairly gloated with pride, basking in his newfound
position beside the powerful man who had become his son by
marriage. "I'll give thee a thousand toasts, Henry. I raise my
goblet to my future ally, fellow soldier, friend . . . son. May
fortune shine on both our houses. And may the line of Ravenscrag be blessed by many sons to carry that ancient blood
far into the future."

"Thank you, Father-in-law," Henry said, as he held up his
hand for silence. It took a few minutes for the resounding
cheers to quiet and the ringing in the rafters to stop. "Now,
as a reminder of the joining of our houses, may I present a

banner I had made last month in York.''

On cue, two liveried pages stepped forward bearing a gilt staff around which was rolled a length of velvet. Following a lengthy trumpet fanfare, the pages unfurled the heavy fabric. An exclamation of pleasure echoed around the hall as the guests craned their necks for a glimpse of the dark blue velvet banner. A heavy gold fringe glittered in the candlelight, the light shimmering like water over the gold embroidery on the coat of arms displayed before them. The arms of the De Gere leopard rampant on its flame red ground were quartered with the predatory black raven of Ravenscrag on a sea of midnight blue.

Both touched and impressed, Sir Ismay said, ''I could have asked for no greater gift. The uniting of our houses is my long-cherished dream.''

The two men stood and embraced, displaying their unity to the assembly. Miserably Rosamund watched; each symbol of their united power felt like another coal heaped upon the fire of her shame. When the truth was revealed, how much greater would be their anger after that public show? She wished she could sink through the floor and never face the inevitable day of reckoning.

The soldiers of both armies seated at the lower trestles at the far end of the hall raised their tankards in salute to their lords. Though the men were placed far from the blazing hearth, they had been amply stoked by steaming cauldrons of mulled ale. The toast to their lords was followed by a toast to their new lady, during which Rosamund stood and smiled as was expected. The following resounding cheer echoed through the room and set metal pots jingling on the tables. The sudden noise also disturbed pigeons roosting in the rafters. The startled birds fluttered overhead, their flight eliciting squeals of dismay from the ladies, who frantically tried to protect both their heads and their trenchers from bird droppings.

Once the commotion was quieted, Sir Ismay turned to his son-in-law and asked, ''Have I not given you a beautiful bride?'' With this he leaned around Henry's broad shoulders to smile benevolently at Rosamund, his humor softened by wine and pleasure. "See how healthy she is. She'll give you a dozen sons."

Henry turned to his wife, his face betraying little emotion. "Aye, she is a beauty indeed." This was all he said before he signaled to the castle steward to send in the servers with the food.

Rosamund smarted beneath his rejection as the grand procession began. Great platters bearing the feast dishes were held high, steaming and fragrant. The delicacies were borne around the room before coming to the lord's table. There were roasted peacocks still with their splendid iridescent tail feathers, crackling haunches of beef swimming in purple wine sauce, spit-roasted venison, and golden capons stuffed with oysters. The meats were followed by gilded fish in seas of sauce and greenery, side dishes of fish and meat pastes, turnips and swedes glazed with honey. All was accompanied by long loaves of bread whiter than any Rosamund had seen before, even on Thorpe's table. Dishes of fresh-churned butter molded into the arms of both houses stood beside the loaves. Sweetened flummeries of whipped cream and fruit, spiced cakes, and gilded marchpane figures appeared next. And there was wine—great flagons of it, goblets filled to overflowing with it, spilling in narrow red streams to the rushes as the servers' arms were jostled. All the riches the great castle of Ravenscrag could boast were heaped before the wedding party, first going to the lord's table before being passed to the other guests in order of their importance.

Servers refilled the ale cups and trenchers of the common retainers far down the hall, their fare plainer and more easily identified. Wistfully Rosamund wished she could eat the food of the common men. There were so many unfamiliar spices in the sauces and rubbed into the roasted meat she could not identify what she was eating.

As the wine flowed, some male guests began to noisily chide Henry about his seeming indifference to his lovely bride. He quickly assured them she would not lack attention in the bridal chamber. And those privy to his tryst with the delectable stranger in the early hours of this morning wondered aloud if there were aught left in the treasure chest to do justice to the marriage bed. Not taking offense at their boldness, Henry laughingly assured them there was an abundant supply to cement the bond of their merging families.

Accustomed to rough talk, Rosamund was not bothered by their ribald comments, yet she could not help wondering how the real Rosamund, fresh from a convent, would feel. Should she pretend to be shocked? As it was, her face flamed from heat and wine. Before she had decided on the appropriate emotion, a singing troupe of women danced inside the hall.

All attention switched to the women wearing filmy green-and-gold draperies and beribboned evergreen wreaths on their heads. Many men paused with goblets and spoons halfway to their mouths as they realized the women's garments were purposely provocative. Each movement allowed glimpses of bare breasts, thighs, and hips amid the floating gauzy green fabric. As the women danced, they sang an old Christmas round, weaving and twisting gold-ribboned garlands in their hands. One by one, as they ended their dance, the wenches came to the dais to lay beribboned tributes before their lord, making sure he had his fill of their charms as they knelt before him. For their pains, Henry laughingly threw each wench a gold coin.

After the dancers, the servants began to move benches and push back trestles in the lower end of the hall to make room for the guests to dance. A great sugar confection depicting both a raven and a leopard rampant appeared at the lord's table, signaling the end of the wedding feast. The glistening confection was colored pink with sandalwood. Great mountains of gilded marchpane had been frosted at the summit to represent snow; on these sugar crags perched a raven looking down on the smaller leopard, who tried to climb the mountain.

Rosamund wondered if Sir Ismay would be offended by the unspoken message—obviously a reminder that the mighty House of Ravenscrag had achieved the pinnacle and the House of De Gere merely strove for that ascension.

The hidden meaning behind the innocent tableau was not lost on Sir Ismay. When Rosamund looked around her husband's shoulder, she saw her father was scowling; he also drank thirstily from his goblet. He had noted well the pointed reminder that, though their fortunes had been united, Henry of Ravenscrag was still his superior in both rank and power.

"We must dance at least one round before we can retire," Henry said in Rosamund's ear, the first words he had spoken to her since they had been seated at the table.

In disappointment Rosamund saw no eagerness on his face, no burning desire in his eyes, which appeared unnaturally dark in the gloom. Retire, she knew, was a polite reference to their bedding. The maids had explained the procedure to her that morning. The guests would sing them to their chamber, and after seeing the bride and groom bedded, they would withdraw. While the wedding guests danced and made merry, the ancient houses of Ravenscrag and De Gere would become one.

Rosamund stood, stiff as an old woman. She felt little joy in anticipation of the dance or of what was to follow. It was as if all pleasure had been drained from her, leaving in its stead fear of discovery and the punishment to follow. Sir Ismay might even be forced into telling him the entire truth. She shuddered at that thought. Surely she would not live to see the morrow if that came about.

Henry led her through the laughing throng to the middle of the hall. In the minstrel gallery, the musicians struck up a lively tune. With leaden feet Rosamund followed Henry's lead as they headed the long line of dancers moving around the great hall. Far from graceful, she stumbled over the rushes as if they were deep brush. Weariness and dread for what was to follow made her head throb.

Aware that some of the guests had begun tittering at her, perhaps imagining that the convent-bred wench's apparent malaise sprang from fear of the impending coupling, Rosamund held her head high in defiance and fixed a stiff smile on her lips. Damn them all! In a way she would enjoy seeing their shocked faces when they discovered they had been duped by a washerwoman's daughter. But that small pleasure could never repay her for her suffering.

At last the dance was over. The tipsy guests prepared to escort the bride and groom to their bedchamber. A noisy procession was forming: first Henry and his bride, then dignitaries, guests, musicians, and servants, pushing their way through the chill stone corridors, singing, laughing and joking.

At last, they reached the bridal chamber, and with much jostling and cursing, the motley rabble halted there. Rosamund's stomach churned when she recognized the room's distinctive studded door. It had indeed been to the bridal chamber Henry had taken her the night before. Tears pricked her eyes at the thought of what might have been. Then the door swung open and the newlyweds were propelled inside. Weak winter sunshine lit the lofty room, revealing the bed's grand velvet hangings and the cloth of gold edging the velvet bedcover with its familiar raven's crest.

The women guests crowded around Rosamund to help her disrobe, blocking the view of their lady from the men's curious gaze. In turn the male guests assisted their lord out of his fine doublet and shirt, likewise shielding his nakedness from curious noblewomen who envied the bride her handsome groom. Those ladies in the room who were privy to the Lord of Ravenscrag's lovemaking smiled knowingly, envying the bride that night's passion, which they doubted she would have the wit to appreciate since she was fresh from a convent.

Rosamund was led up the steps to the big bed. The covers had been turned back to display pristine sheets sprinkled with fragrant lavender and rosemary. Numbly she slipped inside the covers, glad of the warming pan at the bottom of the bed since her feet were like ice. She had to clasp her hands to stop their trembling. Laughing delightedly at what they assumed to be wedding night nerves, the women brushed her thick chestnut hair, spreading it unbound across the pillows. The more kindly amongst them assured her she need not be afraid, promising her that nine months hence she would present his lordship with a beautiful son.

Next it was Henry's turn to ascend the steps to the bed. The gentlemen led him forth clad in a wine damask dressing gown with furred hem. There was an audible groan of disappointment from the women when, as the robe was slipped off, a long, concealing nightshirt was revealed. Many had been secretly hoping for a glimpse of Harry Ravenscrag's much touted virility.

The newlyweds were officially bedded and propped against heaped feather pillows, sitting side by side, hands neatly clasped atop the folded covers. Their task accomplished, the wedding guests backed away from the bed and launched into a song so bawdy that some of the ladies blushed at its explicit words. Hiccuping, belching, and snorting, the rowdy guests formed a long, sinuous line and, with hands on the waist of the person in front of them, sang their way toward the door. Hands sometimes strayed higher, causing squeals of protest as the slow-moving serpent wound out the door and along the corridor. Only the body servants remained in the room.

When the last guest had departed, Henry breathed a great sigh of relief. He waved the servants away.

"You can go. My lady wife and I have no further need of you. Is there wine?" He glanced toward the chest and with satisfaction saw the silver tray covered by a cloth—a repast to revive lagging strength. "You are dismissed."

Bowing, the servants backed to the door and slipped outside. The door closed and heavy silence enveloped the room. Rosamund found an uncontrollable wave of grief welling through her body as her eyes filled with tears. In vain she tried to swallow the lump in her throat. She felt thoroughly defeated.

Henry slid out of bed and pulled on his dressing gown before slipping his feet into short furred boots. "Oh, for Christ's sake, stop crying," he said, glancing back at her as he poured himself a cup of wine.

Numbly she licked tears from her lips, feeling so devastated she did not know how to stop. All her dreams had been destroyed.

"Why are you still crying?" he demanded as he perched on the edge of the bed.

Rosamund swallowed and, finding her voice, she croaked, "Why are you still so angry with me?"

He glowered at her and swung off the bed. "You don't know, do you, you stupid chit?" he growled as he began to pace the room.

"No, 'tis the reason I asked," she said more boldly, her courage gradually returning. Since there was nothing she could do to fix matters, why cry? Tears were no help at such a late date. She was tempted to confess all to Henry, yet she held back.

"Here." Henry handed her a cup of wine and sat atop the velvet coverlet at the end of the bed. Watching the fire blazing merrily in the corner hearth, he finally said, "There's much I can't explain . . . not even to myself. Last night's foolishness could have been a disaster. Thank God, you weren't discovered. Luckily I was able to convince Lady Terlton some drunken fool had locked her in that privy. I had to give her a seat in the chapel to mollify her."

"Is that the only reason?" Rosamund asked incredulously. At his words her heart had leapt in relief.

"No, just a portion." He stopped and sipped his wine, still keeping his attention on the fire. He had to purposely avert his gaze. As the sunlight vanished and the day turned cloudy, the half-light made Rosamund look like the woman from the night before. And he did not want that reminder.

Abruptly Henry stood, then began to pace the room. "What would your father have done had he known? What would the bishop have said? Or half-a-dozen equally important guests? A man does not seduce his own wife. It isn't done, not anywhere, anytime."

"You did."

"Aye, to my eternal shame. But you forget I thought you were another."

"You seemed to enjoy me immensely."

He wanted to dispute her words, but in all honesty could not. "That is beside the point, Rosamund. I would not have treated you so had I known you were not Jane."

Her heart felt lighter as she understood he had no real reason for his anger beyond shattered masculine pride. "It doesn't matter what name you call me. Oh, Henry, there's no shame to it. I enjoyed last night immensely. You made me very happy. And now that we're married there can be no wrong to it. You're my husband."

"I've been your husband by proxy for over six months," he said, dismissing her argument. "That's got little to do with it."

Rosamund stared at him in surprise as she learned he had already been married to her—or more accurately, to his true betrothed—long before she had arrived in England. Only the religious ceremony must have been needed to complete the union. "Then why?"

"Look, Rosamund. Damn it. I've nothing against you personally. You're a beautiful woman—a bonus I didn't expect. I never even thought I'd find you attractive, let alone lust after you. Oh, damn, this is all wrong! You're my wife. It's your duty to beget sons who will inherit my lands and titles. That's all. We bed only out of duty. Surely you must have known this was no love match. I've never even laid eyes on you since you were a little lass. Your father and I signed an agreement."

"Well, none of that's changed."

Henry thumped his fist into his palm in exasperation. "You stubborn wench, why won't you try to understand?"

"I'm trying. You aren't making it very plain."

"I intended that kind of relationship between us—nothing more. My own life is already set. Your task is to bear sons and be lady of this castle."

"And now you've lusted after me can I not still do that?"

Henry's head snapped up as he heard the amusement in her voice. He wanted to be angry with her, but she was so damned appealing that he grew angry with himself for the unwanted—

well, perhaps unexpected—stirring in his blood. Henry shook his head to clear the treacherous thoughts and he resumed his pacing.

"I'm trying to explain that what happened last night was purely of the flesh—like lovers, not like husbands and wives," he said, striving for patience. "It was nothing more than a pleasant dalliance."

"It was pleasant indeed." Rosamund smiled at him, her tongue unconsciously moving over her lips as she recalled how very pleasant their lovemaking had been.

Henry groaned and strode over to the fire, keeping his back to her.

"We can start anew today as husband and wife," Rosamund said happily, not really understanding the fine difference between the two. "The only change will be that you're making love to Rosamund and last night you made love to Jane."

"No! That's impossible."

"You made love to me and it didn't matter that I was your wife. Don't you see? That woman from last night's still here, but her name isn't Jane."

He swallowed and clenched his fists. That was just what he was afraid of. Such events weren't supposed to happen. Their marriage was just a business arrangement, a dispersal of land and the sharing of soldiers, two houses united to strengthen the region. Instead it had become a weakness of his will—of his very soul!

Rosamund sipped the heavy sweet wine as she watched Henry struggling with his conscience. She had known it would be hard for him to go against all he believed. She was overjoyed to learn the paltry excuses that made him withold his affection from her. Then she remembered the lack of that important proof of virginity and she blanched; there was no way to overcome that problem.

Finally Henry came and perched again on the edge of the bed. He nervously fingered the velvet cover as he tried to compose his thoughts despite his jangling nerves and rising blood. Though Rosamund wore a nunlike shift with a high neckline, she had pushed down the covers to expose the mounds of her breasts, which were firmly inviting beneath the fine linen. Her nipples made peaks in the soft fabric and his heart thundered as he recalled how responsive she had been to his touch.

Henry cleared his throat and purposely looked away. When he spoke, his voice was tight. "You're not making this any easier for me. Wife or no, you're one of the most beautiful women I've ever seen. You have to understand there can be no more between us than duty. Say you understand me, Rosamund."

"I hear what you're saying, but I don't understand you. Why can't there be love? Why not passion?"

Henry stiffened as she reached for his arm, her hand insistent against his embroidered sleeve. Steeling himself not to react to her touch, he finally turned to look at her.

"There will be mutual respect, perhaps even affection between us," he said, quickly averting his gaze from her lush mouth. "Your purpose is to bear sons. For that, as you know, we can't stay strangers." He smiled, trying to make light of his remark, but when she smiled too at the reminder, his heart quickened over the invitation he saw in her face. "You're the damnedest convent-bred wench I've ever met," he growled, helplessly leaning toward her before he caught himself and pulled back. "Because of last night's shame, it was ... is ... my intention to let you sleep undisturbed."

"No," she said, "this is our wedding day. You owe me that much, husband. Besides," she added, stroking the warm velvet bedrobe, where it pulled against his thigh, "you know you can't stay away from me forever. So stop this senseless game."

"I play no game," he snarled, trying to quell the heat rising in his body. "Last night was a mistake. It mustn't be repeated. I'm not free to—" He stopped, biting back those betraying words.

"I've already told you I love you. And even though you've treated me ill since you learned I was your wife, I'll forgive you, Henry,'' she whispered, her eyes softly luminous in the half-light.

"You can't love me. You don't know me," he croaked in protest, trying to ignore her hand kneading the muscle in his thigh.

Rosamund smiled and reached up to his shoulder, touching the hard square mass, remembering what his bare flesh felt like. "Oh, I know you . . . after last night possibly better than any other. You are my love."

Henry groaned, closing his eyes. "No, Rosamund, don't say that. No," he protested feebly, allowing her to draw him against her.

"Yes," she said, pulling his unresisting body into her arms. Her heart soared as she held the hot substance of his body against her own, becoming aware of his accelerated passion as his breathing grew ragged.

"This isn't what I intended," he said, still protesting, though his hand stole into her hair, and gulping like a drowning man, he pulled her face to his and kissed her eager mouth, shuddering at the fire ignited between them.

"You see, you've already changed your mind," she said, smiling at his stubborn resolve. Her hands went to his hair and she smoothed the crisp black curls springing to life beneath her fingers. "We'll start afresh today. I am Rosamund, your wife, but I promise you'll know no difference from Jane. Oh, Harry, I want you more than life itself."

Her voice cracked as she momentarily returned to earth, aware this man could cost her her life. Then she thrust away the thought almost as soon as it came. His hot mouth was on hers, awakening the sweetest pleasure she had ever known. He shook beneath her hands, tremors of passion transferring from his body to hers.

"Yes, you are Rosamund, my wife," he whispered in defeat. He closed his eyes to reality and allowed himself to be drawn into that magical world of warm arms and lips and flickering firelight.

Rosamund's heart soared at his words and she cast aside all

doubt and worry, losing herself in passion, desperate to regain the wonder of the night before. Perhaps it was not to be cruelly snatched from her after all. She was going to bind him to her so completely he was beyond redemption. Rosamund shuddered as Henry's hot mouth swept down her neck to her shoulders. Impatiently he unfastened her shift, his hands trembling as he fumbled with the ties. Finally the garment was undone and he pushed the soft fabric from her body. Her creamy shoulders and full breasts emerged from the white folds. They were so perfect and inviting that a cry of passion died in his throat as he gave himself up to the moment.

The hot constriction of Henry's hands and mouth made Rosamund shudder with delight. He kissed the globes of her breasts; then he fastened his lips around her nipple, drawing the life from her, and she melted with passion. As if the two were connected, a searing stab of delight plunged deep between her legs, tugging and insistant, reaching, clamoring. . . .

The bedcovers were all churned about the lovers as they slipped inside their warmth. Henry had pulled off his bedrobe and his nightshirt followed; both garments were pitched carelessly on the rushes. Rosamund shuddered at the arousing sight of his muscular body, finding his flesh hot to her touch. She slid her hand into the tangle of dark hair on his chest, twining damp ringlets about her fingers. She ached for the hot taste of his mouth until she finally pulled his head up from her breasts, eagerly seeking his lips.

They rolled over together and her thighs strained against his in silent invitation. She could feel the demanding pressure of his fiery arousal against her body and she slipped her hand between them, fondling his hot, smooth flesh. Henry gasped in surprise at her unexpected touch, shuddering until he stayed her hand, slowing her caresses.

"Oh, sweeting, you're the loveliest woman in the world. I can't believe you're real," he whispered, finally drawing away to admire her. The flickering fire cast shadows over her milky flesh, turned now light, now dark, creating a magical, unreal scene. She seemed so perfect as to be unattainable and he quickly pulled her against him, capturing her lest she be taken from him. Unaccountably his heart thudded in distress at the very thought.

"There's no difference now, is there, love?" she asked him throatily, nuzzling against the fragrant warmth of his neck.

"Nay, except that today is even better because I have all my senses." He chuckled, enmeshing his hands in her hair, taking handfuls of the silky mass to his mouth and kissing the perfumed strands. He placed thick locks of hair across her chest and twined them around her full breasts, thereby adding empthasis and contrast to their creamy fullness. "Dear God," he whispered, aroused anew, "would that you could wear gowns with a bodice like that."

"For all the other men to see."

He frowned and pulled her possessively in his arms. "No, for my eyes only. Mayhap I will commission an artist to paint you thus and I will keep the portrait secretly in my apartment. Or perhaps I could keep you prisoner like the infidels who allow no other man to look upon their women."

"Then what would I do all day?"

He shrugged before burying his face in the soft heat of her neck. "I know not, but I can tell you what you would do all night."

Rosamund giggled at his suggestion, gladly allowing him to roll her over so that his weight pressed her deep into the feather mattress. Henry rose up on his hands and looked down at her, his eyes dark with passion. How much she loved him. Rosamund shivered in anticipation, aware that by prolonging the final delight they would merely deepen their pleasure. Henry drew his mouth over her breasts, placing feather-light kisses as he traced a burning passage down her soft belly until he came to that secret place between her legs. When his tongue made contact with her quivering flesh, Rosamund cried out in delighted surprise. Gently at first, he bathed her sensitive core in moist heat, his tongue and mouth tenderly teasing until she almost wept with pleasure. Then he withdrew the torment and

105

moved slowly up her body, leaving a trail of kisses in his wake.

Shaking with delight, she clung to his hard body, her mouth pressed against his shoulder, her teeth snagging his flesh. Of their own accord, her fingers molded the hot, throbbing length of his passion, tracing the swollen veins, the velvet smooth tip, aching to feel his strength swelling inside her. Her thighs strained against his and his kisses grew hard. His mouth bruised her lips, yet she did not draw back. She merely pressed harder, longing for them to become one.

Sliding into position above her, Henry stroked her flesh with the swollen length of his passion, withdrawing when she gasped in pleasure, then renewing the onslaught until she crushed him to her. Again and again he withdrew until she begged him to have done.

Rosamund opened her legs eagerly, receiving first his inquisitive fingers. Her muscles clamped on the obstruction and this blatant invitation was more than he could endure. Trying to use his utmost control, Henry gladly breached the portals of her body, sinking deep inside her while she strained to take the length of him inside her. When he lifted her hips with his strong hands enabling him to go deeper, their pelvic bones finally ground together. The molten heat of their passion became a fiery, plunging dance. He no longer consciously held back, nor did she strive to contain him. Together they melted as one in a wonderful, thrilling ascent with no awareness of time and place. They soared to the stars, going through blackness into light until finally their desire exploded, making her cry out in ecstasy. She matched her lover's deep groans of satisfaction with her own moans of total surrender.

After what seemed like an eternity, they floated back to earth, spent and delirious. Henry did not move from the bed, but held Rosamund close, gently kissing her eyelids, tasting tears shed at the peak of fulfillment. His lips moved gently over her face; his hot breath blew comforting against her cheek. In his strong arms she felt safe and deeply loved. The steady beat of his heart was sweet music to her ears. They murmured and kissed until they drowsily sank into oblivion.

It was full dark when Rosamund awoke. Sleepily she reached for Henry only to find the bed empty. The discovery shocked her awake. In alarm she sat up and looked about the room. To her relief she saw he was at the hearth, mending the fire; she also noted uneasily that he was dressed. He looked up when she called his name. As he turned toward the bed Rosamund gasped in fear as she saw steel gleam in his hand, the dagger blade molten in the firelight.

"Ah, you're awake. You can go back to sleep, sweeting."

"What are you going to do with a dagger?"

He laughed at her wide-eyed expression. "Not going to cut out your heart, though I'd probably be well advised to do so." He chuckled, coming to the bed. He had also lit candles from the hearth and he placed the silver-branched candelabra on the chest beside the bed. "No, my love, I'm going to take care of an omission for which you are responsible."

She was almost afraid to ask what Henry meant. When she reached out to him, he took her hand in his. "What are you going to do?"

He grinned and purposely pulled up the covers to hide her charms. "Because of your hot little body, this is a painful alternative."

To Rosamund's surprise, Henry rolled up his shirt sleeve and laid the blade against his skin, nicking his arm. She watched in horror as blood trickled down his wrist.

"Oh, you're bleeding!" she cried in concern, reaching to ward him. But he shook his head.

"Silly goose, I'm bleeding because you did not."

He laid his arm against the white linen sheet, watching as the fabric quickly absorbed his blood, the stain spreading. "There," he said in satisfaction, stanching the cut with a kerchief. "That should satisfy even the most inquisitive amongst them."

Finally Rosamund understood. He was protecting her honor! There would be blood on the sheets after all. "Oh, Harry, you wounded yourself for me,'' she whispered, deeply moved by his action.

"Surely you didn't expect to still be virgin after last night, did you, Jane dearest?"

Still chuckling, he crossed to the chest and poured wine over the cut. When he was satisfied the blood was stanched, he threw the soiled kerchief in the flames.

Realization dawned and Rosamund wanted to laugh in sheer relief. What a fool she had been, afraid Henry would publicly denounce her for the loss of her virginity. He had played the trick for their guests' benefit. Her amusement soon changed to tears of guilty relief as she watched him bind his arm, then fasten his shirt and pull on his doublet.

"Where are you going? It's still night."

He glanced at her, an unfathomable expression crossing his face. "Aye, close to midnight. Don't concern yourself with me. We'll display the sheets tomorrow. Our secret's safe."

He pulled on his boots and gathered his cloak and gauntlets from the bench beside the hearth. He ate a piece of bread and rinsed it down with a half cup of malmsey.

"Don't leave me yet. We have the rest of the night," she whispered invitingly, puzzled by his actions.

"I must. I have other obligations. Don't be afraid. All's still well between us. Just go back to sleep."

"But I want you to stay. We can make love again. Don't leave me alone on our wedding night."

His face was set as he flung his cloak around his shoulders. "Good night, wife. I'll see you tomorrow." Stooping, he kissed the top of her head as if she were a child.

Aghast, Rosamund started to scramble from the bed, reaching out to him. Firmly, and none too gently, he put her hands from him, purposely averting his gaze from her naked charms. Her first inclination was to rail at him, shrilly protesting his treatment of her, but one glance at his set face, where she recognized that cold mask of indifference, kept her from following through.

"Please," she whispered, making one final bid for his attention. "stay with me."

"Much as I'd like to, I cannot," he said with a sigh. Then he walked to the door. He did not even look back.

Rosamund sank down into the feather bed in defeat. Henry had left her on their wedding night as if all the shared love and passion of the past hours had never taken place. Tears of pain for her abandonment welled to her eyes and she angrily dashed them away. Her new, love-smitten self was fast becoming a whining fool. Never in her life had Rosamund cried so easily, but never before had her emotions run so deeply beyond control.

Though she willed it not to be, her heart ached for Henry's love. She gritted her teeth, fighting tears at the realization he had never said he loved her! He had made love to her magnificently, it was true, but even during those moments of passion, he had never once said the words she longed to hear.

Restless, Rosamund got out of bed and went to the window. The cold night air hit her in a reviving slap and she wiped her eyes, sniffling piteously. Why had he made love to her, then walked away with such indifference? There was so much about Henry of Ravenscrag she did not understand. Were all noblemen like him? It could be so. Until that Christmastide she had seen nobles merely from a distance. Mayhap they were unlike other men. Sir Ismay had been a big disappointment to her. Was her husband going to be just as disillusioning?

It was cold at the window, but she did not move. Bright moonlight shone across the battlements, bathing the stonework in silver light. Moonlight was called the light of lovers. Her mouth twisted bitterly at the thought. Only she was in love— Henry was ensnared by desire.

Voices below attracted Rosamund's attention and she looked down. From there she could see the postern gate in the west wall. A cloaked rider astride a huge black horse was approaching the gate. Her heart lurched as she realized the big horse looked very much like the one Sir Ismay rode, but she knew instinctively the night rider was not he. Could that horse

Patricia Phillips

be kin to the one her father owned? She recalled his boasting
how as part of her dowry he had presented a magnificent horse
to Ravenscrag to help sweeten his mood.

Rosamund craned forward as the rider moved into a beam
of moonlight. Someone stepped from the shadows—a servant,
undoubtedly: since he touched his forelock before taking the
animal's reins. So big was the beast that the rider had to duck
to pass under the arch. Her heart ached; she was sure it was
Henry she was watching. Her suspicions proved true a few
moments later as his voice drifted up to her on the clear night
air. He merely said good night, but that was enough for her
to identify him.

He was through the passage and moving along the bank of
the moat, crossing at the ford. He could have been any of a
hundred men with his cloak pulled close, head down against
the cold wind, but she knew it was he. Why was he leaving
the castle so late on that cold December night? His wedding
night, she added bitterly. He was picking up speed: She heard
splashing, followed by the thud of hooves as he reached dry
ground. Was he going to visit another woman? The very idea
made her heart plunge before resuming a sickening thud. Naturally he would not want to alert the garrison by letting down
the drawbridge. Far better was the cooperation of a trusted
body servant who likely was an old hand at this maneuver.
By his stealth none would be the wiser, least of all his wife!

Tears of pain and rage spilled down her face. Damn him!
She had thought their problems resolved. It was as if lately
her mind no longer functioned. Hysterical laughter rocked her
again as she recalled her overwhelming fear of being exposed
as unchaste. Had she used her wits, she would have known
her husband could not possibly expect her to be virgin after
they had already bedded. Even the most addle-witted wench
should have realized that. And trusting half-wit that she was,
she had also thought a rich and powerful lord like Henry of
Ravenscrag could be faithful to one woman. She should have
understood that was not the way of his world. It was not important that he be faithful, least of all to his wife, the despised

110

creature whose role in life seemed merely to act as her lord's brood mare. How could she have thought such a thing? But she had, making the pain of her discovery harder to bear.

Sadly Rosamund went back to bed, aware there was little she could do. When she turned back the covers she saw that dark stain and she thanked her guardian angel for Henry's forethought in taking care of the matter. She would not be cast as unchaste. No one would be any the wiser, least of all, Sir Ismay. Her course was set. Just what that course would be, she did not know. She knew only that what she had wanted and what she had been given were not the same. True love had not accompanied her newfound wealth and privilege.

There, in the privacy of the grand bridal chamber, Rosamund sobbed herself to sleep, aching for love found and lost in the space of a few days.

Chapter Six

Moonlight glistened like shards of ice across the grass in front of the manor house. Blanche watched the curving drive through a slit in the shuttered window, finding it bright as day and still empty. She waited. Long hours had already gone by and no hoofbeats had shattered the moonlit peace of Enderly. As time passed she had grown more tense until her jaw was clenched in aggravation. She gripped her hands so tight her fingers ached. With each passing hour her anger had mounted until she felt like a coiled spring. "Henry will pay for this insult," she vowed, "By God, if I won't make him pay."

She stood at last, legs stiff with cold, and crossed to the hearth to stir the fire before throwing on more logs. Great bursts of sparks shot upward and she caught her breath at what she glimpsed in the formation before it disappeared up the chimney. Blanche took a handful of powder from a chest on the mantel and cast it into the fire, watching as diverse colors leapt up the black chimney. In those dancing flames she saw the outline of a man between two women; however that scene quickly changed to show a toppled crown, great discord, bloodshed, and war!

Reeling from the shock of what she had just seen, she turned away, vowing to learn no more. Divining the future was sometimes painful and she could not always count on the powers of darkness to aid her. Then she heard a distant hoofbeat, coming closer, drumming insistently against the iron-hard ground. He had come at last.

Blanche ran to the door, her anger temporarily forgotten. She fluffed her mass of gleaming red hair, which hung unbound down her back, artfully placing some of the bright locks over her creamy shoulders. She had drawn her hair through the crown of a purple velvet turban. Ever since Walter had brought back the fashion from the Holy Land, she had claimed it as her own. Always anxious to please her in those days, her husband had ordered a dozen more turbans made, all fashioned from rich fabrics, padded, and jeweled. Her especial favorite was of black velvet embellished with crescents and stars; she usually wore it when she dabbled in the black arts.

Voices sounded outside as a groom came to take his horse, then the door creaked on its hinge and more muffled voices spoke as Henry was admitted. Composing herself, Blanche was careful not to let him see how his tardiness had angered her. Timing her greeting just right, she turned to him as he stepped inside the room, taking off his cloak and handing it to a servant. At her hand signal, the woman brought a special flagon of ale and some cakes before making herself scarce.

"Darling, I thought you'd never come," Blanche said, making her voice invitingly husky.

"It was a cold journey," he said as he came to warm himself at the hearth. Then he sniffed the air, aware of that curious, familiar scent from the fire. Blanche had been up to her magical tricks again.

"So what did you divine for our future tonight?" Henry asked, slipping his arm about her fleshy shoulders as she came to his side. Absently he kneaded her pliable flesh.

"What I saw was too puzzling. I don't want to interpret it." She reached up to stroke his cold cheek. She could feel his prickling growth of beard harsh against her fingers. "Now you are a married man," she said, finding it hard to keep the emotion from her voice. "Did all go well?"

Henry moved away from her, flexing his shoulders. "God, I'm stiff with cold. What have you for refreshment?"

Crossing gracefully to the side table, Blanche took a pewter dish and filled it with meat, sliced bread, and small pink sugar cakes. She also brought Henry a tankard of mulled ale. Gratefully he accepted the food and went back to the hearth, where he sprawled on the settle to enjoy his meal.

"Well, now you've supped mayhap you can answer my questions," Blanche said after he had eaten his fill. She sipped from her own tankard, watching him with narrowed eyes above the rim of her cup.

"Aye, it went well, but we'll be months replenishing the larder. 'Tis almost as bad as the king's visit."

"I didn't mean the provisions," she said sharply. "I meant the wench." Did she imagine it? Or did he deliberately look away, as if he did not want to meet her gaze.

"What do you want to know? She's fresh from a French convent. There's little else to say."

His response was too glib. Blanche drew in her breath, feeling the first swirls of unease begin in her belly. "Is she pretty and biddable?"

When he nodded, still careful to look only at the fire, she asked, "And did you bed her?"

His head came up. His blue eyes were hooded and she could read nothing there. "Do you think me a monk? Of course I bedded her. There's no other way to get an heir."

"And that's your purpose for taking a wife?"

"It's every landholder's purpose."

"Mayhap the little French chit is barren."

"She's English, and as for being barren, we'll see."

"I'm far from barren, as well you know," she said as she came to sit beside him on the settle.

Henry smiled at her sharp reminder, but he only said, "Did you think I wasn't coming?"

"You're hours past the time I was expecting you. But it doesn't matter, love. You're here now," Blanche whispered, taking his empty plate and tankard and putting them beside the hearth. "I won't hold it against you. But I still think you should have let me come to the wedding. She wouldn't have known who I am."

"I would have known. That was reason enough," he said sternly, shifting her weight off his shoulder. "Besides, the ceremony's over, the feast past. We need speak of it no more."

The Rose of Ravenscrag

She pressed her breasts against his chest, annoyed to find he wore such a thick doublet he could barely feel the pressure. "Meade Ireton lets his mistress wait on his wife," she said, stroking his hand where it rested on his knee.

"Had I suggested such an arrangement you'd have screamed to high heaven at the insult."

"I didn't mean I wanted to be a maid. I meant he cared enough for her to flaunt her at his castle. He doesn't keep her hidden away."

"I'm not Meade Ireton," Henry said, aware his neighbor to the north had such an arrangement in his household. "Enderly is hardly hidden away. 'Tis my best manor. If you've developed a dislike for it, perchance you'd prefer other lodging. Northcot is still vacant, awaiting Walter's return, if you've a mind you can go back there."

Blanche bit her lip. Henry was in a surly mood. The convent bride must not have provided good bed sport. "Walter won't return. He's dead," she said, a little too quickly.

"We don't know that—or do we?" he asked sharply, pulling away to study her face. "You always sound so sure, more sure than the papal legate or even the king himself. Your husband's still said to be held prisoner in the Holy Land, is he not?"

Blanche shrugged. "So I've been told. Nobody's heard from him for years. We could have had him declared dead and wed each other, Harry Ravenscrag."

"Not while your husband lives, be it in a Saracen prison or not. Besides, the situation's different now. I already have a wife and that's an end of it."

"She doesn't change matters between us, does she?"

Again he hesitated a little too long before replying. "No, though I mightn't be able to come to you as often."

An icy chill gripped Blanche's heart. Was she being cast aside? "Why not?"

"By taking a wife I've assumed more obligations. Besides, there's much unrest and talk of war. I have to get my men armed and in shape to fight if needed. A messenger came just

115

last week from the Percys warning me the Northern lords are looking to their swords. The king's much beset by York's plots.''

''That won't stop us loving, sweet,'' she said seductively, stroking his muscular thigh. His blue-and-silver doublet was very fine and Blanche jealously wondered if he had worn it to wed the French chit. ''You still love me, don't you? Your wife's not altered that.''

Again she thought he paused too long before answering and her unease increased. She could feel his tension lessening as the potion she had slipped into the ale soothed his ill humor. But she couldn't give him potions indefinitely. The more time he spent away from Enderly, the more room he was given for independant action. So far she had not learned how to control his will, though it was not for want of trying.

Henry slipped his arms about her. Perfumed clouds of her hair spilled over his doublet and settled against his face. Sitting before the hearth and enjoying the simple refreshment had put him in a much better mood. Earlier, he had been in half a mind to stay at Ravenscrag. Yet he had promised Blanche that, if she stayed away from the celebrations and did naught to cause trouble or embarrassment, he would visit her on his wedding night. He had made that vow, yet when the time had come to keep it he had had to fight a battle with himself not to break it.

Blanche felt delectable in his arms. As the firelit minutes elapsed, she felt more pliable to his will and increasingly hot and desirable. His head buzzed and her face swam above him, lovely features mistily alluring, full breasts partially exposed above her bodice. His eyes already burned and the silver spangles on her violet gown reflected the fire, dazzling his eyes until flames appeared to surround and consume her. Through the glare Blanche smiled invitingly. She slipped her hand inside his doublet, stealing beneath his shirt to softly stroke his chest and shoulders.

At last! She could feel the sexual tension quivering through his body. The potion was working, though at first she had begun to doubt its effectiveness.

"Make love to me," she said, pulling her breasts free from the spangled bodice, spilling the treasures into his waiting hands. Blanche was rewarded by the increased heat of his mouth as his hands kneaded her flesh and she could feel his rising organ brushing her thigh. Against his will, his desire had been fired.

Chillingly she repeated the words to herself: against his will! What a curious thing to say. Yet everything had seemed to be against his will: each word, each caress, each kiss. Or mayhap it was more that Harry Ravenscrag had expended so much energy plowing that virgin field his potency had ebbed.

Blanche's questing fingers found his swollen manhood and with quickened breath she outlined the flesh beneath his hose. "Aha, then he is still alive," she said. "I'd thought you wouldn't be able to rise to the occasion."

Henry chuckled at her words and he pressed her down on the padded settle, imprisoning her there. "Taunting me now, are you, wicked one? I'll show you how well I can rise to the occasion." He crushed her soft thighs beneath his. He buried his face in her ample bosom and his voice was muffled when he said, "You've no need of your black magic to arouse me, woman."

She smiled against his crisp, tickling hair, saying nothing. How little he knew. Even a man as virile as Henry could use assistance at times. She pulled his face to hers and plunged her hot tongue inside his mouth.

His lovemaking was rough and demanding, a turn of affairs she did not welcome. Mayhap she had put a pinch too much potion in his cup. Pressing her knee between them, she forced him to slow, making a barrier to his eager coupling. "Not yet, sweet. See how high I've banked the fire, it wasn't meant for a quick plunge."

Henry's head was too confused to catch the malice in her voice and he laughed at her insistence for slower lovemaking. Reluctantly he tried to oblige by holding back, but he did not try too hard for too long.

*   *   *

Rosamund did not see Henry until the noon meal. When she went inside the great hall she found him already seated at the table with Sir Ismay and several other men. To her horror she saw the blood-stained linen sheet from the marriage bed hanging from the minstrel gallery like some battle trophy. Her face flushed and she gulped with surprise at the blatant proclamation of her chastity on view for all the castle to see. As the page led her to her chair, she purposely averted her gaze from the amused guests, some of whom chuckled openly over her appearance so late in the day, assuming she had to stay abed to recover from her husband's lovemaking.

"Here, wife. See. All's as I promised," Henry said in a whisper and he winked at her, reminding her of their shared secret.

Rosamund smiled at him and even managed to greet Sir Ismay pleasantly. Her father fairly beamed his approval and she knew his happiness was an expression of relief and gratitude for the obvious proof of her virginity. If he only knew. That thought made her smile, cheering her mood. She had no cause to hang her head in shame. She must remember she was lady of the great castle.

If only she could speak to her husband alone. Granted, first she would ask him where he had gone the night before, but she would also tell him how painful his desertion had been to her. She hoped none of the noble wedding guests were aware she and her new husband had spent the best part of their wedding night apart. She would be ashamed to have them know such secrets.

A platter of fine white bread and spiced meat paste was set before her, accompanying a steaming pottage of vegetables. After the grand feasts of the past days, the meal was very plain, yet Rosamund found it delicious. Accustomed to eating only one substantial meal a day, she knew she would soon be spoiled by the rich bounty of Ravenscrag's table.

There was no opportunity for private speech with Henry since his own captain of the guard was seated at the table with

Hartley, Sir Ismay's captain; those men monopolized his attention. No one paid much attention to her, or to what they were eating. Henry, her father, and their captains spent most of their meal moving the salt cellar, cups, and knives around the cloth to represent troops and battle positions. Nobody smiled or laughed, making the noon meal decidedly sober.

When Rosamund glanced about the hall, she saw that many guests had already left the castle. There were many empty places at the trestle tables. There had been many rattling wagons and clopping hooves that morning while she waited in her tower chamber. It must have been their guests departing. How strange that they should leave so soon; she had expected the revel to last through the 12 days of Christmas.

It had not been pleasant spending the morning alone. First of all, her maids had come to dress her and take her back to her own chamber. While they were tidying the bridal suite the girls had giggled about their lord's lustiness. At her approach their conversation immediately stopped, but not before she had heard telltale snatches of gossip that made her heart ache. They had spoken of a place called Enderly and the Red Witch, crossing themselves at the mention of the woman as protection from evil. Their gossipy whispering suggested it was to Enderly her husband had ridden the night before. Their references to his sexual prowess probably meant he was the lover of whoever lived there. After the past night's prolonged weeping, the confirmation of her worst fears did not make her cry anew; it merely deepened the chill that gripped her heart as she sat in her remote tower room sadly contemplating her future at Ravenscrag.

The meal dragged on. Rosamund's sadness lifted when she found Henry smiling at her and she was aware he covertly watched her over the rim of his cup. But he still said nothing to her that did not pertain to the meal. When the men were done with their discussion, they pushed back their chairs and stood, signaling the meal was over. Rosamund's faithful page, Pip, came scurrying to her side to lead her back to her chamber.

119

Annoyed that her husband had so shamefully ignored her, Rosamund ran after Henry, catching up to him at the foot of the stair leading to the solar. "Henry, wait!"

He stopped and turned around, displaying not the anger she had been prepared for, but a smile of pleasure at the sight of her. "I'm sorry I ignored you, sweet. We've had disturbing news. Come upstairs. We can talk there."

His unexpected good humor flustered Rosamund and her heart raced as she followed him up the stairs to the solar. There a welcoming fire blazed in the hooded hearth. At one end of the room was a huge window through which light poured, yet the cold wind did not. The high window was arched in stone like the windows in the parish church. Tentatively Rosamund touched the panes, looking out through the greenish horn window at the panorama of winter countryside beyond.

"There you have the lands of Ravenscrag," Henry said, coming to her side. "Far to the north lies Scotland, which has its own king, James Stewart."

"Is everything I can see through the window yours?"

Henry chuckled at her astonishment. "Aye, and much beyond, unless you have eyes like an eagle. Between us and Scotland lies Ireton land, that of the lords Clifford and Roos, and the kingdom of the Percys. To the south are a few lesser lords, tenants of mine, then your father's lands and his tenants. 'Tis true that the North Country is owned by a handful of powerful men."

Rosamund listened in amazement at the recital of his importance in the land. Suddenly she understood why Sir Ismay had been eager to ally himself by marriage with the great Lord of Ravenscrag.

"Are they all your friends?"

Henry pulled a wry face. "Hardly. Oh, some pretend friendship, but I always watch my back."

"Would they kill you?"

"Some would, given half a chance. If you mean, are we on the same side politically? The answer is yes. Most Northern lords are a power unto themselves. We're far from the controlling influence of Henry's parliament and much too far for a rescue by the king's troops; so we've learned to fight our own battles with our own men. We usually unite only against the Scots when they start feeling brave."

"Henry's the king's name? Just like yours."

"It is for him I am named. Yet I'm afraid this Henry is a poor excuse for a king. Half the time he has not his wits. But he is rightful King of England and because of that I've sworn to support him against his enemies."

Recalling the men's mealtime talk of war, Rosamund asked innocently, "And has he many enemies?"

Her naivete made Henry laugh, yet his humor was not unkind. When she pouted slightly at his laughter, he seized her for a swift embrace. Then, almost as if he had forgotten himself, he put her from him and indicated she was to sit on the blue padded bench before the hearth. He stood watching her, leaning against the hearthstone as he talked.

"Poor lamb, they did keep you in ignorance at that convent. Our king's beset by a nation of enemies. Thus far they've been driven to ground, but they won't lie low forever. His cousin York wants his throne. It's rumored Henry's young son is not his, but was sired instead by the queen's paramour. Henry himself marvels at the miracle conception, considering his son must be a child of the Holy Ghost. So that tells you something, both about the boy's doubtful legitimacy and the state of the king's mind. As it happens, York offers fine strong sons for the line instead of that puny little lad. He would form his own dynasty putting the two great houses of York and Lancaster at war. This present uneasy truce won't hold."

"And you're for the king? What house is he?"

Henry smiled at her increasing ignorance. "Lancaster—the white rose of Lancaster, descendant of the great John of Gaunt. Unfortunately, this Lancaster's no Gaunt. Between them they form a pitiful triumvate, poor addled Henry, his French vixen of a queen, and their puny, bastard lad," he said bitterly, glancing about quickly to make sure they were still alone. "I can't believe you had no knowledge of any of this."

"Nay, none," she said, alarmed by the imminent prospect of war. "Will you have to fight?"

He smiled grimly. "Yes, and in all likelihood before the new year's much older. I leave today to go recruiting. My tenants on the outlying lands must be prepared. They owe their loyalty to me."

Rosamund sat quietly digesting the alarming facts while Henry outlined what route his recruiting would take. Long weeks of harsh winter lay ahead, during which she would be left at the castle by herself. In Whitton she had been blissfully unaware of this political turmoil, isolated from the mainstream of events. In a way that life of ignorance was preferable to taking a hand in shaping the nation's destiny.

"And what of me? Can I come with you?" she asked.

Gravely he shook his head. "Nay, it's too harsh, too dangerous, sweet. The bogs and moors are full of lawless men; in fact the whole country swarms with old soldiers, runaway peasants. It's not safe for you to leave the castle."

"I'll be like a prisoner! What will I do all that time?" she wailed in dismay.

"What do you want to do?"

"For a start I need to learn how to run your household."

"Then I'll arrange it. You also have a new white palfrey to ride in the stables—my wedding gift to you. But you mustn't go abroad alone. You'll have a riding master and grooms to accompany you at all times. Do you understand?"

Rosamund nodded. Little did he know she could barely stay in the saddle. "I'll learn to ride well so we can ride together when you return."

Her words pleased him and he rested his hand on her head, stroking her glossy hair. "I'd like that. Do you like dogs? I remember we talked about such things on that fateful night, but my head was so mussed I've no recollection of your answer."

"I don't know much about dogs. If they're important to you, I'll learn to like them," she said eagerly, wondering if these dogs were the huge mastiffs she had seen lounging before the hearth in the great hall. Their teeth and fierce expressions had frightened her; she remembered well the tales told in the village about Goody Clark's mastiff tearing men's flesh to ribbons.

"If only we had more time. I wanted to show you my dogs, my hawks, to take you riding on the moor, to show you the winter falls. 'Tis a mass of ice sparkling like diamonds in the sun." He stopped abruptly and straightened up, as if growing aware of his own enthusiasm and nipping it in the bud. "Someday, when the danger's past, we'll go there. Now I've much to do before I leave. I'll send the servants to you and they can explain their duties. You may study the accounts, see the lists of provisions, tour the castle—whatever you want. It was my intention to show you around, but now I must leave that to another."

Henry moved from the hearth, seeming impatient to leave. When Rosamund came to him and took his hand, he grew tense. She could see the tension in his lean jaw and feel the tremor in his arm as she held it against her.

"Henry, is there a place called Enderly nearby?" she asked, looking up at him.

He drew in his breath and his expression turned guarded. "Aye, it's a manor to the north of here."

"Who owns it?"

"I do."

"Who lives there?"

He paused, aware some loose-tongued servant must have let the truth slip out. Inwardly he cursed. He had been going to tell her about Blanche in his own time. She was no fool. It was likely she already knew far more than she revealed.

"Lady Blanche."

Rosamund asked no more, believing he had told her the truth, but believing also that her worst fears were founded. When she mentioned Enderly he had looked so uncomfortable. Then that familiar cold, angry expression had tightened his face and she was almost sorry she had asked. There seemed no more to be said since he turned on his heel and strode to the stair.

"Am I to stay up here?" Rosamund asked.

"If you wish. The light in the window seat is good. I can have the women bring linen and silks for embroidery if you'd like."

She nodded, suddenly feeling small and alone. "You'll tell them how much I need their help?"

"Of course. None shall treat you harsh for your ignorance or they'll answer to me. They are to be as open and helpful as possible. The steward, Thurgood, shall come to see you. There should be friendship between you since he'll be your right hand while I'm away. Now I really must go. God keep you."

Then Henry sprinted down the stair and was gone. Rosamund leaned against the cold stonework, watching him stride across the hall. He did not look back at her and that omission made her heart ache. Was he so possessed with his plans for war that he had no further interest in loving her? Or was it more that his night at Enderly had stripped him of all desire for her?

Sadly she considered her position there. Retreating inside the warm solar, she became freshly determined to make the most of what was offered to her. She would learn all she could about running the great household. Perhaps by doing that, and also by learning how to ride well and to be affectionate to his dogs, she could worm her way inside Henry's heart. To have enslaved his body was pleasant, but it was the allegiance of his heart she craved.

Rosamund was delighted with the quality of the bleached linen and the basketful of brilliant silk embroidery threads he sent to her. A young seamstress named Con brought them to the solar. Rosamund found the freckle-faced redhead was skilled at sketching an outline; so together they devised a pleasing design of birds and wild flowers.

When finished, the piece of embroidery would be a cover for the chest beside her bed. Con suggested that, if they stitched identical pieces, both chests in the bedchamber would have matching cloths. Skeins of gold and silver thread winked amid the brightly colored silks and Rosamund drew them admiringly between her fingers, never having handled such precious materials before. Altar cloths were often stitched with that thread. Perhaps, when she was sufficiently skilled, she would make a cloth for the altar in the castle chapel.

Together they stitched in the window nook, enjoying the pale December sunshine. Rosamund found it very pleasant to have a companion to sew with. Con came from a village like Whitton that lay to the east and she entertained Rosamund with amusing stories about her home. Rosamund had to be careful not to appear too familiar with village life lest she betray herself.

Later in the afternoon the young page, Pip, hurried inside the solar to tell Rosamund her lord was soon to depart and if she wanted to see him go she must hurry. Her stomach lurched at the thought of the danger facing Henry in the lawless countryside; yet she also knew he would travel with an armed guard and take all precautions necessary for his safety. But his leaving gave her time to put her plans into action. With enough time, she was sure she could astound him with her knowledge of the workings of the castle and, she hoped, her newfound skills in the saddle. The prospect of the big undertaking lifted her flagging spirits.

The page held out a fur-lined cloak for her, reminding her it would be cold on the battlements. Rosamund thanked him and pulled the softly lined garment around her shoulders, nestling in the luxurious fur. The lad blushed to the roots of his yellow hair upon receiving her thanks. Then Rosamund mounted the winding stone staircase leading up to the battlements. She had made two friends at Ravenscrag, Con and young Pip. Already she felt like less of a stranger in the teeming household.

Searing cold wind buffeted Rosamund's face as she stepped out onto the battlements. Several sentries touched their forelocks in respect, bidding her good day as they passed. There was a great commotion coming from the bailey as men and supply wagons formed a column before streaming into the outer bailey, headed for the drawbridge. Bright pennants fluttered in the sharp wind, bearing both the arms of De Gere and Ravenscrag. Rosamund wondered if Sir Ismay would ride with his new son-in-law, but she could not see him among the men.

It was easy to spot Henry's black stallion. Rosamund's heart thudded as she looked at him. His breastplate gleamed as he turned to take his helm from his young squire who stood at his saddlebow. As if he felt her gaze on him, he turned, looking around the battlements until he spotted her.

Rosamund's heart pitched when Henry stood in the stirrups to wave; then he gestured with his gauntleted hand, as if blowing her a kiss. She shouted good-bye to him but the wind blew her voice away. After waving one last time, he crammed on his helmet and turned his horse's head toward the gate.

Their pennants streaming, the troop of men and wagons clattered over the wooden bridge to assemble on the far side. Henry rode to the head of the column and turned back toward the battlements. He waved again, though he was so far away Rosamund doubted he could still see her fluttering kerchief. She watched until the soldiers appeared as no more than mere specks, like a column of ants weaving their way across the undulating moorland toward the Hambleton Hills.

When Henry was gone, a great emptiness filled Rosamund's heart. She realized she was almost completely alone in the strange castle.

"You've done well, daughter," a familiar gravelly voice said.

Startled, Rosamund found Sir Ismay standing behind her, booted and spurred, his cloak billowing in the strong wind.

"Aren't you going with them?" she asked in surprise.

"No, I'm heading south to alert some of my own tenants."

"Will I see you again?"

"Most assuredly," he said, his hard face seamed with amusement. "Likely when you drop your first babe, if not before."

A flicker of dislike for the nobleman who had fathered her

126

stirred in her breast. "You're most trusting of me, aren't you?" she asked as they began the descent from the battlements.

"What do you mean by that? Shouldn't I be?"

"I could lay your scheme open."

"Ah, but you won't. You're no fool. Besides, it's far too late for that. Even a blind man could see Harry Ravenscrag's stolen more than your maidenhead. You fairly pant whenever he comes near."

How she hated his sly smile and intimate knowledge. But she could not deny his observation. They paused in the passage below, momentarily alone.

"Did you send them the gold?" she asked, wanting to make sure Sir Ismay had kept his part of the bargain.

"Aye, and Joan has a basket of goods to boot. You should be going down on your knees to thank me. You not only instantly bettered your station, but you've also got a man half the women in the county want to bed. Of course, their pining won't go unrequited, but that's something you'll have to accept. Now, kiss me good-bye, sweet," he said, raising his voice as steps sounded in the corridor.

Dutifully she kissed his leathery cheek, and he pulled her against him to kiss her brow. "Good-bye, Father."

"Good-bye, dearest Rosamund, mine."

His hard mouth quirked in a smile as he turned away and headed toward the great hall. Several servants had witnessed the affectionate parting of father and daughter and it pleased him greatly.

Several days later, Rosamund began her lessons in earnest. December 25 was a quarter day and the gathering of rents and goods took much time. Once that task was completed, Thurgood began her formal education in household management.

The castle steward was a middle-aged man of medium height with little to make him stand out from the rest, except his steely eyes, which ferreted out every inconsistancy, each slovenly servant, or missing provision. Rosamund discovered the running of the castle was divided into different areas, each under the care of different servants who in turn answered to Master Thurgood.

A treasurer, Hoke, had charge of accounts and keeping detailed records of all expenditures. The all-important captain-of-the-guard traveled with Henry, but Rosamund met young Chrysty Dane, who was the second-in-command. The old chaplain, Father John, who had performed the wedding, was assisted by two pimply clerks, who also wrote letters for their lord. The cook, Salton, ruled the kitchen while Parret, the butler, had charge of the buttery, where the wine and ale were kept. There was a stable marshall in charge of the grooms and horses; Rafe, the huntsman, trained the castle hunting dogs. Ben was the young falconer. There were also carters to drive the wagons, farriers to shoe the horses, coopers to make barrels, and masons to repair the castle stonework. Fletchers made arrows, bowyers made bows; there were lorimers, billers. . . . Rosamund's head spun from all the unfamiliar positions employed inside the castle walls.

Apart from those important people, there were a multitude of laundresses, seamstresses, maids, and scullions. A half-dozen pages, sons of noble households, also served in the great household in order to educate and prepare them for their coming knighthood. Pip, the lad assigned to her, was the son of Sir Meade Ireton.

Rosamund made copious notes during Thurgood's lengthy explanations, laboring over the penmanship she learned at Thorpe Abbey. Finally those tedious lessons taught to her by Sister Magdalene had proved useful. In Whitton she had not been called upon to either read or write; for the most part the villagers were blissfully illiterate. Hour after hour she studied what she had written until she was able to put names with faces, running down the long list of Henry's dependants. Rosamund could not say she felt welcome in her endeavour, though she was treated politely and the servants answered her questions. She was aware of an undercurrent of resentment for her determination to learn the workings of this household. Probably the more she learned about their duties, the less easily the servants would take advantage of her.

Once Rosamund felt familiar with life inside the castle, she ventured out to the stables. There she found the huge warhorses; the mighty animals made her uneasy when they tossed their heads and stamped their massive hooves. Though she was used to seeing cart horses in the fields, these creatures had been out in the open, not confined inside murky stalls where they barely had room to move, leaving her vulnerable to the vagaries of the beasts' collective tempers. Aelfred, the grizzled stable master, made sure she was acquainted with each of his charges before he finally led her to the stall where her new silver palfrey was kept.

A fine delicate head and silvery mane popped above the partition and the two ladies studied each other. Tentatively Rosamund put out her hand and touched the mare's velvety muzzle. The mare did not toss its head nor try to bite her; greatly encouraged, Rosamund moved closer to stroke its neck.

"Name's Luna—some foreign jargon for moon, his lordship said. Had her from a merchant who claimed she belonged to royalty. She's a fine lass—gentle, but she's got spirit if needed. She'll take to you, I can tell."

Once they were left alone, Rosamund whispered to the white horse that she did not really know how to ride and she hoped Luna would cooperate and not make her look like too much of a fool. Luna whickered and nuzzled Rosamund's face as if she understood.

When the time came to ride her palfrey, Rosamund was forced to confess to Aelfred that she was not a very experienced rider. To her amazement, he laughed and nodded his agreement.

"Aye, lady, I knowed that from the first," he said, laughing at her shocked expression. "I may be a poor man, but I'm no simpleton. Reckon you didn't get much chance to ride in that there convent."

"No, most of our time was spent indoors," she mumbled, hoping he was not going to ask her about her supposed French upbringing. To her relief he did not.

"Get aboard then, lady, and we'll go for a ride round the bailey."

It took over a week of daily rides for Rosamund to feel confident in the saddle. Without Sir Ismay's scorn, nor the need to hurry, she could progress at her own pace. With Luna's cooperation she relaxed and her confidence grew.

A heavy snowfall delayed her proposed first expedition beyond the walls. As she watched the snowflakes drifting past her turret window, Rosamund wondered if Henry was still on the road or if he had sheltered in the safety of some castle or manor. For many days the wind moaned piteously around the tower and the world beyond the window lay silent and white.

The snow had melted long ago and the green leaves of spring had already appeared when a messenger arrived to announce that his lordship would be home within a fortnight. At the news a great flurry of activity began both inside and outside the castle.

Henry's impending arrival caused Rosamund to step up her riding lessons, and she became increasingly nervous as the day of his arrival grew near. On mild days she went out on the moorland. Riding Luna proved such a pleasant diversion she wondered why she had so disliked the idea of riding. She soon grew to love and trust her palfrey. Following his lord's wishes, Aelfred always accompanied Rosamund beyond the walls, taking two strong young grooms with them in case of trouble.

Another guest also tagged along on these outings: a black mixed-breed hound. The dog was a present from Rafe, the castle huntsman. Dimples was the gangly pup's name, so called because, when he gave his canine grin, his face dimpled. Rafe's young son had christened him thus. The pup already came to the command, blissfully unaware of the unsuitability of the name of Dimples for a hunting dog. He gamboled at the palfrey's hooves, falling in mud, splashing through becks and puddles, all in a relentless quest for rabbits. When Rosamund was in the great hall, Dimples lolled at her feet, whining a noisy greeting at the sight of her, his heart smitten with love for his new lady.

One day, the crimson blooms on the elms glowed in the sunshine while a light wind stirred the birch branches against the wall. Rosamund sat sunning herself on the stone bench in the sheltered angle of the bailey wall. How much she enjoyed the unexpected spring warmth. There were even spear-shaped daffodil leaves sprouting amid the yellow crocus in the small garden beside the bench, their new leaves thrusting out of the black earth.

Rosamund was still sitting contentedly on the bench when the rider came, thumping over the moor, sent on ahead to alert the castle to his lord's return. Excited by the longed-for news of Henry's arrival, Rosamund bathed and perfumed her hair. She put on a new gown, which her favorite seamstress had finished just in time. Over the yellow silk she wore a green-and-yellow damask surcoat edged with gold brocade. The gown's oversleeves hung close to the ground while the tight-fitted undersleeve formed a gold-edged point on the back of her hand. Unlike the others in her wardrobe, the gown had not been altered from someone else's garment, but made expressly for her. Rosamund twirled and spun about the room, admiring her reflection in the strip of polished steel used for a mirror. The maids had wound her long braids inside gold cauls, which attached to a headband worn over a short veil. In her splendid attire, Rosamund looked every inch the Lady of Ravenscrag.

She waited nervously for Henry's return. Finally she heard the clopping hooves and creaking wagons announcing his arrival. She had not watched from the battlements, preferring to stand at the door to meet him. She could feel the warmth of the sun on her back, penetrating her thin silk gown. Though outwardly she appeared composed, Rosamund had to clasp her hands together to stop their trembling. The thought of seeing Henry again, of being able to touch and talk to him, made her heart pound. For a panicky instant she suddenly could not recall his face. Then he was before her, astride his snorting black horse.

His heavy plate clanking and creaking, Henry removed his helmet to reveal his matted dark hair and the red pressure mark of his helmet seaming his brow. Almost as if he did not remember her either, Henry stared dumbstruck.

Unable to stand the suspense any longer, Rosamund ran toward him amid the men and horses. Henry came out of the saddle and she was in his arms; he held her close, his cold breastplate bruising her soft slesh.

"Rosamund, by all that's holy—it is you! How different you look today," Henry said against her ear, his breath tickling her face.

"Oh, sweetheart, welcome back. It's been so long."

Her joyous greeting evidently pleased him because Henry held her a long time, his mouth hot against her neck, making her shiver with delight at the awakened memory of his kiss.

Finally handing his horse to a groom, Henry left the sunlit bailey and walked inside the gloomy castle with Rosamund on his arm. As they entered the great hall a resounding cheer of welcome came from the assembled retainers, who were relieved to have their lord returned safely from his journey.

To Rosamund's dismay other men joined them in the hall. Henry turned to welcome his guests and he ordered refreshment for them. Their important neighbor, Sir Meade Ireton, and his uncle, Sir John of Thurlston, were introduced first. Rosamund felt quite pleased with herself when she sweetly told them how glad she was to meet them and managed a graceful curtsy. Next were two Percy relatives from Northumberland; several lesser guests of little importance were not introduced. The formal courtesy over, the men followed Henry to the lord's table.

Pleasantly aware of their guests' approving glances, Rosamund was disappointed to learn she was not expected to join them at table. Instead Henry led her to a bench beside the hearth before joining the others. Already the men were unfolding maps and diagrams, beginning again their important discussion of battle tactics.

Rosamund fought mingled anger and tears of disappointment as she sat on the bench by the hearth, smarting under the unexpected snub. Since she was the Lady of Ravenscrag, she had thought she would be treated as an intelligent adult instead of being relogated to the background like a pretty child. Dimples pressed against Rosamund's skirts and she fondled his velvety ears, thankful to have his undivided attention though he was just a dog.

When the servants brought food Rosamund rightly guessed she was not expected to join them at the lord's table to share the hastily prepared meal. The refreshment was only for the men. Later she would eat the welcome-home feast she had planned in honor of Henry's return. The dishes had been chosen with the help of Salton, the cook, a fat, red-faced man with a hearty humor who knew far more about his lord's taste in food than Rosamund. She had also arranged for a bath to be drawn for Henry at his leisure and fresh clothing laid out for him. When she had made those plans how much she had been anticipating their wonderful reunion. Everything had been spoiled, however, by the perpetual planning for war.

In the past she had thought a nobleman's life was a nonstop round of pleasure. She had imagined the well-dressed, well-fed creatures had naught to occupy them but amusement. Since coming to live at Ravenscrag Castle she had discovered how wrong she had been. The lord of the castle spent his time arming, recruiting, and training his men, meting out justice, gathering rents, visiting his far-flung manors—and other women!

That unpleasant thought crept into Rosamund's mind. It was painful to recall Sir Ismay's remark that many women thirsted for her husband and that their desires did not go unrequited. She turned to look at Henry's dark head bent over a map spread between the wine cups and the platters. He was undeniably very handsome and she could understand why other women wanted him, yet she had hoped he would want no other but she. It was possible he had not spent one night alone since leaving Ravenscrag, never pining for the sight of the beloved. . . .

Dimples whimpered as Rosamund's caresses stopped. Rosamund forced away those painful thoughts, reminding herself Henry was there and she must make the most of the time he spent with her, not ruin his homecoming with jealousy.

Some time later, their discussion over, the guests bid their farewells. Henry walked from the hall with the men, sparing nary a glance for Rosamund, who still waited beside the hearth. Gnawing fear that he did not care deeply for her surfaced again and she tried in vain to squash the disturbing thought. An outer door clanged, briefly admitting the clamor of men and horses, before slamming shut. The ensuing silence made her feel even more isolated. Rosamund waited for close to an hour for Henry's return before going in search of his body servant, Jem, whom she found stuffing himself in the kitchen.

"Did your lord leave with the others?" she asked him.

Guiltily gulping down his food and trying to swallow as he talked, Jem said, "Nay, lady, he bathed and is sleeping. He's not to be disturbed," he added, raising his voice as she headed toward the door.

Anger flared inside her. "Were those his orders?" she asked incredulously.

"Aye, lady, he said he was not to be disturbed on any account."

Fighting to maintain her composure as the kitchen staff gawked at her, taking in every word, Rosamund nodded and turned away. Her heart ached afresh for her husband's seeming indifference. After all the time she had spent preparing to astound Henry with her newfound skills, dressing herself like a princess for his pleasure, and even ordering a celebration meal with his favorite foods—all was for naught!

Blinded by tears, it was more by sense than sight that Rosamund left the castle's chilly precincts, stepping out into the warm sunshine. Early afternoon light shone golden over the stonework, casting fretwork shadows of new leafed trees on the walls. Dimples walked at Rosamund's side, brushing against her, anxious for attention, but her mind was too full of pain to notice him. She had finally admitted she must come close to the bottom of Lord Henry's list of matters of importance.

Perchance he had passed much of the winter's inclement weather at Enderly or one of a dozen other manors with accommodating mistresses. The thought made Rosamund grit her teeth in a vain effort to stop her hot, angry tears. When was she going to accept the truth? It was only she who loved.

Birch leaves swam mistily before her eyes as she leaned her burning cheek against the cold stone wall. How stifling the lordly surroundings had become once she discovered the luxurious life was only a sham. People of quality moved like actors in a play, politely condescending to each other, saying one thing while thinking another. She had to get out of the castle, to go where the air was fresh and she was free from the prying eyes and ears of a hundred people who lived inside the walls. The gossiping maids were probably already laughing about her foolish naivete in thinking Lord Henry had thirsted for her charms alone when the whole county of Yorkshire was full of women only too eager to welcome him to their beds.

Rosamund stumbled on the steps to her room, tripping over the skirts of her yellow festival gown. She almost hated the dress; it was an unpleasant reminder of her own stupidity in thinking Henry and she would enjoy a romantic evening alone, of her stupidity in ever thinking she could make him love her.

Rosamund almost slammed the door on Dimple's nose and he looked quite woebegone as he slinked inside the room at her heels. With little regard for her lovely new gown, Rosamund pulled it off as quickly as she could, given its many lacings and fastening. Next she took off the gold filet and cauls, tumbling her braids down her back. Angrily she bound the two braids with a ribbon, visciously knotting the bright red silk. Not caring about her appearance, she took the first gown she came to in the clothes chest, a dark purple wool patterned in loden. Over it she wore a plain dark cloak. If only for a little while she had to be free of the castle and the new identity she had assumed, with all its obligations—and disappointments.

Rosamund first intended to ride out on Luna. She had even pulled on her soft deerskin riding boots, but then she changed her mind because she knew the horse would attract too much attention. Dressed in the dark wool garments, she should be able to blend unnoticed with the laundresses and departing retainers of the visiting lords who still milled about the outer bailey and drawbridge.

Pulling the hood of her cloak down over her face, Rosamund started out the door with Dimples still following at her heels. No one would mistake her for a laundress if the dog came with her. Much to Dimple's distress, she ordered him to stay. He whimpered and groveled on the rushes, desperate to accompany her, but she quickly shut the door. He yelped a few times, then was quiet. Fortunately the tower seemed deserted since most of the staff was either preparing the meal or unpacking their lord's wagons.

Quickly she crossed the bailey and walked across the lowered bridge, keeping her head down. None of the guards gave her a second glance. Rosamund could hardly believe her good fortune as she moved away from the towering stone walls, keeping the hood around her face until she was at a safe distance. Most of the others headed toward nearby villages; only she turned out onto the open moor.

When she was far enough away from the castle, Rosamund threw off her hood, enjoying the cool breeze on her face. As her pace increased she unfastened the cloak and, before going much farther, finally took it off. Her building temperature probably had more to do with anger than the heat of the sun.

How far was it to Whitton? she wondered, looking across the open countryside of undulating moorland marked by craggy limestone outcroppings and stands of trees. Because of the length of her journey to Ravenscrag, she knew she could not walk to Whitton in a day or even two. Then reality took over, jolting her with the truth. Nothing of her former life in Whitton remained. Rosamund, daughter of Joan, lay beneath a headstone in Whitton churchyard.

Leave it to her noble father to have taken care of that contingency. She had no life beyond the one ordained for her inside the castle walls. Sometimes in the past she had fantasized that her mysterious noble father would one day acknowledge her as his own. Well, that event had taken place and it was a great disappointment to her. Why then should she have expected life with Henry Ravenscrag to be any less disappointing? He was a man of his class. From the very beginning he had never hidden his feelings about a wife. She had become that scorned creature—no longer Jane, the giddy, sensual bedmate, but Rosamund, the dull and dutiful wife.

"Damn you, Henry Ravenscrag!" she yelled so loud she wondered that her lungs did not burst. Startled by the noise, a flock of birds circled overhead, uttering raucous cries of alarm.

Rosamund's head hurt and her feet ached from her long walk. She had no idea how far she had come. Uneasily she wondered if she could find her way back or if she would have to spend the night on the moors. She also wondered if there were any desperate men lurking in the sparse stands of trees dotting the landscape.

Finally she stopped to rest beside a gurgling beck, and pulling off her boots, she dangled her feet in the cold water. Its iciness made her gasp, but soon her tired feet began to feel better. She sat on the mossy bank soaking her feet and watching birds fluttering about the white flowering thorn thicket beyond the beck. When she felt somewhat restored, she dried her feet on her skirts and prepared to go on.

She stood in the shelter of elms and willows growing beside the water, surveying the empty expanse of moorland. Perhaps she had ridden so far before. The beck looked familiar, yet she couldn't be sure because in that terrain one place looked like another. In the distance she could hear gulls calling and she wondered if she was close to the sea. On the moorland the wind had a cold edge to it, but she did not know if she smelled sea salt on the breeze or merely the fragrance of spring on the Yorkshire moor.

Rosamund leaned against the gnarled trunk of a hazel hanging over the water. At her feet were small, star-shaped white flowers; shy primroses hid amidst the scrubby grass at the base of the tree. That far north, the flowers did not bloom until late. It was already April. Had it really been that long since she had been with Henry?

Tears, no longer needing to be suppressed, trickled down Rosamund's face, which was hot after her brisk walk. In a way the tears were comforting. She slid down to the rough grass, and leaning against the tree trunk, she rested her face against her wool cloak, sobbing for all she could not change.

The unexpected thud of hooves startled her. Rosamund jerked her head up to listen, aware she must have dozed since the sun hung far lower in the sky. She pulled her dark cloak around her, hoping to blend with the tree trunk. Was the unseen rider one of the thieves roaming the moor? Though she had little of value to steal, she had few illusions about the payment the man would extract.

The horse's hooves thumped closer, squelching through mud at the edge of the beck. Then silence. Rosamund dared not move from her hiding place, though it afforded little cover beyond a few blackthorn bushes and a circle of gorse. Perhaps the rider merely came to water his horse.

"By all that's holy! What are you doing here?"

She recognized the voice at once. Henry had come in search of her. Rosamund saw the angry set of his face as he slung his cloak across his saddle and came toward her. He wore a simple dark jerkin and hose over a plain white shirt; his tall black boots reached up to his thighs. When she looked into the sun the white shirt was so bright it dazzled her eyes; the sleeves flapped in the wind blowing fresh and chill from the east.

"I had to get away from the castle. I was suffocating," Rosamund said angrily.

With as much dignity as she could muster, she struggled to

her feet. Squaring her shoulders, she faced him, determined not to be cowed by his superior strength and rank. Let him be angry. She was angry too and with far more cause.

"After all I've told you about the danger of leaving the castle, I can't believe you came out here alone, and so late in the day."

"It wasn't late when I started."

"Indeed, and what time was that?"

"What do you care, my lord? You were too busy entertaining your important guests to spare any thought for me. And when they left, you bathed and went to sleep."

"I needed to bathe and change clothes after such a hard ride. Believe me, you'd not have welcomed me."

"I'd have welcomed you after being down a mine shaft!" she shouted, the wind sending her voice echoing about the moor.

"Walking alone on the moor is sheer stupidity. I thought you had more sense than that. If you needed air why didn't you bring a groom with you or even that misbred hound?"

"Dimples? Is he all right?"

"Aye, but he damned near howled the castle down. The servants thought it was a banshee. It took some time to find out where he was holed up."

She glared at Henry defiantly. So Dimples had betrayed her. But she could not be angry with him, poor dog.

"If it hadn't been for him I'd probably still be sleeping. I'd never have known you'd come out here alone," Henry said.

"Of that I've no doubt. You might even have slept through the night without any thought to me. As your wife, I seem to be a necessary evil in your household."

"What makes you say a foolish thing like that? Didn't I greet you right warmly?"

"And promptly forgot me."

"I had pressing business. The others needed my time. We could have been together later."

"Oh, really, and when might that have been? After everyone had gone to bed and there was naught left to entertain

139

you? Would you have had time for me then? I expected to
share a meal. My gown was made just for your homecoming.
This was to be our special night together. Oh, damn you, Harry
Ravenscrag, for treating me so cruel!''

Henry appeared genuinely surprised by her anger. "Don't
you think I wanted to be with you after all those weeks
apart?"

Rosamund sniffed loudly and tried to gulp down her angry
tears. "Why? From what I hear you never lack for women's
favors even without your mistress at Enderly." She had cast
that barbed remark at random; when he winced, she knew it
had hit its mark. But she had not wanted it to be true. She
looked at him through a mist of tears. "Oh, go to hell, Harry
Ravenscrag. I should be flogged for ever thinking you would
love me."

Unable to say more without crying, Rosamund turned and
stumbled away over the uneven ground, anxious to put distance between them.

Henry leapt after her, grasping her arms and spinning her
about. "Listen to me, woman," he cried, his jaw tense. "What
happened before I knew you cannot be changed. You have no
cause to flay me with it."

"Did knowing me change anything on our wedding night?"
she said, then felt his arms go rigid. Again she had hit the
mark. How much she had wanted that not to be true also. She
had clung to the faint hope that he could have gone somewhere
innocent and far away from the hated manor of Enderly. The
lump in her throat threatened to burst and she struggled to be
free of him. Why had she ever thought the man was her dream
come true? Life with him was fast becoming a nightmare.

Henry held her tight, though he did not meet her gaze. "I'm
sorry for that, Rosamund. It wasn't supposed to matter."

"Not matter! To who? Me?"

"No, to me."

"I didn't know it did."

His fingers bit into her arms in a bruising grip and he forced
her against him, though she struggled to be free. Tension hard-

ened his face and Rosamund felt a flicker of fear as she saw his rage.

"There's much you don't know," he said, giving her a little shake. "You've no idea how much I wanted to change things . . . or how hard I tried not to—"

"Not to what?"

The changing expression on his face surprised her so she stopped struggling and looked up into his dark-fringed eyes, trying to interpret his thoughts. But the fading light cast shadows across his lean face.

"Not to what?" she demanded again.

"Not to love you," he whispered.

Stunned by what she thought he had said, Rosamund decided her imagination must have been playing tricks on her. He could not have said he loved her. Perhaps the whine of the wind had just made it seem as if he had said those words. "Did you say you love me?"

"Aye, 'tis true, God help me. No other wench can hold a candle to you. That was a hard admission to make. I've fought long against it. This wasn't supposed to happen with you, but it did. During this time apart I've finally had to admit the truth."

Her determination to hate him evaporated before the beauty of his confession. His lips were close to hers, yet still he hesitated, unsure if she would welcome him.

"Oh, Harry, this can't really be happening. 'Tis my dream come true."

"Rosamund, sweetheart, how much I've missed you. Say you're not angry with me."

His warm breath caressed her face and it seemed as if she needed his strength to hold her upright. The hard pressure of his body against hers became precious torment. Then his mouth covered hers and it was the sweetest kiss she had ever known.

"I love you, Rosamund," he whispered against her ear, his tongue tantalizing her earlobe. "You are my wife, but you are also my lover."

141

That statement was the one she had longed to hear, the very one he had withheld from her. Melting into his arms, Rosamund lost all sense of time and place. They stood locked in an embrace, buffeted by the wind swirling over the moor. Curlews and gulls circled overhead, their noisy cries heralding a storm.

"Come home. Let's eat our feast and have a night to remember," Rosamund said.

Henry smiled at her invitation. Then he kissed her hair and her brow. "You can wear your new yellow gown after all and I'll enjoy taking it off you," he said, sliding his hands down her back, caressing the firm contours of her buttocks through the purple wool gown.

"I'd like that, Harry. 'Tis what I hoped would happen."

"Sweetheart, I'm sorry if I neglected you. None of it was meant to hurt you."

"I know now," she said, forgiving him for causing her pain.

His passionate kisses smothered her words and she felt the hard pressure of his desire rising between them. As if by mutual consent, he took her down gently to the ground, rolling them close to the birches, the gorse and blackthorn thickets sheltering them from the wind. Beneath her back the heather felt springy. Rosamund delighted in the arousing pressure of his hands on her breasts and she shuddered, recalling how she had ached with longing for him all those lonely weeks apart. So swift and intense was their desire, there was little time for love play. She knew from his labored breathing and fiery kisses that their lovemaking would be quick and hot. Her legs ached as she strained against him, going weak with desire.

"I love you, sweetheart. I love you," he whispered over and over again, as he caressed her thighs and moved higher. With an eager sob she spread her legs, not prepared to wait any longer to receive him. Henry welded his hot mouth over hers, delaying a moment to free the burning brand that made her gasp with delight as its heat impaled her chill body. Straining upward, she wrapped her legs about his narrow waist, pulling him closer, causing the heat to sear through her belly to her very heart. Clawing at his clothing, Rosamund dug her fingers into his jerkin, anchoring him there for her delight. Once, twice, he plunged hard and she cried out in ecstasy as she lost control and gave herself over completely to passion.

Never before had they been so hot, so eager, so unwilling to wait; the tumultuous climax was different from any Rosamund had known. And later, as they lay entwined in the heather with the cold air whipping across them, she gave thanks for the beauty of their heated coupling. Henry had finally said he loved her. Just as she had always hoped he would, Henry Ravenscrag had truly become her lover, giving her his heart as well as his body.

"Are you ready to go home, sweet?" he asked at last, smiling lazily, his face softened by spent passion.

"Yes. We still have to enjoy your welcome-home feast."

Henry chuckled as he helped her up and pulled her into his arms for a final embrace. "There isn't a meal in all Christendom I could enjoy any more than the one I've just tasted," he whispered against her ear. Then he turned her face up for a tender kiss. "Thank you, sweetheart, for loving me so well."

"No, 'tis I who must thank you," she said, leaning against him as he led her toward his horse, which was cropping grass nearby.

"Come. Let me take you back like a conquering hero with his prize slung across his saddlebow."

"Nay." she laughed, shaking her head. "I'd much prefer to sit before you, love."

He placed his hands on her waist and swung her to the saddle; than he mounted behind her, pulling her inside his cloak. Rosamund sighed in contentment, finding his warmth a welcome barrier against the cold wind, his strength a comfort against life's trials. She smiled as she leaned back against him while they galloped over the moor, reveling in the knowledge that Henry, Lord of Ravenscrag, was hers at last.

PART II

PART II

Chapter Seven

During the autumn of 1460, while the Yorkist army headed
north, their leader, the Duke of York, stayed in London trying
to legitimize his claim to the throne. He considered himself
the rightful claimant, and though he had the king's promise
of the succession after his death, it was not enough. That waste
of precious time enabled the Lancastrians to rally after their
defeat at Northhampton in July, drawing many new supporters
to their cause.

December of that year was cold but dry, a welcome change
from the wet summer. In the past months, the king's supporters had moved tirelessly about the north recruiting men and
conferring with Queen Margaret in her makeshift court at Pontefract, readying their ranks for the intended march on London.

After much thought, Henry sent a letter home to Ravenscrag
asking Rosamund to join him for Christmas at Pontefract Castle. Though he doubted there would be much celebrating that
year, Christmas would be made joyous be having her by his
side. It was several weeks since he sent a letter by a trusted
man; so far there had been no reply. He knew winter was not
the best of times to travel through the North Country, but as
the battle plans were not his, he had to abide by another's
timetable.

The day was cold and grains of sleet stung Henry's face as
he rode across open country with a handful of men, scanning
the horizon for his returning messenger. He felt uneasy about
having left Rosamund alone for so long. Some lords had
brought their wives with them, but he had not wanted to put
Rosamund in danger. Most of the summer had been spent in

the field; so he had been home only a few weeks before he had had to leave again. Autumn had been much the same. As the weeks dragged on, he ached for the sight of her until he grew reckless when there was still no sign of action by asking her to join him. The Duke of York was reportedly holed up in Sandal Castle outside Wakefield awaiting reinforcements under the command of his eldest son, Edward, Earl of March, who had been campaigning in Wales. It was quite possible they would spend the entire winter playing the cat-and-mouse game.

The light was fading when Henry finally abandoned his watch. He turned around and galloped back to the safety of Pontefract. Maybe he would hear from her on the morrow.

The wild terrain was heavily wooded. The straggling Yorkist troops set up camp in the shelter of the trees, building their fires in a clearing. The army's ranks were swelled by many local men looking for adventure and the booty of war. During the day, those new recruits halfheartedly practiced warfare as their leaders tried to shape rough plowmen into soldiers. A few among them showed a natural talent by quickly mastering the weapons of war; those men were put in charge of their fellows.

As time went by without the promised excitement, boredom gradually set in. The archers still practiced at makeshift butts and the armorers honed weapons and mended equipment. Yet for the most part, the green soldiers lay around, complaining about the slim pickings their foraging had so far produced. They also doubted there was an enemy within a week's march of them.

A number of women traveled with the army, some coming to cook and wash for their own men, while others had followed the troops from London, intent on cheering the cold winter's nights. One of the London camp followers was Nell, a pinched-faced young blonde who chose a group of local Yorkshire men as traveling companions.

"Reckon we be getting close to York, now, eh?" she asked,

pushing between the men to warm herself at the fire.

"Reckon."

"I hear tell the French queen's at Pontefract."

The big blond man hunched over the fire gnawed on a joint of rabbit and paid no attention to her. Finally he pushed Nell away when she put her arms round his neck and tried to kiss him.

"Aw, leave him be, hinny. He's still moping for his lost sweetheart," one of the others said. Winking at her, he added, "Now I be ready for a bit of a lark, if you've a mind."

"Poor Steven," Nell said. "Why don't you tell me about it, love? Sometimes makes things better to talk," she said. Then, trying a new tack, she asked him, "Were she pretty?"

Steven turned glazed blue eyes on her. "She were like an angel."

His words were met by a loud guffaw from some of the others and he cuffed the nearest man over the head. His huge fist delivered a resounding blow and the man yelped in pained surprise. "There's no other woman for me now."

"He's took 'im a vow," someone hissed, hiding his humor. Many a man nursed bruises when he ran afoul of Steven of the Forge.

"Naw, go on. You're never going to 'ave any ever again?" Nell asked him incredulously.

"She were the only woman I ever loved and now she's dead. I've vowed to wed no other."

"Well, wed and bed's two different things," Nell said, encouraged. She stroked his arm, remarking on the knotted muscles under his shirt. "I could soon make yer forget."

"No one can make me forget." He stood abruptly and spilled rabbit bones on the ground. "We's to be up early tomorrow. You'd best turn in."

The others seated around the campfire watched as he plodded away through the trees.

"He's been a bit touched in the 'ead ever since she died," Hodge said, relishing being the center of attention. "She were a beauty all right, that Rosamund. She were daughter to my

Joan. Died real mysterious like. He wouldn't leave the churchyard. Sat by 'er headstone day and night. A right nice stone
she got, like some princess, all carved and such with her
name.''

The others were suitably impressed. Hodge licked his thick
lips, studying Nell. There were other parts to his story, some
real, some imaginary, which would make good entertainment
for many nights to come. Around him men were rolling themselves in blankets beside the embers of the campfire. Hodge
pulled at Nell's arm, offering her a ribbon he had kept after
ransacking a cottage the week before.

Nell had moved from man to man since following the army
north. Though she very much fancied the blond leader Steven,
she also wanted a red ribbon. She nodded her assent and put
the ribbon in her pouch. Hodge was as good as the next man.

Rosamund was glad the weather had stayed dry. She was
already tired of riding, but she knew there were many miles
to go before they reached Pontefract. To pass the time while
she rode, she repeatedly pictured her joyous reunion with
Henry, what they would say and do, how they would feel.
When Henry's letter had arrived asking her to join him for
Christmas, Rosamund had wanted to dance with delight.
Aware of her newfound station, she only allowed herself
smiles in public, then danced around her room like a mad
woman once she was alone, hugging his letter to her breast,
kissing the parchment as she pictured him writing those impassioned words.

My darling wife, how much I've longed to see you. My
days and nights are empty without you.

She had repeated the sentences again and again until she
knew them by heart. His handwriting was hard to decipher
and she had even wondered if Henry had written the letter
himself or if he had dictated it to a clerk. Though she had
never seen him write, she assumed as an important lord he

knew how. After struggling through the two pages of bold, evenly shaped letters, she decided he would not have trusted such intimate sentiments to another. Therefore, maintaining the same secrecy, she had chosen not to ask Gregory, the pleasanter of Father John's clerks, to read the letter for her. It took Rosamund several hours to wade through the sentences until she had made enough sense of them to learn that Henry wanted her to come to Pontefract. How far was that? No matter, she would go to the ends of the earth to be with him.

The small party of riders moved down the gentle hillside to water their horses at a gurgling beck. Swaledale sheep grazed in the valley. The surrounding countryside was littered with boulders as if some giant had slung them from the top of the hill.

Huddled as she was inside her fur-lined cloak, Rosamund was reasonably warm, yet she still thought longingly of her destination. Not only was she anxious for the warmth of Henry's arms and lips; she was also looking forward to a warm fire and hot food when she reached Pontefract.

"Look, lady, over there," shouted one of the men-at-arms riding with her for protection.

On the stone bridge crossing the beck lay a bundle of clothing. On closer inspection the bundle proved to be a man. Rosamund gasped as she recognized the messenger who had brought Henry's letter and taken back her reply. Quickly she turned away as the soldier pushed the man over and she saw the gaping wound in his throat. Both his pouch and horse were missing.

"Robbers most likely, my lady. We'd best not tarry here. We'll make for the nearest town."

"There's no town, nobbut a village close by," the older soldier in charge said.

They glanced warily about the rough moorland, which appeared to be deserted except for the sheep. Rosamund's party was small, consisting of three men-at-arms, a groom, Pip, the page, and Margery, the maid. They also had two mules to carry the baggage. When they left Ravenscrag their number had seemed ample for protection, but since they were faced with the possibility of a band of robbers lurking nearby, the party seemed very inadequate.

For the past three nights they had lodged at manors belonging to Sir Ismay. Though Rosamund was not comfortable seeking shelter at the manors, it was expected that she should stay at her father's holdings. In fact, Forest, the soldier in charge of their party, had a map showing both Sir Ismay's and the Ravenscrag properties, even down to the abbeys and manors who owed favors to their lords. Though Rosamund found it strange, she supposed that practice must be how journeys were conducted amongst the nobility. Once they turned east they ran out of De Gere land, leaving behind the comparative safety of Langley Hutton.

Nervously they increased their pace, riding hard, anxious to leave the boulder-strewn valley. No one accosted them and they rode as far as the next low upland range without incident. From her vantage point Rosamund looked down on the countryside spread before them like a patchwork quilt. What she saw made her stomach heave with apprehension. The land was so familiar.

"Where are we headed?" she asked Forest, maneuvering her mare beside his.

"To Boughton Abbey, lady. We'll spend the night there. 'Tis a pity we couldn't have gone to Thorpe, seeing as how your family has ties to the abbey, but it was too far out of our way. Boughton owes favors to Lord Henry; so we'll be welcomed, have no fear."

Rosamund nodded and smiled politely. It was not their reception at the abbey that bothered her. Boughton Abbey was close to Whitton. She had walked past the abbey's tall, ivy-covered walls several times, sometimes glimpsing the black-robed monks tending sheep and working the land. While part of her longed to see Whitton village green and the familiar cottages surrounding it, part of her was repelled by the thought.

During the latter part of the journey Rosamund worried that

Henry would leave Pontefract before she arrived. The messenger's death meant he was unaware she had left Ravenscrag.

The party of travelers reached Boughton Abbey well before dusk. A mist was coming down, wreathing the buildings and treetops and giving the surroundings an eerie appearance. When the abbey guest master learned their identity, they were warmly received. They were seated before a roaring fire, where they were served platters of spiced meat and cups of mulled ale, accompanied by thick slices of bread covered with honey.

Though Rosamund greatly enjoyed the warmth and the meal, she was still tormented by the thought that her old home lay within walking distance. She dreaded meeting Hodge, but she wanted to see the others, especially Mary. She knew Sir Ismay had sent them food and gold, but she really wanted to take her sister away from End Cottage. If she could just see Mary alone and show her she was not really dead after all. But how could she do that? Her transformation was too great a secret to entrust to a child.

Rosamund puzzled over her dilemma throughout her meal, and by the time they retired to bed, she had already formed a plan. The abbey was short several kitchen staff in the guest-house and she had secured one of these places for Mary. There she would be fed and housed and most important of all she would be safe from Hodge's advances.

After her maid fell asleep, Rosamund pulled her cloak over her gown and tiptoed from the room to go in search of Pip, who was sharing a room with the other men in their party. She was afraid she would wake the sleeping men as she stepped carefully across them sprawled on straw pallets beside the warm hearth.

Pip woke easily and at first he stared wide-eyed at Rosamund before comprehending she wanted him to get up and accompany her. Wondering at her strange request, yet not questioning it, he picked up his cloak and soft-soled shoes and followed his mistress.

They slipped unnoticed through the side door into the court-

153

yard, where Rosamund sent Pip to saddle their horses, then waited impatiently in the shadows for his return. After what seemed like hours she heard hooves clopping over the cobblestoned yard. The horses' shoes made so much noise she was afraid someone would come to investigate the clatter. When they passed the snoring gatekeeper without detection, she could hardly believe their good fortune.

"There's a little wench in the village who's treated cruelly. I've spoken to the abbot about her and he can use another pair of hands in the guesthouse. I've left money so she'll be cared for," Rosamund said when Pip's curiosity overcame his training and he asked where they were bound.

Pip nodded, not finding the idea strange, though he did ask why they must go in such secrecy in the dark.

"Her stepfather would never let her go. If she comes with us now she can ride with you. She's small and light."

Pip agreed to the suggestion, though he did not relish the idea of carrying a smelly peasant girl in such close proximity to his own person. It was because of his unusual fastidiousness that his father had sent him to Ravenscrag, hoping that service in the great household would help him overcome his squeamish nature and make a man of him. However distasteful Pip personally found the idea of riding with a peasant wench, he would obey his lady's commands. It was his duty, but more to the point, he had fallen madly in love with the beautiful Lady of Ravenscrag.

They neared Whitton parish church, which was set apart from the rest of the village beside a meandering stream. There, because of the water, the mist was heavier, swirling about them and bowling along the path from the nearby beck like a living being. When Pip saw gravestones emerging through the mist, he shuddered and crossed himself. To his horror his lady turned onto the track leading through the churchyard.

"Surely the lass doesn't live here," he said in fright, drawing his mount closer to Rosamund's.

"No, there's a grave here I want to see," she said, glancing about at the recently dug ground. Several villagers had found a home there in the past year, she discovered, surprised by the number of fresh-turned mounds of earth. Then she saw a large headstone by itself under the yews against the stone wall. Her stomach clenched and her heart began to race in apprehension. She knew on that stone she would find her own name.

Above the hovering mist the moon was shining, and over the churchyard the mist had taken on a whitish glow. Again Pip crossed himself, glancing fearfully over his shoulder; his knees began to shake.

Rosamund dismounted and crossed the frozen ground to the plot, where some dead flowers lay atop the mound. Who amongst the villagers had put flowers there? Maybe young Mary. Or it could have been Steven. They were the only two souls who she thought would truly mourn her. Swallowing her apprehension, Rosamund forced herself to read the words on the freshly chiseled stone marker.

Here lies Rosamund, daughter of Joan Havelock, died this day, December 18, in the Year Of Our Lord, 1459.

"Lady, someone's coming," Pip said, sincerely hoping the unseen presence was of his world.

Rosamund turned toward the sound of the footsteps to see a small, cloak-swathed figure hurrying along the path from the priest's house, carrying a cloth-covered basket. The figure drew closer and the quickened gait changed to a run. Rosamund gasped in delight when she recognized Mary. Sometimes her sister cleaned for the priest and in payment he gave her a supper of bread and cheese for the family. Even her cloak looked like that same ugly, rough garment shared by all the family members. Rosamund could not have asked for better luck. Stepping on to the path, she called, "Mary."

The girl skidded to a halt. Her eyes were huge as she gaped at the apparition rising from the mist. She froze to the spot with terror.

"Don't be afraid. It's only Rosamund."

Mary screamed and dropped her basket, spilling loaves and

cheese on the ground. Still screaming, she finally found her feet, and stumbling and sobbing in fright, she raced toward the village street.

Shocked by her sister's reaction, Rosamund called after Mary, running to the cemetary wall to wave and call her back. After one terrified glance over her shoulder, Mary kept on running. Pip chuckled over the girl's fright, forgetting his own fear in his enjoyment of the incident.

"The lass thinks you're a ghost, lady. You should see the way the mist wreathes around you, all glowing. She'll tell this story for years to come."

A ghost! Rosamund gasped at her own stupidity. Of course Mary would think she was a ghost. There had been no need of mist to make Mary sure the apparition was Rosamund risen from her own grave, which she stood beside. The mist had wisped about her. Her face had been concealed by her hood until she had stepped forward and it had slipped back. That was when Mary had seen her face. Far from soothing the child's fears, her recognition had taken away all doubt that the figure was Rosamund risen from the dead.

Feeling defeated, Rosamund turned her back on her own grave. All her plans had gone awry. There was little chance of taking Mary into her confidence. She had never meant to frighten the child. Even Luna's white coat gleamed eerily in the mist. Many a village legend was spawned by such an incident. Whitton villagers would be terrified to pass the grave-yard on a winter's night for fear of seeing Rosamund's restless shade with her ghostly steed.

Pip was still chuckling when they remounted and rode out of the churchyard. "Where does this lass live, lady," he asked in surprise as she turned back onto the abbey road.

"I've lost my stomach for adventure, Pip. Let's go back to our beds." Rosamund urged Luna forward, picking up speed, eager to put time and space between herself and the horrid reminder of her own fate.

Surprised, but again not questioning his mistress's actions, Pip was only too pleased to comply, having little stomach himself for such nocturnal visits.

"They can bring the wench to the abbey during the day. I'll have the abbot send his servant," Rosamund said as they neared the abbey gates.

"That's a splendid idea, Lady Rosamund," Pip said, breathing a sigh of relief to be safe inside the protective walls of Boughton Abbey.

Rosamund stayed at Boughton only long enough to be assured Mary was brought safely inside the religious community. After her disasterous attempt to speak to her young sister at the churchyard, she did not want to frighten her again or risk exposing her own charade.

Through a peephole Rosamund watched as the abbot's servant brought Mary inside the guest master's chamber. Mary had grown several inches taller since last Rosamund had seen her, though she still looked very pale and thin. At times she burst into fits of weeping and Rosamund felt guilty when the abbot's servant relayed a tale of the frightening apparition the child had witnessed the previous night. At Rosamund's request Mary had been told only that the Lady of Ravenscrag had made a donation to the abbey to care for deserving girls. It was a tale that satisfied all concerned.

When they resumed their journey to Pontefract, Rosamund shed a few bitter tears for a past that was no longer hers. Finally she squared her shoulders and looked straight ahead. The future lay along this meandering road; Henry and Ravenscrag Castle were her life. It was pointless to mourn for that which no longer belonged to her.

The small party of travelers lost precious time on the road. A bridge ahead was impassable, forcing them to detour many miles out of their way. Then a horse went lame. By the time they neared Pontefract, the 12-day Christmas celebration was almost over. More bad luck was to come. Rosamund was devastated to learn Henry had ridden to battle with the Lancastrian Army.

She was stranded in the strange town. A kindly mother superior from a nearby convent offered hospitality to Lord Henry's lady. Though her suggestion that Rosamund seek shelter inside the convent walls until the hostilities were past was sensible, Rosamund was reluctant to agree. Finally she decided to stay at Setterforth Convent, where she waited apprehensively for news of the outcome of the latest clash between Lancaster and York, fearful Henry might be wounded or killed and aware she was powerless to change whatever fate had in store.

The late December night was cold and dark. Frost nipped the air. Henry sprawled on a makeshift bed in his tent, where a brief council of war had recently taken place. The plan put forth seemed fair enough, given their meager choices. York was keeping Christmas at Sandal Magna near Wakefield while awaiting the arrival of reinforcements. Sandal Castle was not provisioned to support an army of 8,000, limiting the time York could hole up there, which was fortunate, Although the Lancastrian force outnumbered York's, they lacked siege equipment. It was a stalemate unless York could be persuaded to leave his stronghold to do battle in the open. And therein lay their plan.

Much of the castle's surrounding terrain was heavily wooded. The Lancastrian force numbered close to 10,000. If they split the troops, having a few thousand marching forward in full view toward the castle, while the others lay in wait in the woods, they might be able to persuade their enemy to leave his lair and do battle. There would certainly be much temptation on York's part to make short work of so small a force. With seeming reluctance to make a stand, the Lancastrian troops would keep falling back, drawing their opponents farther from the castle and closer to the trees. Once in position, the hidden troops would come out of the woods and cut off their escape.

It was a bold plan that just might work. If they waited too long for York to starve himself out, half their own troops would have wandered away. They were also not anxious to wait for his reinforcements to arrive; if they did so, they themselves would be in the unenviable position of being outnumbered.

Somerset, Clifford, Percy, Dacre—Henry reviewed the powerful families represented there who had shared a bumper of Malmsey with him, drinking to victory on the morrow. The flower of the North had assembled outside Wakefield on that winter night. The December quiet was suddenly shattered by a woman's high-pitched laughter. It appeared that not all rested in preparation for the morrow.

Henry thrust aside a vivid mental picture of the probable activity in the nearby tent, and his thoughts immediately turned to Rosamund. Sadly he realized there was little hope of his seeing her. All his plans had gone afoul. Either the messenger had been captured or set upon by thieves. There was no sign of either the man or the letters. Perhaps it had worked out for the best since Henry's situation had become more dangerous. The surrounding countryside swarmed with troops of both sides and it was not a comforting thought that Rosamund might have been traveling across country where she would be at the mercy of both armies.

Again the woman laughed and Henry rolled onto his stomach in an attempt to quell his rising blood, which was fired by intimate thoughts. There was little chance of sleep while his mind followed that course. Sometimes he found it hard to believe he was actually in love with his wife. Had his friends known, they would have found his plight highly amusing. They brought him women until he was forced to invent a vow wherein he had promised celibacy into the new year in return for a special intention. One of the priests had blessed him for his piety, making him feel despicable for lying about a sacred vow. Yet the invention was needed to stop the steady stream of wenches being provided for his pleasure by well-meaning friends.

Steps sounded outside; then the tent flap was lifted. Sir Ismay entered, swathed in a thick cloak.

"Will you share a bumper with me, Harry?" the older man asked, coming to warm himself at the glowing brazier. "I'm getting too old for this. The cold seeps into my bones.''

"Gladly. Are you ready for battle?"

Sir Ismay shrugged as he crouched on a stool. He leaned over the brazier while Henry poured the wine. "Is a man ever ready to die?"

"Dear God, die! What gloomy thoughts are these? We're going to be victorious.'' Henry laughed, touching his goblet to that of the other man. "Here's to victory."

"Victory."

"What makes you so gloomy of late?"

Sir Ismay sighed, not anxious to reveal what plagued him, yet no longer wanting to keep it to himself. "I had a dream . . . a vision, if you will, and—''

Alerted, Henry swung his feet to the ground. "What are you trying to tell me?"

"Oh, it had a little bearing on the outcome of tomorrow's fight. It was more of a personal nature."

Henry breathed a sigh of relief. "Good. Well, don't torment me. What is this dire prediction?"

"I saw riders bearing a body across a saddlebow," Sir Ismay said, staring unseeing into the brazier's glowing embers. "The De Gere arms were on the saddlecloth."

"Gloomy imagining, nothing more, Father," Henry said good-naturedly, hoping there was no more to the vision than that. Sir Ismay was never the most cheerful of men, though since they had become allied by marriage he had seemed much more at ease.

"Aye, perchance you're right. What news from Ravenscrag?" Sir Ismay asked, trying to cast off his gloom. "Is there a bun in the oven yet?"

Henry ran his hands through his dark hair and shook his head. "Hardly. We've not had much time together. I'd hoped to spend Christmas with Rosamund at Pontefract. Ismay, thank you for giving me your daughter. At first it meant little more than an alliance, but now—well, now I feel otherwise.'' Henry ended gruffly, finding it difficult to put his deepest feelings into words.

Sir Ismay's dark eyes widened. "Dear God," he said a tight smile lifting his hard mouth. "You're both bewitched."

"Both?"

"Aye. The wench is besotted with you, lad. Didn't you know that?"

Henry grinned and nodded. "Aye, and every day I thank heaven for her."

Sir Ismay stood, clutching his cloak around his broad shoulders. "May circumstance never make you change your mind," he said darkly, brows drawn together. "Sleep well, Harry. We'll ride together on the morrow."

They shook hands and Sir Ismay ducked beneath the tent flap and was gone.

The great walls of Sandal Castle appeared shadowy in the morning gloom. Everything was unnaturally quiet, as if the thousands of soldiers were spellbound, awaiting the release of an ancient curse to bring them to life. Henry shivered in apprehension. He did not like the quiet. He drew on his gauntlets and secured the straps on his helm. And he waited.

From the battlements the opposing side had watched the Lancastrian force moving over the open ground beyond the castle walls. It was a far smaller force than expected, and stung by taunts that he lacked courage by hiding away safe inside Sandal, the Duke of York decided he would make short work of them, thereby falling into the trap so cleverly laid for him.

Excitement rippled through the assembled troops as they heard the castle garrison preparing to come outside. The din made by the readying Yorkist force drifted across the open ground, stirring the waiting men's excitement. The horses stamped their hooves, whickering and tossing their heads, fired by the current of emotion rippling through the ranks. The great drawbridge came down; the gates opened.

"Here they come!" Henry cried, alerting his men to the enemy's approach. Waiting for that moment, the archers loosed a volley of arrows. A second volley followed. Still the bulk of the Lancastrian force made no move to engage. The opposing sides faced each other across the stretch of open ground known locally as Wakefield Green. A chill wind stirred pennants and furled flags against their poles. The lethargic force did not put up much of a fight; instead they shifted backward, giving ground, still moving as if they were bewitched, slowly, methodically, ever backward.

The Yorkist troops coud not believe their good fortune! Not only were the Lancastrians in much smaller numbers than expected; they were also of no great courage, seeming reluctant to give battle. A great shout of triumph went up from the Yorkist troops as they derided the lackluster performance of their enemy.

Thinking it prudent to remind his men that they were not retreating, merely performing a tactical exercise, Henry sent the word through his troops and on to the De Gere men at his right, and to the Iretons on his left, as the conflict moved ever closer to the trees, leading the Yorkists into the trap until they were much too far from Sandal Castle to retreat to safety.

Henry circled a knot of fighting men, leaning down from his saddle to dispatch a couple, swinging his great sword in a wide arc, lopping quickly before he moved on. Behind him Sir Ismay was shouting excitedly, engaging with gusto, the past night's trepidation had been forgotten in the face of the enemy.

As was their custom, men fought on foot, keeping their horses at the rear. The plan neared completion, and Henry and Sir Ismay followed suit, their blood quickening at the sound of clashing steel and the cries of the combatants echoing over Wakefield Green. Yet even though the pace was picking up, everything still moved far more slowly than expected and in much smaller magnitude, as if the bewitched were coming but slowly to life.

Just when the Yorkist troops thought to close in for the kill, a horn blew, followed by a second blast. Except to those who listened for it, the signal went unnoticed above the general clamor.

Henry pulled his troops around, signaling for them to move to the right as the rest of the Lancastrian army spilled out of the woods. Thousands of shouting, screaming men descended on Wakefield Green eager to do battle. In alarm the Yorkists turned about, suddenly seeing the trap. The Duke of York's men were surrounded on all sides. Too late they saw the error of their bravery. They would have to fight to the death.

That short, bloody battle lasted no more than 30 minutes. The Lancastrian casualties numbered in the hundreds, the Yorkist casualties in the thousands. The great Duke of York fell, as did many of his supporters. Powerful Salisbury was captured and delivered into the hands of his bitter enemy, Percy of Northumberland. York's young son, the 17-year-old Duke of Rutland, was killed by Lord Clifford in payment for the Yorkist murder of his father at St. Albans. Many old scores were settled on the field, forever destroying what shreds of chivalry remained. The battle fought that last day of December, 1460, set the vengeful tone for the remainder of the bloody dynastic wars.

In the aftermath of the fight, the victorious Lancastrian army trickled inside the great city of York to make merry and celebrate their victory. They were greeted by the severed heads of their enemies set high above Micklegate Bar so none should forget their triumph. The great Duke of York, whom many had considered to be the rightful claimant to England's throne, wore a paper crown and his head was flanked by the gory heads of Salisbury and Rutland.

The crimson sun hung low in the sky as the travelers toiled uphill to York's city gate. Rosamund stared in wonder at the stone walls looming before them, washed golden by the rays of the sun. A flock of crows cawed above the main arch, pecking at something atop the gate; they perched in rows on the crenellations and on the turrets flanking the entrance.

The walled city of York would dwarf the fortress of Ravenscrag, with its many turrets and battlements. Rosamund had never been inside a city before and the sheer number of people moving in and out of the gates astounded her. They would never find Henry in that crowded place.

News of the latest battle had reached Setterforth the previous week, relayed to the religious community by a wandering minstrel: The man had been unable to tell Rosamund about casualties, beyond the names of the mighty who had fallen on the opposing side.

With her heart in her mouth Rosamund waited at the guard post, allowing the captain of her small guard to ask for admittance for their party. Around them the crowd jostled impatiently, anxious to be allowed inside the city before curfew. Carts loaded with kegs and barrels to satisfy the thirst of the victors rattled through the wide central gate. The vendors paid their toll and were waved through. When Rosamund noticed the guards seemed to be admitting all comers, her apprehension vanished.

As she had hoped, they were quickly passed through the gates and found themselves inside the crowded cobbled streets of the second city of England. The sheer press of people thronging the main street propelled them forward. It seemed just as many people were anxious to leave York before curfew. Beyond the city stood the great forest of Galtres, its mighty trees blackening the landscape. Rosamund had been relieved when she learned the road to York did not go through the forest. It was said straggling troops from both sides camped there, as well as the usual cutthroats and brigands.

It was so crowded in the streets Rosamund could scarcely draw breath. Tall buildings hemmed the travelers in on either side. When once she paused to stare in wonder at an impressive building, she was nearly run down by the relentless movement of humanity. Some houses had carved wooden gables painted in bright colors and gilded like gingerbread; coats of arms were displayed over their doorways. The house timbers creaked in the wind as the party passed. Buildings leaned against each other at such precarious angles it seemed as if they kept each other from falling down. In many places the upper stories overhung the street until they virtually met in the middle, blocking out the sky. There were shops at street level and many of the shopkeepers were putting up their shutters for the night.

Eventually the travelers came to a sluggish river; once they had crossed the water, narrow streets led them deep into the heart of the city. Rosamund held her breath when traversing the butchers' shambles, where offal and other debris choked the open ditch in the middle of the street. The stench of blood mingled with that of putrefying flesh added to the ever present odor of middens and stables coming off the slippery mire underfoot. Many streets were unpaved, making travel even more hazardous. Even the appetizing smells of roast meat, baking pastry, and fragrant wood smoke wafting out of the dwellings could not mask the noxious odor of the narrow streets.

From time to time on their journey, the men-at-arms stopped to make inquiries of passersby about the lodgings of the Lord of Ravenscrag. To Rosamund's dismay, no one had heard of him, though some of the soldiers wore the Lancastrian badge. Their quest seemed as hopeless as seeking a needle in a haystack. After the long ride Rosamund was bone weary. As each stranger shook his head in bewilderment at their question, her hope dwindled until she finally decided to wait till the morrow to resume their search. She told her captain to find them lodging for the night.

Her request had seemed simple enough, yet so crowded was the city, every inn where they stopped was already full. She had begun to give up hope of finding either Henry or a room, when Pip suddenly spotted an Ireton man drinking ale outside a tavern door.

The man told them that Lord Henry was lodged close by the great church of St. Peter. The man did not know the name of the street, but he was sure it would be near St. Leonard's Hospital, where many of the wounded had been taken.

When Rosamund heard Henry really was inside the city and unharmed, she breathed a great sigh of relief. It was dusk and a cold wind gusted between the buildings as they headed towards Goodramgate, knowing they were on the right track when they passed Holy Trinity Parish Church. One of the

men-at-arms had lived in York as a boy, so he was able to
lead them by a roundabout route into the district of St. Leonard's. Rosamund was thankful she was not traveling alone.
Though the main streets were wide enough to allow them to
ride two abreast, the dark, winding side streets were barely
passable.

At last they came to the area they sought. The enormous
church of St. Peter towered above all else, making the huddled
stone-and-timber dwellings look like toys beside the grandeur
of its walls. Scaffolding was still in place since, after 200 years
of construction, York's glorious minster was not yet complete.
The central tower had still to be finished. The workman's
cooking fires glimmered around the church's precincts as itin-
erant masons and carpenters prepared their evening meal.

After making many inquiries, the travelers finally located
the inn where the Lord of Ravenscrag was staying. It was
called the Nag's Head and was located off Lop Lane. Rosamund shook with excitement and fatigue as she dismounted
to enter the old inn; her legs were stiff and trembling after so
many hours in the saddle. To her disappointment, Henry was
not in his room.

Though reluctant to do so, the landlord finally agreed to let
Rosamund stay in her husband's room to wait for his return.
Lodgings were found in the stables for the men, while Margery
was to share an attic room with several other maids.

After helping her mistress undress and unpack some of her
clothes, young Margery was virtually asleep on her feet. Rosamund sent her off to bed, assuring her she could manage
quite well by herself.

Rosamund lit a candle. She looked around the sparsely fur-
nished room with its heavy-wood-beamed ceiling and rush-
strewn floor. A narrow window overlooked the street. When
Rosamund lifted the leather curtain, she saw several figures
moving through the shadows in the street below, but she
doubted any of them could be Henry. More likely they were
thieves setting out for a night's work.

She turned away from the window and tested the large bed

that almost filled the room. It was heaped high with wool blankets and woven coverlets and hung with heavy, dark hangings. There was also a chest beside the bed and a bench before the hearth, where a fire was blazing merrily. It was a pleasant room, yet it did not seem welcoming. Fatigue had made Rosamund vulnerable and she blinked back her tears of disappointment. How excited she had felt when the landlord had finally said the Lord of Ravenscrag was lodged there. Her hopes had been dashed a few minutes later when she found not only was Henry not in his room, but he had not been there for much of the day.

Huddled in her cloak, Rosamund sat before the fire, wondering when he would return. An unpleasant thought kept stealing her peace of mind: When Henry did come back, he might not be alone. To have to sit there and see him with his arms about some easy wench would break her heart. Yet she had to admit such an event was distinctly possible. In fact, if she was completely honest, it was very likely Henry was not spending the evening alone. Men often considered feeding their sexual appetite little different from eating and drinking. But not her own love. Please, not Harry, she whispered in a fervent prayer for his faithfulness. It would be too cruel, after coming so far, to have to witness such a devastating truth.

On the pegs above the bed hung several articles of clothing; his trunk stood in the corner. Rosamund touched the hard leather and cold metal of his jack. Then she lovingly stroked the soft silky pile of his velvet doublet. Time crawled by and she had trouble keeping her eyes open. Finally she abandoned her watch, and pulling off her shift, she climbed into bed.

How her weary limbs delighted in the soft mattress. Ignoring the lumps and the chill covers, she spread her arms and legs wide and lay there, enjoying the luxury of stretching out, of having her tired body supported by something other than a jouncing nag and of having fat feather pillows to cradle her aching neck. The warmth of her body gradually swallowed the chill from the covers and she sighed in contentment.

Why didn't Henry come back to his room? she thought wistfully, wishing she could make him appear through sheer will-power. What could he be doing in the noisy, smelly city? The probable answer to that question did not cheer her mood; so she dwelled on the idea of their being together soon. How she ached for his arms and trembled at the thought of touching and kissing him. Her nipples hardened as she thought about lovemaking, and pangs of desire stabbed between her legs. However much she longed for Henry the truth remained: He was not there and he might not return before morning.

The late hour and her own weariness joined forces against her as her steadfast belief in him began to crumble. Tears squeezed from under her closed lids. She did not admonish herself for disloyal thought, nor did she indulge in anger at the idea he might have betrayed her with another woman. The ache of desire blended with the ache of loneliness and the ache of weary limbs as she began to sob into the pillow.

Soon Rosamund felt even too tired to cry and her sobs gradually died in her throat. Her mind drifted in the firelit room, thinking about him and trying not to think about him, wanting him, yet at the same time wanting to hate him. It was not wise to be enslaved in such a fashion, she reminded herself drowsily. Not good, not prudent, not. . . .

Banging and thumping outside the door woke her. For an instant she did not know where she was. Then Rosamund remembered she was in York, waiting for Henry at the Nag's Head. Outside in the passage she could hear several muffled male voices. Then her blood ran cold as she heard a woman unsuccessfully trying to stifle her mirth.

Fists clenched beneath the blankets, Rosamund waited stiffly in the flickering firelight. More steps sounded. The latch lifted. She did not move; her eyes were fixed on the door, waiting for Henry to come inside. The door banged shut and a single dark shadow crossed the golden pool of firelight. Gradually Rosamund let out her breath, unaware till that instant that she had been holding it. He was alone.

The dark male figure cast a huge shadow in the small room as the man flung off his cloak and crossed to the hearth. He bent over the blaze to warm himself, then stirred the logs with the poker. The fire blazed high, lighting his face, and Rosamund was relieved to see it really was Henry. The woman may not have been with him after all since she had heard other men's voices outside. Wistfully she clung to that thought, needing to believe it.

Firelight glowed on Henry's face, softening his stern profile, gilding his flesh until it appeared to have been cast from gold. His dark curly hair tumbled untidily about his collar far longer than he usually wore it. He was so handsome she shivered in pleasure as she looked at him. Each time she saw him was as thrilling as the first.

Rosamund did not speak. She just lay there, waiting to surprise him. Wide awake, she trembled in expectation of him slipping inside the covers, totally unaware of her presence. Though her trunk had been brought to his room, she doubted he would notice it in the dim light from the fire and a single candle. She lay very still and waited.

Finally Henry dropped his heavy boots on the rushes with a thud. His doublet, shirt, and hose, he slung on the bench. He was going to bed. Though his back had been toward her, Rosamund thrilled at the sight of broad, smooth shoulders tapering to a narrow waist. Her gaze moved over the compact curve of his buttocks and down to his strong sinewed thighs. She imagined running her hands over his body and it was all she could do not to call out to him.

Henry snuffed the candle, leaving the room lit only by dancing flames. Great shadows wavered over the ceiling, making a grotesque caricature of his body, showing great branching shoulders on a towering frame and long, thin legs striding across the wall toward the bed.

Henry threw the covers back and the bed dipped as he slid inside. He sprawled there, the bed wide enough to keep them from touching. The side where Rosamund lay was in darkness, yet she could not believe he had not noticed the mounded covers. Already Henry's breathing grew deep and even. Surely he was not asleep.

Tentatively Rosamund slid her hand across the cold covers to meet the aura of warmth radiating from his body. Reaching out, she shivered in delight as she grasped the thick length of his manhood in her hand. She gently fondled its substance until suddenly it was flaccid no longer.

With an angry oath, Henry jerked upright and flung aside the covers. He leapt from the bed. "Who the hell are you, wench? Get out of here! God damn them. I've told them all time and again."

In agitation he fumbled to light the candle, cursing under his breath. Back at the bed, he tried to snatch away the covers while Rosamund battled to keep them.

"Who are you?" he demanded again.

Then she suddenly sat up, her hair spilling loose about her shoulders. The candle cast a halo of light over her face and she thrilled as she saw his incredulous expression. The candle wavered dangerously in his hand, threatening to fall on the rushes. Rosamund squeaked in alarm, reaching out to save it.

"Don't you know your own wife, Harry Ravenscrag?" she asked him when he did not speak.

Stunned, he didn't move. Finally, he very carefully set down the candleholder on the chest beside the bed. "Rosamund?"

"Yes, sweetheart, it's Rosamund."

She could not keep her eyes off his engorged organ thrusting so close to her face, throbbing even as she watched. She had only to lean forward a little to touch the tip, laving her tongue around its fullness, gently massaging the velvety soft flesh until he groaned aloud with desire. She could already taste the first sweet drops of his passion.

"Oh, dear God, Rosamund, my love!" he croaked, finally dropping on the bed beside her.

They rolled about in a tumble of bedcovers. Henry dragged her into his arms, covering her face with kisses. How hot he was, how strong. Rosamund could feel the blood thundering in his veins as he enfolded her close against his smooth flesh, afire with need. The rigidity of his muscular arms told her how hard he strove to wait, tremors vibrating between them.

The heat of his mouth covered hers as his impassioned kisses fired her to great desire.

They rolled about together amid the sheets and blankets until she was on top of him, stroking his strong muscled chest, straddling his hips with her legs. Rosamund gently squeezed his dark nipples. Then she leaned forward so that her full breasts were suspended above him like fruit ripe for the plucking.

Henry groaned as he captured her breasts in his eager hands, sobs of desire choking in his throat. He kissed those alabaster globes passionately, trembling to have his most cherished dream come alive before his eyes. He sucked her engorged nipples, setting her on fire.

They did not wait. By mutual agreement, she rose up until she had sheathed that magnificent throbbing strength inside her body. With a muffled cry, Henry grasped her hips, straining up while Rosamund drove down, sobbing with ecstasy as she felt his searing strength filling her body. Then she rode him like a wild mare until the dam burst and he flooded her belly with liquid heat making her cry aloud with passion.

They rolled over together until Henry was on top. His lips were searing hot against hers, his tongue invading her mouth. The interval between lovemaking was short. He seemed only to move a few thrusts before he was full and ready to take her again. Rosamund delighted in the pressure of his hands on her breasts. How she had ached to feel his caressing hands on her, imagining the thrill of passion in the dark solitude of her tower room all those nights when he was away.

"Oh, Rosamund, sweetheart, how much I love you," he whispered against her ear, his breath like fire. The trail of kisses he pressed along her jawline burned into the flesh.

"I've waited for so long to be held like this," she whispered back, her voice husky with desire. "You are my love, Harry. Nothing will change that—not time nor space."

His mouth muffled her words. Then he absorbed her sudden shout of ecstasy as he repeatedly plunged deep inside her, touching the very core of her being, so that Rosamund screamed in pleasure, hardly able to bear the devastating sensations he aroused.

They drifted on a sea of passion, sometimes coming ashore to doze, then lazily kiss, until once more they were cast adrift on the relentless waves of desire. Again and again Henry made love to her until he had no more strength. Never before had he made love to a woman with such heat and intensity or for so great a time.

Chapter Eight

A short burst of snow fluttered past them, borne on the brisk north wind, which funnelled between the buildings. Rosamund and Henry walked back to the Nag's Head from the cathedral, where they had attended a Mass to offer thanks for the Lancastrian victory.

Rosamund found the sheer grandeur of the great minster overwhelming. She had spent much of the Mass admiring the enormous stained-glass windows and the intricate wood carving in the church's candlelit interior. An array of gold plate gleamed on the high altar; the priest's rich brocade vestments, which were embroidered in gold, were lavish enough for a king.

"Would you like to go riding outside the walls when we've supped?" Henry asked as he slipped his arm about her shoulders.

"Oh, could we?" Rosamund said in delight. How wonderful it would be to ride beneath sky and trees with enough space to move without the constant racket of the hundreds of people who seemed to spend their entire lives on the narrow streets.

"I guessed you were also in need of fresh air," Henry said, dodging a rush seller whose wares flapped in his face as, bent double under the heavy load, the vendor pushed his way through busy Lop Lane.

"I can't wait to feel the wind in my face and be able to move without rubbing elbows with all these people. A ride in the country sounds like heaven, even though it's freezing out."

"A little cold won't hurt us. You have your choice, lady: frostbite or suffocation."

Rosamund pulled a wry face at the choices offered her. "Then I choose frostbite, though it seems a poor alternative."

A gate leading to the cathedral precincts stood at the end of Lop Lane; so their walk back to the inn was short. Inside the inn's common room a welcoming fire blazed. They supped lightly off roasted mutton, bread, and mulled ale, with a handful of sweet almond comfits for dessert. The bread provided for the lord's table was soft and white. Some of the common travelers were eyeing Rosamund and Henry's dinner enviously since they were served dark rye bread and sour ale.

Henry ordered a more substantial meal to be prepared on their return. Then he and Rosamund went up the narrow stairs to their room. A fire crackled in the hearth and a tray of wine and sweet cakes had been left on the chest. Rosamund also noticed that, beside the bed, there was a second chest that had not been there earlier.

"Oh, look. They must think we need more space to store our clothes," she said, stooping to examine the carved-and-painted piece of furniture. When at first Henry did not answer, Rosamund did not find his silence strange since he was sipping a cup of malmsey before the hearth. Then she glanced up at him and saw his betraying grin, and she realized he knew far more about the chest than she.

"Is it a gift?" she asked in surprise, coming to him and sliding her hand inside the unbuttoned neck of his doublet to caress his smooth skin. "Tell me, my lord, or I'll throttle you."

"Nay, surely not after tracking me down," he said, capturing her hands. "You wanton woman, following a man halfway across Yorkshire."

"You invited me."

"Aye, but I didn't think you were coming."

"That's not my fault. I wrote to tell you. I didn't know the poor lad bearing my note would be killed by robbers."

"Having you waiting here was a wonderful surprise. It's fortunate I don't have a weak heart. Hiding naked in my bed, indeed! At first I thought you some strumpet the others had sent to my room.''

"Because you often entertain strumpets in your room?'' Rosamund asked, pretending to jest, but the pain behind that question was too acute for humor.

"Nay, because I don't. My friends have feared for my sanity, considering it unhealthy to stay celibate all this time.''

How much she wanted to accept his easy jesting explanation. "You were faithful to me?'' she asked, her voice breaking with emotion.

"Of course I've been faithful, silly goose.''

Henry pulled her into his arms and kissed the cold tip of Rosamund's nose. Her eyes glistened with moisture. Not wanting him to know how much the subject of his possible infidelity hurt her, she buried her face against his soft green velvet doublet.

"Go on. Look in the chest,'' Henry said. "There's something there for you.''

Together they opened the stiff silver filigree clasps. A dark folded bundle of fabric virtually filled the chest. Henry took one end, Rosamund the other, and they pulled out the heavy garment. Thick fur spread over the rushes as Henry shook the folds from the forest-green velvet cloak. Rosamund gasped in delight at its beauty, seeing the hooded garment was lined with luxurious vair.

"This is my Christmas gift to you, wife,'' he said gravely, draping the cloak about her shoulders.

"You bought it for me?'' She sank her hands into the silky warm lining. It felt rich and soft. Rosamund had never seen such a wonderful cloak in all her life.

"When I thought you weren't to join me in Pontefract, I had it packed away. I bought this from a foreign merchant and I've been hoarding it like precious gold.''

"Oh, Henry, it's so beautiful. How can I thank you?'' she cried, straining up to kiss him.

"Thanking me's never been much of a problem in the past,'' he said with a grin as he turned her about to admire

175

her velvet cloak. The dark green made her hair look almost red. He reached out and pulled off her headdress, sending the rippling, silky mass cascading over her shoulders. "There, that's how it should be worn."

Feeling beautiful, Rosamund pirouetted before him, nestled inside the lovely cloak. "Am I to wear this on our ride?"

"Of course. It's designed to chase away the winter chill. There are matching gauntlets at the bottom of the chest. They might be too big for you. I wasn't sure of your hand size."

Exclaiming over the second gift, Rosamund slipped her hands inside the green leather gauntlets, which were also lined and trimmed with vair. "Oh, I'll be warm as a summer's day! People will think I'm a princess in this grand cloak. But, Harry, I've a gift for you that I spent all summer making. 'Tis not nearly as magnificent as this. I'm almost ashamed to give it to you now."

"Whatever it is, I'll cherish it," he said with an indulgent smile, drawing her into his arms and kissing her tenderly. "If you made it, it'll be a treasure indeed."

Rosamund searched inside her trunk for the gift, which she shyly gave to him. The black velvet purse was intricately stitched in crimson, green, and gold. She had labored over the purse for many weeks, embroidering a design of birds and vines that Con had drawn for her. The singing birds were worked in bright gold thread and the encircling vines were green with gold and red blossoms. It was a fanciful scene unlike the real birds and flowers found in the Yorkshire countryside, yet the artistic interpretation reminded her of an illuminated manuscript she had admired at Thorpe Abbey. By his expression, she could tell Henry was pleased.

"Sweetheart, it's beautiful! I'd no idea you were such a skilled needlewoman. Of course, I already know how skilled you are in other ways," he said, pulling her back into his arms. "Thank you. It's truly a work of art and I'll treasure it for its beauty, but more especially because you made it for me."

Rosamund beamed in delight at his praise and she leaned against his strong body, sighing in contentment. She felt her marriage was complete. The past two days had been like a wonderful dream. Just by coming to York she had entered another world, and the added thrill of finally being with Henry again made the trip complete. That first night they had made love until they could no longer function; then they had slept contentedly in each other's arms. Their inn room was made special by the precious memories of the love she had known there. Finally she felt as if she belonged in Henry's world.

They stood wrapped in each other's arms until he sighed and reluctantly put her aside. "This will never do if we're to go riding today. I must go down to order the animal's saddled. We'll take some men with us and leave your maid and the lad behind."

Henry left, sprinting down the stair to the stables. Back in their room, Rosamund snuggled inside the cloak, smiling in contentment as she wondered what to wear. She had worn her best yellow silk to Mass. It was too fine for riding; so she must change it for something more serviceable. She smiled as she stroked the fur and nestled her cheek against its softness. When she thought about the fact that Henry had given her the special gift, her heart filled with love. Against the cloak her embroidered purse seemed small and insignificant.

Sometimes Rosamund loved Henry so much her heart felt close to bursting. She smiled as she looked down on the street jammed with people on that cold noon. The teeming city was such an unlikely place to have found contentment. There could be no greater pleasure than to love and be loved in return. Henry had been faithful to her out of love, not obligation. All her doubts and suspicions were spawned by her own jealous nature; in the future she would take care not to let that emotion get the better of her.

At last she turned from the window and took off her cloak. Immediately she felt its absence since the room was uncomfortably chilly. She took a wine-colored wool gown out of the chest, it being her only clean gown, and she laid the garment across the bed.

For some time Rosamund struggled with the lacings of her

yellow silk gown, which Margery had carefully fastened that morning. She knew she could have called the maid, who would be awaiting a summons. But an exciting plan formed in her mind and she did not want young Margery there to spoil the mood. Rosamund was glad neither Henry nor she kept a body servant in the bedchamber because the arrangement heightened their intimacy.

At last she had undone the gown sufficiently to pull it off; her shift, slippers, and silk hose followed. The air in the room was icy against her naked body. Quickly Rosamund pulled the fur-lined cloak around her shoulders, finding it warm and soft as thistledown against her bare skin. She was done none too soon. Already she heard Henry's distinctive step on the stair. Quickly Rosamund put her clothing out of sight and went to the hearth.

When Henry strode inside the room he was surprised to see her standing where he had left her. "Are you ready?" he asked, closing the door behind him. "You look as if you've never moved."

Rosamund smiled, running the tip of her tongue invitingly over her full lips. "Oh, I've moved, sweetheart. I've been waiting for you."

As Henry spoke he was unfastening his fine velvet doublet, which he discarded for a more serviceable garment. He turned, carrying a russet wool jerkin over his arm, and nearly bumped into Rosamund, who stood directly behind him.

"You won't need that yet, love," she said.

Henry started to argue with her, but she took the doublet from him and dropped it back on the chest. Then, turning about, Rosamund slowly opened her cloak to reveal smooth flesh curving in gleaming perfection against the fur. Henry's eyes widened and his breath tangled in his chest. For an instant he did not move; then his arms automatically reached for her.

"Oh, sweetheart, what a welcome." He slid his arms inside the fur cloak to enfold her body. He buried his mouth in her neck, his lips hotly demanding. With shaking hands he began to caress her, first molding her heavy breasts, then sliding his palms over the tantalizing curves of her buttocks.

"I've already ordered the horses saddled. We're to leave in a few minutes," he said weakly, his breathing growing ragged.

"I doubt you'll take much longer than that," she whispered wickedly, aware he was already highly aroused. Rosamund backed toward the bed, where she dropped the fur cloak on the covers, spreading it so she could lie on its silky softness.

Henry stood admiring her, enraptured by the perfect picture of her curving white flesh against the fur, ripely inviting and his for the taking. He swallowed, fighting against arousal, wanting to prolong the moment, loath to destroy the highly seductive mood she had created.

"You're like some wonderful pagan goddess," he said in admiration, not daring to touch her. He merely looked and adored.

"Then come and worship at my shrine," she said, holding out her shapely arms to him.

Henry could stand the suspense no longer. His breathing grew ragged as he pulled off his boots, then fumbled with the fastening of his tights until he finally pulled them loose. Rosamund had knelt to help him and the proximity of her ripe mouth and breasts considerably delayed the swift negotiation of the fastenings. Finally, with his shirt hanging open and his linen drawers stretching to contain him, Henry fell beside her on the bed.

Rosamund eagerly slipped into his arms, nestling against him. She buried her face in his chest hair, where she sucked his nipples to tease him and squirmed against him while she pushed down his drawers, finally releasing his organ from all restriction. His pulsing flesh was heavily engorged and hot as fire. Joyfully Rosamund slid the burning brand between her legs, capturing him with her thighs while he kissed her passionately. His tongue plundered her mouth. They were no longer aware of what caresses they bestowed. Instead they moved instinctively, as Henry's throbbing manhood sought Rosamund's moist entrance and she eagerly opened to him,

Patricia Phillips

drawing his heated flesh deep inside her, straining to contain all of him.

Arms wrapped tight, mouths welded together, they began to move rythmically. Glorious release came in seconds; shuddering, they fell back against the fur cloak, marveling at the depth and swiftness of their passion.

"There," Rosamund whispered breathlessly against his ear, "we took no more time than the blinking of an eye. None will be the wiser."

Henry grinned at her observation as he lazily stroked her smooth back. "Oh, won't they? I doubt they'll believe I'm this winded from climbing the stair. They're probably freezing down there in the yard, wondering why their master takes so long about his dress."

"Then let me help you, sweet, speed you on your way," she said, still not moving, basking in the pleasure of total satisfaction.

"Aye, a good idea," he whispered, while he continued to lazily stroke her shoulders and kiss her face, and smooth aside bright strands of hair. "And I'll assist you, my lady, if you promise to stage no more seductions."

"I'll promise, if you'll promise not to behave like a randy stallion," she said, seeking and finding his organ still partially erect. Giggling as her fingers spanned the heated girth, which pulsed and filled at her touch, she stroked the blue-veined surface, finding it soft as velvet.

"That's cheating! No more until we return. Then there'll be no quick coupling like this. I vow to make love to you till you beg me to stop."

"Oh, that sounds like such a wonderful promise. I mightn't go riding after all."

Henry grinned as, with a reluctant sigh, he moved away from temptation and swung his feet to the rushes. "Of course, that's after we've supped with Lord Stokes and his lady, and Meade Ireton, without his lady, but with a wench whom you must accept without question." He winked at her and Rosamund smiled, recalling the stories she had heard about Ireton and his mistress.

"If you insist. Only I'd thought we were to sup alone."

"Tomorrow, sweet. But first we're going to explore the city. There's much to see once you overcome the smell and the crowds."

Rosamund pulled a face as she reluctantly knelt on the bed. "If you say so, my lord, though much of what I want to see is already here in this room."

Henry laughed as she jumped from the bed and ran into his arms. When they kissed, his body responded. Shaking his head, he sternly put her aside. "Now, you temptress, get dressed and we'll take our ride. Later you can feast your eyes on that which you enjoy seeing above all else."

Smiling, Rosamund bent to kiss the moist head of his organ. "Only if you promise," she said as he captured her face between his hands, "that we'll have an entire day to ourselves."

He smiled down at her and kissed her brow. "Done. Rosamund, you've made me happy since you came into my life. I never expected it, sweet. We can be back here in bed before you know it. The Eagle and Child's only a stone's throw away."

Pouting at the reminder of their obligation, she nodded in agreement. "All right, but no boozy war stories till the wee hours."

"I promise."

After several more embraces and lingering kisses, Henry resolutely put Rosamund from him. Trying to ignore her obvious delights, he played lady's maid with fumbling hands and muttered curses. After much laughter and false starts, they finally pronounced themselves ready for their ride.

Narrow Lop Lane was crowded with noisy street vendors, basket-laden housewives, and sightseeing soldiers. All pressed so close to the horses it was a miracle their feet were not trampled under their hooves.

On the way along Petergate to Bootham Bar, the city's northern entrance, Henry stopped to speak to the captain of his guard, who had billeted Ravenscrag troops in the district. That duty finished, the riders quickened their pace, passing unchallenged beneath Bootham Bar as they headed for open country.

A sharp wind buffeted their faces as they rode over scrubby pastureland, where shaggy sheep were grazing. Stinging moisture whipped past them in the wind's icy blast. Rosamund found her cloak marvelously warm, its dense fur blocking the wind. Henry pulled ahead, his black cloak billowing behind him like a sail as he set his restless stallion at a gallop, giving him his head along a beaten track. Soon he came back, his horse more willing to move at a manageable canter.

"Poor lad, he's been in his stable all this time. I thought he'd enjoy a treat. Likewise this poor lad's also been chafing at the bit to feel the wind in my face and see open space again. You couldn't give me enough gold to live in a city like York."

"It looks small from here," Rosamund said, reining in on a hillock to look back at the city, which was girdled on two sides by seething gray water. In the gloomy afternoon light its fortifications were darkly forbidding.

"Why didn't we leave by the other gate?" she asked Henry later as they jogged companionably, breathing in great gulps of sharp cold air. "Through the main gate. I don't want to ride in the forest. There are robbers and soldiers camping there."

"They won't bother us. We have our own soldiers to protect us. Besides, I didn't want you to see the grisly trophies stuck on pikes over that gate."

"Trophies? I don't remember seeing anything."

He glanced at her. "The severed heads of York and his son, young Rutland, plus several others of importance, are rotting there. It's as well you didn't notice them."

Rosamund paled as she recalled the flock of crows pecking at something over the entrance. While feasting on the spoils the carrion crows had hidden the gruesome sight from view.

"Why did they put their heads over the gates?"

"For all to see the vanquished, I suppose. Some say it was

done at Queen Margaret's order because she hated York so, but I can't think that. She was in Scotland with Mary of Guelders. To do such a thing violates the code of honor. Honorable dead are not to be treated like common criminals. This war's taken a bloody turn. There were many who avenged past wrongs at Wakefield Green. There's little chivalry left.''

As they rode along Rosamund digested his bitter words. She knew nothing about battle. The idea of the soldier's actions being ruled by a chivalric code of honor seemed strangely at odds with the nature of their venture. In battle one killed. Surely it was as simple as that.

''A code of honor—you mean like a knight lives by?'' she asked, recalling something she had been told.

Henry threw back his head and laughed heartily. ''Dear little girl, your convent background's showing. True, knights take an oath, yet few uphold it when it's contrary to their desires. The purification, the night-long vigil, the oath of chivalry—we've all taken that, but it seems to matter little when you've an enemy on the point of your sword. Maybe those ideals are more for men who stay home to plot wars than for those who have to fight them.''

''You're a knight?''

''Yes, but I'm no Sir Galahad. Too much living gets in the way of the romantic stuff of legends.''

Rosamund did not know who Sir Galahad was, but she declined to show her ignorance, afraid she should have known.

They skirted a dense wood and came out on a stretch of open country, marshy in places with thickets of gorse and blackthorn tangling beside the path. The open landscape rolled far to the north, forested ridges black against a gun-metal sky.

''Will we be past this forest soon?'' Rosamund asked. She glanced warily at the dense trees, fancying she saw movement there. ''Are there wild beasts in the forest?''

Henry laughed and reached out to grip her hand reassuringly. ''Don't be afraid, sweet. We've ten armed men with us. There are deer and boars, though I'll wager the most dangerous beasts of all are the soldiers camping there. The Forest of

Galtres stretches a good ten miles.''

No one challenged the party, though Rosamund noticed that, when they again came to a thickly forested stretch, the soldiers regrouped, not allowing their lord and lady to ride exposed. A few minutes later, when they headed toward another clear stretch, the soldiers visibly relaxed.

"Do you feel comfortable enough on your nag to race me?" Henry asked presently.

Though she doubted Luna could begin to keep pace with Henry's stallion, Rosamund agreed. She had never raced anyone on horseback. As she picked up speed the wind whipped her hood off her head and quickly untangled her hair-fastening until her tresses streamed loose behind her. Rosamund was surprised by the mare's spirit, though she suspected Henry held his stallion in check since he seemed unable to pull ahead. She vowed one day to ride well enough to truly hold her own in a race.

Looking over her shoulders while the mare still pulled ahead, she called, "See who's winning, my lord."

When Rosamund turned about, she screamed in alarm because she was headed for a mass of undergrowth backed by a dense thicket of trees. Desperately she tried to either rein in or pull the mare to the side. Finally they slowed before veering to the right. Then horse and rider crashed through dense brush.

Henry thundered after Rosamund, afraid for her safety. He kept shouting to her, but when she failed to respond, he assumed the mare galloped out of control. He doubled his pace in an effort to save her.

Spiny gorse branches snatched at Rosamund's skirts and etched a bloody tracery on the mare's silvery flanks. A sudden shout from the thicket startled them both as a man leapt into her path. Thinking he intended to attack her, Rosamund screamed in fright. The startled mare reared and plunged desperately until the man grabbed her reins and a few minutes later he had calmed the frightened mare.

"There ye be, lady. Her not be used to such thick undergrowth," he said, his voice kind, his accent deeply Yorkshire.

"Thank you. At first you startled me, but I can see you're used to handling horses."

"Oh, aye, me and me dad looks after 'em for—"

His story was cut short as Henry thundered alongside and protectively moved to shield Rosamund from danger. He was about to challenge the scoundrel when a glance at the man's open face told him no harm was meant.

"Thank you, lad, for saving my wife."

Henry flung the man a coin. He grasped Luna's reins intending to lead the mare back with him, while his own soldiers waited in the background, alert in case of trouble. The path between the thickets was so narrow the horses were unable to maneuver about. Trained for war, Henry's stallion obediently backed along the trail, but Luna was terrified of the strange maneuver and she balked, whinnying and rolling her eyes, resisting his effort to lead her. The stranger reached up, and taking her bridle, he gentled the mare before coaxing her to follow the bigger horse. They were soon out of the tangled brush and safe on open ground.

Impressed by the lad's skill, Henry leaned from the saddle to say, "If you ever get tired of playing soldier, lad, I could use you in my stables." The young man's brown eyes lit with surprise at the offer and he politely touched his forelock in acknowledgment. "I'm Henry of Ravenscrag if you've a mind to take me up on my offer."

With that Henry wheeled about, preparing to leave. It was at that point he saw a dozen shadowy figures watching from the trees. Unsure on whose side the troops had fought, he did not feel inclined to ask in case he did not like their answer. The smell of cookfires blew in the wind and he guessed the soldiers' camp was nearby. Wary of ambush, he quickly turned about, taking the mare with him.

Tears of fright trickled down Rosamund's pink cheeks while her heart thundered so hard she thought it would burst. Henry smiled reassuringly at her, pausing to allow their guard to regroup. He leaned from the saddle, finding their mounts were still long enough for a quick kiss while he whispered encouragement to her.

Rosamund sniffled, blinking away tears, which were seized by the wind. They moved swiftly along the trail, away from the tangled thickets of the Forest of Galtres. Rosamund was relieved to leave behind the dark forbidding forest. There were ragged men moving in the brush and she had sensed danger beneath the tall trees; feelings of foreboding had come over her so swiftly she could not ride away fast enough to suit her. Henry laughed at her eagerness to return to the city, which earlier she could not wait to leave.

Behind them, the bedraggled men stood in the shelter of the trees, watching the action unfold before them as if they were an audience at a play.

"Bloody rich bastard, that," one of the men muttered as he rapidly assessed the value of the trappings and horseflesh, not to mention the party's fine clothing.

"What'd 'e give yer, Jake?" another asked as the hero returned, holding a silver coin in his dirty fist.

Suddenly Jake found himself pulled about, almost losing his balance. A brawny yellow-haired man loomed over him, snarling face close to his. "What'd 'e say to 'e?"

Jake swallowed uneasily as he held out the coin. "He gave me this, Steven."

The other man barely glanced at the coin. "What did 'e say?" he repeated through clenched teeth, watching the party of riders clopping away toward York.

"Said as 'ow if I got tired of fighting 'e could use me in 'is stables."

"And where might that be?"

"Don't know. Never seed 'im before. What was the name he said? Ravenshead? Naw, not that. Mebbe Ravenscrag. Aye, that's it. 'I'm Henry of Ravenscrag,' says 'e."

The others guffawed at Jake's imitation of the nobleman's speech. Only Steven did not smile. He still watched the party of riders though they grew small in the distance.

"And what about 'er?"

"She were a pretty 'un, weren't she?"

"What about her. Were she a lady?" Steven said, gripping Jake's arms until he yelped.

" 'Ere, 'old on. I don't know. She were his wife. Lady of Ravenscrag, I s'pose. She were that frightened 'er eyes was big as pennies."

"Did she 'ave hazel eyes flecked over with green and lashes thick as brambles, all long and curling, and her hair's the color of chestnuts?"

"Oh, aye, all of that," Jake said, "bright as copper and streaming loose down 'er back."

"Good tits too. I seen em when 'er cloak come open," a man named Will said.

Steven glowered at the maker of that observation. "And you're sure she's the Lady of Ravenscrag?"

"Well, Steven, 'e didn't really say so, but 'e did call her his wife, and if he's the lord, I reckon she must be the lady."

The others noisily agreed. Steven released Jake, who rubbed his bruised arm but knew better than to object too strongly. Steven of the Forge was a rum one. The fighting had just made him worse. He had no fear of death, and he always led his men right into the thick of battle. He was a might too brave for most of the others.

Steven turned about and lunged into the trees, running till he headed out on the far side of the wood. The party of riders were just coming abreast of him since they had to follow the path that skirted the wood. Standing well back in the trees, he pulled his ragged hood down to hide his face and waited, his heart thundering with excitement. What if she really was Rosamund? Likely it was just a noblewoman who looked like her, but he had to find out.

First came the soldiers, riding two abreast before their master, behind him and on either side of him. If they saw Steven watching from the trees they gave no sign. There she was, riding on this side of the path. Steven craned his neck, trying to see past the burly soldier riding beside her. He could clearly see the great lord wearing his fine black cloak and a plumed rolled velvet hat on his dark hair. Gypsy dark he looked in the fading light, powerful, hook nosed, and arrogant. Steven hated him.

The woman turned in the saddle until Steven was able to gaze full upon her, his heart thundering in his chest. Almost as if she knew he was there in the trees she looked his way, her face pale, her full mouth tense. Steven blinked, rubbing his eyes; then he looked again. She had to be Rosamund! There was no mistaking those high cheekbones above softly curving cheeks, pink as ripe apples, and her smooth skin the color of fresh cream. Will was right: She did have good tits. Steven could see them making mounds in her cloak, just as he remembered. That cloak was a fine garment, likely something her husband had bought her, Steven decided, his mouth curling in a snarl. A rich bastard like that could buy anything he chose, take anything, even steal a poor man's sweetheart if he wanted. And that woman was his sweetheart. There could not be two women on earth who looked like her.

Steven's heart was pounding so hard he had to lean against a tree while he shut his eyes, fighting for composure. When next he opened his eyes, the riders had already moved off along the path.

How could that woman be Rosamund? Steven had watched her burial in Whitton churchyard. She'd been all wan and pale, thin as a rail. Yet she was there, full fleshed again, all decked out in velvet and fur and riding a fine palfrey—with Henry of Ravenscrag! Steven spat on the ground in contempt. By God he'd remember that name till his dying day. Though Steven did not know how the bastard had done it, he realized the nobleman had stolen his Rosamund. Henry of Ravenscrag had tricked everyone into thinking she was dead. All the village had wondered why she had been given such a fancy headstone. It all made sense. Henry of Ravenscrag paid for it. Joan had said the stone was paid for by Rosamund's noble father. Joan had kept wailing and blubbering in her ale cup and Hodge, daft as he was, had believed the tale. Come to think of it, Joan had had new clothing and the family had had good food on the table for a while. Likely the old bitch was in on it, selling Steven's sweetheart to that rich bastard for a whore!

Steven pounded his fist against his palm in rage. They'd pay for this, every one of them. He didn't know how, but he would make them pay. And he would rescue Rosamund.

As he headed back to camp, daring plans swirled through his mind. He'd never been to York. It seemed an impossibility to rescue her from a man who kept his own soldiers and from inside a city he did not know, but Steven would do it. He would find a way.

Steven was already within sight of the camp when a brilliant solution crossed his mind. He did not know York, but young Des did. If he was quick he could ride into the city on the cart Des had loaded, in hope of getting through the gates before curfew to exchange rabbits and deer for ale to slake the men's thirst. A handful of men were enough to save Rosamund from her fate at the hands of that powerful lord. So wound up did he become imagining his beloved's suffering, Steven was almost in tears when he joined the others.

"Well, lad, been to see his lordship off—or was it more 'is woman?" Steven's friend, Macky, said with a wink.

The ensuing burst of laughter died abruptly when the other men saw the troubled expression on Steven's face.

"What is it, lad?" Macky asked.

"I just seen a ghost, Macky, a real flesh-and-blood ghost," Steven said before heading for Des and his cargo of spoils.

The cart rumbled along rutted tracks, taking several short-cuts to reach the city before curfew. Their time was so good they were only a few back in line from the grand mounted party awaiting admittance through Bootham Bar. Steven would recognize those riders anywhere. He could see his grand lordship's hat with the feather bobbing about. And he gritted his teeth as he pictured the other man kissing Rosamund or worse.

Gasping at the pain of that picture, Steven placated himself with the reminder that the bastard wouldn't touch her that night. Their fateful afternoon ride would be the last Henry of

Patricia Phillips

Ravenscrag saw of Rosamund. Steven clenched his fists, muttering curses beneath his breath. Rosamund was his; she had been promised to him for a wife. Steven fingered the knife in his belt, itching to plunge it in his treacherous enemy's heart.

"Keep them in sight," he hissed to Des as they rolled forward through the city gate.

Des nodded and told the others to watch which direction the mounted party took. No one was moving very fast along the congested street.

Steven looked about him, awestruck by the buildings. Had he not been about so important a task, he would have liked to have walked the streets and admire the rich houses. The teeming city street was both exciting and frightening. Exploring York would come some other time: That night he had a mission of mercy to complete. He had sworn to rescue his Rosamund.

It was already snowing lightly when the Lord and Lady of Ravenscrag dressed for the evening. Since their return there had been little time for love play; besides, the servants made Rosamund shy. She could not ignore Jem and Margery as they prepared their master and mistress for their dinner party. It amazed her that Henry could stay oblivious to their presence, as if they were sticks of furniture. She supposed his indifference came from a lifetime of being surrounded by servants who supposedly saw and heard nothing. Being closer to their class, Rosamund knew how wrong that assumption could be. A servant's intimate knowledge was often the downfall of the mighty.

Rosamund wore her yellow silk gown and brocade surcoat; her hair was coiled inside a jeweled fret Henry had bought her last summer. When she looked at her husband in his splendid satin doublet she smiled in pleasure. Around his neck dangled a gold medallion and chain and a gold linked belt was slung about his slim hips. His hose were black as were the tall supple boots reaching to his thighs. Best of all he had fastened to his belt the black velvet purse she had given him, considering it

190

handsome enough to wear for the important dinner.

Henry looked at her and smiled, and the special communication made her heart flutter since she knew he was thinking about the time they would be alone later.

Pip and another lad were to light the way on the short walk to the Eagle and Child. Rosamund shivered, but not because she was cold. It was more because she was leaving the safety of the familiar room. She could not explain why that night's dinner made her feel so apprehensive.

"Nervous about tonight?" Henry asked sympathetically, noticing the tension around her mouth.

Rosamund nodded, gripping his hand as they went downstairs. "It must be because I want to make you proud of me."

"Oh, sweetheart, if you sat in the corner all night and said not a word, I'd be proud of you. I promise they'll all be as delighted with you as I am."

She doubted the truth of his statement, but was pleased he had made it. Trying to shake off her feeling of foreboding, she walked with Henry to the inn door. That afternoon's ride had been unsettling. Her near accident on horseback told her she was not the rider she had fondly imagined herself to be. Even the thick forest had made her feel uneasy; it had been such a relief to come back inside the city.

To her amazement, though the hour was late, people still thronged Lop Lane. Partway along the street a cart loading barrels of ale blocked the road. The obstruction caused such a bottleneck that the passing citizens were eager to voice their displeasure. A noisy and profane cursing match was taking place between the cart's driver and several passersby.

As Rosamund walked over the cobbles, keeping close to the buildings, she looked straight ahead, not anxious to make eye contact with the rough-talking strangers. In the city she had found commoner and nobleman alike stared rudely at her as she passed, making her wonder whether they would have accosted her if she had been alone. In the gathering dusk, she was afraid someone would jump out of the shadows to grab her. The thought made her shudder and she moved closer to

Henry as they walked in single file past the cart.

Though Rosamund had not expected to, she found the dinner at the Eagle and Child most enjoyable. She even liked Meade Ireton's golden-haired mistress. Her name was Diana and she singled out Rosamund for friendship probably because she was the only other young woman in the room. Lady Stokes was middle-aged and vaguely disapproving of the flamboyant Diana. To Rosamund Lady Stoke's manner was condescending. She scrutinized Rosamund closely, eager to relay her impression of Harry Ravenscrag's wife to her circle of friends.

Being under Lady Stokes's critical gaze was the worst part of the splendid dinner, which was laid on with many courses and great expense. Their host had hired a singing boy and two dancing girls to entertain the guests with sentimental love ballads sung to the accompaniment of lute and tambor. Beyond the diamond-paned windows Rosamund could see snowflakes lazily drifting past the eaves, illuminated by the lantern hanging over the inn door.

As the night wore on several other men joined them until Rosamund began to despair of making an early retreat. Several times she caught Henry's eye and he shrugged apologetically, knowing it would be rude to leave in the middle of their discussion.

Eventually Diana began to yawn openly and she finally announced she was going home to bed. Meade Ireton winked at her, running his hand through his auburn hair and glancing about at the company. He too found it difficult to excuse himself from the other men's heated discussion of Wakefield Green; so he had to send her home alone. The background music droned on as the boy sang automatically for the assembly, who were paying scant attention to his performance as they talked and quaffed large quantities of wine and ale.

Since the Ireton party was lodged at another inn in Lop Lane, halfway between the Nag's Head and the Eagle and Child, Meade suggested Diana go back to the inn ahead of him, taking with her a page and manservant. He would join her when he could.

When Diana asked Rosamund if she would like to leave and walk with her, Rosamund found the perfect excuse to leave the crowded, overheated inn room. It might also break up the nonstop round of heroic tales. Rosamund caught Henry's eye and he nodded his approval of the suggestion.

"Ale-sodden old fools," Diana muttered as they headed downstairs. The servants assisted them with their cloaks. "Half an hour 'e's got before I'm going to sleep. Then he's lost his chance," she said with a giggle, glancing back to where Meade Ireton and Henry sat pouring a fresh round of drinks.

Rosamund agreed as she wistfully watched Henry from the stair, seeing him bending close to hear Lord Stokes above the din. Their plans for an early departure seemed doomed to failure. The noisy dinner party showed no sign of being over soon.

"We can shop in the market tomorrow if you'd like," Diana said, waiting for her page to open the door for them. The chill night air gusted inside the passageway and a few snowflakes settled on the flagstones.

"Yes, I'd like that," Rosamund said, not sure what plans for the day Henry had made. "I'll have to let you know."

"Right. I need a bit of life. Those old sticks bore me to death. A lot like the sainted lady of Ireton Manor, if you ask me. As old as rain, that woman is, but very rich. She brought Meade most of his money; so I can't object too much to her, now can I? 'Specially when I get to spend a lot of it.'' She winked and squeezed Rosamund's arm. "At least Henry married a woman he couldn't be ashamed to keep for a mistress," Diana said, digging Rosamund in the ribs as they stepped outside into the street.

Traces of snow-frosted windowsills and doorsteps and settled in crevices of roofs and walls. It was very dark in Lop Lane, making them glad of the swinging lanterns held by their pages. In no time at all they reached the door of the Leather Bottle Inn. From inside could be heard the drunken singing and laughter of a celebration taking place in the inn's upper rooms. It seemed as if that night all York was celebrating the Lancastrian victory.

Pip shivered apprehensively as he waited for Rosamund to say good-bye, highly aware they stood alone in the street since the other page and footman were inside the Leather Bottle.

Diana kissed Rosamund's cheek before she too went inside the inn. A great feeling of unease swept over Rosamund as she, like Pip, was made aware of their vulnerability on the street. She could tell the page was nervous because his lantern had begun to swing excessively atop the pole.

"Come on, Pip. Be brave. We can see the inn door from here," Rosamund said in an effort to bolster the lad's courage. A lantern illuminated the sign outside the Nag's Head and cast a yellow glow across the snow-sprinkled cobbles. The twin clipped bushes growing in tubs before the inn's entrance each wore haloes of white.

Rosamund picked up the pace, striding out, eager to reach the warmth and shelter of the inn. In a couple of minutes they would be safe inside and Pip could breathe easily again.

They passed shadowed doorways and alleyways that seemed to seethe with life. They walked close together in the bright pool of lantern light. Suddenly, as they neared the entrance to a narrow, ill-smelling entryway, a dark figure stepped forward. Pip squealed in surprise as the lantern was grabbed from his hand. Almost in the same breath, Rosamund found a hand clamped over her mouth, stifling her screams as she was forced into the alleyway. Pip lay on the ground, his cries muffled by his cloak as his assailant kicked him until he lay still.

Rosamund struggled and tried to scream for help, but the crushing hand bruising her face allowed only muffled sounds to escape. She could see several dark figures crowding around her. As soon as the hand was taken away, she tried to scream for help, but a cloth was wrapped around her face. Still trying to shout for help, Rosamund's voice became little more than a mumble borne away on the wind moaning down the dark alleys. Her captors bound her arms at her sides. She was raced along, her feet barely touching the cobbles. When she stumbled, she was yanked back on her feet as her abductors ran through the twisting alleyways of York, moving far away from Lop Lane, dragging her with them.

They finally reached an open doorway and Rosamund was taken inside. She fought a dirty sack the men put over her head. But her struggles were to no avail. Not only could she not cry out, but she could not see where she was going. Gasping for air inside the confining sack, she was propelled along before being hoisted inside a vehicle. She kept fighting as best she could on the flight, while her captors cursed her roundly before they finally cuffed her into submission and blackness descended.

The next sensation Rosamund felt was cold. She woke to total blackness and found her body stiff and her head throbbing. At first she could not remember what had happened. When she did, she was sick with dread. Did these robbers intend to murder her? Beyond cuffing her over the head, they had not actually harmed her. She supposed that would come later. She shuddered at the thought of being passed around a gang of cutthroats to slake their lust. Surely Henry knew she was missing. The prospect of rescue cheered her. If anyone had the means to rescue her it was Henry. She must cling to that hope.

Voices in the background alerted her to the arrival of her captors. When the ground moved beneath her, she realized she lay in a moving cart. She could hear horses' hooves clopping over the cobbles and the creak and groan of the cart's wooden sides. The men's rumbling voices were muffled by other sounds until at last the cart slowed and stopped. A great noise surrounded her, clopping, braying, mooing, as if they were stopped at some market. Then she heard a man's rough voice telling them to move along and she realized where she was. A chill came over her when she discovered it was the voice of the guard at the city gates.

Desperately she struggled to sit up and call for help. She found she had been bound around both arms and legs. She still wore her fur-lined cloak and for that consideration she was glad

195

since she had been left outside all night in the cold. Whoever had captured her was leaving the city. Henry would never find her. Where could they be taking her? People told terrible tales of women being captured to work as slaves in the London stews. Surely that horror was not to be her fate, not when she and Henry were finally happy together.

Tears welled beneath her lids and trickled inside her gag. The sacking smelled of earth and blood; she hated the feel of it against her face. She closed her eyes, trying to overcome her dread, trying to be brave and maintain hope, but the task was hard. She could also smell human sweat; so she knew at least some of her captors rode beside her. Eventually she began to doze as the cart jogged along.

Chapter Nine

"You bloody fool, I told you not to harm her!" Steven growled, interrupting Des's account of the previous night's abduction.

Steven himself had ridden out of York alone in a stolen cart. The donkey and cart had been standing in the yard at the Nag's Head. In case the others failed to abduct Rosamund, he had been waiting at the inn for her return. Full of bravado, he had intended to climb the drainpipe to her room and snatch her from under Ravenscrag's nose, planting a dagger in the nobleman's ribs in payment for his deceit. In fact, so much had he relished the plan, he had been greatly disappointed to learn their original plan had gone off without a hitch. Steven had been tempted to go to Rosamund just to reassure himself she was safe, but in case she screamed and raised an alarm, he decided against doing so.

"She's not hurt. Nothing more than a bump on the 'ead," Des said, scowling at his comrade. He had been uneasy about taking the woman from the start, considering the abduction to be one of Steven's more foolish plans. Well, they had her and it was up to Steven to make sense out of the situation.

"She'd better not be hurt, or you'll pay for it," Steven said. "Where is she?"

"In the tent. Nell's looking after her."

Steven nodded, pleased. That was a smart move. Poor Rosamund would be in need of a woman's company. "Did anyone see you do it?"

"Naw, 'cept the lad with the lantern. We shut 'im up good."

"He's not dead? I didn't want that."

"Could be. More likely he's just got a sore head. What does it matter about 'im anyway?"

"It matters! We only wanted her. No one else was to be hurt." Except his fine lordship, given the opportunity, Steven added mentally. He had not told the others about his backup plan. Most of the men were cowards, afraid of crossing the gentry.

"Right, well, no one was, Steven," Des said. "What does you want with his lordship's woman anyway?"

"You're a marrowhead, young Des," Macky said, playfully pushing the other man's shoulder. "Steven's got big plans. Right?"

Steven nodded, glancing warily at Macky, unsure what the other man meant. He had told no one the real reason he was abducting Rosamund.

"What'll bring 'is grand lordship running quicker than stealing 'is piece of tail?" Macky said.

A dawning smile spread over Des's flat face. "Then when 'e gets here, we get money for her?"

"We do better'n that. We capture 'im too. A lord like that's worth a big ransom," Macky said.

"Ransom?" Steven said, considering Macky's surprising proposal.

"Aw, go on, Steven. You can't fool me. His lordship's for Lancaster and rich with it. They'll pay a pretty penny to get 'im back. It's done all the time."

Several of the others in earshot gasped at the audacity of the scheme, marveling at Steven's ingenuity. Uneasily Steven let them think ransom had been his goal. His plotting had gone no further than to rescue Rosamund and take her back to Whitton as his wife. Still, asking a ransom was not such a bad idea. Let the other men think he was holding her for money. That way they'd keep their hands off her and save Steven the trouble of having to kill someone.

"Well, now, I can't keep much from you, lads, can I?"

Steven said jovially. "Show me where she is. I must keep her 'appy until we get paid."

Steven could hardly control himself as they crossed the clearing. He wanted to run to the patched tent under the oaks where Rosamund waited. He mustn't seem too eager, he told himself, or the others would soon smell a rat. Maybe if he got a lot of money for the lord, he wouldn't go back to Whitton after all. Since he'd seen a bit of the country, he fancied a change. Surely there would be employment for a good blacksmith in York. He could buy a forge and start afresh. No one would know if he and Rosamund slipped away before dawn.

" 'Ow much you reckon she's worth?" Des asked, his voice slightly hushed with awe as he considered Steven's daring scheme. And he'd thought his leader only wanted to mount the woman. It was that intention that made him so uneasy since he knew well the swift retribution for crossing the rich and powerful. If Steven had told them his real plan, few would have gone along with him, considering the action far too dangerous.

"I haven't thought about it yet," Steven mumbled as they reached the tattered tent and he pushed up the flap.

The interior of the tent was gloomy since little light penetrated these tall trees. Inside, Nell scrambled to her feet.

"Take those things off her," Steven said when he saw his lovely Rosamund wrapped in the sacks they'd used to haul dead rabbits.

When Nell struggled to unfasten the sacking, Des stepped forward and slashed the rope with his knife. As soon as her mouth was clear, Rosamund began to shout for help. Quickly Des slapped his hand over her mouth and he looked pleadingly at his leader.

"Go on, you two, leave her to me," Steven said.

Obediently, Nell and Des scurried from the tent. Then Steven bent double under the low canvas roof because his bulk seemed to fill the confined space. Rosamund was trembling. There was enough light for Steven to make that out. His Rosamund was afraid of him. His heart went out to her. Dropping to his knees, Steven thrust back his ragged hood.

"Look, Rosamund, love. It's me," he said hoarsely.

Rosamund froze as she recognized his voice. She blinked and shook her head to clear her vision, wondering if she was delirious. Then the man moved closer to her and she knew she was not dreaming.

"Steven," she said through parched lips, "is it really you?"

"Aye, lass, it's me. Oh, Rosamund, you're still alive. It's a miracle! Don't fret. You're safe now." He took her hand and cradled it in his huge callused palm.

"Safe? You mean you attacked me?"

"Nay, lass, but my men done it on my order. I'm important now. I'm not just Steven of the Forge. I'm in charge of these men," he said, puffing out his chest. "Sorry if the lads treated you rough. Oh, Rosamund, love, I can't believe I've found you again," he whispered, his voice shaking with emotion as he reached out to stroke her hair.

Rosamund shuddered, drawing away from his caressing hand. "This can't be happening," she muttered, trying to rise, then stumbling back since her ankles were still tied.

" 'Ere, lass, let me undo the rope. Damn them. I didn't want you harmed in any way," he said angrily as he slit her bonds with his knife. Someone called to him from outside the tent, and he rocked back on his heels. "I have to go. I'll send you some food."

"I'm not hungry," Rosamund said, her swirling stomach making the thought of food unbearable.

"You'll feel better by and by," he said, ducking out of the tent. When Steven had gone, Nell returned to her post. Rosamund no longer appealed to the silent woman to release her. She slumped back against the canvas and shut her eyes, trying to think of a way out. Why was Steven near York? He must have joined the army, or he would not be camped in the forest with the soldiers. More puzzling than that was how he had known she was alive, let alone in York. He must have been with the men watching when she and Henry had ridden there the day before. Of all the men in England—what ill luck had placed him here? He knew her so well he could easily destroy her make-believe life.

Though meeting Steven was a daunting event, Rosamund was unprepared for a second shock that made her flesh crawl. When her promised meal arrived within the hour—a wooden bowl of rabbit stew—she was horrified to see it was Hodge who brought it. Rosamund could not stifle her shocked cries as she stared at his thick features, his wet slack mouth, and close-set eyes.

"Lord, it is you!" Hodge said, equally stunned.

He bent closer to look at her face and Rosamund was almost overcome by his body odor of mingled dirt, sweat, and ale. The smell stirred sickening memories she had hoped were hidden forever.

"How can you be here and in Whitton churchyard too? I thought the lad was barmy." Hodge gestured impatiently for Nell to leave them alone and she obediently ducked under the tent flap.

The appearance of Rosamund's hated stepfather only intensified her nightmare. She gasped as Hodge ran his grimy, callused hands over her ankles, remarking on the pressure marks made by the rope.

"Come nightfall, girlie, we'll 'ave us a time," he said, licking his thick lips in anticipation. "Reckon now that the rich lord's dipped into the well, there's no 'arm in me 'aving a few drinks."

"Don't you dare touch me," Rosamund said, her eyes narrowing in anger.

"Or what'll 'appen to me this time? Is that rich father of yourn still going to string me balls round me neck?" he asked, chuckling as he recalled one of her former threats. "You don't scare me now, Rosie. I'm a soldier. I've killed men. Fought in battles. People don't push me around anymore."

"My husband will have you hanged."

"Oh, pretending he's your husband, are you? I never really believed that fairy story about you dying from some sudden sickness. The money Joan got was what he paid for you, weren't it? The bastard must've wanted you bloody bad to go to all the trouble of pretend funerals and such. Reckon there's something worth having between your legs after all.''

Hodge yelled in surprise as he was yanked backward and flung into the dirt outside the tent.

"Get away from her! Don't even think about touching her!" Steven yelled, his face contorted with rage.

The others gathered about and fell silent as they watched Hodge pick himself up, rubbing his shoulder.

"Listen, all of you! If anyone so much as lays a hand on her, I'll cut it off. Your payment for lusting after her's going to be a knife in the heart," Steven said.

"Aye, lads, we don't want her used. Reckon that rich lord won't pay what we asks then," Macky said, chuckling at Hodge's foolhardiness in blustering up to Steven, hands on his hips.

"I've got a right, after all, she is—"

Steven cuffed Hodge across the mouth, sending a spray of blood from his lip as it cut against his teeth. "Shut up! I'm in charge here. What I say goes.''

Nursing his injured lip, Hodge glared belligerently at Steven, but he wisely held his tongue. Inwardly he quailed, aware Steven dared him to reveal the identity of the woman in the tent. Always a coward, Hodge did not want to openly cross the younger, stronger man. The lads would be surprised all right when they found out she wasn't a lady at all, just his stepdaughter. The time would come for Hodge to tell them everything. But maybe he'd wait till her rich lover had paid her ransom.

A cacophony of sound filled the inn room as if all the bells of York were pealing on the cold and murky January morn. The church bells made a constant din, clanging for many minutes until all citizens were wakened from their sleep.

Henry turned away from the small leaded window, his face as gray as the lowering sky. Morning already and still no word of Rosamund! For the hundredth time he cursed himself, considering it his fault she had come to harm. What would it matter if Rob Stokes had taken umbrage, or if Ireton or Carlton were angry with him for leaving their tiresome dinner early? Not a whit when measured against losing Rosamund. By staying until he had felt it would not be impolite to leave, he had let her be abducted off the street. God, how could he have been such a fool? When he had finally left the Eagle and Child and hastened back to the Nag's Head, visions of what he would do for the rest of the night had stirred his blood and quickened his steps until his lantern bearer nearly had to run to keep up. It was all for naught! Rosamund was gone.

He pulled on his cloak, glancing through the window at the gray sky. It was light enough to begin the search anew. She must be somewhere near at hand; she could not just have vanished into thin air. The men woud be waiting for him downstairs. Last night he had wakened Benton from a boozy sleep, telling his captain to ready the men to begin a search of the surrounding streets for Lady Rosamund.

The cobbles were icy in spots. People had already begun to stir and shutters were coming down all over the city. Vendors and carters were delivering their goods. Cages of cackling hens and flopping gray scaled fish, fresh from the past night's nets, were being offered for sale at nearby stalls. Even the general stench of the streets was sweetened by the fragrance of baking bread and roasting meats. On that winter morn York was alive and well. Nothing there had outwardly changed while Henry's whole life had been turned upside down.

Capt. Benton took the liberty of laying a comforting hand on his lord's arm, concerned for his well-being. Dark circles and lines of fatigue altered his master's handsome face, aging him ten years. In his plain jerkin, cloak, and hose, Henry could have been one of a hundred lesser nobles filling the city instead of the great Lord of Ravenscrag.

"Rest assured, my lord, we'll find her. It takes time. Why don't we question the lad again? Maybe he can remember something."

Henry nodded his agreement. Wearily he ran his hand over

203

his face, rubbing the stubble on his chin. "It can't hurt."

Inside the inn, Pip lay on a cot beside the window. The gray morning light made his pallor seem all the more deathlike. Henry stood looking down at the lad a long time, wondering what he knew. That afternoon his father was taking him home; so if Henry did not learn something within the next couple of hours, his only lead would be out of reach in North Yorkshire.

Thumping his fist inside his palm as he paced beside the bed, Henry was relieved to see the lad was still alive. Sometimes Pip stirred in his sleep, but there seemed little hope he would regain consciousness soon—if at all! Under the cooling cloths soaked with linament, Pip was a mass of black swollen bruises. Whoever had abducted Rosamund had punished the daylights out of the young page entrusted to Henry's care. Henry's guilt was doubled when he considered the poor lad could die. Ireton had assured Henry he laid no blame at his feet; the Iretons had other sons and Pip had never been his favorite. Yet Henry's neighbor's generosity did not absolve him of blame.

By afternoon Henry felt weary beyond belief. Knowing nowhere else to look for her, he was contemplating catching a few hours' sleep when a messenger arrived. A prentice lad in shabby clothing had come to the inn clutching an unsealed note to be given only into the hands of the Lord of Ravenscrag.

Hope and fear swirled through Henry's brain as he accepted the note, which was what he had been waiting for. His hands shaking, he opened the grubby paper and went to the fire to read it.

Lord Henry of Ravenscrag. Yewer lady is in the forest. The place yew was yesterday. Come by yewerself. Bring gold.

The note was unsigned, poorly written, and misspelled, yet it could have been a missive from angels so delighted did it make Henry. The prentice lad was paid and sent on his way.

Within minutes Henry was pulling on his riding boots. Money—he must have money. He had a purse of gold, probably not enough, but it was all he had with him. He had jewels, though he expected that rabble would prefer something more easily negotiable.

As Henry dressed, he vacillated between vengeance and compliance. With an unusually lenient turn of mind, he decided Rosamund's abductors were starving soldiers brought there by York and abandoned with no means to get home. If it meant getting his darling back, he could well afford to be charitable.

"By heaven, Ravenscrag, you're not going to parley with the scoundrels," Ireton said from the doorway, the news having already circulated through the inn.

"I'm doing worse than that. I'm going to pay them." Henry's lip twitched at Ireton's expression of stunned surprise. "If it brings Rosamund back, it's worth it," he added, strapping on his sword and thrusting several daggers in his belt.

"Harry," Ireton said, his manner softening, "I know love drives out common sense, but think, man. This could be a trap. Stokes is all for mounting an attack. Between us we've the men. What say you to that?"

"That the old bastard must be itching for a fight," Henry said dryly, checking through his weapons one last time. "How do you propose to find the right ones? They all look alike. We can't kill all the men in Galtres Forest."

"How do you propose to find the right ones?"

"They'll be on the lookout for me and my gold. I've a good idea which paths lead to that part of the forest."

"And what if she's already dead?"

Henry caught his breath. He must admit that thought had crossed his mind and been as quickly dismissed. Somehow hearing Ireton voice it aloud gave it more substance. "No, I have to believe she's unharmed."

Ireton nodded sympathetically, stepping aside to let Henry pass. "I don't understand it. Diana says when she left them they were a stone's throw from the inn. How could the scoundrels have got to her?''

''Easy. This whole city's honeycombed with alleys and entryways. Everywhere's black as hell. They had only to lie low till she was alone, then pounce. Young Pip's always been a cowardly lad. Besides, what chance would he have against them?''

Meade Ireton commiserated glumly. It was hard to admit his son lacked courage, but it was true nonetheless. Though Pip appeared devoted to his lady, a more unlikely champion could not have been found.

''Take care, Harry,'' Ireton said, his voice gruff. ''Will you consider letting me come with you?''

Henry smiled and shook his head. ''I'll take a couple of my men. Apparently the money's what the bastards are interested in, not me.''

Finally his horse was saddled ready to leave. For every delay Henry cursed and chafed at the bit, knowing it would take some hard riding to get to the Forest of Galtres and back before nightfall. He had chosen two young, burly soldiers to accompany him, refusing to let Benton risk going himself. The captain's expertise would be needed to command the men left behind if matters did not go as planned.

A group of Henry's friends again asked him to reconsider the proposal of mounting a small army to flush the rabble out of Galtres. They warned him he could be heading into a trap. They beseeched him to take care. Then they let him go. It was to no avail to advise Harry Ravenscrag to take caution. He had taken part in too many escapades requiring luck and bravery to be talked out of such a venture. Besides, the stakes in the present instance were of immeasurable value to him. Ravenscrag was enamored of his wife, and though his comrades still had not stopped shaking their heads in bewilderment over the astounding fact, they were aware wisdom had lost out to passion.

Dressed in a plain black cloak and leather jack, his coat of arms hidden from view, Henry and his two armed companions

206

attracted little attention as they rode along Petergate to Bootham Bar as fast as the press of people would allow. He had contemplated bringing Rosamund's mare, but decided against doing so. She could ride with him on Diablo. When he thought about holding her against him he was overcome with longing. How he wanted to press her soft body against his, to put his arms round her and kiss her lips. When he considered the possibility she had been harmed, his heart lurched and pounded sickeningly. He knew the rabble of common soldiery was bestial. How could he expect chivalric courtesy from them? His only hope lay in the notion that their greed for gold was stronger than their lust.

Slanting rays of watery sunlight penetrated the gray sky as Henry pounded along the path. Through the trees he saw groups of ragged men hunched around campfires. Some soldiers glanced up at the sound of riders, but seeing little remarkable about the newcomers, they went back to their meal. Henry knew he was close to the camp he had seen the day before because he began to recognize the surrounding terrain. He had been counting the number of clearings they crossed, the thickets of fir, oak, ash, and birch they skirted to get to that point. There the tangled underbrush grew denser, the forest thicker. His pulse quickened as he neared the rendezvous.

Over the past few minutes he had become aware of dark shapes moving among the trees, and though he acted as if he had not seen them, he was aware they were following him. Those men knew he had disobeyed their command by not coming alone. Though against the ragged horde he might as well have been alone. Three armed men facing several score had little chance of winning a battle.

Henry suddenly drew rein as a man stepped into his path to block the way. The tall blond man had a thick-chested build and powerful limbs. Henry noticed the stranger's bulging muscles and sinewy arms as he reached for Diablo's reins. One quick nudge of Henry's knee sent the stallion rearing. When the horse's hooves flailed in the giant's face, he stumbled back in surprise.

"Keep your distance. Where is she?" Henry asked tersely, scanning the gathering force with unease. In a matter of minutes the escape route was blocked and Henry cursed himself for walking into a trap. He should have made the abductors come to him.

"Henry of Ravenscrag?" the blond man said.

"I am he." He noticed the speaker gave him no title.

"Did yer bring the gold?"

"Possibly."

" 'Ere, there's no possibly about it. Did yer?"

Henry was aware of his soldier's tension as more men grouped about to watch the spectacle. He had already scanned the surroundings and saw no permanent buildings. Several crude huts made out of branches and a dilapidated tent housed the men. If only Henry knew where they were keeping Rosamund. He considered the wisdom of storming through the rabble, but decided not to do so.

"Git down and talk with me fairlike," the giant said.

There was little wisdom to that proposal either, so Henry sat immobile in the saddle. "Where is she?"

"We's got to see gold first," someone shouted.

"Not until I see her. How do I know she's even here?" Henry said.

The blond leader conferred with several others before finally sending someone to the tent. So that was where the men were keeping Rosamund. Henry's hand closed over his sword hilt as he saw a blindfolded woman pushed through the tent flap. From such a distance he could not see the woman's face, but she was the right height and her gown was yellow. He was about to ask the men to bring her close when she was yanked back inside the tent.

"Now you've seen her. Where's the gold?"

"Not so fast. How do I know she's unharmed?"

The blond man shrugged. "You have my word."

He spoke with such conviction, Henry was taken back. Though it was probably a foolish assumption, he decided he could rely on this man's word. "Let me speak to her."

"You'll have to get down for that."

Stalemate. Henry sat astride his horse, considering the other man, who refused to flinch, boldly returning his gaze.

"Don't do it, my lord," one of his men hissed in warning, moving closer to protect his master.

For a few more minutes Henry sat there, raking his stern gaze over the ragged crowd. Several men still wore filthy bandages and there were others with crude crutches. They must have fought at Wakefield Green. Their wounds were fresh, the rags binding their injuries stained with blood. They were desperate men. They also had weapons. Henry could see pikes and staves, clubs and knives clutched in their filthy hands. Though he and his men were also well armed, they were badly outnumbered. If they put up a fight they'd take some of these yokels with them, but with those odds, a score, more of less, would still leave too much opposition.

All things considered, Henry finally made his move, swinging his leg over the saddle, aware of his own soldiers' groans of dismay at his action. The ground felt spongy underfoot, his legs unsteady with weariness. Bracing himself against his horse, Henry found his spurs were sinking into the loam.

"Take me to her. If she's unharmed, you'll have your gold."

Open hostility was plain in the blond man's face. Henry did not like the uncomfortable feeling of being looked down on. The giant of a man was a good hand taller than he and broad as a barn. Other men drew close, awaiting the word from their leader. Then suddenly Henry saw several men on the fringe of the crowd moving stealthily toward the horses; out of the corner of his eye he saw them raise staves to strike the riders. Too late he yelled a warning to his men. One man toppled from the saddle in one swoop. Collie's foot still hung in the stirrup when his horse bolted, dragging him through the brush. The other man, however, was only dazed and he wheeled about, his horse rearing, catching men painfully about the arms and head. Turning about, he set his spurs into his horse's flanks and raced back along the path to York.

Henry watched in amazement. That was not a maneuver he had taught the lad. Henry hoped the lad was headed for York to alert others to his master's danger.

Shouting in rage over the botched attack, the blond leader sent men after the fleeing rider. When one man tried to mount Diablo to join in the chase, the stallion shied, catching him on the temple and knocking him down.

"Leave him! He won't be ridden. I don't call him Devil for naught," Henry cried.

His statement effectively backed the men off. No one was eager to be trampled. The big man started to argue; plainly used to horses, he was not afraid of the stallion, though he did not try to mount Diablo himself. It was possible he did not know how to ride. Instead he sent some of the others to capture the riderless horse.

Turning to Henry, he held out his hand. "Now we'll have that gold, your lordship."

Henry smiled grimly. "Only if you can catch yon rider. He carries the money in a pouch round his waist."

Their dirty faces were a study of incredulity, which Henry would have found amusing in less dangerous circumstances. His story was not strictly true: Findlay had only half the gold; Henry and the fallen Collie shared the rest.

Their faces darkening in anger, his captors abandoned all pretense of civility. Henry was grasped from behind, and though he pulled his dagger and sliced a couple of the men for their pains, it was not long before they had subdued him.

"You're going to stay with us till yon soldier brings the gold."

"You might have a long wait," Henry said, aware Findlay might take the gold and keep on riding. Loyalty to the Ravenscrag family would be all that kept the lad honest.

"We won't wait long," the blond man snarled.

Henry was dragged struggling to the hut farthest from the patched blue tent. As a safeguard the men bound his arms and legs. It was obvious Henry was not going be treated as an honored guest when his captors slammed him down on a bed of bracken and told him to shut up or be gagged.

It didn't take the men long to find Collie's purse since he lay with his skull caved in amidst the gorse bushes. Next they rescued his runaway horse; Henry could hear them exclaiming over the quality of the animal. Someone was also talking to Diablo. Through the crude branch wall he could see the stallion's gleaming flanks and a man patting and soothing him. Was it the lad who had stopped Rosamund's wild flight, the one Henry had offered to place in his stable? That man could be an ally; he had seemed less brutish than the rest. Henry lay there in the gloom and tried to devise an escape plan.

The men finally came back inside the hut and roughly searched Henry, dragging off his belt and taking the purse of gold with it. One man greedily eyed his rings, but he had not the courage to take them. Then they left Henry alone.

Across the camp, in the patched blue tent, Rosamund lay back on the sacking that served as her bed, wondering what was happening. There had been unusual activity in the camp that day. Since her captors had pulled her out of the tent and quickly pushed her back in, they had not returned. Had Henry come to rescue her? Excitement rippled through her veins at the thought. Could all that commotion have been caused by Henry and his soldiers? Yet if that was so, why was she still tied up in there, sitting on the smelly bed? There had been shouts and scuffling, followed by sharp cries of pain. She had even heard Steven's angry voice before the commotion had died down. Perhaps it was just a fight among her abductors. Surely Henry would not have been reckless enough to come alone? Her heart swooped into her belly at the thought. If that were true, he must be a captive also.

Tossing about on the rough sacking, Rosamund waited for news as the afternoon dragged to a close. Only the usual sounds of camp life filtered inside the tent. Blindfolded as she was, she could only guess what was going on. She had no success in trying to work the bandages free or loosen the bonds on her hands and feet. Tears of frustration pricked her eyes as she realized that she was solely at Steven's mercy.

Rosamund tensed as she heard rustling outside. Someone was coming to the tent. She sniffed the air, using her sense of smell like a blind person. It was the woman. She smelled different from the men, not any more pleasant, just different.

"Have you come to untie me" Rosamund asked eagerly, "or at least to take off this blindfold?"

Silence. Rosamund sighed. She was not surprised. The woman had never spoken to her. Rosamund assumed she must belong to one of the soldiers. There were other women in the camp—Rosamund had heard their voices—but they never came to the tent. That one had sole charge of her.

Nell knelt beside the captive, longing to speak to her. What would it matter? Steven would never know. She put down the bowl of stew and reached out to pull off the blindfold.

"Listen, you. If you're quiet, I'll let you see."

The unexpected voice so close to her face startled Rosamund and she jumped in surprise. She nodded vigorously, eager to gain that privilege. When the pressure of the bandage came off, her head and eyes were sore. She fluttered her lids, then shut them because they hurt.

The woman knelt there, looking at her. She was thin faced with straggling blond hair; she was also much younger than Rosamund had supposed. Tentatively she smiled at her jailor.

"Thank you. What's your name?"

"Nell."

"I'm Rosamund. Tell me what's happening. What was all that commotion about?"

Nell rocked back on her heels, considering the request. She yearned to talk to the captive lady in her fine clothing despite Steven's admonition to the contrary. She wanted to tell the captive about the man who had ridden into camp and the dead soldier and the bag of gold she had only glimpsed. . . .

Rosamund accepted the stew after Nell had untied her wrists. Then Nell grinned. "Is 'e your 'usband, that great lord?"

Rosamund's stomach lurched. So she had been right: Henry

had come for her! Trying not to seem too eager, she asked, "Is he still here?"

"They've got 'im tied up as well now. They'll get even more gold for 'im."

"Is he Henry of Ravenscrag?" Rosamund asked, just to make sure the captive man was really Henry.

Nell nodded vigorously, her face coming alive. "That's right. They've got 'im tied inside the hut down by the hollies. Wouldn't let me go see 'im—only Steven's allowed inside."

Rosamund mentally reviewed her surroundings. There had been several hollies near the entrance to the clearing. And she had seen a hut nearby. She knew the place they were keeping him, for what good that would do. Unless she could untie Henry and help him escape—No, she had to stop that dangerous and exciting train of thought.

"Is he hurt?" Rosamund asked carefully, her heart in her mouth as she waited for the woman's answer.

"Naw, but they's not treated 'im kind. He fought 'em you see, and that made Steven angry."

Rosamund would have guessed Henry would not go quietly. That he was not wounded was a relief. But if no one sent gold to ransom him—she refused to contemplate Steven's next move.

Turning her most winning smile on Nell, she asked, "Will you let me see him?"

Nell laughed in scorn at her request. " 'Ere, you want to get me throat slit? 'Course I won't." Then she leaned closer, her face brightening. "He's like a prince, isn't he? I seed a foreign prince once in London, all decked out in jewels and such, riding a big 'orse, sitting as proud as you please. Oh, he did set me heart racing." Nell stopped when she heard steps crunching through the leaves.

Hodge poked his head inside the tent. "You been talkin' to 'er. I heard you. Wait till I tell Steven. You'll catch it then."

"Naw, Hodge, you wouldn't do that," Nell said, her face paling. "I meant no 'arm. It didn't hurt none, what I said."

"Mebbe not, but rules is rules. Now, if you'll let me talk

to her alone for a couple o' minutes, maybe I won't tell.'' Hodge ran his tongue over his lips in anticipation.

"Naw, you know I can't do that," Nell said firmly as she retied Rosamund's bonds. She picked up the empty bowl. "You know what 'e says about that."

Hodge's thick lips curled in contempt. "Yeah, I heard, but see, I'm different. I got special rights," he said, coming into the tent where he crouched against the canvas. "Go on, just five minutes, Nell. 'Appen I can get you a gold piece. I knows where the money's kept."

Nell gasped in delight. She knew what Hodge intended, but for a gold piece, she might let him alone. She weighed her probable punishment for turning a blind eye against what a gold piece would buy. The gold won.

"Aw right then, but you'd better be quick about it—and you'd better come through with the gold, lad."

Appalled, Rosamund watched as Nell slipped outside into the gathering dusk.

"Well, Rosie, I told you we'd 'ave us a time tonight, didn't I?" Hodge asked, leering at her, his voice slurred. He had drunk ale. Rosamund could smell it, but she guessed excitement and not drunkenness thickened his speech. As he looked down at her he panted, his lips hanging wet and slack.

Suddenly he fell on her and Rosamund struggled to be free of his weight. A wave of nausea washed over her as she recalled all those other times he had forced his attentions on her—only then she had had the luxury of flight and not been bound hand and foot. Though she was a captive, she was no longer blindfolded or gagged. Rosamund opened her mouth to scream for help and Hodge muffled her cries with his dirty hand.

"None of that, you bitch! This'll be quick. Reckon you haven't done it with a real man for a while and might like it better than you done with 'is fancy lordship."

Rosamund sank her teeth into his fleshy hand, hating the taste of his dirty skin. Hodge yelped and he retaliated by cuffing her across the head with his doubled fist. He pressed her

214

back, his hand roaming freely under her gown. Doubling up her knees, Rosamund tried to push him off; she didn't succeed, but she made his task harder. Next, with her bound hands, she clouted him soundly across the ear. Hodge was panting as he pulled up her skirts and fumbled with his own clothing. Desperately she tried to heave him off, constantly thrashing about.

Hodge growled and spat at Rosamund, dropping his bulk over her legs and effectively stopping her defense. He was frustrated in his effort to rape her, having to keep one hand over her mouth. Angrily he grasped her bound hands, wrenching her arms back above her head until Rosamund thought they would be torn from their sockets.

"Now, then, our Rosie, we'll see who's master. I have rights."

She gagged as his wet organ battered her thigh; he loomed above her, struggling to hold her down and get into position at the same time. Rosamund continued to cry out, fighting to be free of his clamped hand, which so far had muffled her voice. She fought hard, aware she was rapidly losing ground. The horrid feel of his erect organ brushing her thighs told her he was winning the battle as he effectively used his bulk to pin her down.

"Damn you," a man's voice suddenly said.

Hodge blinked stupidly in the lantern light that flooded the tent. Then he was grasped from behind and yanked back, his errection already beginning to dwindle as he saw Steven's angry face.

His face contorted with rage, Steven set down the lantern. He grasped Hodge, lifting him off his feet and dangling him in his huge fists. Hodge kicked and struggled, whining piteously for Steven to put him down.

"I told you," Steven said.

"She's not hurt none, Steven. I didn't do nothing," Hodge said as he was bounced up and down like a marionette. Finally Steven dropped him on the ground. Hodge tried to scramble to safety through the open tent flap. Steven went after him; in his free hand he held a knife, the silver blade quivering as he glared at Hodge.

"You knew what I'd do if I found you with her. All of you's been warned."

Hodge's eyes grew big with fear, and his fleshy lips quivered as he began to blubber incoherently.

"You knew what I'd do," Steven said. "She wasn't to be touched."

Then suddenly Steven's hand moved. Firelight gleamed an instant on the steel blade before it plunged into Hodge's sagging belly, ripping up with such force, Hodge was knocked backward. Hodge squealed, then gurgled as he fell. Steven's face was a mask of hatred as he pulled out the knife only to plunge it back into Hodge's chest. The two men scrabbled on the ground, their flailing limbs kicking against the tent canvas until Hodge lay still, stretched full length beside the tent, a knife hilt protruding from his chest.

The others who had gathered about the tent to watch fell strangely silent as justice was meted out. They were all aware of Steven's promise of a knife in the heart to anyone who touched the captive woman. They were also aware of Hodge's appetites and, seeing his garments undone, were in little doubt he had been caught in the act.

"Leave him," Steven shouted when several men stepped forward to tend Hodge. "He's got no need of you now."

The men looked at Hodge's bleeding body, which appeared much smaller in death than in life. The winter wind moaned between the trees in the ensuing lull, fluttering dead leaves along the branches. Some men shivered in fear at the sight of Steven's wrathful face, wondering what would happen next.

"Leave him, I say," Steven growled as the men came to cover Hodge, where he lay on the blood-soaked ground. "And just as I left him," he added, when someone grasped the hilt of the knife, preparing to draw it out. "It'll be a reminder to the rest of you."

A rumble of displeasure came from the men as one by one they began to melt away, casting furtive glances at the bloody corpse beside the tent. They were afraid their leader had stepped across the line into the shadowy world of insanity. No one killed a comrade over a captive woman. They shook their heads, muttering amongst themselves, but they had not the courage to condemn Steven to his face. No one wanted to be his next victim.

Steven finally went back inside the tent. Rosamund lay weeping—not for Hodge, because she had always loathed her stepfather, but for her own helplessness. Nell slunk back in the shadows to avoid Steven's wrath, though for the moment Steven seemed to have forgotten her.

"Did he?"

Rosamund shook her head, trying to push down her skirts with her bound wrists.

"Oh, love, I'm sorry. After what I said and all, I didn't think he'd dare," Steven said remorsefully as he helped Rosamund to sit, then modestly arranged her skirts to cover her legs. Next he pulled a dagger from his belt and slit her bonds, chafing her wrists to restore circulation where the rope had cut red bracelets in her flesh. He undid her ankle bonds, all the while crooning in sympathy, appalled at the livid marks on her slender white ankles.

"Get 'er shoes," he growled at Nell, who quickly found the flat-soled velvet slippers. Steven admired the saffron velvet, stroking its softness before he slipped the shoes on Rosamund's feet. Rosamund still wore her snagged, dirty silk hose, but her captors had always hidden her shoes.

"And find 'er other stuff," Steven said sharply. Nell had hidden the fine fur cloak, thinking to keep it for herself. Reluctantly she complied, amazed as she saw Steven gently settle the garment about the woman's shoulders.

"There, love, that'll be better. Keep you warm," he said, sweeping back Rosamund's dangling hair from her hot face. "Not long now before you'll be off home," he said, still keeping his distance.

Exercising great personal restraint, he had not kissed or embraced her. Rosamund must stay pure until they were wed. A picture of the hated Lord of Ravenscrag flickered through his troubled mind and he scowled at the reminder that she was no longer pure. For the moment he'd forgotten that bastard had already stolen her maidenhead, but he wouldn't hold that against her. He damned the nobleman for touching her and he damned Joan and Hodge for selling her. In a way what had happened that night was fair justice. Steven smiled in satisfaction as he recalled Hodge with his fat belly slit open. It was just punishment for Hodge's greed in selling Steven's lovely Rosamund.

For her part, Rosamund realized that something was terribly wrong with Steven. In the past he had always been gentle and kind. Rosamund saw the love shining in his eyes as he treated her tenderly. But for how much longer would that love be there? Once she told Steven she was married to Henry and could never be his wife, his rage would turn on her. So far she had kept her mouth shut about the matter, hoping she need never explain herself. All along she had expected to be rescued. But time was running out. Considering the punishment Steven had meted out to one of his own for attempting to rape her, she could not bear thinking about what torture might be in store for Henry. Her heart began a frenzied beat as she wondered if Steven had already killed Henry in payment for loving her.

"Do you still keep Lord Ravenscrag captive?"

Steven grinned. "For a while, till the gold comes."

Rosamund gasped in relief, her heart soaring. "You're only holding us for ransom?"

"He's held for ransom. You'll come home with me."

After a while Steven left, and Rosamund lay back on her bedding, uncomfortably aware of her pounding heart. Her worst fears were founded. Steven wanted to pick up where they had left off, just as if nothing had happened. That must be his reason for protecting her from his comrades and for not laying a hand on her himself. She was to be his wife!

A wave of nausea churned through Rosamund's stomach. What would become of Henry if no gold was sent to ransom him? She already knew the answer to that question: Steven would kill him.

"You'd best be careful. Don't seem to me as if 'e's in 'is right mind," Nell said before she slipped out of the tent. She had several invitations for the night, and after the lesson Steven had just taught, it was safe to assume no one would bother the woman.

Rosamund sat alone in the dark. Steven had taken the lantern with him, and her eyes didn't readjust to the dark for some time. When she closed them, fire specks still danced beneath her lids. The camp had grown quiet and she assumed the men had packed up for the night. A huge orange ball from the cookfire was reflected on the tent wall. She stretched her feet and arms, remembering she had not thanked Steven for untying her. Could she persuade him to do the same for Henry? Maybe then he could escape. Since Henry was a knight and soldier, she imagined he knew all manner of tricks to evade captors. If she had a knife to slit Henry's bonds, she would not need to wait for Steven's good graces. She could slip out and free Henry herself.

A startling idea shot though her mind: She had access to a knife! Turning, she looked at the ghastly silhouette splashed across the tent canvas in the firelight. The dagger still jutted out from Hodge's chest. All she had to do was pull it out. The idea was so revolting she shuddered to contemplate it. To get the knife she would have to touch Hodge! Rosamund fought down a surge of nausea. She couldn't do it. But if Henry was to escape, she must!

Stealthily Rosamund crept out of the tent. The fire had died down a little, and its light didn't reach as far as it had earlier. Pressed against the tent, she looked in all directions for guards. Two men huddled beside the fire talking while several more moved about. For the most part the men were asleep. She recognized Steven's unmistakable build as he sat talking beside the fire and she wondered uneasily if she could slip past him. The wind rustling through the dead leaves helped muffle her steps.

Rosamund shuddered in revulsion as she neared Hodge's corpse. Leaning over him, she closed her eyes as she gripped the wet dagger hilt and tugged. Nothing happened. Quickly she snatched away her hand as if it had been burned. Shuddering she wiped the sticky blood on her skirts.

Men's voices sounded closer and she saw Steven and his companion were walking behind the tent to relieve themselves. She held her breath, anxious to slip back inside her prison until they had gone. They were too busy with their discussion to notice her move back inside the tent.

"Don't do it, Steven. 'E be too powerful," the other man was saying.

"I don't give a tinker's damn about 'is power. It's simple: We want gold; they want 'im. Besides who can say we done anything?"

"Aye, but he's a grand lord. Someone'll guess we killed him, won't they?"

"Don't be a coward, Macky. How will they guess if he leaves us in good faith and is robbed on the way back. Now that's not our fault, is it?"

Rosamund's heart thudded in fear when she realized what and whom they discussed. Steven was going to kill Henry after the ransom had been paid.

"Well, are you with me or not?"

Still doubting the wisdom of the plan, Macky reluctantly agreed. "Who else is in on it?"

"We don't need no one else. There'll be all the more for us that way."

Macky slapped Steven's shoulder. "Right then. Let's go have a drink on it."

The two men moved away, leaving Rosamund trembling in the darkness as she wondered what to do. More wood was thrown on the fire, and the blaze leapt high, casting great hunched shadows across the canvas wall, obliterating Hodge's grisly image.

Rosamund had to free Henry while she had the chance. The morrow could be too late. Once the ransom was paid his fate would be sealed. Taking a deep breath, Rosamund mustered her courage and stepped out into the cold night.

Rosamund knelt beside the corpse. With her eyes shut, she grasped the knife again and she pulled hard. A sickening, squelching sound ensued and the sucking drag on the knife made her want to vomit. Then, after a final gurgle, the knife was suddenly free in her hand. She dropped back, swallowing down the bitterness in her mouth. Sweat beaded on her brow and she was so light-headed she thought she would faint. Closing her eyes, Rosamund held her breath, fighting down the unpleasant sensations. The wind cooled her hot face and chilled the sweat trickling off her brow. When she stood her legs felt unsteady, but they grew stronger by the minute. In her hand she had the knife. The worst part was over.

Fortunately there was no moon and the shadowy trees fringing the camp gave her cover. It seemed no time at all before she stood behind the lean-to beside the hollies. What if there were guards posted outside? Her heart skipped a beat. She had not thought about that.

Working her way closer to the wall, Rosamund looked through the woven branches. There was a dark bulk on the floor. She took a twig and kneeling pushed it through an opening in the wall until she heard movement inside.

"Henry," she whispered hoarsely, her mouth close to the rough bark. Again she jabbed the twig, pushing it almost all the way through "Henry," she said again, as loud as she dared. Then her heart leapt with joy as he answered.

"Where's the guard?" she asked.

"Doorway," he whispered hoarsely.

Rosamund could feel his breath warm against her ear. "Is he sleeping?" she whispered back.

"Yes."

"I'm coming in."

It seemed an eternity before she worked her way to the front of the lean-to. Fortunately the wind had risen and it moaned through the tree branches masking the sounds she made. There were two guards! One hunched beside the hut, his head on his knees, while the other lay across the doorway. A duet of snores told her they were both asleep.

Glancing about the camp to make sure no one was stirring, she moved into the open. The first guard snored loudly, jerking his head. Terrified he would wake himself, she froze against the wall until the snores were even again. The other man was rolled in a blanket in the doorway. She stepped over him, lifting her skirts to prevent the trailing fabric from waking him.

Henry sat against the far wall, his hands and feet bound. After a whispered greeting, Rosamund fumbled with the knife, trying to saw through the thick rope binding his wrists. Her fingers ached with the effort and she thought she would never cut through the rope when it suddenly gave way. Henry sawed through his own ankle bonds. Though it was dark and he could not clearly see her face, he reached out and tenderly stroked her cheek.

''Thank you for saving my life, sweetheart.''

She gripped his hand, her eyes filling with tears. He did not know how true that statement was.

The man in the doorway stirred and they froze, alarmed to think they might be caught so close to freedom. A few minutes later he was snoring again and they breathed a sigh of relief. Henry slid the knife in his belt. They had taken his own weapons; so he would make do with that knife.

They stepped over the sleeping man, then stealthily moved away from the hut. Henry grasped Rosamund's hand, leading her to the primitive lean-to where the horses were kept. He had guessed at the direction of the building by the strong smell of horse. The lad who had befriended Diablo had been carrying water in that direction.

Leaving Rosamund in the shelter of a stand of saplings, Henry moved silently to the building. He could see Jake's slumped form lying inside.

At the sound of his master's voice, Diablo whickered in greeting, though Henry had barely whispered his name. Diablo turned his big black head, snorting and pawing the ground, his broad back thumping against the makeshift partition that divided him from his beloved master.

Jake snapped up, alerted by the animal's changed mood. Henry did not want to harm the lad, nor did he want to sacrifice his chance of escape. No sooner had Jake scrambled to his feet than he was grasped from behind and a knife grazed his throat.

"Don't say a word, lad, if you want to live."

Jake's eyes grew round as he recognized the speaker, but he did not say anything.

"Saddle them."

Keeping the knife against Jake's back, Henry moved with Jake to get the saddles. First Diablo, who made such a racket Henry winced at the horse's joyous greeting, afraid he would betray them. Henry reached up to fondle his head in an effort to pacify him. Then Jake saddled the other horse, his hands shaking as he cinched the girth.

Henry watched him work through narrowed eyes. He did not want to have to commit murder, but he was not sure he could trust the lad. "Thank you for taking care of him," he said in an undertone, patting Diablo's silky side. "If you've a mind to come with me, I've a stable full of beasts to care for."

Jake hesitated and Henry moved the knife higher. "Remember, your life won't be worth much when he learns it was you who helped me. But be sharp, I've not got all night."

"Aye, milord, I'll come. I've nothing to lose," Jake said, tossing back his shaggy hair.

"Do I have your word?"

Jake nodded, surprised he was being trusted.

They walked the horses out, trying to move quietly. In the doorway Henry paused, making sure everything was still. Fortunately the lean-to was set apart from the rest of the camp. Most of the men were already asleep, rolled up in their blankets beside the fire.

Henry nudged Jake forward along the track, highly aware of leaves crackling underfoot. "Rosamund," he hissed as he neared the stand of trees.

She stepped from the cover, surprised to see he had another man with him. As quietly as possible they walked the horses to an open patch. Henry swept Rosamund into the saddle, then leapt up behind her. Jake hesitated before he mounted the other horse. His movements were so ungainly that he revealed, though he had cared for many horses, he had not ridden many.

"Do you know the way out of here?" Henry asked the lad.

Jake nodded and headed west, bouncing in the saddle as he desperately held on. So far so good. Every crackling leaf and twig made Henry look behind them, fearing a hue and cry would begin any minute.

When they reached the safety of the first clearing, they picked up speed. Henry recognized the path that turned back to the east, bound for York. They had been on the road only a few minutes before a commotion sounded behind them. Lantern light moved amid the bare trees as men were roused from sleep to search the brush for the captives. As Henry nudged Diablo into a gallop, a shout told him they had already been spotted. Then an arrow whistled past his ear and harmlessly embedded itself in a nearby tree trunk. Faster, faster, they went, desperate to get out of arrow range. Several more shafts landed harmlessly in the gorse thickets beside the path before they finally pulled ahead, galloping to freedom.

Henry did not slacken the pace until he could see the walls of York. The sky was lightening by the minute as sunrise approached. The first golden glimmers of light speared the heavy clouds, tipping the crenellated walls with shafts of gold. The enormous Mickelgate stood before them, already yawning wide like some giant maw ready to admit the day's traffic.

Rosamund had never been more pleased to see the dirty, smelly city. She leaned back against Henry's comforting strength and gave a deep sigh of relief.

"We're safe at last," she said, turning to kiss his cheek, which tasted of wind and moorland. Heavy black stubble covered his jaw, making him appear a dark, mysterious stranger.

"Thank heaven. What say you to going home, love, after

we've supped and packed? We've been away from Ravenscrag far too long.''

"Oh, Harry, yes, let's go home." She nestled back against his warmth. To be able to go with him to Ravenscrag was the most wonderful thing she could imagine. The noisy city and the dangers of battle would be left behind for the clean, sweeping moor and endless sky; they would be returning to the craggy land where Henry Ravenscrag was the undisputed king.

Around them the gloomy city streets were coming to life. They cantered across the city, serenaded by clanging church bells and rumbling carts. As they turned into Lop Lane the Nag's Head sign came into view and Rosamund thought it the most welcome sight she had ever seen.

Chapter Ten

Firelight flickered over the gray stone walls. The tower room was warmly inviting though outside the winter wind howled around the battlements like a lost soul. Rosamund sighed and stretched in the bed, happy to be nestled in a sea of down with Henry sleeping beside her. That day he had to leave to recruit men from among their recalcitrant neighbors to fight for the king's cause. It was an unpleasant reminder of the warlike times. When they had returned to Ravenscrag she had thought they would leave the war behind, but she had been wrong. As the most powerful landowner in the region, Henry was expected to recruit and recruit and recruit until no living male from there to the Scottish border had not heard of the king's call to arms. Or rather, it had become Queen Margaret's rallying cry because she, rather than her husband, directed Lancaster's force. It was said the poor addled king slipped in and out of sanity, granting the Yorkists far too many concessions to suit his fiery French queen.

When it was full light, Rosamund turned to look at her sleeping husband and saw how peaceful and young he appeared in his sleep. It was unfortunate he must take to the road again just when the cut he had received at Wakefield Green was mending. The healing slash had been split asunder under the rough treatment of Steven's men. Henry had laughed at Rosamund's concern, saying the wound was little more than a scratch and accusing her of unnecessary fussing. Even though he complained about her attentions, she knew he enjoyed them.

Rosamund bent to place a gentle kiss above the clean band-

226

age she had insisted on him wearing. Then she squeaked in surprise when his arms moved to capture her. He had only pretended to sleep.

'You're awake,'' she said. "Then up you get, you cheat. 'Tis already daylight.''

Henry pulled her down beside him, kissing her lips and fondling her breasts, which peeked invitingly from the neck of her cambric shift. "Would that I could stay in bed with you all day. Surely we can let old John of Thurlston rest secure in his tower for a few more days.''

Rosamund's heart leapt in excitement at the prospect of having Henry to herself for a whole day. Then her hopes were dashed when he sighed and resolutely put her from him.

"No, my duty's clear. But I promise, love, I'll be back with you tonight.''

"It might be too wet and muddy for travel,'' she said. It was only a few days since a light snow had fallen and the moorland tracks took a long time to clear. Again her hopes soared only to be dashed.

"Nay, remember, we rode that way yesterday. The roads are clear enough.''

She nodded, disappointed, but knowing he was right. The men had arranged to meet when the weather cleared and she knew Henry must go. They had made love for much of the past night, aware their time together was fleeting. Since their return from York, Rosamund had not told her husband that she knew Steven, letting him think her abduction had been a crime of opportunity with money as its sole purpose. Her conscience pricked her over her deceit, but to reveal she knew Steven of the Forge meant she would have to reveal all, she had argued silently, knowing she could not do that. Besides Sir Ismay's possible retribution for betraying their deception, she was not secure enough as the Lady of Ravenscrag to want to take such a risk.

Nuzzling against Henry's warm, smooth neck, Rosamund slid her hand under the covers to stroke his shoulders. Gently she slipped her fingers amid his abundant chest hair, playfully caressing his nipples before she moved her hand lower, down his taut belly until she finally held the soft, full flesh of his organ in her hand. She shivered in delight when she recalled how very skillfully he had pleasured her last night. As if by magic, his flesh pulsed to life at her touch.

Henry captured her hands. "Now, nice as this is, you must stop. No trickery to tempt me to stay here when you know my duty is elsewhere."

Rosamund giggled at the mock severity of his tone and she reluctantly let him get out of bed, then moved into the warm hollow where his body had been. She lay back contentedly as she admired the smooth perfection of his muscular body. His broad shoulders and powerful back sloped to a narrow waist and firm, compact hips. Henry crossed to the hearth in search of his robe, which he had discarded when they had made love before the fire. The firelight burnished his skin and Rosamund dreamily likened him to a statue cast in gold. Her blood stirred when she looked at him. She was as desirous as ever of his lovemaking. She would never tire of admiring him, she vowed happily, sighing in sheer contentment.

In the safety of their room, the nightmare that had taken place in the Forest of Galtres seemed to belong to another time. Whenever she considered their narrow escape she gave fervent thanks to her Maker for His aid. Even Henry, never unduly pious, lit candles in thanks for their deliverance and he gave a generous donation to a nearby abbey in payment for their safe return.

Jem, Henry's body servant, came to dress and shave his lord for the day. Rosamund watched the procedure from the bed, feeling like a spectator at an erotic play. Her mind was filled with memories of the previous night, freshly awakened by the arousing sight of Henry's body. Sometimes he glanced up and winked or smiled at her affectionately, and their silent communication made her heart pitch with love.

When it was finally time for him to leave, they held each other passionately. Rosamund suddenly clung to him, afraid to let him out of her sight in such dangerous times. Each time he left the castle, she was never sure when, or if, he would come back.

"Till tonight, sweetheart. I promise we'll sup together first, and then—"

"It's the and then I'm looking forward to most," she said, hiding her discomfort as she gave him a final embrace. "God-speed and return safely to me."

Henry had been gone for several hours when Rosamund was told she had visitors. She was sitting sewing in the solar with Dimples lying at her feet. The dog raised his head and gave a warning growl at the intruder. Rosamund had to scold the dog, though she shared his dislike of the man who stood before her. Last week Thurgood, the castle steward, had taken to his bed and it was Hoke, the castle treasurer, who had assumed temporary command of the household.

"Shall I admit the visitors, Lady Rosamund?" Hoke asked, his sly face bland.

Rosamund agreed, puzzling over the man's curious expression. She was not sure she trusted Hoke to have her best interests at heart. He was a calculating and deceitful man. He said a noble lady and her children had come to pay their respects. Rosamund assumed the noble lady was the wife of a neighboring lord come to welcome her home, though it seemed strange for such a woman to be traveling in winter without her husband. Possibly the visitor's husband was one of the men who had joined Henry for that day's recruitment.

Rosamund glanced at her reflection in the polished steel mirror and nervously smoothed her rose brocade surcoat, which was worn over a plain white wool gown. Her braided hair was covered by a simple veil and chaplet. Not splendid, but she assumed her dress was suitable for the visiting wife of some lesser gentry. Rosamund had already ordered a tray of cakes and wine to be brought to the solar, where a cheerful fire blazed in the hooded fireplace. The room was far more hospitable than the smoky great hall below, with its roosting pigeons and noisy soldiers.

While she waited, Rosamund took up her embroidery again,

wondering why it was taking so long for her guests to appear. Finally she heard children's voices drifting up the stair.

Two small children swathed in fur-lined cloaks appeared at the top of the stairs, standing there hesitantly as they waited for their mother to join them. Rosamund smiled at her young guests, holding out both hands in welcome. Shyly the children came forward to greet her and allowed her to kiss their cheeks before she led them to the hearth to warm themselves. Dimples rolled on his back, his big tail thumping in pleasure against the floor. He seemed pleased to have unexpected company. The children clapped their hands and laughed at the big dog.

A servantwoman bustled upstairs to take off the children's cloaks. Rosamund glanced up to find the children's mother watching her from the doorway. So striking was the stranger's appearance that Rosamund was at a loss for words. Her guest was tall; her fiery red hair tumbled to her shoulders as it spilled out of her lilac hood. However, the beautiful, fine-boned face framed by a swansdown-edged hood was calculating and forbidding. Rosamund felt very ill at ease as the woman moved gracefully across the room after she had waved the servant away.

"Welcome to Ravenscrag, Lady—" Rosamund paused, not knowing the woman's name and sensing the hostility in her continued silence. The stranger seemed to be sizing Rosamund up from head to toe.

"It is Pomeroy. Lady Blanche."

Mentally Rosamund reviewed her neighbors as she and the woman curtsied politely, but she was unable to recall anyone named Pomeroy nearby, though the name sounded familiar. The children were staring up at her with round blue eyes. They were such beautiful children; naturally, with such a striking mother, one could expect nothing less. Yet it was not the red-headed beauty they resembled. There was something in their soft cherubic faces that tugged at Rosamund's memory, yet she was at odds to place the hauntingly familiar likeness.

"Lady Rosamund, allow me to introduce my children to you. This is Henry, and the baby, Elinore."

The children bowed or curtsied politely, as they had been taught.

"They are such lovely children, Lady Blanche. You are most fortunate."

"Do you have no children of your own then, my lady?" the other woman asked. Her question was unnecessary since everyone thereabouts knew Henry had no heir.

Rosamund shook her head. For some unknown reason the strangely arresting woman made her feel like a stranger in her own home. Rosamund motioned for Blanche to join her on the cushioned bench beside the hearth. Blanche casually tossed her swansdown-trimmed cloak across a nearby chest before coming to the hearth to warm her hands. Rosamund noticed the other woman's ringless hands were long, slender, and very white, the skin almost transparent. Her very presence disturbed Rosamund, who wondered why she had come to visit since her aloof manner suggested little eagerness for friendship. Rosamund had to admit that the other woman's beauty of face and form made her feel inadequate. Blanche was dressed to perfection in purple silk trimmed in marten, and the creamy swell of her bosom was revealed above a low, fur-trimmed neckline.

"Your children are a credit to you, my lady," Rosamund murmured politely as she tried to stimulate conversation. She turned to watch the small boy and girl playing with wooden blocks and hoops that the servant had left on the rushes. The children good-naturedly retrieved their toys from Dimples, who was determined to join their game.

"Yes," Blanche said with a smug smile. "For three and four they are most well behaved, don't you think?"

She turned to admire the picture-perfect black-haired girl and boy in their rich garments. The children were dressed in matching outfits of wine velvet, though the boy wore a doublet and the girl a gown. Had it not been for the difference in their height one would have thought them twins.

"I'm sorry my husband's not at home today. He's gone recruiting for the king," Rosamund said awkwardly as she

231

poured wine and handed cakes to her guest.

Daintily Blanche bit into a rich cake. Her small, even white teeth reminded Rosamund of a cat; her green almond-shaped eyes were ablaze with flickering yellow light. Mesmerized by the other woman's startlingly feline appearance, Rosamund wondered if it was just the reflection of the fire that made Blanche's eyes seem so unusual.

"I had to come to see Henry's wife. You're far more lovely than I imagined, dear Rosamund," Blanche said at last as she fastidiously dusted crumbs to the rushes. Suddenly she snapped her fingers to summon her servant, making Rosamund start in surprise. The woman, who must have been waiting on the stair, appeared at once. "Take the children to the kitchens and get them some food. And take that hound with you."

Rosamund told Dimples to go downstairs and he reluctantly obeyed. Though Rosamund held her tongue, not wanting to be rude to her guest, she resented her taking charge. The children trotted obediently after the servant, whispering among themselves, never once glancing back at their mother.

"I'm pleased that you came to visit," Rosamund said, aware such a polite remark was expected. Yet in truth she could not wait for her uninvited guest to leave.

"Really?" Blanche said, smoothing her skirts as she watched Rosamund intently. "In that case, you must not know who I am."

Surprised by her strange statement, Rosamund swallowed uneasily. "Why is that?"

"Because, my dear, I'm the woman Henry loves."

Rosamund stared in shock at her guest, hardly able to comprehend what she had just heard.

Blanche gave a brittle, unpleasant laugh, enjoying her rival's shocked expression. "Now I've upset you. I'm so sorry."

"My lady, you have me at a disadvantage," Rosamund said stiffly. "Explain yourself."

"I live at the manor of Enderly."

That name alone was explanation enough. She was that

Blanche! Rosamund knew why the name had seemed familiar. She had never dreamed her rival would dare come there. A pain stabbed her heart, making Rosamund catch her breath. She was looking at the infamous mistress of Enderly—Henry's whore! Rosamund drew herself to her full height as she stood stiffly before the hearth.

"What do you want with me?" Rosamund said.

"Isn't it natural for me to be curious about you? I've waited a long time for this meeting. We thought it wisest that I not come to the wedding, but that was a long time ago. You've had plenty of time to get used to my existence."

"I was aware of your existence. There was no need for me to meet you."

"Weren't you just the least bit curious? Didn't you want to see what kind of woman Henry enjoys?"

Rosamund gritted her teeth to prevent herself from saying something she would later regret. "I am the kind of woman Henry enjoys."

Blanche threw back her head and her cruel laughter pealed out, while her mane of red hair tossed about her creamy shoulders. "Oh, my dear, how naive you are."

"Henry loves me."

"But you're his wife!"

"Now we've both satisfied our curiosity, we've nothing to say to each other," Rosamund said after a long pause, during which she tried to gather her wits.

"Oh, but you're wrong. I've much to say to you," Blanche hissed, leaning closer.

The musky perfume that wafted from Blanche's clothing dried Rosamund's throat and made her feel dizzy. Rosamund swallowed uncomfortably, longing to tell the other woman to go, yet she was not sure if Henry would be angry if she did. She had already learned the nobility played life by a different set of rules from Whitton villagers; so far the rules concerning a visiting mistress had not been explained to her.

"Then say it and be gone," Rosamund said.

Blanche smiled smugly and leaned back against the padded

settle. "You mustn't be jealous. I've been Henry's lover for a number of years. And I assure you he has no intention of giving me up. So you'd better get used to the idea."

"How dare you?" Rosamund cried, no longer able to maintain her composure in the face of the other woman's insolence. She longed to strike Blanche's smug face. "He's already given you up."

"Is that what he told you? You'll learn not to put such faith in a man's word, dear heart, or you're going to be hurt. You see, I've something that keeps him coming back to me, something you don't have."

Stonily Rosamund met the other woman's gaze, her heart beating erratically, her rising anger making her legs shake under her white skirt. "And what magical thing is that, my lady?"

"I have his son and daughter, Lady Rosamund."

Time stood still. Rosamund was acutely aware of the wind moaning beyond the big windows, of the crackling logs, and much closer, of the pounding of her own heart.

"You liar!" she hissed, itching to slap that smug, catlike face, to rip out by the handful that billowing hair. "You liar!"

"Don't you wish that were so. Rest assured, they are his children. Surely you can see the likeness."

Stunned, Rosamund considered the strange feeling of familiarity that had tugged at the back of her mind when she had first seen the lovely blue-eyed, dark-haired children.

"You only need look at the portrait over there to know I speak the truth."

Numbly Rosamund turned to look where Blanche pointed. In the corner hung a portrait of three young children, Henry and his two younger brothers, who were both dead, playing with a hound in that very room. It was not a very skillful painting, but the artist had captured their likeness. Rosamund's heart sank. That likeness was what she had been trying to recall when she had looked into the boy's angelic face and found that his large, dark-lashed blue eyes and softly rounded pink cheeks reminded her of someone. Blanche's son was the image of Henry's youngest brother, Fenton, who had been around that same age when the portrait was painted.

Watching her rival's stricken expression was not triumph enough for Blanche, who was not nearly as secure in Henry's affection as she pretended. Following up for the kill, she said with feigned sweetness, "You mustn't mind that Henry comes to me still. Did you know that? Even on your wedding night, it was to my bed he came."

"I knew about that night. So you see, it's no great surprise," Rosamund whispered, sitting suddenly on the settle as her legs grew too weak to hold her.

Blanche scowled. She had not expected Rosamund to know. "And do you really think that's the only time he's been with me at Enderly? Consider how many nights he's spent away from home since you've been wed."

Rosamund hated to admit just how many there had been. Weeks'—months'—worth of nights were all unaccounted for.

"He's never stopped coming to me," Blanche said, rewarded by Rosamund's gasp. Pushing her advantage, she drove on relentlessly. "In fact, though he might prefer I not tell you this, I lost his child just this past Christmas. Henry stays with me regularly and he has ever since—"

Rosamund no longer heard Blanche's voice relating detail after painful detail. Her ears buzzed and her head felt close to exploding.

"You don't know how to please a man like Henry. He's not just satisfied with ordinary lovemaking. I know how to please him with secret potions that excite him beyond belief. He's a stallion serving me again and again."

"Get out!" Rosamund said through set teeth, finally finding her voice.

As if on cue, the servantwoman appeared at the door with the two children, each holding a shiny red apple. As Rosamund stared at them, her heart pitched. They were both so like Henry there was no mistaking their paternity. Those big blue eyes, the dark curls, and the shape of their faces owed nothing to Blanche Pomeroy's catlike features. They were both pure Ravenscrag.

"We're leaving now. Dress the children," Blanche said. Then turning back to Rosamund, she said, "I hope you'll remember our visit for a very long time, Lady Rosamund."

"You can rest assured of that, Lady Pomeroy," Rosamund said, her jaw aching with the effort of maintaining her dignity. Rosamund, the washerwoman's daughter, would have leapt on her rival, sobbing with rage. Lady Ravenscrag had to stem the tears burning at the back of her eyes and battle to control her murderous temper. Swallowing the choking lump in her throat, she said, "I'll remember this as one of the most hateful days of my life."

Blanche smiled icily as she fastened her cloak; then shepherding the children before her, she sailed downstairs.

Rosamund was still not to be allowed the luxury of tears. She stiffened as she heard Hoke's solicitous inquiry, laughter barely hidden behind his voice.

"May I be of service, Lady Rosamund?"

She turned quickly and saw his gloating expression before he cleverly masked it. Damn him! He had known exactly who that woman was. It had been his intention that she should be shocked and hurt; she could see the truth in his face.

"No, Hoke. Any business I have can wait until Thurgood recovers," she said coldly before she turned her back on him.

She stood looking out at the winter landscape a long time before she heard him move away, his tread heavy on the stair. She could imagine Hoke regaling the rest of the staff with all the details of Lady Blanche's visit. He had appeared so rapidly after her departure that he must have been listening on the stairs. The very walls of the castle pressed in on her. She had to get out where the air was fresh, where no one listened and spied.

Though Rosamund was not the rider she wished to be, she was skilled enough to be able to temporarily escape on horseback. She had to be alone to think, alone to grow familiar with the new ache in her heart so that in public she could act as if nothing was amiss, thereby cheating people like Hoke of the pleasure of watching her pain. A searing gallop over the moor would help blow away the cobwebs of grief.

The icy wind whipped away her bitter tears, stinging her cheeks until they glowed red with cold. That morning, as she had lain drowsily in her bed, she had felt so happy, content and loved; only a few hours later, she felt totally bereft. Why had Henry let her believe he no longer visited Enderly? True, she had never actually pinned him down with that question. How clever men were, hiding behind the letter of the word: not actually lying, yet not actually telling the truth either.

Oh, damn him! Damn him for betraying their love with that red-haired bitch! Everything she had ever heard about Blanche Pomeroy had come back to haunt her. One of the servantgirls had told her of Blanche's reputation for witchcraft, something Lord Henry had always laughingly discounted when he was warned against her. Folks said the Red Witch ensnared him with magic spells. When Blanche spoke of secrets that made him serve her like a stallion, was she talking about black magic? In Whitton the people whispered about witches potions that created such an unnatural state of arousal men became insatiable.

A vivid picture of Blanche and Henry writhing naked in each other's arms flashed through Rosamund's mind, causing a hot wave of nausea. Henry's vows of love had enhanced his passionate lovemaking. The idea of that intimacy being shared with another, of Blanche arousing Henry and being aroused in turn as she enmeshed him in her net of flaming hair, only increased Rosamund's nausea. Such intimate caresses and passionate kisses were Rosamund's alone, not some paltry favor to be squandered on the devil's handmaiden.

Feeling suddenly as if she was going to faint, Rosamund reined in. Slumping forward she pressed her hands over her eyes and tried to stop her head from pounding. How could Henry have deceived her so? How could he have been bedding another while he made such impassioned vows to her? Had all those lovely words been lies? Ah, no, no, she groaned, he loved her. He was her own fairy-tale prince.

The cold ring of that phrase made her raise her head. Had she just unwittingly discovered the truth? Was their passionate love a fairy tale existing only in her own imagination, like all those splendid fantasies she had invented to brighten her days?

Tears trickled down her cheeks as she moved over the moor, barely noticing the buffeting wind. Finally, as the sky grew gloomy, she turned the mare's head toward home.

There was a chance that the other woman lied about Henry coming to her still. Sense had already told Rosamund those children belonged to no other man. They were both too much like Henry for that. Yet they were aged three and four, conceived long before Henry had met Rosamund De Gere.

At that startling reminder, she tried to sort through the possibilities. She looked out across the craggy landscape, which was devoid of life except for the shaggy, bleating sheep. She slowly digested the facts. She was not foolish enough to expect Henry to have been faithful to her before they had met. That cheering boost to her spirits was dashed a moment later when she considered Blanche's claims that he still slept with her. Rosamund knew Henry had spent their wedding night at Enderly; it was also possible he had been with Blanche during the first winter when he had been away for weeks, riding about his manors. He had told Rosamund he had tried everything in his power to keep from loving her. Wistfully she recalled his tormented expression the night he had confided those sentiments to her and how much she had loved him in return. Had everything in his power included sleeping with Blanche?

It was entirely possible, Rosamund argued anew, as she went indoors seeking the warm hearth, that Henry had not visited Blanche since then. But the woman claimed to have miscarried Henry's child at Christmastide, which was far too late for a winter's liaison. That child would have to have been conceived in autumn or late summer, both times Henry had been away from home. He had purportedly been assembling an army for the king, but instead he could have spent those sunny weeks in Blanche Pomeroy's bed?

The hours till Henry's return were an eternity. Rosamund could not decide whether to confront him when he arrived, wait until they had supped, or wait till they were in the privacy of their bedchamber. To have to eat in the great hall before all those people while pretending nothing was amiss would be torment. Far better to get it over with when he came home.

While Rosamund waited she tried not to picture Henry in Blanche's arms or, worse still, in her bed. She tried, but did not succeed. She tortured herself, wondering if there were times Henry had come to her straight from Blanche's bed.

It was almost a relief when she heard the general stir around the castle following the arrival of a soldier who had ridden ahead to alert them to their lord's approach. Rosamund threw on the fur-lined cloak Henry had given her, freshly reminded of his betrayal as the fur caressed her, soft as a lover's hand. That gift had been so special; suddenly it too was spoiled. Everything about their love was tarnished since she knew he had shared it with another.

The wind raked the stone walk as she stood on the battlements looking across the moor. A winding ribbon of light moved like a glowing serpent around hillocks and gorse thickets, coming closer. The flaring torches glowed orange in the darkness as the riders approached the drawbridge, which had been lowered to admit Henry and his men. How much she had longed for this moment. Her feet dragged as she went down the stair, wanting to delay their confrontation for as long as she could. During a weak moment she had even considered greeting him as if that afternoon's hateful meeting had never taken place. How much easier it would have been to turn a blind eye to her husband's philandering, as she was sure many wives did. But that approach would not work for her. Above all else there must be honesty between them!

Honesty! The word ignited a weak fit of laughter until she had to lean against the cold stone to compose herself. The hypocrisy of that righteous thought was laughable. From the beginning there had never been honesty on her part. So how could she demand it from him? But although she had deceived him, she had not done so with her heart or body. That was the same emotional honesty she wanted from her lover. What a deceitful pair they had become. Henry hiding his love affairs while she hid her identity. And she could not even scorn those children for being illegitimate when she herself was Sir Ismay's bastard!

Henry strode inside the great hall booted and spurred, his dark cloak tossed back over his shoulders. His gaze raked the shadows as he searched for her. He seemed surprised Rosamund had not met him at the door.

Taking a deep breath for courage, Rosamund finally moved from the pillar behind which she stood, her tread solemnly measured. She walked with as much joy as if she went to her own execution. Over her shimmering gown of magenta silk she wore a silk damask surcoat trimmed in vair. In her rich gown, with a sparkling coronet and billowing veil atop her coiled hair, she looked like a princess. A bitter smile lifted her mouth as she heard Henry's audible gasp when he saw her. Though she had dressed for his homecoming in her splendid new festival gown, she might as well have worn sackcloth for all the pleasure it gave her.

"Rosamund, sweetheart, you're a vision! If I'd known this was a special night, I'd have come home much sooner," he said, holding out his arms to her.

She moved into his embrace, her heart filled with pain, tears throbbing behind her eyes. Why couldn't everything be the way it had been that morning? Why did her happiness have to end? When they kissed, his mouth was warm and passionate. The promise behind his ardent kiss was just another painful reminder of what might have been.

"Welcome home, husband," she said stiffly, her voice strained.

When Henry held her he knew something was wrong; he felt the resistance in her body. His eyes narrowing, he looked closely at Rosamund's composed, unsmiling face and saw strain lines about her mouth.

"What's wrong? What's happened?" he demanded, catching her by the arm when she began to walk away. "Tell me."

No more waiting to decide about the best time to broach the subject. Rosamund gave him an agonized look before she pulled free, moving as fast as she could toward the safety of the solar. Henry strode after her.

When he caught up to her, she kept her voice low as she said, "There's something wc have to talk about."

"Can't it wait until I'm bathed and dressed? We did a lot of hard riding today."

"After what I have to say that probably won't matter," she replied sharply.

"Very well."

Henry signaled his men to go about thcir business. Some he sent to oversee the care of the horses, while the rest drifted away to the lower tables and sat waiting for their meal. Grimly Henry followed Rosamund upstairs to the solar, racking his brain for the probable reason behind her strange behavior. Though the firelit solar was usually welcoming with its padded benches and flickering candles, that night the room had all the chill of a tomb. Rosamund's icy mood sapped its warmth. Henry closed the door behind him and waited.

Rosamund went to the darkened windows and stared out into the black night. Below in the bailey lights flickered sporadically and a guard on the battlements carried a torch as he walked the circumference of the walls. Apart from the firefly chinks of light, all she could see was black sky and open moor stretching endlessly to the border; the bleak landscape matched the desolation inside her heart.

"Well, speak your piece. I'm waiting," Henry said impatiently from the doorway.

Rosamund started in surprise as she heard his voice. She had momentarily forgotten he was there, so locked in her own misery had shc bccn. Rosamund heard his boots clumping across the floor as he strode to the window. He did not touch her but she could feel the warmth radiating from his body, so near and yet so very far away. How she longed to be able to turn to him and melt into his arms, to bc held and comforted.

She wanted everything back the way it had been that morning, but she knew nothing would ever be quite the same between them again.

Rosamund swallowed repeatedly, trying to rid herself of the lump in her throat. Finally she turned to Henry, seeing the dark scowl that knitted his brows and tightened his jaw. Henry might not know what she had to reveal, but he was clearly prepared for the worst.

"I had a visitor today while you were gone."

"Yes," he said impatiently, "go on."

"Lady Blanche Pomeroy."

He swore beneath his breath, angered by the discovery. "Damn it. I told her—Rosamund, I'm sorry she upset you."

"Lady Blanche wanted me to meet her children."

Henry was clearly startled by that piece of news. He started before he gathered his wits and stepped forward to take her in his arms. She pulled away.

"*Your* children, Henry."

"Rosamund, I meant to tell you. It just never seemed to be the right time."

"The right time!" she cried, clenching her fists in anger. "And when would that have been, when the lad was old enough to fight? You always said you had no heir. What about him?"

"He's not my heir."

"But he's your son."

He nodded, his mouth set. He sighed before he finally said, "Yes, he is mine."

"Then why isn't he your heir?"

"Because Lady Blanche has a husband. Under the law the lad's his heir, not mine."

"She has a husband!" Rosamund cried in shock. "What kind of man is he to let her whore with you?"

Henry winced at her choice of words. Then he turned away and began to pace the room. "Her husband's imprisoned in some godforsaken hole. Some say France, some the Holy Land. I don't know where he is, nor do I really care. And for your information, Blanche is not my whore. Besides, you already knew about the mistress of Enderly. This can't be that much of a surprise.''

''Not a surprise! She walks in here with two mirror images of you and you think I'm not going to be surprised?''

''I grant you that it's all my fault for not being honest. I never wanted to deceive you. It was done more to keep from hurting you.''

''Why didn't you think about that before you went whoring with her?''

''I've known Blanche for years, long before Walter's capture. He's my tenant at Northcot. We even fought together at one time. Don't you understand, sweet? My life with Blanche happened before I met you.''

''Is that so? Then what of the child she miscarried at Christmas?'' Rosamund said, her voice shaking with anger.

''What child?''

''She says she miscarried your babe.''

''At Christmas? Then she lies! I can count as well as the next man and if she miscarried then, it was no babe of mine.''

''She says you still go to her.''

He looked stonily at her flushed face. ''Who are you going to believe—her or me?''

''Oh, Henry.'' Rosamund groaned at his unfair question, clasping her hands to stop their trembling. ''I want to believe you.''

''It sounds like it when you challenge me with that bitch's lies.''

''Ah, but you see, she already told me you'd lie about it.''

''When I said it was over between Blanche and me, I meant it. Nothing's changed. You're still the woman I want.''

''But you went to her on our wedding night.''

''Dear God, Rosamund, that's over a year ago. Yes, it's true. I did go to Enderly then and I've been there since.''

''I knew it!'' she cried out, her hand flying to her mouth to keep back the torrent of angry words poised on the tip of her tongue.

Henry grabbed her arm and swung her about. "Listen, Rosamund. Hear me out. I've been there two other nights, both during that tormenting time I was trying not to fall in love with you."

"You slept with her then too?" she whispered, tears spilling down her cheeks. "Do you love her?"

"No, I probably never did. Blanche satisfied a need. That's how I knew everything with you was different. You were no easy quenching because I loved you with my heart as well as my body."

How much she wanted to believe him. Rosamund saw his angry face through a blur of tears. Men lied so easily, their protests of innocence often unraveling with the next breath. "How do I know you're telling me the truth?" she whispered, swallowing down tears.

He glared back at her, his fist clenched. "You don't. And by God, if you're fool enough to believe that treacherous bitch instead of me, that's your choice."

"Damn you! Don't call me a fool! Don't twist this to your advantage. You have wronged me! Don't you think I want to believe you? With her husband gone and no land of her own, she has to be supported by someone. Am I also a fool for thinking that someone is you?"

He looked stonily at her before turning his back on her anger. "I won't see her out on the street and of course it's my duty to support the children."

"Something else I don't understand is why you were so desperate to get an heir. All you needed to do was marry her and your heir was ready-made."

"You forgot she can't remarry until her husband's declared dead," he said as he strode over to the fire. Henry plunged a poker in the logs and viciously stoked them until flames leapt up the sooty chimney.

"That's the only reason you didn't marry her instead of me?"

"No, I never considered marrying Blanche. I admit she did broach the subject. But poor Walter refused to cooperate."

"Is that because she didn't bring an army and strategic holdings to the marriage?"

"Well, now you mention it—"

"Dear Lord! You wanted the alliance just as much as Sir Ismay. You wanted the De Gere land," she whispered incredulously, fighting the insane desire to laugh at the sheer stupidity of the lordly dealings.

"Oh, for God's sake, Rosamund, stop it! Can't you find anything else to belabor me with? That's how life works, or have you forgotten? We're fortunate that we have more than our alliance to keep us together. The facts are simply these: Before I knew you I had a mistress who bore me two children." He held up his hand for silence when she started to interrupt. "That's not unusual for a man in my position. In fact, had I no women in my past, men would likely have thought me a lover of boys. You wouldn't have welcomed that vice any more than you do an ex-mistress."

"That she is your ex-mistress is my concern."

"You have my word on it. If Walter fails to surface, we can take the children into our household when they are of an age."

"No! How can you even suggest it?"

"Because, dear wife, that's also not unusual. Even if I don't take the girl, I'll be expected to take the boy."

"As your heir?"

"No, he stays a bastard unless I publicly recognize him as my own. He'll join the household as a soldier, a cleric, whatever suits his talents."

"And what of our children?"

"They'll be my heirs. I'll explain to them who he is and they'll accept the truth. There's no great shame to the matter. Most noble households make similar arrangements."

Rosamund tried to keep her lips from trembling, to fight back the tears that slid onto her cheeks. "I'll never be able to look at him without remembering his mother."

Henry shrugged. "If it annoys you, we'll board him at a neighbor's. Now that's enough of this. I'm sorry you were hurt. And I promise Blanche will hear about this and it'll not happen again. It's my fault for not telling you about the children. I'm truly sorry about that and I apologize.''

She glared at him, not wanting the matter to end there. ''How many more bastards have you sired around the countryside?''

He smiled cynically at her angry question. ''I'm not a child, Rosamund. I've lived at Ravenscrag most of my life. Don't torment yourself with the past. Let it go.''

He brushed his hands together as if disposing of the problem, making her seethe in anger at his easy dismissal. ''Is that all you've got to say?'' she said.

''What do you want me to say? I'm tired. I'm hungry. I've been in the blasted saddle most of the day. Let's go down to sup and have done with this.''

''You may be able to dismiss the subject that easily, but I can't. Have you forgotten I saved your life? Is this the thanks I get?''

He stared at her in amazement, seeing no connection between the two matters.

''And didn't I thank you right gladly for it? Be reasonable, Rosamund. What's done is done. It can't be undone.''

''Believe me, I'd have thought twice about saving your neck had I known about this,'' she said, her anger getting the better of her. ''I could have died trying to free you, but I didn't think about that. All I thought about was saving you. Only then I thought you were true to me, and now, damn you, I find you have children about the countryside and a redhaired bitch who swears you still make love to her because she has many tricks to arouse you.''

''Stop it! We'll have no more of this! Believe Blanche or believe me—it's immaterial. I'll be back on the road tomorrow. So you'll have ample time to come to a decision.''

Henry strode across the room and wrenched open the door. The wooden door crashed shut, rattling in its frame as his heavy tread thumped down the stairs.

Stunned, Rosamund stood before the window, feeling the

cold on her back. He was leaving on the morrow and they'd wasted their last night in anger. Tears trickled down her cheeks. They had just quarreled bitterly over Blanche Pomeroy. Had it been the bitch's intention to thrust a wedge between them? Henry could be telling the truth. She'd never caught him in lies in all the time she'd known him. Yet the cynical side of her character reminded her that up to then there had been little of importance worth lying about.

Rosamund rested her head against the window's icy surface, hoping the cold would help stop the pain throbbing through her temples. She had even surprised herself by her petty reminder that she had saved his life. Deep in her heart she knew that, if there had been a dozen women in his bed, she would still have saved him because she loved him far too much to let him die.

Her mouth quirked in a bitter smile at the thought. Henry may well have had a dozen women in his bed, or even a few hundred, if Sir Ismay was to be believed, yet those casual relationships did not disturb her half as much as his attachment to Blanche Pomeroy. Blanche was not some cottager's nubile daughter who considered it a privilege to share the lord's bed. She was a noblewoman. Blanche lived less than ten miles from Ravenscrag, and worse even than that, she was the mother of his children.

Angrily Rosamund thumped her fist into her open palm. How could Henry even have considered bringing those children into his household? As long as she drew breath she would never allow it. Henry had no need of a bastard son. She would bear him many legitimate sons.

Wounded by that defiant lie, Rosamund crumpled to the rushes where she began to sob quietly. It was likely she would not be given the chance to bear his sons. She could have destroyed his love for her. Henry could even return to his old habits. Surely she had not sacrificed him to appease her own jealousy. For a little while longer she sobbed; then she finally grew angry with her own weakness. Henry almost had her believing their quarrel was her fault. It was he who had slept with Blanche and fathered her children. He might even still be seeing the woman and lying about it. Rosamund had no fault in the matter.

Rosamund stood and shook out her crumpled skirts. Defiantly she straightened her shoulders, marched to the chest, and took out her embroidery. She shared no blame in the matter; so Henry must be the one to make amends. She would not go crawling to him, begging for his attention. Let him come to her. After he had supped and had time to measure his guilt, perhaps he would come up to the solar and apologize. She knew that, if he swore he loved her and vowed he would not go to Blanche again, she would forgive him.

Rosamund sewed a long time while the fire burned low and the candles guttered. Henry did not come. When the hour had grown late and the sounds from the great hall quieted, she put away her embroidery. Rosamund looked down into the great hall, where she could see men sleeping on pallets on the floor. No one stirred, nor was there any sign of Henry. The fire was blazing high; a tree trunk had been thrown there to keep it through the night. The remains of a meal were still on the high table, possibly left there at Henry's request in case she was hungry. Had he waited there for her to join him as isolated in his pride as she had been in hers?

Her eyes filled with tears at the thought. She took a torch to light her way to bed. Did he wait for her in their chamber? She hurried, eager to see him because she had decided to forgive him. Anything would be better than enduring such terrible isolation.

The tower room was empty. The fire had already been banked for the night and a new candle flickered on the chest. Rosamund's heart thumped sickeningly as she wondered where Henry was. In the castle were many chambers and he could be in any one of them. But she would not go in search of him, because when she found him he might not be alone. In the castle there were many willing women. Henry would have no need of Blanche to quench his lust.

Loneliness and jealousy combined to rob Rosamund of

sleep, as she waited, hoping he would finally come to bed. The cocks had begun to crow, heralding the gray dawn, before she finally lapsed into a fitful sleep, still alone in her tower room.

Chapter Eleven

Rain, sleet, snow, and sun—in the days following Henry's departure the weather ran the gamut. As Rosamund looked at the changing countryside beyond her window she prayed Henry would return soon. The day he left she had not said good-bye, and she bitterly regretted the stubborn act. She had watched his departure from that room, keeping well back from the window so he would not see her. And he had looked for her. That memory above all others tore at her heart. Henry had paused below the window astride Diablo, and he had waited before finally riding on. That scene would be forever etched in her brain. If he did not come back she would never be able to erase her feeling of guilt about that morning. Because of Blanche Pomeroy she had hardened her heart until it had frozen into a chunk of ice.

There had been no word from Henry all week. Rosamund's only consolation was in knowing he was not riding into battle. Yet when a country was at war there was always a threat of battle. She promised herself that, if her prayers were answered and he came back to her, she would welcome him home with open arms. Life was much too short for bitterness.

Without success Rosamund searched in the chest beside the bed for a new candle. She was not surprised. Since Henry had been gone, there had been an unsettling change in the servants attitude toward her. The soldiers under Chrysty Dane had not changed; besides she only knew those few who had been patients in the castle infirmary. It was the castle servants with whom she came in daily contact who showed a lack of respect. Supplies were not replenished and chores were not finished on time. Rosamund had caught both men and women idling away their time gossiping. Some of the gossip was wounding because the servants openly discussed Henry and Blanche or Henry and a dozen other women. Rosamund suspected many accidentally overheard whisperings were not so accidental. Though she could not prove it, she felt Hoke was at the bottom of the servants' changed attitude. Had sympathies toward Lady Blanche made Hoke Rosamund's enemy?

If only Thurgood were well enough to reclaim his place as steward, Rosamund was sure the situation would change. The day before, when she had upbraided a couple of maids for slovenliness, the women had dared walk away before she had finished speaking to them. Foreigner, outsider, they called her, and she guessed there were less polite names used behind her back.

That morning Rosamund dressed herself. Margery had been temporarily assigned to other duties. The woman Hoke sent in Margery's stead was old, and Rosamund often found her snoring in the dressing room. Rosamund smiled grimly as she secured her braided hair beneath a plain band. Hoke thought he was making her life difficult by denying her a maid. Little did he know that the loss of her body servant was a poor way to punish her.

Rosamund decided to visit Thurgood and ask for his help. When she reached the infirmary and saw the castle steward pale as the pillow on his bed, she was filled with dismay. How gaunt and aged he looked; weight had dropped off him since his illness.

"Lady Rosamund, how kind of you to visit me," Thurgood said, brushing back his sparse locks as he politely touched his brow.

"Are you feeling better today?" she asked, sitting beside his bed.

"No worse," he said with a tight smile. "Have you news of Lord Henry?"

She shook her head, and Thurgood said, "Soon then. He's

only gathering men. Take heart, my lady. We've had no word of battles.''

"That's true. No, Thurgood, I came to see you on another matter. I very much need your help.''

"You have as much help as a sick man can give.''

"Is Hoke an ally of Lady Blanche?'' Thurgood's shocked expression made her smile. "Nay, I already know about her. You can speak freely.''

"He's not merely an ally, lady; he's her relative. Why?''

That news was definitely not good. Rosamund swallowed uneasily as another piece of the puzzle dropped in place.

"I think he's turned the staff against me. They've been rude and slovenly. No, don't upset yourself. I tell you this only so you can help me. I ask no more of you than that.''

Thurgood had begun to rise, annoyed by her report; he fell back groaning and clutching his stomach, the effort bringing beads of sweat to his brow.

"That surprises me. He's never been a popular man,'' Thurgood said. "Unless—how much do you know about Lady Blanche?''

"Enough.''

Thurgood glanced warily about the empty room before lowering his voice and saying in hushed tones, "They say she's a witch.''

A shiver of fear crept along Rosamund's spine. "I've heard such whispers.''

"They're far more than whispers, lady. It's said she can change into a cat!''

Rosamund gasped, her eyes widening at the tale. Fear quickly replaced her amazement and she wondered if that was why she had likened Blanche to a cat. A moment later she dismissed the thought. That was superstition. Such things couldn't really happen. The Sisters at Thorpe always had chastised her for believing such nonsense.

"That talent doesn't threaten me,'' Rosamund said, trying to make light of the subject. "What else does she do?''

"Mixes potions and charms. Some of the castle wenches

252

regularly buy love potions from her. Maybe Hoke's using that to bribe the maids into cooperating. Does Lord Henry know?''

"It's only happened since he left.'' Rosamund did not mention Blanche's visit, nor her quarrel with Henry, though she suspected the steward had already been informed about both.

"Take care, Lady Rosamund. She has much power. And though Lord Henry says the charge of witchcraft is nonsense, I'm not so sure. Maybe you should visit your father while your lord's away. You'd feel safer there.''

That suggestion had no appeal since Rosamund was even more of a stranger at Sir Ismay's castle than at Ravenscrag. She was not even sure where Langley Hutton was, but of course, Thurgood was not to know that.

"No, I'll stay here. How else am I to know that Lord Henry's well.''

"Then get me paper and pen. I'll help you by telling the household I'm at the point of recovery. That'll wake them up.''

Rosamund did as she was bidden, though she had not as much faith in the idea as Thurgood. When the note was written and sanded, he said he would send it with one of Father John's clerks to make the announcement more official.

As soon as the note was read to the assembled servants, Rosamund saw an immediate change in their behavior. They were no longer openly insolent, and they took care that she had fresh candles and enough wood to keep her fire burning.

Rosamund was delighted with the outcome; she hoped the improvement would continue. She was in the solar playing with Dimples when Hoke announced the arrival of a guest. Rosamund had such an intense feeling of deja vu they she insisted on knowing the guest's identity before granting admittance.

"It's young Master Ireton, my lady.''

At first Rosamund wondered who young Master Ireton could be until she realized it had to be Pip. She had heard he was up and about after recovering from his injury, though he still suffered headaches and memory loss.

Rosamund was pleased to see her young page again. She swept him into her arms in greeting, making Pip blush with pleasure. Three servants accompanied him and they were sent to wait on the stairs in case he should need them.

Once the greetings were over, Rosamund found Pip unduly serious, a change she put down to his recent misfortune. When she had visited him after her return from York, Pip had regained consciousness and mercifully remembered little about the attack. She decided not to even mention the subject during his present visit.

When Pip had finished his refreshments, he moved restlessly to the window, where he stood surveying the empty moor. "When's Lord Henry expected back?"

"I don't know," Rosamund said, wondering at his abrupt question.

"Pray God it's soon," he muttered as he came back to the hearth. "My father and his men are riding with him. More's the pity."

"What do you mean? Are the Yorkists coming this way?"

"Nay, they're still south of here."

"Then why should we be concerned? We're virtually alone for miles since the neighbors have gone with Lord Henry."

"Not all of them." Pip leaned forward and lowered his voice. "My uncle plans to attack now that the garrison's weak. He also knows the bridge has been left down lately."

Rosamund's heart began an uneasy thud, and her stomach clenched as she considered their dangerous position. "Who is your uncle?"

"John of Thurlston."

"Didn't he go with Henry? I remember Henry mentioning him."

"Nay, he begged off by saying he needed more time to rally his men. I think it's only the changeable weather that's kept him away this long. Take care. He's old and treacherous and he won't hesitate to kill any who stand in his way."

They were leaning close like conspirators. Their voices were hushed lest the waiting servants should overhear their conversation.

"How do you know all this?" Rosamund asked.

"I'm staying with him. He let it slip when he was deep in his cups. I've known these past two days, but they wouldn't let me take to the saddle. 'Tis only because it's sunny today I was able to come. Lady Rosamund, you must get word to Lord Henry. Tell him of your danger and ask him to come home."

"How? I don't know where he is."

"Truly?" Pip asked, his face blanching in shock.

"Truly. I know only that he's riding somewhere about the countryside. We've but a handful of able-bodied men. The rest went with their lord."

"Let's pray my uncle will reconsider. It's a fool plan for an old man. There's no way he can stand against Lord Henry's troops. Though once he makes up his mind, it's hard to change it. I'll have to leave. I didn't tell anyone I was riding this far. It'll be a hard ride to get back without causing suspicion. Take care, Lady Rosamund."

Their good-byes were exchanged and Pip rode away from the castle, leaving Rosamund to her fate. Within the hour further alarming news came from the infirmary. Thurgood was running a high fever. He had seemed to be improving until the midday meal.

Though the sun shone, it gave little warmth as Rosamund hurried across the bailey to the forbidding square keep, where the captain of the guard had his quarters. Uneasily she noticed the drawbridge was still down with men working on the mechanism. So that was why Chrysty Dane had left them dangerously undefended. It seemed he had been given little choice. At the moment any enemy could ride unchallenged into the heart of Ravenscrag Castle. She had intended to ask about the bridge, but she had felt so dispirited since Henry's abrupt departure that she had not actually done so.

The young second-in-command saw Rosamund crossing the bailey and met her at the door. Rosamund was ushered to a chair while he stood, listening intently to what she had to say. Though he appeared undisturbed by the news, Rosamund knew that was not so. A pulse jumped in his right jaw just below the knife scar that marked his young face.

"How many men has he?" Chrysty Dane asked.

"I don't know. I didn't think to ask," Rosamund said.

"Have you told Hoke?"

She shook her head. "What about the drawbridge? Is it broken?"

"I've men reworking the winch and chain. I hope they'll have it finished before dark. I'll send extra men to help them."

Chrysty Dane immediately took care of that task, leaving Rosamund alone in the spartan guardroom, trying to think of a solution to their dilemma. When he returned, Chrysty's fair face bore a grin of relief.

"They say it'll be finished in a couple of hours, lady, so at least that worry's out of the way."

Rosamund realized Chrysty Dane had summoned Hoke when the steward joined them a few minutes later. She tried to hide her dislike of the man when he laughed and ridiculed her startling news.

"Now where did you hear such a preposterous story? Sir John of Thurlston—really, my lady, he's been Lord Henry's ally for many years."

"Pip Ireton told me."

"Ah, well, then, that explains it. Everyone knows the lad's not been right in the head since his accident. I shouldn't worry about it. You go back to your embroidery, Lady Rosamund, and leave such matters to us men." Then he winked broadly at Chrysty, who smiled and nodded in agreement.

Inwardly seething, Rosamund stood, drawing herself up to her full height. "Let's hope, if our danger proves to be real, you men can quickly solve the problem." She nodded curtly to them both and stalked from the keep.

How dare they treat her like a silly child! Chrysty had seemed sensible enough until Hoke appeared. She must hope the second-in-command had merely been appeasing the steward by agreeing with him. Thurgood would have taken her news far more seriously, but Thurgood tossed and turned on his bed, raging with fever. The castle's defense was the farthest thought from the poor man's mind.

That night, Rosamund lay sleepless in her bed, straining to hear the sounds of an approaching enemy force. Rosamund prayed for Henry's swift return with even more fervor than usual. He was needed to defend the castle, not merely to ease the ache in her heart.

The next day was clear and sunny. Two sunny days in a row were a godsend at that time of year. It might also prove to be a godsend for John of Thurlston's troops. At least the bridge was drawn up; Rosamund had heard them winching it the evening before. Fortunately Chrysty Dane had taken her news seriously enough for that. Had it been left up to Hoke, the men would have continued to repair their main defense at the same leisurely pace, assuming, with all their neighbors gone and the enemy far to the south, they had no fear of attack.

Hoke's condescending attitude annoyed Rosamund afresh that morning when she tried to form an accurate picture of their capabilities should they be attacked. There was little she could do to change him; so she continued to pray for Thurgood's recovery and Henry's swift return.

It was early in the day, soon after full sunup, when a lookout on the battlements sounded an alert. With a sinking heart, Rosamund raced around the winding stairs to see what had caused the alarm. To her horror she saw stretching far to the north a dark ribbon of men winding about the hilly terrain. Could her prayers have been answered? Instead of an enemy, the approaching men could be their own. She watched as they came closer, banners waving, and her heart sank more as she saw not the familiar raven, but a silver portcullis against a pine-dark ground. Her palms grew sweaty as she acknowledged the warning she had received had been no fantasy of an addled mind: Sir John of Thurlston led an army in full battle array.

As the force approached the castle, showing its strength as it grew closer, a hasty call to arms was sounded. Grim faced,

Chrysty Dane met her at the door to the tower.

"Now are you convinced?" she asked him sharply.

"I believed you yesterday, lady," he replied gruffly, " 'Tis why I had the bridge put up."

She wondered aloud what they could do to protect themselves from the impressive force beyond the walls.

"As far as I can tell they have no siege equipment. So we could just stay put and wait them out. On the other hand, he has many archers."

"Archers? What difference will that make?" Rosamund said.

"I've so few men, he can pick them off at his leisure, unless we abandon the battlements and stay below."

"Then do that. It's not cowardly, just good sense."

He glared at her, his manhood affronted by the suggestion. "I'll not cower below like some green lad. I'm in charge of these soldiers and we intend to fight. Besides," he added gloomily, "he has scaling ladders, by the look of it. If we leave the battlements unmanned, he can just walk in."

Rosamund turned pale at the dismal news. "How many men do we have?"

"Fifteen able-bodied, another five walking wounded."

"Is that all? What about the servants?"

Chrysty laughed scornfully at her suggestion. "They're all cowards through and through. You'd never get them up on the battlements in the first place."

Rosamund was still trying to think of a plan when she heard a challenge bellowed from outside the castle walls. Then an arrow came sailing over the wall and everyone scattered to avoid its lethal force. The arrow quivered harmlessly in the wooden door of the blacksmith's forge. A paper was attached to the shaft.

Chrysty Dane wrenched the arrow out of the wood and retrieved the note. For a couple of minutes he labored over the message, too proud to send for one of Father John's clerks to read it to him.

"He says we must surrender. They have many archers and

he will pick us off. If we surrender, Sir John says he won't kill us."

"How kind of him," Rosamund said, heading toward the tower stairs.

"Nay, lady, come back. Don't go up there. It's too dangerous."

But Rosamund did not heed him. She wrapped her cloak about her body as she hurried up the twisting stairs, resentful anger burning inside. How dared he threaten them? He had pretended to be Henry's friend. She had entertained him in their own hall, and he was such a coward he was trying to take advantage of her since her husband was away. He had betrayed them by using Henry's leniency to gather an army for his own purpose instead of in support of the king.

Though the sun shone brightly, the wind up on the battlements was cold. Rosamund pulled her cloak as tight as she could about her neck before she strode to the edge of the parapit, much to the distress of the soldiers kneeling there, who begged her to have a care for her safety.

Rosamund looked down at the troops gathered below, deployed in a wide arc on the flat plain facing the castle. To the south, east, and west, the ground was craggy. The moated approach from the moor was the only practical choice for an enemy attack. Rosamund quickly singled out the corpulent, barrel-chested Sir John. His long gray locks fluttered beneath his old-fashioned conical cap and his wildly curling mustache combined to make him look like a savage border raider.

"John of Thurlston," Rosamund shouted, her voice floating over the battlements.

He looked up and a smile crossed his face when he saw her. Motioning to a couple of men to accompany him, he rode forward a few paces and stopped. "Do you want to surrender, my lady?"

"No, I want to tell you to beware. Lord Henry's due back . . . maybe today before sundown. So you'd best take your men and go home while you're still able."

Though he appeared not to be taking her seriously, a change

Patricia Phillips

of expression flitted briefly across his thick features at her words. "Hardly, lady. No messenger has reached the castle today. We saw to that."

Rosamund had not known they would be guarding the road. Thinking quickly, she bluffed her way along. "How do you know? We haven't told all our secrets. You have no idea how many secret ways there are into the castle."

John of Thurlston sat astride his dappled gray considering her words while he shielded his eyes from the sun with a gauntleted hand. Squinting up at her, he could not tell if she stood alone. "You're spinning a yarn," he shouted back at last.

"Believe what you want. Time will tell."

"Aye, it will that, all right." Chuckling, he turned his horse's head around and headed back to his troops.

Desperately Rosamund searched her mind for some ammunition to use against him. There was little she knew about John of Thurlston, except that he was old and corpulent and sometimes he had difficulty walking because of an old leg wound. He was also short-tempered and shortsighted—shortsighted! There was the chance he could not see how many guards manned the battlements, especially with the sun glinting off their armor and causing great flashes to dazzle the eyes. She knew that was so because she had seen many men holding their hands to their brows to shield their eyes from the glare.

To her alarm Rosamund saw her enemies were moving forward a huge shield on wheels. Unfamiliar with war paraphernalia, she did not know what the flat woven screen was used for until someone told her.

"That's to protect their archers, lady," a nearby soldier said. Rubbing his grizzled chin, the man added, "Seems like he has us outfoxed."

"Have we no archers?"

The man shrugged. "Aye, a few."

Chrysty Dane also shrugged at the same question. What was the matter with them? Why did they not give her any credit for thinking?

"Why can't we use our own archers against his?"

Chrysty Dane shook his head. "We've only a handful and they're too far out of range."

"Then why are they getting ready to shoot at us?"

"Because they'll be protected, lady, they can move much closer," he said in exasperation.

Men had taken up position behind the shield as Rosamund and the others spoke, and a sudden volley of arrows sailed over the walls, met by strangled cries from the battlements as men were hit.

"We can't just sit here and let them pick us off. What do you usually do to combat a shield?" Rosamund said.

"Fire the framework. 'Tis only made from woven reeds and branches."

"Then do it!"

"Aye, lady, I'll tell them." Chrysty Dane grinned at her suggestion, as if he had been waiting for word from a higher authority. Inwardly Rosamund quailed. He was the man she trusted to defend them. Obviously he was not used to taking full command and he seemed unable to think what to do.

A flaming arrow was duly dispatched. The first one fell short, as did the second. Rosamund began to despair of them ever reaching their target. Their best archer was finally brought onto the battlements. The man had a crippled leg and other wounds from Wakefield Green, making it difficult for him to come up the twisting stairs. When he finally arrived on the battlements, he took up his position. An arrow dipped in pitch was set alight and it sailed into the air. A cheer went up as the arrow hit its mark.

Rosamund was disappointed when the enemy quickly put out the fire. But the second and third arrows were not as quickly doused. Soon the wicker frame blazed and a great hole appeared in its center, forcing the archers to run to safety out of range of the defenders' bows.

Though round one had been decided to their advantage, Rosamund was dismayed to find four men were wounded and two were already dead. At that rate Sir John would capture the castle before dark. Rosamund tried to think what was best to do because she understood they could not hold out all night with so few men. There were low places in the moat and it was only a matter of time before the defense would be breached. Chrysty told her once their enemies crossed the moat under cover of darkness they would use their scaling ladders to enter the castle.

How she longed to see the flapping banners of the Ravenscrag men coming to their rescue over the horizon, but the moor stayed bleak and empty. Rosamund formulated a plan, aware it was not brilliant, but it was the best they had. She called both Chrysty Dane and Hoke to listen to her idea, glaring down the steward as he started to protest, daring him to challenge her a second time. He was decidedly green around the gills when he thought of Ravenscrag falling into enemy hands while under his control. Such a shameful event could not easily be explained to his lord.

"If we hurry, we can take advantage of the sun. Since they can't know how many men we have, they'll guess from the glinting armor and weapons. Won't they assume the soldiers are protecting themselves behind the stonework?"

The men agreed, frowning and wondering what preposterous suggestion she was going to make.

"Bring all the menservants onto the battlements. Arm them with pots and kettles, the shinier the better. Are there extra weapons in the guardroom?"

"Aye, lady, but I've no men trained to use them. Those yokels don't know the right end of a—"

"They won't have to. This is a terrible gamble and we might lose. I'm the first to admit that, but we can at least try. Distribute weapons. Give them anything shiny that will catch the sun and have them make noise. Put our archers behind the arrow slits. Do we have arrows?"

"Some, but not nearly enough to take that many out."

"Then send a lad to gather all the spent arrows and retrieve them. I know this might not work, but neither of you has a better idea. I agree we could stay put and do nothing, but we

262

might not be able to hold out till Lord Henry returns. At this rate our men will be dead in a couple of days, though I doubt Sir John is willing to invest that much time in conquering a skeleton force. I'll be damned if I'll give away Henry's birthright without a fight.''

The men gave her their grudging admiration and went to do her bidding without further argument. At first the menservants would not cooperate. Then Rosamund told them it was their only chance to live; otherwise, if Sir John stormed the castle, most of them would die. Rosamund did not even feel one pang of guilt for what most likely was a lie. She didn't think even old John of Thurlston would murder pot boys and scullions. Finally, being given little choice, they reluctantly agreed. The men's faces brightened when she told them they need not expose themselves to danger, but were merely to get behind the fortifications wearing whatever armor and carrying whatever weapons they were given. They were also told to bring pots, kitchen tools, and anything else that would shine or sound like armaments to the invaders.

It was a motley assortment swarming the battlements. Arrows flew sporadically over the walls as Sir John's archers tested their range. They had a makeshift cover of sorts, not as good as the first, but they were rapidly finding their mark.

Rosamund found Chrysty Dane strangely buoyed by the sight of the rabble army assembled to defend Ravenscrag. He puffed out his chest as he strode about, ordering the men to their posts. Some of the pot lads also enjoyed the excitement, strutting around proudly in their borrowed armor and brandishing weapons they had not the slightest idea how to use. All the extra bows were distributed and the men were shown the proper stance and grouped at the ready around a skilled archer, who took aim through the arrow slit. There were only five master archers, though the castle fletcher and his lad also knew how to use bows.

Within the hour Sir John rode forward again seeking their surrender. He was well within bow range but he also carried a white cloth at the end of a spear, calling a truce while they discussed strategy.

Rosamund was aware of the chivalric code among soldiers but she simmered in anger at the thought that they could have picked him off easily by ignoring the rules. The enemy could also have killed her when she had first gone on to the battlements, but they had held their fire. She was grudgingly forced to admit chivalric honor was not such a bad thing after all.

"Are you surrendering to us?" she shouted boldly as she stood on the battlements unafraid, or seemingly so, while she prayed the enemy would likewise observe the truce. The wind blew her chestnut hair wildly about her shoulders, tugged at her clothes, and blew her voice toward the assembled troops.

"Surrender? Nay, lass, I come to to try to persuade thee to surrender."

"Never!"

"Tha knows tha can't defend Ravenscrag," he shouted back, lapsing into a thick Yorkshire accent as his temper frayed, "with a handful of lads with wet breeches being led by thee. Admit it."

"Only a handful? You haven't looked closely, Sir John. Our battlements fairly bristle with troops."

Ignoring the uneasy swirling in her stomach, Rosamund signaled to the motley force to make itself known. The sun shone off a dazzling array of gleaming steel and polished brass. There were flashes of fire all around her, winking off scythes and horse trappings. She knew their enemy took note because many of them shielded their eyes against the dazzle.

Chrysty Dane had ordered all and sundry to the battlements dragging pots and pans. The ensuing clanking sounded like the preparations of a large army. Rosamund knew the wind must have carried the sounds to those waiting below. She hoped Sir John was convinced by her trickery. She had no other plan up her sleeve.

They waited while Sir John conferred with his men. Rosamund huddled in her cloak, refusing to leave the battlements.

Chrysty Dane stood beside her and it was he who faced the enemy when Sir John made his next and final foray to seek their surrender.

"You've had enough time. This is your last chance."

"You already have my answer," Rosamund said.

"What about your captain? Or have you taken command, lass?" Sir John scoffed, squinting up at the battlements, making out her fluttering hair.

"Here I am. What do you want with me, Sir John?" Chrysty Dane called back, moving into plain sight in an opening in the stonework. When he spoke, he consciously deepened his voice and his swaggering bravado gave him an air of supreme confidence.

"Where've you been hidin' all day, lad, behind a woman's skirts?" Sir John shouted, his taunt bringing a guffaw of laughter from his men.

"Outfitting my men to defend the castle. Surely you heard them. Or are you deaf as well as blind?"

Rosamund wondered at the wisdom of that taunt, but it was already made.

Sir John glowered at them. "So you're prepared to fight then?"

"For as long as you can take it before you limp home to Thurlston with your tail between your legs," Chrysty said.

Not waiting to hear more, Sir John wheeled about and galloped back to his men. No sooner was he safely out of range than a volley of arrows sailed over the battlements.

The Ravenscrag men crouched low, hugging the walls, and their casualties were minimal. During an ensuing lull, a lad collected all the spent arrows, and they were soon sailing back toward the enemy. Over time their attackers had moved closer and many were in striking distance. The defenders were rewarded by the surprised cries of wounded men as the enemy was temporarily sent into disarray. Repeated volleys followed, their master archers firing off arrows as quickly as possible to give the impression that more men were shooting. It was not enough.

"If that's the worst thee can do, tha'd best pack up and throw out the key," Sir John said scornfully.

"Lady, it won't work," Chrysty Dane told Rosamund a few minutes later. "We must aim for him."

"No, give him a little more time to reconsider," she said, trying to delay the inevitable. Sir John had been Henry's ally over the years.

"Then at least let me take down his horse."

That idea was even less appealing. Rosamund fought against what she came to realize was the most logical move.

"They have three leaders beside Sir John, likely tenants of his. Now we've stopped shooting maybe they think we're spent. Look. They're even moving forward to make it easier." Chrysty ducked, hugging the stone wall as an incoming hail of arrows descended. Some men were hit, and cries of pain followed the barrage. Again the lad gathered the enemy arrows.

"Give me permission to pick off their leaders," Chrysty said.

Rosamund reluctantly agreed. It was a daring plan and they did not know if their archers had the skill to follow through. Though it pained them not to retaliate since they had fresh ammunition, the men were told to hold their fire and let the enemy move closer. Four of the archers had been given targets and told to loose their arrows only on command.

The enemy spread over the flat plain, moving closer. The best archer in Ravenscrag Castle had Sir John for his target, and at Rosamund's request, he was told to wound the old man and not kill him. When the signal finally came, the arrows were let fly. Cries and screams of pain greeted the barrage, and the archers continued shooting until their quivers were empty. One of the captains had fallen from his horse. Another slumped wounded in the saddle. A third had his beast shot out from under him. Sir John was pinned to his pain-crazed mount by an arrow through the thigh, and he bellowed for his men to stop the bolting horse.

The enemy archers quickly replied with volleys of their

own. Again these arrows sped back to them, until the enemy archers finally stopped firing, tired of being wounded by their own arrows.

The sky had clouded over and Rosamund knew she and her men had lost their advantage. The sun no longer struck fire from the array of metal on the battlements. The men clanked and rattled to make up for their loss, but the noise was not nearly as effective.

Sir John's troops had drawn back out of range. To Rosamund's delight she noticed an entire section of the arc break away and ride out onto the moor, going back the way they had come. Some of Sir John's allies had deserted.

The clouds continued to blacken; soon raindrops splashed and plopped against the pots and pans with a rhythmic sound. Faced with the coming deluge to add to their troubles, their enemies finally withdrew some distance off, debating among themselves whether to continue the attack.

Rosamund was cold, tired, and hungry, but she stayed on the battlements with the others. There were even some wenches standing cloaked and helmeted alongside their men. Though Rosamund had never loved them, she began to feel a grudging admiration for her husband's retainers, who had rallied magnificently in their time of need.

The rain came down harder. The sky was black with cloud and the rising wind buffeted their clothing, making it hard to stay covered against the onslaught. It was so cold Rosamund began to shiver and she crouched in the doorway to the tower, trying to stay dry.

A cheer came from the men on the wall and she roused herself to investigate. To her relief, Rosamund saw their enemies had turned tail. They were riding onto the moor with their heads down against the driving rain. Below the walls, enemy soldiers were gathering the dead and wounded, and the men inside Ravenscrag Castle allowed them to work without hindrance. With their fallen comrades slung across their saddlebows, the men of Thurlston rode hard after their leader.

It was over! Rosamund could hardly believe they had won.

She began to shake, partially from cold, partially from nervous exhaustion. Chrysty Dane insisted she go indoors to the fire.

Later that evening, Rosamund wore her festival gown and sat at the high table, though when Henry was away she usually ate in her room. She invited Chrysty Dane and his archers to sup with her. The men were greatly honored by her generosity, though they were ill at ease, unused to the formality of the lord's table. Their meal was no feast, merely bread, haunches of meat, and bowls of soup washed down with ale. Yet to all who ate that night in the great hall, the victory meal was as sumptuous as any banquet.

All the castle retainers were gathered in the dark, hammer-beamed hall. Rain drummed on the roof and swooshed down the wide chimney, sizzling on the logs. For the first time since she had entered the castle, Rosamund actually felt as if she belonged. When she came into the hall she was met with a resounding cheer, and everywhere she looked she saw approving smiles. Even Hoke grudgingly thanked her for her brave role in saving Ravenscrag.

Many toasts were drunk to her and Rosamund stood at the table, mingled tears of fatigue and happiness filling her eyes. She had defied their enemy for Henry, not for these men and women who had shown her little affection. But in doing so, she had earned their admiration. The cheers were long and hard. Rosamund's waiting tears spilled down her cheeks, so moved was she by their great show of affection. If only Henry were there to share the moment. But she knew had he been there, the moment would not have taken place. The victory was something she had planned alone. It had not been calculated to please him, yet she hoped when he learned of her role in saving his beloved Ravenscrag he would be pleased.

Chapter Twelve

Henry's letter arrived on a gray day when the sky was heavy with snow. Rosamund's heart pounded with excitement as she read and reread his loving words. He wrote that he was staying at Burnham Manor in Cheshire and longed to have her at his side. Again he begged her forgiveness for causing her heartache, and he promised he would try to make it up to her when next they met.

An insane idea gripped her as she sat beside a roaring fire, listening to sleet tinkling against the window. If it wasn't winter she would have traveled to Cheshire. But why let a little cold weather stop her? One of their soldiers was a Cheshireman and he could surely take her there. Rosamund's longing for her lover's arms was so deep that she decided not to let the prospect of winter weather discourage her. As long as the roads were passable, she could endure the cold. It was a reckless proposal, but after her recent success at defending Ravenscrag Castle, Rosamund was feeling reckless.

After delivering a cautionary warning about the dangers of her proposed journey, the Cheshire soldier finally agreed to lead the party to Burnham. He warned her there would be much hard riding ahead, and even though they would head south, where the weather was less severe, he could not guarantee a clear passage.

Moving as if in a dream, Rosamund hurriedly made arrangements for her journey. Dressed in her warmest clothes, she set out at first light the following day, accompanied by Margery, the maid, and four men-at-arms. Overnight the snow-banked clouds had miraculously drifted north, leaving the roads damp but clear for travel.

As if charmed, the first three days continued dry and the traveling party made excellent time. Their small group of six encountered no resistance. Though the soldiers had been apprehensive about meeting the Yorkist army, they saw no sign of enemy soldiers. Fortunately their small party was of little interest to the few groups of armed men they met along the way, and they traveled toward Burnham with rising spirits.

They had already entered Lancashire before the rain began. January was almost at an end. Country people called the following month Filldyke because of its heavy rains. Rosamund assumed the notoriously wet month must be off to an early start that year.

The farther south they went, the heavier the rain became. Finally when the driving rain changed to squalls of sleet, Rosamund decided to put up for the night at an inn on the Macclesfield Road. There had been increased activity on the roads during the past couple of days, and her escort reported both sides were building up their forces for a coming battle. That news was alarming. Rosamund hoped they would not be caught in the middle of a fight. She also wondered whether, when they eventually reached Burnham, Henry would still be there. Nothing was sure two days in a row.

Though Rosamund hated to sup in so public a place, Margery and she ate their meal in the inn's common room beside the roaring fire, where they were able to dry their clothes. They were so wet that great clouds of steam rose from their clothing. When Rosamund took off her riding boots, water poured from them. How she would have loved a warm scented bath and the comfort of clean sheets and a feather bed. That her straw pallet was not alive with fleas was the most she could hope for at the Drover's Rest.

They were not far from Burnham Manor and she longed to see Henry. How many days would it be until she saw him? Just the thought of kissing and holding him set her heart racing. She carried his letter inside her bodice in an oilskin pouch to keep it dry. It was tattered from so much folding and un-folding and water spotted from her tears. How could she have let her jealousy of Blanche make her shut her heart to him?

"My lady," a man's voice said at her elbow.

Shaking herself out of a doze induced by the warm fire and hot food, Rosamund looked up to see who was speaking to her. A stranger in a dark cloak, his hood pulled low on his brow, stood beside her.

"Yes?" she said.

"Lady Rosamund of Ravenscrag?" he asked politely.

"Yes, I am she." Rosamund's heart began to thump un-easily as she wondered how the stranger had known her iden-tity and what he wanted with her.

"They said I'd find you beside the hearth. Terrible weather for traveling, it is an' all. I'm sorry to have to tell you, but one of your men's hurt in the stables and we need you."

Alarmed by the news, Rosamund struggled wearily to her feet. Her legs ached and she felt unsteady. Margery was asleep, resting her head against the settle; so Rosamund did not wake her.

The man led Rosamund through the crowded common room toward the back of the inn, conversing easily with servants they met along the way. The rain had stopped but a gusty cold wind swept inside when the man politely held open the door for her.

In the innyard there were many horses and wagons. The stables lay to the right and the man pointed that way, stopping first to pick up a lantern he had left at the door. Uneasily Rosamund wondered which of her soldiers had been injured. Whichever man it was, she hoped his injury was not serious enough to delay them. She feared that the injured man might be Will, her guide. She doubted the other men would be able to follow the crude map he had drawn for the journey.

"What happened to him?" she asked the stranger, quick-ening her pace to keep up as he strode ahead, weaving between loaded wagons. She hurried after him, following the bobbing lantern light.

"Over here, lady, lying in the straw," the man said, his voice muffled.

Uneasily Rosamund stepped into the dark stable. The man set the lantern down on the flagged floor, where it cast a dim yellow circle of light. In a shadowed stall nearby she could see a dark shape lying in the straw, but she could not tell who it was. She moved forward and knelt down.

Leaning over the man, she peered through the gloom as she asked, "Will, is that you?"

Then her words changed to a scream, quickly muffled, as the man came up out of the straw and grabbed her.

"Nay, lass, it's not Will," Steven said, holding Rosamund down in the straw.

Rosamund's eyes were wide with sheer panic. She saw several of Steven's men standing around the stable. How could she have been such a fool? Too late, she knew she had been tricked. Yet how could Steven be there? How could he have known where to find her?

She was not given any further chance to raise the alarm. A gag was tied roughly around her mouth. Steven sat up, brushing straw off her damp cloak.

"We're together at last. I was beginning to give up hope, but me prayers was answered," he said with uncharacteristic piety.

Rosamund grunted, frantically trying to cry out for help. She hit out at Steven when he tried to pull her to her feet, but he only smiled the same besotted smile she had seen in the forest, the smile that made her blood run cold. It was as if he was deaf and blind to her protests, living in some make-believe world of his own making.

"Bet you're wondering how I knowed where you was. Love, I've known where you was every day since you left York. I couldn't have asked for better luck. I've seen you on the road. I knowed which inn you was staying at. But all that doesn't matter now. All that matters is that we're together."

Steven scrambled up and towered over her, his solid bulk blocking the light. "We're bound farther south; so I'm taking you with me. You won't get the chance to give me the slip this time.''

Rosamund was roughly bundled in a blanket before being hoisted aboard a wagon. Within an hour they were pulling out of the innyard into the cold January night. Sleet pelted the wagon's canvas top as the men huddled together, trying to get shelter from the elements.

Rosamund's world became a chill, dark cavern wedged between sacks of grain. Where she was bound, she did not know. The nightmare had begun again.

Henry slumped in the saddle, his eyes drifting closed until he forcefully jerked himself awake. Damn, he was tired. They had been riding through much of the night, trying to connect with the main body of Lancastrian troops. He had word Queen Margaret's forces were heading south, cutting a 30-mile-wide swath of destruction in their wake. The spoils of war were the only payment the wild Scots she had enlisted could hope to get. Henry would have thought they would have come across some evidence of the army's march sooner, but perhaps they were too far west. That past week they had strayed off course, close to Chester, detouring around swollen rivers and streams. He hated to admit it, but they were lost.

Someone ahead shouted that a movement of troops had been spotted and he held up his hand to halt his men. The main body of his troops were camped with the De Gere and Ireton men several miles back.

The force winding along the narrow road below was considerable. They moved in an orderly fashion with banners waving, but Henry could not discern their insignia because the wind dropped, furling the silks around their poles. Gambling that those troops were not Yorkist since they were crossing the Welsh borderlands, he motioned for his men to head down hill to meet them. They carried a white pennant as a safeguard against attack because the soldiers fairly bristled with weapons.

To Henry's relief he found the troops were Lancastrian, under the command of the earls of Pembroke and Wiltshire. He quickly assembled his own forces and those of De Gere and Ireton, and they tagged along at the rear of the army, who also sought the main Lancastrian force.

Many of the men Henry had recruited in Yorkshire had melted away, deserting for the most part, though a few had linked up with other troops. Few men could stay in the field too long; they were needed at home. Besides, many still clung to the old feudal custom of 40 days' service a year for their lord. Counting the months before Wakefield, they were long past that figure. Henry did not blame them. Many lords had already pulled their troops out of the army and headed home, a move he himself had considered on more than one occasion.

Their scouts soon located an army, but it was that of Edward, Earl of March, York's oldest son and contender for the throne. He was camped in Herefordshire and hot to intercept their force from Wales. Pembroke's troops were not only Welsh; there were Bretons, French, and Irish among the ranks. Young Edward knew that, if they were allowed to join Queen Margaret's army, they would make a formidable enemy. After the Yorkists' recent defeat at Wakefield, meeting such an army would likely be the end of his cause.

The Yorkist forces were farther south near Wigmore. Henry received the news of an impending battle philosophically. It had to be expected. They had been in and out of the field for a year with only Wakefield under their belt. He could not expect Edward to lie down and play dead, especially with the death of his father and brother to avenge.

Once Henry would have welcomed the chance to cross swords with the enemy, but that was before he had met Rosamund. Whenever he considered the depth of his love for her, he had to question his sanity. Never in his life had he thought he would love someone so intensely, certainly not his wife, nor even a mistress, though he had had his share of those. Henry wondered if Rosamund had received the letter he had written that lonely night at Burnham, when his heart and other parts of his anatomy had ached for her. There had been plenty of available wenches; once he would not have hesitated to use one of them to relieve his heat. But his concern for Rosamund's feelings dampened his lust, and she had made him aware of how the pain of his infidelity wounded her. When he listened to a minstrel's heart-tugging lay about lost love, the words moved him to a depth of emotion he had not known possible. The thought of losing Rosamund's love was more than he could stand.

Was he getting old? Was that also the reason his will to fight had dwindled? Would he soon be like Sir Ismay, picturing his own death each time he faced the enemy? He frowned, uneasily considering that, unlike in his youth, he no longer felt immortal. The change scared the hell out of him.

Pulling on his cloak, Henry strode across the marshy ground to Sir Ismay's tent. In the background he could hear Welshmen singing and someone played a harp.

"Come in, lad. Share a cup with me," the old campaigner said. He sat soaking his feet in a basin of hot water, trying to relieve the ache the cold weather caused him. "Damn fools, you'd think they'd at least have the sense to confine their fighting to warmer weather."

"Unforgiveable of them, isn't it?" Henry laughed as he sprawled on the blanketed bunk in his father-in-law's tent. As he studied the other man he was shocked to see De Gere suddenly looked old. Deep furrows lined his toughened face; his mouth was little more than an embittered line. When he spoke his dark eyes still glowed, but that was the only sign of youth. Rheumatic legs and feet had slowed him over the past year and the cold winter months of the campaign had only intensified his discomfort.

"It's hell to grow old," Sir Ismay growled, impatiently motioning for the serving lad to pour them both a bumper of mulled ale.

The spiced ale was strong and hot. Henry drank it with relish, aware of the heated brew curling pleasantly through his stomach, the welcome warmth creeping along his limbs.

Outside the Welshmen's singing grew louder and Sir Ismay

curled his lip in displeasure. "Damned caterwauling foreigners. what ails them anyway?"

"Possibly a lament for their homeland—or a lost love."

Sir Ismay snorted in derision. "Love—a highly overrated emotion used to stir a boy's blood and give him a goal to fight for."

For some time they discussed the campaign and the coming fight, not mentioning the fact that the morrow might be their last, though Henry could tell it was on the older man's mind by his brooding expression and the way he sat with his head sunk on his chest.

"God fare thee well tomorrow, Harry," Sir Ismay said gruffly, hobbling to his feet when it was time for Henry to leave. "Stay close to me, if you're able."

Henry gripped his hand hard. They looked deep in each other's faces, momentarily somber. "You have my word, Father."

The use of that term pleased Sir Ismay. "Thank you, son." Unexpectedly he embraced Henry, lightly brushing the younger man's cheek with his hard mouth.

"Good night."

Henry cleared his throat as he walked out into the misty night. White trails wisped between the tents and bowled along the nearby road. They were in a damp, unhealthy place, and he shivered in the chill air. What had just taken place in Sir Ismay's tent had moved him, and he was surprised. When the older man had embraced him, it was almost as if he had been saying good-bye. Henry shuddered as the morbid specter of death crept into his thoughts. It was nothing more than pre-battle anxiety. He refused to think abut death again.

The Yorkists were deployed at a crossroads on Wig Marsh beside the River Lugg, which at that time of year was about 20 feet across. The date was Candlemas Day, February 2, and the troops were apprehensive about fighting on a holy day. The enemy forces took up their positions amid the strip fields of Kingsland village. They were both well rested and well fed since they had traveled barely three miles from Edward's castle at Wigmore.

The morning was cold, and white clouds of mist hovered over the marshy ground. It was almost ten o'clock before glimmers of sunlight penetrated the mist; then a strange phenomenom appeared in the heavens: There were three suns! Groans of dismay came from the ranks, the men considering the anomaly a heavenly warning against fighting on the holy day. Young Edward of March swiftly turned the unusual sight to his advantage by telling his men it represented the Trinity and ensured them of victory.

The Lancastrian army moved along the road from Presteigne, wondering where the enemy forces were hiding. Suddenly cries of awe and fear echoed through their ranks as the mist parted to reveal three suns glowing unnaturally in the heavens. Directly below the spectacular sight, shrouded by floating mist, thousands of men knelt. All were praying in thanks for the heavenly promise of victory.

Stunned by both the triple suns and the vast ranks of Yorkist troops, the Lancastrians halted. No one had expected Edward to rally such a large force after the debacle at Wakefield. The enemy spread far over the marshy ground beside the river.

Henry led his men forward, not impressed by the heavenly spectacle. He cursed under his breath for the untenable position in which they found themselves. They either had to find a way across the river or move far to the right, close to Leominster, to come around the enemy troops. When the praying Yorkists stood, the Lancastrians came on and the battle, later known as Mortimer's Cross, began.

Henry went with the right flank and found a shallow ford to cross the river. Hails of arows bombarded them, shot by Yorkist archers under cover on the high ground. The sudden onslaught assured him their position was the best place to cross the River Lugg or Edward would not be guarding it so well. They soon made it to the other side, but took heavy casualties.

The fighting began in earnest when they were face-to-face

with the enemy on Wig Marsh. The soldiers engaged on all sides; the fighting was bloody and furious. As was the English custom, Herny dismounted and fought alongside Sir Ismay and Meade Ireton. Between them they brought down hordes of men, losing many of their own in the process. They were in a treacherous place to fight. Men slipped on the marshy ground, their steel-shod feet sinking to the ankles in the cold ooze. They fought for hours with opposing sides hacking furiously at each other with sword, poleax, pike, and mace. The terrible clang of metal battering against metal filled the air and mingled with the cries of the wounded and dying. They fought so hard that many were staggering with weariness, but still no decisive ground was taken, no goal attained. The fight was merely to annihilate the opposition.

As they stumbled about the bloody marsh, Henry's men moved farther and farther to the right, fighting as if on an island, completely cut off from the Lancastrian center under Pembroke. Henry could neither say they were winning or losing. The men merely kept battering and trying to hold their ground. Henry's plate was badly dented and had developed dangerous weak spots. His helm had been caved in on one side by a giant wielding a mace; his head still buzzed from the din.

Beside him, Meade Ireton fought gamely, though blood from his wounds trickled on the ground while his crushed left arm dangled uselessly at his side. Even Sir Ismay staggered on, his face grim inside his steel helm. He barely kept track of his allies through the narrow eyeslit. Arrows repeatedly glanced off the soldiers' plate, seeking an unprotected place, and frequently finding their marks, evidenced by the cries of pain as men fell in the churned mud, which was becoming harder and harder to fight over.

Directly behind him, Henry heard a bellow of pain and turned in time to see Sir Ismay stumble. A handful of the enemy leapt upon the older man, battering, stabbing, and trying to pry off his helmet. Hartley, De Gere's captain, was killed trying to protect his lord. Yelling for support, Henry plunged forward, toppling a couple of the enemy with a mighty blow from the sword chained to his belt. Seizing the two-handed weapon in a death grip, Henry hacked his way through to the fallen man, slashing unprotected arms and legs until the enemy finally gave way.

Henry knelt in the mud beside his father-in-law and tried to pry off his battered helm, which was broken in a dozen places and crushed against his skull. When he finally pulled the smashed steel loose, Henry found that Sir Ismay's head and face bore a dozen deep, bloody gashes. Around Henry, his men held back the enemy, making a safe place for them. In fact, the fight seemed to have moved farther away in the past few minutes.

Henry cradled Sir Ismay on his lap, mopping away the blood with his surcoat and trying to determine how badly the other man was hurt. Sir Ismay was still conscious. His lids fluttered open and he smiled up at Henry grimly through bruised and bleeding lips.

"Thank God for you, lad," he croaked.

Finally able to take a breather, Henry pulled off his helm and wiped his sweating face on his surcoat. When he looked up at the sky, he was surprised to find the sun already low. Not wanting to chance behing hit by a stray arrow, Henry quickly put back his dented helm and secured it.

Suddenly, galloping hooves sprayed bloody mud over them as a young soldier yelled, "The center's broken. We're giving ground. Flee for your lives." Then he galloped away over the sea of mud.

Dazed with fatigue, Henry didn't at first comprehend what the lad had said; then he acted. With the help of several of his men, he bore the injured man toward the rear of the battle. They joined the mad scramble to the horses tethered alongside the baggage wagons. Men caught their mounts and, if they were able, scrambled into the saddle and wheeled about, leaping over heaps of the slain, floundering along the muddy river bank. When he was mounted, Henry could see more of what was going on. The fighting at ground level had been no more than a noisy, bloody conflict with nothing clear save the faces of the men who tried to kill him. The battlefield was in shambles. Men running here and there, desperate to escape. One thing was certain: The Lancastrians were running for their lives.

"Careful," Henry shouted when Sir Ismay's men helped put their lord in the saddle.

"I can still ride," the wounded man said, managing a sickly grin. Grotesque rivers of blood coursed down his stubbled cheeks.

"Tie him on," Henry said, just to be on the safe side.

Then he grabbed Sir Ismay's bridle and led him away. Meade Ireton was already in the saddle, momentarily doubled over in pain from the effort and trying to support his broken arm. Some of their neighbors lay on the ground, their helmets pried off. Henry had not the time to retrieve their bodies, but as he passed, he told the soldiers to take care of their masters, hoping they would obey him. In the short time he had, Henry assembled pitifully few of his men before they galloped from the field while they were still able.

Their enemies were actively pursuing the fleeing Lancastrians to Leominster and along the Hereford Road, taking prisoners who were worth ransoming and murdering the rest. Knowing they stood little chance if they followed those well-marked routes, Henry branched off across open country, bypassing both cities. He headed instead for an abbey he had seen from the high ground when they had passed that way the day before. Of the men who accompanied him, many began to fall back, seeking their own escape routes. Henry let them go. As it was, he was gambling that the enemy would not search so far afield just yet, having enough sport within a couple of miles of the field. Henry hoped the monks could patch up the wounded before they were driven back on the road.

Nightfall was already settling over the fields when Henry and his men hammered on the studded oak door of the small abbey. Precious time elapsed before shuffling feet finally announced someone had come in answer to their summons.

"We've wounded men in need of care," Henry told the hesitant servant who opened a small iron grille in the door. "Tell the abbot I'll pay well for their care."

The latter statement seemed to convince the servant to let them in because the man could be heard unbolting doors until they finally stood wide enough to admit the small, weary party of horsemen. Ten men were all who arrived at the abbey, and they were soon swallowed up inside its dark ivy-covered walls. The door was refastened and the servant led them across the dim courtyard and into the building.

It was a battered, bone-weary group of men who huddled beside the welcome hearth, supping off bread, meat, and ale. Henry had given the old abbot a purse of gold for their care and the abbot seemed well pleased, not asking on whose side they had fought, caring only that they were in need of nursing.

After he had supped, Henry went to Sir Ismay, who lay atop a straw pallet on the stone floor. He offered his father-in-law a sip of ale and a honey-dipped wad of bread, carefully inserting the food inside his bleeding lips. A robed monk sponged Sir Ismay's brow while another put salve on the livid wounds crisscrossing his face and neck. They had stopped the bleeding from all but the deepest gash, where metal splinters still protruded. Sir Ismay had lost a lot of blood and his sagging face was the color of parchment, making the deep red gashes all the more noticeable.

"Harry, are you wounded?" Sir Ismay asked, turning his head, his voice little more than a croak.

"A couple of gashes, some pulled muscles. I'll soon mend. And you, you old war-horse, look like they've been using you for target practice."

The older man tried to grin and he gripped Henry's hand. "Don't leave me here, Harry."

"I won't. See if you can sleep."

Henry moved to Sir Ismay's other side to kneel beside Nathan Bennet, whose bearded face was even whiter than Sir Ismay's. A monk was trying to spoon broth between his stiff lips. One glance told Henry that Sir Nathan would be lucky to live through the night. Blood pooled around him. A novice with a pail and brush came to scrub the flagstones clean. Nathan had been wounded in the neck and thigh. Blood had collected inside his plate, and not until the monks had pried it off to release a gush of blood did anyone see the severity of Sir Nathan's wounds.

Meade Ireton was propped against the stone hearth, a cup of wine in his hand. The monks had already dressed and splinted his arm, though from the extent of the damage Henry doubted Meade would be much use with a sword for some time, if ever. Shards of splintered bone penetrated the flesh and the entire limb was swollen.

"I'm not going to help the cause much like this, am I?" Meade asked, his lips tight against the pain. "As soon as I'm able, I'm for home."

"I'll ride with you," Henry said, knowing he could not let Ireton go home alone.

"Don't leave me here, Harry," Sir Ismay said plaintively, overhearing their conversation. "Let me go with you."

"You shall, I promise," Henry said, sinking down on the flagstones in relief, not caring about the hard, chill surface as he stretched his tired limbs. In a few minutes he was asleep.

The monks woke Henry sometime in the night. A young novice shook his arm, whispering urgently to him. It was like trying to wake the dead. Finally, reluctantly, Henry came back from the satisfying place he had been and opened his eyes to find a smooth, beardless face close to his own.

"My lord, you must come now."

Henry got to his feet with difficulty. His arm felt useless as pain burned through his shoulder. He must have injured it during that last frantic bout of swordplay to save Sir Ismay's life.

"What is it? Are they here?" Henry asked.

"No, the old one's asking for you."

Henry glanced around the room and discovered that Sir Ismay had been moved. The novice hurried ahead of him, his sandaled feet barely whispering over the stones while Henry's mail-shod feet clanged and rattled, echoing through the lofty rooms. Sir Ismay lay in a small side room. A monk was seated beside his bed, sponging his face. Although Sir Ismay had a raging fever he seemed coherent at the moment.

"I'm come," Henry said, taking his hand. The answering grip was feeble, but it was a response.

"Leave us," Sir Ismay said, his voice strengthening as he issued the order. The young monk shrugged and put down his cloth and basin and walked from the room.

"What's this?" Henry asked, not liking the look of the other man. There was no way he would be able to ride with them at first light. They would have to leave him behind. Henry felt guilty about the need to break his promise. "You're supposed to be getting better, not worse."

"The poison's already in me, lad. I won't last long. No, don't say anything. Just listen."

Grimly Henry pulled up a stool and sat beside the bed, bending low to catch Sir Ismay's words. Sir Ismay appeared to be lucid and Henry assumed the older man was going to instruct him about the disposition of his property. To his knowledge Rosamund was the only heir. Rosamund—just the thought of her brought Henry a stab of pain. Her lovely face seemed to float above them in the stark chamber, which reeked of sickness and blood.

"You love Rosamund well, don't you, Harry?"

"Better than life itself," Henry said.

"Good, good. She's my only heir. I left instructions at Thorpe in case."

"I'll carry them out as best I can."

"Yes, I trust you to do that, Harry. But first there's something I must explain about—"

"Rosamund," Henry said. Out of the corner of his eye he saw a priest come to the door prepared to give extreme unction. Sir Ismay saw him too and he frantically tried to sit up before he fell back, feebly waving his arms.

"Begone! By God, they're in a hurry to shrive me."

Henry signaled to the priest to leave. "He's gone now. Go on. What about Rosamund?"

Sir Ismay turned his face on the pillow. "She's not who she seems," he whispered.

Henry took the cloth and sponged the other man's brow, trying to keep water from tricking down his neck. "Who is she then?" he asked, humoring the other man, paying little attention to his muttering.

"Not from France."

Henry stopped sponging and leaned closer. "Not from France. Where is she from?"

There was a long pause before Sir Ismay whispered, "Whitton. I deceived you, lad. I can't die with this lie on my soul. I've deceived you. The first Rosamund died. This one's also my daughter, but she's not noble. Her mother's a tanner's daughter. I'm sorry, Harry. Say you forgive me."

Henry drew back, stunned by what he had heard. Sir Ismay's voice was weak, but he was coherent. Sir Ismay had deceived Henry. How was that possible? How could Rosamund be the daughter of some village wench? She could read and write; she'd wit enough to master the castle ways. It could not be true. Yet if it was true, not only had Sir Ismay deceived him, but Rosamund as well. That realization was even harder to bear. He understood that Sir Ismay had not wanted to sever a profitable alliance, but what was Rosamund's reason for the deceit? Surely Henry should have seen through such a gross deception, yet God knows, once he had set eyes on lovely Rosamund, she was all he could think about day and night.

He sat there in shock, vaguely aware of Sir Ismay's rasping breathing as he considered the far-reaching consequences of the deception. His wife, the Lady of Ravenscrag and future mother of his heir, was a peasant woman's get! The village Sir Ismay had named was barely elevated from a pigsty, yet that treacherous old man had tricked him into accepting Rosamund as his daughter fresh out of a convent. What a fool he had been! No wonder he had found her the strangest convent-raised girl he had ever known.

But why was Henry blaming them? He was to blame for not being able to get beyond the ache in his loins, which had rapidly become an ache in his heart. It did not matter where Rosamund had been born, or to whom. He loved her. In all honesty it probably would not have mattered if Sir Ismay had not sired her. But at least Henry was grateful for that small blessing. There was even the chance the old man was delirious, his tale no more than fevered rambling. Yet much as Henry would have liked that to be the case, he believed in his heart of hearts that the story was true.

Henry stood and tried to resolve his anger. He looked down at the grizzled campaigner, who seemed to be resting easy since he had unburdened his conscience. The old devil had wanted the match so desperately he had stopped at nothing. Henry wanted to seize him, drag him from his sickbed, and force him to listen to his outpouring of anger at being deceived. It would do no good. A man as close to his Maker as Sir Ismay had far more important matters on his mind than double-crossing an ally.

Henry left Sir Ismay to the ministrations of the priest who hurried inside the room to give him the last rites. Feeling restless and not knowing what to think or what course, if any, to take, Henry wandered about the abbey precincts. He had to force himself to move because the growing pain in his body gnawed at his self-control.

When at last he reentered the cold stone cloisters and worked his way around to the north walls adjoining the church, he saw a young monk seated at a desk inside a cubicle built into the wall. The monk was laboriously inscribing a page of a manuscript beautifully decorated with birds, fruit, and flowers in glowing, jewel-bright colors.

"Good morning, brother. That's a fine work of art."

"Thank you, my lord," the tonsured monk said, trying unsuccessfully to hide a smile of pleasure at the unusual praise.

"Could you devise a coat of arms for me?"

"I can try. What shall it be: unicorns or leopards rampant?"

Henry shook his head. "Nay, a raven with a rose in its beak.

285

The coat of arms is for my wife.'' There, it was done. Henry
swallowed. He had long contemplated the project. After what
he had just learned from Sir Ismay, it seemed even more important. His gift would assure her that, despite her humble
birth, he loved her. By having her own coat of arms he would
show her she was still his love and the Lady of Ravenscrag.

Henry sketched a crude rendition of his shield bearing the
arms of Ravenscrag, adding a full-blown rose to the raven's
beak to symbolize the protection of his own Rose of Ravenscrag, his darling Rosamund. Henry told the monk the colors
of his arms and asked that the rose be colored white and gold
for purity. The young monk welcomed the unexpected project
since it was a departure from his usual holy themes.

It would be ready the next day at the earliest. Could Henry
wait here another day? So far there had been no sign of re-
taliatory troops, yet each day's delay made their position more
dangerous. His own body begged for rest and a glance at the
others told him they too needed time to recuperate. One more
day, then they would leave.

Sir Ismay died that night. Though Henry had been prepared
for the inevitable, the death was still a shock when it happened.
That was two of their small party gone; Nathan Bennet died before dawn the day before. Sir Ismay's dream of a body carried
on horse with a De Gere saddlecloth had been prophetic after
all. It was as well they had delayed an extra day since Henry
could bear his father-in-law's body home to Langley Hutton.

Henry's shoulder and arm felt as if they had been torn from
the socket. A monk rubbed salve into his muscles, telling him
that there were probably deep tears that rest and time alone
would heal. Henry was offered a poppy infusion to deaden the
pain, but he declined. He needed a clear head to plan their
route if they were to arrive home safely. Pain would keep him
alert.

Henry waited for the monks to finish their lengthy prayers for
the dead in their small chapter house, impatient to be on the
road. Sir Ismay's body had been wrapped in canvas and fastened to his saddle. If they still had their baggage wagons their

journey would have been much easier, but those wagons were probably nothing more than burned-out hulls on Wig Marsh.

The countryside teemed with soldiers from both sides. Henry had his work cut out to lead his party to safety and elude capture. Not familiar with that part of the country, he relied on a crude map drawn by one of the monks to find his way home to Ravenscrag. The long journey was grueling for the wounded. Though the long hours in the saddle did not constitute rest, the pain in Henry's arm gradually began to abate.

Frost iced the plowed ridges of the fields as the party began their final ascent to Ravenscrag. Henry did not know how long it had taken them to reach Yorkshire, but he guessed that February was well advanced. As he headed north he had left Sir Ismay's body at his manor; he had already taken the corpse of Nathan Bennet to his home. The other men who rode alongside him were Ravenscrag men, and though they were battered and weary, they were delighted to see the familiar countryside. It did not matter that the wind howled like a lost soul over the bleak winter moors. Sharp, fresh moorland air seared their lungs, and as they moved higher, flocks of gulls and curlews screeched a welcoming chorus overhead.

Henry's standard flew from the castle towers, just as it had the day he left. The place was his. Henry felt a great surge of pride as he surveyed his sprawling lands, with the mighty castle perched atop the craggy landscape like a great bird of prey. In his saddlebags Henry carried the rolled parchment bearing Rosamund's coat of arms in blue, gold, and white. The young monk had produced a beautiful rendition of his design; all that was needed was a skilled seamstress to sew the banner in silk. But he would not wait until it was sewn; he wanted to give Rosamund the coat of arms that very day. When he thought about revealing his knowledge of Sir Ismay's secret he felt uneasy, wondering what she would say in her own defense. Whatever it was, he realized he did not care. He was in love with Rosamund the person, not the woman he had supposed her to be.

The closer they came to Ravenscrag, the straighter Henry

sat in the saddle, forcing his painful shoulder back as he rode proudly toward the drawbridge. A soldier rode before him carrying his banner, which was quickly identified by the men on the battlements.

Henry waved his gauntleted hand in greeting to the guard on the nearest tower, who returned his salute. Then he heard the winch squalling as they let down the bridge. Soon the small party of riders crossed the wooden planking, and the horse's hooves thudded dully over the sodden wood. Ridges of snow had drifted against the base of the walls and etched the roof tiles in white.

Henry's heart thumped in excitement at the thought of seeing Rosamund again. He could hardly wait to hold her in his arms. The closer he had come to Ravenscrag, the less her past mattered to him. Their secret was known to only a few. Hartley must have known since he was Sir Ismay's shadow. That left two others beside Henry and Rosamund and those two had already taken the secret with them to the grave.

A lowering sky of gun-metal gray promised more snow. Henry looked up at the tower and tried to see Rosamund in the gloom. Uncomfortably he recalled how she had purposely stayed hidden when he rode away. Pain and hurt had made her withdraw from him. Still, he had given her enough time to recover from that unpleasant discovery and he hoped, she, like he, was ready to forgive and forget.

There she was! He could see fluttering lavender skirts billowing from under her dark-furred cloak as she ran out from the shadowed north tower. Henry gritted his teeth as he swung himself from the saddle, the pain in his shoulder making sweat bead on his brow. She was running toward him, coming out of the deep gray shadows like a ray of spring sunshine. He stretched out his arms to her and she ran headlong into them, hitting him with such force that he staggered slightly under the onslaught.

His arms went round her and her hood fell back. Mountains of curling red hair spilled out. The woman in his arms was Blanche Pomeroy!

Chapter Thirteen

Henry slumped wearily at the high table, listening to a recitation of woe from Hoke, whom, to his surprise, he had found acting in Thurgood's stead. Henry had not been expecting his usually healthy steward to become deathly ill. He was immensely touched and very grateful for Rosamund's bravery and fortitude in rallying the castle servants to save Ravenscrag, and his heart warmed at the thought of her doing so out of love since she knew how much the land meant to him. But he couldn't understand why she had left. His outrage at old mad John's puffed-up foray to capture Ravenscrag faded before the growing ache in his heart.

Finally tiring of Hoke's litany of complaints, Henry waved him away with assurances that the more pressing problems would be dealt with on the morrow. Since he arrived to find Rosamund gone, the sheer bone weariness of his long journey and nagging injuries had set in until he found it hard to think clearly. The thought of being with Rosamund again had been enough to keep his spirits high. Without her there, he had no reason to force bravado. He felt like hell and he probably looked that way as well.

"Here, love, drink up," Blanche said.

She stirred the wine in his goblet, supposedly sweetening it with honey, but Henry suspected the addition to be something else. Too short-tempered to be a party to her tricks, Henry demanded a fresh goblet and had the young server fill it in front of him. Blanche pouted at his apparent distrust, but dared not object; Henry noticed she did not touch the other goblet of wine herself.

Blanche was dressed in a lavender gown with a billowing gauzy overlay and a daringly low-cut bodice. Her flaming hair was drawn through a padded silver-and-purple turban. In another mood he would have found her appearance stunning, but her obvious attempt to seduce him had the opposite effect.

Blanche studied him, her green eyes slitted. He looked grizzled and travel weary, beyond that there didn't seem to be anything she could not remedy, given the chance. It was a godsend having that bitch flitting about the countryside, leaving Henry alone and vulnerable.

"I can't imagine why you're in such an ill humor," she said when Henry moved away from her soothing caress.

"Can't you? Then let me explain," Henry said, scowling at her. "I'm bone weary from traveling across country and trying to stay one jump ahead of the enemy. Before that I fought a hell of a battle. I lost half my men somewhere between here and Ludlow. Then after I finally get home, I find Thurgood sick and Hoke in charge with Rosamund gone and you here overseeing the household as if you were Lady of Ravenscrag. Now why shouldn't I be in an ill humor?"

Blanche pouted, feigning hurt at his angry words. "You should be pleased I'm here to help you run the castle now she's left you."

"Saving the garrison's hardly the work of someone who's planning to leave me."

"Then why isn't she here?"

Henry could not answer that. He spooned steaming soup in his mouth, relishing its meaty flavor. The food was the best he'd had since taking to the road.

"Oh, face the truth: She's left you! She never loved you the way I do. Your son and daughter are asleep upstairs and I'm here presiding over your hall."

"Damn it, Blanche. I don't want you presiding over my hall," he snapped, pushing aside his empty bowl. A server came forward to ladle gravy over the bread and meat on his trencher.

"Well, someone has to do it," Blanche said.

290

"I have a competent staff, and they can manage by themselves. It's bad enough having your nephew, Hoke, as steward, without finding you here as well. I might even suspect a conspiracy."

Blanche's tinkling laughter cut him short. "A conspiracy? Oh, don't be so dramatic. I stepped in because there was no one else to do so after she left without a word. I was only helping poor Hoke, who had everything dropped into his lap. Now where's the conspiracy in that?"

Again Henry had no answer. He felt that there was something underhanded brewing and that Blanche as well as Hoke were up to their necks in it. On the day he left he knew Rosamund had been hurt and angry with him, but surely she would not leave him over Blanche, would she? As weariness and pain overcame him, Henry was no longer sure of anything. First, Hoke had told him Rosamund left no message and no one knew where she had gone. Then Henry heard from Chrysty Dane that Rosamund had taken four men-at-arms and the woman, Margery, with her. None of her actions made sense. Could it be possible that she had set out to join him after receiving his letter? Yet if that were the case, what had happened to her?

Glumly Henry finished his wine and refused more. Blanche was looking highly annoyed and he guessed the evening had not gone according to her plans. Well, let her be annoyed. She would be out of there on the morrow. And he also intended to go to the infirmary to see for himself just how ill Thurgood was. There appeared to be a connection he did not want to make. Each time Thurgood ate, he grew worse, and though that was consistent with a stomach ailment, it was also consistent with poisoning. Were Blanche and Hoke in league against his steward? Even worse, had they conspired to be rid of Rosamund?

Henry grasped Blanche's arm, his fingers biting in to the white flesh. "By the rood, woman, if you've done any harm to Rosamund, you'll pay dearly."

Blanche flinched before the sheer malice in his face. Then

she made a great show of rubbing her arm where, when the sleeve was stripped back, red patches marked the milky-white skin. "How dare you accuse me of such a thing?"

Henry did not answer; instead he pushed back his chair and strode from the table. Blanche hurried after him, finally catching up to him and grabbing his arm to turn him about. She pressed her soft, full breasts against him, provocatively licking her lips with the tip of her pink tongue.

"What's the hurry, love? Wait for me," she whispered.

Henry looked down at her stonily; then he shook her from his arm. "I'm going to my chamber alone. I suggest you do the same."

Her green eyes flashed in anger. "You fool man, why can't you accept the truth? She's got no need of you now she's heiress to Langley Hutton and its manors. We belong together. She knows that. I have your son and she can't compete. She's left you, Harry Ravenscrag."

Angrily he grasped her shoulders as he glared down at her. "I warn you, Blanche. Take care or you'll be sorry."

Then Henry flung Blanche away from him and she bounced against the wall. Ruffled and angry, she tried to calm her temper as she watched him stride away. Blanche saw no use playing into his foolish wife's hand; she must be sweetness personified. Henry would be made to see her worth. The longer that wretched woman was gone, the more time Blanche would have to change his mind.

In his empty bedchamber, Henry stood, finding the room cold and bare despite the fire blazing in the hearth. The shutters were in place at the window and he struggled to unfasten them.

"We've been keeping them shut of late, my lord," the servant stoking the fire said. "There's a big white cat been prowling the battlements."

"What's that got to do with it?"

"The cat was here in the room. We thought it best to keep it out."

"I see." Henry opened the wooden boards and flung them

aside to look out at the black night. There was no moon and the surrounding landscape looked shadowy and alien.

It was strange that a cat should be prowling the battlements, but he found such an occurrence no cause for alarm. "Have someone throw the creature in the moat or take it back to the moors. That shouldn't be a problem."

The servant hesitated before he said, "One of the soldiers tried to kill the cat last week. He injured the animal's foot but it escaped. No one knows where it lives. It's large and wild, my lord."

"Oh, all right, I'll close the shutters before I go to bed."

"It would be wisest. Good night, my lord."

After the man had gone Henry leaned against the cold stonework, looking out without seeing. He felt tired and utterly defeated. His shoulder hurt like hell, but that pain was easily overshadowed by the ache in his heart. Why had Rosamund left him without a word? Had Blanche schemed to rid herself of her rival? The thought was too painful to contemplate. It had not pleased him to find Blanche there, though she had tried to make his homecoming pleasant. Doing so was not without sacrifice, she had been swift to point out, since she claimed she'd had to leave her sickbed earlier in the week.

"Oh, Rosamund, sweetheart," he groaned to the empty black night, "come back to me."

Since Sir Ismay was dead, did she have no further obligation to him? The very idea made him feel sick to his stomach. Could Rosamund have gone back to Whitton? Or could she be at Langley Hutton? After all, those lands and manors were hers now and that would be a big temptation for a poor peasant girl. Yet Henry had been sure she loved him. He could not imagine her going anywhere without leaving word. He would send someone to both Whitton and Langley Hutton to see if anyone there knew where to find Lady Rosamund.

For a long time Henry lay wakeful in the bed with the shutters closed. He liked to look out at the stars when he lay here and fall asleep to the song of the moorland wind and the scent of rain and heather. Be damned to it! Wild cat or not, he was going to open the shutters.

Angrily he got up and slammed back the wooden shutters. Then he marched back to bed, after first laying his knife beside him on the chest. If the cat jumped on the bed he'd make short work of it.

As he lay there going back and forth over the puzzling day, Henry recalled Blanche saying she had hurt her foot. A chill crept over him and he barely stopped short of making the sign of the cross. God, he was growing as fearful as the rest of the household. He knew the locals swore Blanche Pomeroy was a witch who could turn herself into a cat. Oh, be damned to them! All he needed was a good night's sleep. On the morrow he'd be able to think things through more clearly.

Henry blew out the candle and lay there, aching and throbbing for Rosamund, longing to hear her whispered endearments, to smell her hair, and to feel her soft breasts pressed against him. Then a sudden thought jerked him out of this painful reverie. How had Blanche known Sir Ismay was dead? He'd not told anyone yet. Certainly when Rosamund had left Ravenscrag, she could not have known because he doubted he and his men had even fought Mortimer's Cross then. So the greed of possessing her own property could not be the reason behind her leaving as Blanche had suggested. Only one reason was left: She no longer wanted him and had run away from Ravenscrag. But if that were the case why had she taken five people with her? A runaway didn't usually advertise the fact.

Angrily he thumped at his pillow, which felt like a sack of rocks. He lay on his stomach in a futile effort to get comfortable. Surely the morrow would bring him answers to the mystery. It had to.

The breeze blowing across the meadow was soft and warm. Rosamund stretched on the sun-splashed grass, listening to the chorus of birdsong in the trees. March was warmer and gentler there than in Yorkshire. The countryside was dotted with woodland interspersed with stretches of rolling meadow, where black and white cows grazed. From the abundance of apple orchards where the trees already swelled with buds, Rosamund guessed she was in cider country.

The land was so lovely that its beauty made her heart ache. Yet she still longed for the sharp smell of the wind blowing off the moors and the raucous cries of gulls and curlews; most of all, she longed for Henry. Those things meant home to her, and home was where her heart lay. Henry must wonder where she was. She could not trust Hoke to tell him the truth about her journey. It was anyone's guess what tale had been concocted between Hoke and Blanche to blacken her name. Her heart ached to see Henry again, to have his reassurance that nothing had changed between them.

The land stirred to life after its winter sleep, but her own life had stopped one icy winter night in Cheshire. She had lost count of the time she had meandered back and forth with Steven's ragged band of men. Sometimes the soldiers harried small bands of opposing troops who put up little fight; then Steven's men stole anything of value. A few women traveled with them and Rosamund had forged a tenuous friendship with Nell, her former jailor. Steven gave her little opportunity to escape; he kept her near him at all times.

At first Rosamund dreaded each night, waiting for Steven to make sexual advances toward her. That had not happened and she was grateful for her deliverance. So far Steven continued to treat her with respect, threatening dire consequences to anyone who touched her, reminding them of Hodge's fate. Though he kept her safe from assault, he also kept her isolated. Some days she was so lonely she could weep.

People spoke of a battle fought nearby in the rolling borderland with many left dead on the field, and she prayed earnestly that, if Henry had fought, he was safe. One day a priest came to minister to the ragged soldiers. Rosamund tried to tell him she was kept prisoner, but after one glance at her dirty, disheveled appearance, he backed away, convinced she was a madwoman.

That afternoon Steven's men lay dozing in the warm sun,

sprawled lazily about the sweet meadow grass. Several times when Rosamund started to get up, Steven had cocked an eye open as if some extra sense had told him of her every move. At night her hands and feet were tied as a safeguard, but it no longer concerned her; she was used to being a captive.

Steven finally came across the grass to offer her a crust of bread smeared with goose fat. "Here, lass, sup off this before we get back on the road," he said, crouching down beside her. His massive thighs strained the fabric of his thick wool tights, a fresh reminder of his strength, lest she fancy challenging his power over her.

Rosamund accepted the bread and forced it down. The grease tasted rancid and made her gag.

"We'll get better once we're home. Not far to Whitton now," Steven said as he stood.

In truth he had no idea where they were. They had wandered back and forth through the pleasant countryside for weeks. The easy spoils had begun to dwindle, telling him it was time to strike out for new ground. Some straggling soldiers informed him that both armies were building up strength in preparation for another battle. He had already grown disillusioned with that style of warfare. It was all so futile. Fight, disband, fight, disband—if a man was lucky he lived through the fighting. But on the whole, Steven found the disbanding worse. Men had to fend for themselves and live off the land, and the people thereabouts weren't generous with the scarecrow rabble invading their meadows.

"Not still mooning about 'is lordship, are yer?" Steven demanded gruffly, noticing tears gleaming in Rosamund's eyes. "You'd best forget him. 'E be nowt but crowbait on yon battlefield." He waved his hand vaguely towards the east. "Come on. Get up. We're moving."

Rosamund traveled the roads in a creaking ramshackle wagon pulled by an ancient donkey. She could have walked faster, but she was in no hurry to reach their destination. As long as they were on the road she still had a chance to escape. When they got to Whitton, her life would be over.

But, the chance to escape came far sooner than she expected. One warm afternoon she and Nell had gone to wash away the grime of travel in a pleasant gurgling brook running through the meadow. They had already redressed behind a stand of sallow willows when guffaws of laughter and a chorus of hoots and whistles startled them. Thinking the gawkers were their own men, Nell marched into the open, her hands on her hips, prepared to give the interlopers a piece of her mind. To her surprise she found a group of strangers.

"Here, lass, want to come keep us warm," one of the men shouted. "Bring her along too," he added, nodding toward Rosamund, who was hanging back in the shadow of the willow.

"Aye, lass, especially bring her along. She'll 'ave us singing all the way 'ome," another man said.

The last speaker had a heavy Yorkshire accent, and his speech alerted Rosamund to a new possibility. Even the clothing of these men was different from most of the stragglers she'd seen. They were dressed uniformly in brown and tawny. Though ragged, their clothing appeared to be some form of livery.

"Where are you from?" Rosamund asked, stepping out into the meadow, tossing back her damp hair.

"Up north yonder, not far from York" a man replied, pulling off his cap and making a mock bow. "And where be you from, my pretty?"

"The same place, lad."

"Then it's a bloody miracle, in't it?"

At that point several of Steven's men came running over the field to battle the strangers if needs be. Not intimidated, the strangers swaggered over to meet them, introducing themselves by their first names and making a peace offering of some fowls they had captured at a nearby farm.

Glad of the fresh food, Steven's men fell into easy stride with the strangers. From that point on, the two groups traveled together. Rosamund did not consider the meeting fortuitous. But at dusk a few days later, after they had made camp for the night, one of the men brought her a pewter plate of food.

"Here, lass, wrap your ears round this."

Rosamund enjoyed the hearty roast meat; it was spiced to hide the fact the meat was past its prime. While she ate, the young man crouched against a nearby tree, chatting pleasantly and keeping his distance. Rosamund was aware that Steven watched them, but as the lad showed due respect Steven chose not to interrupt at first.

"Why are you their captive?" the man asked her in an undertone. "A lady like you."

Startled, Rosamund looked up, food poised on the way to her mouth. "The big man, Steven, is taking me back to his village. Can you help me escape?"

"I might," the lad said without changing expression. "We be going ourselves tomorrow, heading home. There are more of us up along the way. Where be you from then?"

"Ravenscrag."

"By gaw! That's only a stone's throw from us. We're Ireton men."

Rosamund had a hard time not changing expression, nor registering joy at the startling revelation. "Did you fight in the big battle hereabouts? Do you know if the Lord of Ravenscrag escaped?"

The man shook his head. "Nay, we was separated from the rest. T'other lads might know. Some of them's already gone home. We couldn't get round the enemy and had to hole up. Will you trust us to take you back, lady?"

Rosamund smiled. "I've had to trust this rabble. You can't be any less trustworthy."

The lad grinned in reply. "You must be Lady Rosamund then, aren't yer?"

She gasped in delight that he knew of her and she nodded vigorously. But Steven was coming toward them, growing suspicious about their continued conversation. Scowling at the man, Steven's voice was surly when he said, "This lass has her own man."

The Ireton man grinned and he touched his forelock in respect. "Right, sir. My master wanted the lady to taste his special roast fowl spiced with thyme and rosemary."

"Aye, well, tell him thanks," Steven said as the man backed away before returning to his fellows. "What was he saying?"

"He just wanted to know where we were from."

"Why?"

Rosamund shrugged, growing uneasy seeing Steven's face set in that telltale scowl, which usually boded ill. She couldn't risk him sending the Ireton men away in a jealous rage, not when she had new hope for escape. Desperate, Rosamund did something she later despised, but she could think of no other way to quickly alter Steven's mood. She laid her hand on his arm, gently stroking his sleeve as she asked, "Will we be home in Whitton soon?"

A light seemed to go on in his eyes and his expression softened, his mouth parting in a gasp of pleasure. She had never before indicated anything close to affection for him, let alone love.

"Soon, I promise," he said, his voice husky with emotion. He took her hand in his giant fist and smoothed the roughened skin with a dirty finger. "Getting eager for us to be together, are yer?"

Alarmed by his sudden switch of focus, Rosamund tried to back off. She had not meant to stir his emotions. Doing so might prove dangerous. "I'm just tired of all this moving about," she said. Her reply might not have altered his romantic fantasies, but it did halt his softening mood.

Clearing his throat, Steven stood, and he rubbed his brow, puzzling over his answer. "Reckon it can't be more'n a couple weeks before we gets there. I'll try to find out how far it is."

When Steven walked away Rosamund let out a sigh of relief. Her heart was pounding with excitement and dread. She realized her false show of affection had not been wise, but it had been necessary. She was possibly putting herself in greater danger by agreeing to travel with strangers, yet she had to take that chance. She knew why their clothing had seemed vaguely familiar; the Ireton livery was brown and tawny edged with silver. She assumed that, since the men's silver trimmings had been stripped off, they had used them to barter for food along the way.

Rosamund could tell the strangers were in a serious discussion with their heads together, their voices low; when they glanced in her direction several times she hoped their plan included her. The men finally made camp for the night. Though friendly with Steven's band of soldiers on the road, the Ireton men always kept a separate sleeping camp, mindful of Steven's erratic moods and not eager to rouse his anger.

Earlier in the day a couple of tinkers had fallen in with them on the road; they were presently regaling Steven's men with tales, either real or imagined, of the great spoils they had taken on the battlefield. When the soldiers scoffed at their boasting, the tinkers unwisely set out to prove they spoke the truth. From the furtive glances exchanged by Steven's men, Rosamund guessed they planned to relieve the tinkers of their loot. When she saw the spoils out of the tinkers' packs spread over the ground, she looked for something she recognized. To her relief there was nothing of Henry's amongst the gold buttons, rings, and jeweled knives the tinkers had scrounged from the dead. Not to be outdone, the other man brought out pieces of plate, broken weapons, and some jeweled daggers and sword hilts. As she saw the greed in the faces of Steven's men, Rosamund realized the foolish tinkers had just signed their own death warrants.

If she tried to warn them of the danger, her own life would be at stake. The tinkers had also captured a group of horses they were taking to sell in the closest town. To her relief Diablo was not among the animals. Sense told her that, because Henry's possessions weren't there, it was not proof he was still alive, but she still took comfort from the discovery.

Night had fallen, the campfires burned low, and most men had already rolled themselves in their blankets. Silently and treacherously, Steven and two of his men crept up to the tinkers and slit their throats after they had lain down to sleep.

From where she lay inside Steven's tent, Rosamund heard their muffled cries, followed by the agitated instructions from Steven about disposing of the loot. Then came silence.

Rosamund closed her eyes and began to pray, hearing the bumping and the muttering of the assassins as they dragged the tinkers' bodies off into the underbrush. Rosamund huddled in the corner of Steven's tent, where she usually spent her nights wrapped in a scratchy blanket and lying on a pillow filled with chicken feathers.

Much later when Steven finally came inside the tent, she could smell spirits on him. There must have been a flask hidden in one of the tinkers' packs. His voice was slurred when he spoke to her. Rosamund answered, reassuring him she was safely where she was supposed to be. Steven rolled himself in his blanket and lay in the tent opening. A few minutes later he was asleep.

Rosamund could not believe her good fortune. Steven had not thought to tie her hands and feet! Maybe she could escape on one of the captive horses. It was a wild, insane idea and immensely appealing to her. She did not know where she was or how to get home from there, but her vision of freedom was so tantalizing that she had to try.

Stealthily she got to her feet. In the back of the tent she had been working on a threadbare place, making a hole big enough to escape through. To her disappointment not even her head would fit through the hole, let alone her shoulders. Since the tent was pegged, she could not slip underneath the canvas. Disappointed, she sank down on her blanket, trying to plan her escape. Suddenly a dark form loomed in the tent opening and she gulped at the realization that some of the others might be taking advantage of Steven's condition to try their luck with her. She clenched her fists, prepared to do battle to keep from being raped.

"Lady." It was the man who had spoken to her this afternoon.

"Yes."

"We're ready. Are you bound?"

"No."

"Step careful then. Best bring your blanket."

Moving slowly, she stepped up and across Steven's broad body, holding her breath in case she woke him. She wore the blanket about her shoulders like a cloak. There, she was actually stepping on the cold grass, the slick blades poking through her threadbare slippers. Her escape had been too easy. With thumping heart she looked behind her, expecting to see Steven watching her. To her delight she found he had not moved.

The Ireton man grasped her arm and pulled her behind the tent before they were seen. Placing his finger against his lips to signal silence, he motioned for her to follow him. No one had noticed. The few men who lolled around the dwindling fire were draining flasks and throwing them on the ground. Rosamund offered a prayer of thanks for the contraband liquor they filched from one of the tinkers' packs.

Shadows moved about under the trees in the Ireton camp. It was very dark there and Rosamund kept stumbling over rocks and branches. There was a moon, but banks of cloud scudded overhead to obscure its light. Rosamund's heart began to race in excitement. She smelled horses and realized the Ireton men had already confiscated the tinkers' captives.

"Lady Rosamund, Jebson Lynche at your service," the Iretons' captain said as he bowed politely. "My master's Lord Henry's ally. It's our duty to take you safely home."

"Thank you," she whispered, tears of joy filling her eyes. A few minutes later Rosamund was being helped into the saddle. She wrapped the blanket more closely around herself to keep off the night chill. The men had even had the forethought to wrap the horses' hooves, sacrificing pieces of their own clothing for the added safeguard. Quietly, they moved from the meadow to the roadway. Laughter and drunken voices echoed sporadically from the camp, but no one came after them.

The clouds tossed the moon about like a ship in stormy seas, sending bursts of silver light flickering across the roadway. Rosamund looked up at the heavens, thinking what a lovely sight they were, made even more beautiful by her own freedom. The wind sang through her hair as they picked up speed. They left Steven's camp far behind as they galloped down the main highway, heading north.

During the following week Henry found his tenants returning in small bands. Some men were already home when he rode about his lands to determine his losses; though he suspected they had deserted before Mortimer's Cross, he did not chastise them. There were already rumblings that he would soon need to muster his army again to fight for the king. He would give the men a breather before he broke the bad news.

As Henry rode home to Ravenscrag, fluffy white clouds bowled across the clear blue sky. Though the air was cool, there were already signs of spring. The heavens seemed to stretch to infinity and he reined in on a hillock to look over his land. So vast, so empty—a mirror of his own emotions. As he did countless times each day, he wondered where Rosamund was. He had prayed and lit candles in the chapel, as Father John had advised, seeking some news of her. All was in vain. His messengers had come back without any news from either Whitton or Langley Hutton. Rosamund had apparently disappeared from the face of the earth. As the fruitless days stretched into weeks, he became even more suspicious that Blanche had had a hand in Rosamund's disappearance.

Henry turned about and rode home. Clouds scudded overhead, fleecy and silvered by sunlight. He squinted against the glare as something caught his eyes: A kerchief fluttered from the north tower! His heart lurched before beginning a frenzied beat. Had Rosamund come home?

Henry spurred forward, galloping the last few hundred yards. His gallop ended in disappointment; it was Blanche who met him in the bailey.

"Welcome back, my lord," she said, curtsying formally to him. "There's a messenger come from Meade Ireton."

"A messenger?" he said sourly, trying to hide his disappointment. He had left Ireton's only that morning. The mes-

303

sage must be the call to arms they had been expecting.
"Where is he?" he demanded, jumping from the saddle and
handing Diablo to a groom. "What is the news?"

Blanche shrugged, her mouth turning down petulently as
she said, "He wouldn't tell me."

Good for him, Henry thought, striding ahead. Blanche was
a growing nuisance. She was supposed to have left Ravenscrag
days earlier. She was determined to worm her way back into
his good graces, even suggesting she would accompany him
on his next journey about the king's business. He had not said
yea or nay. In truth, he did not know what to tell her. If
Rosamund never returned, he did not expect to live like a
monk for the rest of his days. And in the past Blanche had
been a pleasant sexual diversion. Yet his heart throbbed with
precious memories of Rosamund, and he clung to the hope
that she had not actually left him, that her disappearance was
explicable.

Blanche never let Henry rest. She kept up a constant barrage
against his emotions, snidely reminding him about Rosamund's departure, eager to seed his distrust of her rival. To
Blanche's great annoyance, Henry still had not given her an
answer, despite the fact that she frequently tried to drug him
into compliance. Mostly he avoided her powders and potions,
though once, when his lust soared to alarming heights, he
knew he had inadvertantly taken an aphrodisiac.

"I thought you were supposed to be leaving this morning,"
he snapped, angry with himself for his weakness in succumb-
ing to her wiles.

"I was ready to leave when the messenger arrived, but I
waited for you to come back."

"Good, then as I've no further need of you, you can leave
as planned. Godspeed. Take some of my men with you to
assure a safe journey."

When he turned away and searched the gloomy hall for the
messenger, Blanche scowled, her mouth forming a bitter line.
His stubborn refusal to give in to his desires baffled her. It
was going to take desperate measures to bring Henry back to

heel. That bitch's hold on him was much stronger than she expected. It certainly called for stronger potions than she had brought with her, reminding her it was time to go home to Enderly. She dare not trust a servant to bring her grimoire and the special ingredients she kept locked in the attic room.

The children had been home over a week, their visit to Ravenscrag lasting just long enough to remind Henry of his obligations. He had played with the lad, she had to admit, showing him how to hold a sword and shoot a bow, skills she supposed a boy's father ought to teach him, but even that attention annoyed her. She had been disappointed to discover that Henry was not much different from Walter in that respect, perpetually concerned with warfare, wasting both his youth and his strength in the service of some addled old man who had barely the wit to know his own name.

"Very well, my love, I'm leaving now," she said loudly to recapture Henry's attention because he was already halfway across the hall.

He had spotted the Ireton messenger sitting at a trestle. He waved absently in farewell before turning his back on Blanche. She seethed inwardly at his indifference. Damn him! It was as if all her spells and potions had suddenly lost their power. Only once had she managed to lure him to her bed and even then he had fallen asleep before he had made love to her. That night her fury had known no bounds. She had made the mistake of giving him too much wine with the potion. She was careful not to repeat that mistake, yet maddeningly, he avoided any food or wine he suspected of being doctored, leaving her at her wit's end about what to do next.

"Lord Henry." The messenger bowed over his arm, doffing his cap.

Both men glanced toward the doorway where Blanche stood listening. They waited for her to leave before they continued. Snorting in displeasure as she realized she was not going to learn the content of the message, she finally stormed away in a flurry of skirts.

"Never be kind to old mistresses, lad. They become damned

hard to get rid of,'' Henry said, swinging his booted leg over the bench to sit beside the messenger, eager to hear what the man had to say. ''Have you news from the king?''

The messenger took a sealed paper from his pouch and Henry broke the wax Ireton seal. As he suspected, the note from Meade Ireton told him that Queen Margaret was summoning the Yorkshire lords to rejoin the army at York and to prepare to face Edward, Earl of March, who had mustered his troops outside Pontefract.

''Thank you, lad. Have you supped?''

The Ireton man said he had. Glancing about the hall, the man first made sure Lady Blanche was not still within earshot before he spoke.

''Is there something else?'' Henry asked as he leaned forward. ''By God, have you news of Lady Rosamund?''

''Aye, my lord. She's safe. And she should get here before nightfall.''

Henry made the man repeat twice what he had said, hardly able to believe he had really heard the exciting news. Almost as if he too had understood, the leggy hound, Dimples, began to career madly round the table, tongue lolling, panting in excitement.

''God be praised! Is she well?''

''Aye, but in great need of rest.''

''How can I thank you?'' Henry said, rising and beckoning a nearby servant. ''Let me give you a reward.''

''That's not needed, my lord,'' the lad said, blushing. ''Your people have treated me well. And now I must get back on the road. I've my lord's messages to deliver before dark.''

It began to rain close to midnight. Rosamund wrapped her cloak tighter against the wind-driven onslaught. She was so weary she could barely stay in the saddle. The men had offered to put up for the night, but she knew they did not want to. Not wanting to delay them further, she insisted she could go on, encouraged as the miles to Ravenscrag slipped away. They had already been delayed, first when one of the horses had gone lame, then later when a man had been thrown and broken his arm and they had had to stop to splint the limb. What should have been a journey over by dark had been prolonged by fate into the wee hours.

As they toiled uphill through the driving rain Rosamund beheld a sight she had thought never to see again: the turrets of Ravenscrag Castle! Rain trickled down her neck and slashed her face; her man-size leather gloves, which had kept her hands from blistering under the reins, were sodden.

Overhead the proud Ravenscrag standard flapped wetly in the wind as her companions hailed the watch on the battlements. After they had identified themselves, the party of riders was warmly greeted. Rosamund's heart leapt for joy when she found that they were expected. Henry had been told she was coming; he was waiting for her. Though she could barely keep her eyes open, Rosamund sat straighter in the saddle, freshly aware what a bedraggled mess she must look. She had to hope, in that instance, love truly was blind.

Servants ran to greet them after they had crossed the drawbridge and the outer bailey. Rosamund was quickly wrapped in a warm dry cloak after she dismounted. Bright torches flamed overhead as all around her stood beaming tenants eager to greet her, joyfully thanking her escort for rescuing their lady. Their reaction had far more enthusiasm than she had expected and she was delighted. The sounds went round and round in her head as her ears buzzed and her feet seemed to barely touch the ground as she was hastened under the stone archway out of the rain. In the jumble of noise and people she searched for Henry, but she did not see him. Stumbling with weariness, Rosamund was glad of the men's support as she was led inside the castle.

"Where's my husband?" she finally asked. "Is he not here to greet me?"

"Lord Henry waited for you till dark, my lady. He had to ride out to summon his tenants for the king. He'll be back before dawn. He waited till dark," the man said, defending his master.

Rosamund felt as if she had been struck a blow in the chest. Could Henry wait only that long for her after so long a time? Daily she had pined for him, aching for his arms, wondering if he was safe after the battle. Well, at least she had the answer to that question. He must not have been wounded, if he had even been near Hereford. Then a thought struck her, plucked from the muddled swirl that filled her mind. Had he gone to visit Blanche? Or was Blanche already there, taking her place beside Henry?

"I'm surprised no one's here to meet me, not even Lady Blanche," she said to her escort.

"The Lady Blanche left this afternoon, lady," the man said as he helped her upstairs.

His unwitting words were a knife thrust in Rosamund's heart. So all her worst suspicions were founded. Henry had not waited more than a few weeks before bringing that scheming redhead to his bed. Tears welled up in her eyes, and in her utter weariness she could no longer contain them as they slid down her cheek and dripped on her already sodden clothing. All her joy at being back at Ravenscrag was rapidly buried under an avalanche of pain over Henry's continued infidelity.

Rosamund was met at the door to her room by a flurry of joyous women eager to attend their lady. They fussed and cried over her and she cried with them, though the servants did not know her tears were for her lost love.

The women washed her face and brushed her hair, throwing aside her old ragged garments and dressing her in a clean linen shift. On the morrow, she assured them, she would bathe properly. Then she would wash her hair and soak her aching limbs in scented water. That night all she wanted to do was sink into oblivion in the hope that rest would soothe her broken heart.

When weak sunlight speared arrowshafts across the bed, Rosamund woke in the unfamiiar surroundings, wondering at first if all had been a dream. No, the clean linen sheets assured her she was back at Ravenscrag! Her mood soared, only to be dashed a moment later when she came full awake and remembered she had arrived home just in time to discover her husband's infidelity. The reminder was like a pronouncement of doom.

She had cried herself to sleep; but she vowed to cry no more. She should have expected no less. Henry was a nobleman used to having his every whim fulfilled; when the fire burned too intensely in his loins, he quenched it with any available woman. That behavior in itself was not as much cause for distress as knowing that the woman he chose was the treacherous Blanche. Rosamund had little ammunition to fight the Red Witch, if that is what Blanche truly was. A chill went down her spine as she thought about Blanche weaving evil spells and mixing magic potions. Henry always laughed at the tales, considering them no more than servants' gossip. Yet Rosamund was not convinced the legends were only gossip. Men had the ability to become deaf, dumb, and blind when aroused, and though Rosamund hated to admit it, Blanche was both beautiful and desirable.

Chapter Fourteen

Henry stopped in the doorway and his heart began to race as he heard Rosamund's voice. She was singing to herself as she splashed in a copper tub before the blazing hearth. Heaps of towels, flagons of scent, and clean underclothes surrounded her. He glanced around the room, pleased to see that for the moment at least they were alone. The servingwomen must have gone for hot water.

Though Henry had not expected to take Rosamund by surprise, doing so would be an added pleasure. He shivered in delight at the sight of her shapely arms and her mane of bright hair, coiling in sodden strands down her back as she bent to soap her legs. Though he had accepted the story as true, he still found it hard to believe Sir Ismay's tale of Rosamund's begetting. That tanner's daughter must have been a goddess! Moving quietly across the rushes, Henry stood behind her and waited until she leaned back to squeeze warm scented water on her hair before he slid his hands over her eyes.

Rosamund squealed in surprise, though in an instant she knew her visitor had to be Henry. Pain stabbed her heart as she realized how much she had longed for him, yet all morning she had dreaded this meeting.

"Husband, I trust you're rested," she said coldly, forcing her best noblewoman's voice, her words formal and distant.

Henry took away his hands, startled by her chill greeting. "Rosamund, sweetheart, is that all you have to say?" he asked in disbelief, his throat constricting with emotion.

When he moved to the side of the bath, she slipped lower

in the pink-tinted water until only her head and shoulders showed.

"You're angry because I wasn't there to meet you. Oh, love, there's no need. I can explain that."

"I'm sure you can," she said, thrusting her hands under the water, not wanting him to see they trembled.

"What's that supposed to mean?" he said, his face hardening.

"You're always so good at explaining things to me. I'm sure this time will be no different."

"I spent the night riding the moors to present the Queen's call to arms to my tenants. You act as if I was out bedding a whore!" he said angrily. "This is hardly the loving reunion I was anticipating. What's the matter with you?"

"I'll ask you the same question?"

"There's nothing wrong with me."

"Oh, so you don't find it odd that, after I'm gone only a few days, you bring another woman to your bed almost as if you couldn't wait to see the back of me."

"Don't be ridiculous! That woman—and I assume you mean Blanche—came here of her own accord. She left yesterday for Enderly. I've not taken her back as my mistress, whether you believe me or not."

Rosamund stared ahead, desperately trying to hold back her tears. The pain of disillusionment after all the longing she had felt for Henry was almost more than she could bear. "I could have died for all you cared," she whispered, licking treacherous tears from her lips. "It was only by the grace of God that the Ireton men rescued me. The least you could have done was meet me at the door."

"Rosamund, love, don't do this. I waited—"

"Till dark. Yes, so I was told."

"The messenger said you'd arrive before dark; so I waited as long as I dared. Then I had to go out to alert the men. As it was, they were dragged from their beds and didn't take too kindly to the news. Like it or not, Rosamund, I have a responsibility to the Crown. You've no reason to be angry. If

311

you only knew how much I've ached for you and how many messengers I sent trying to learn where you'd gone. I'm the one who should be angry with you for leaving without telling anyone where you were going.''

"You angry! I left word, though I suppose loyal Hoke didn't tell you."

"No, in fact he—well, no matter, I'll deal with him later."

Clanking pots and pans at the door announced the arrival of hot water. To Rosamund's dismay, Henry waved the servants away.

"Lady Rosamund has no need of you. We'll ring if you're wanted," he said at the door, before shutting it in the servants' faces.

"How dare you! The bath's getting cold. I need that hot water."

"No, you don't. If the bath's cold, get out."

"Not with you here!"

"Why? I've seen you naked before."

"Henry—"

Ignoring her protests, he latched the door. Then, drawing up a stool, he leaned back against the bed and spread his booted legs. "I'm prepared to wait just as long as you are."

The glared at each other. He was stern, his mouth set in that intractable line; she was white faced, her lips trembling.

"Damn you!"

"Curse me all you want. Doubtless you know more colorful oaths than that, coming from Whitton."

Her gasp was audible in the quiet room. "What?" she whispered, thinking perhaps she had misunderstood him.

"You see, my love, I know far more about you than you suspect. I know you're really Rosamund of Whitton, Sir Ismay's get from the local tanner's daughter."

His words stunned Rosamund. Her heart began a frightened, frenzied beat. "I don't know what you mean," she stammered, desperately playing for time as she searched for some plausible explanation of her deceit.

"Mean? Oh, I think you do. By the way, your doting father's dead."

Rosamund showed surprise, but beyond that she registered little emotion at the unexpected news, which in itself condemned her.

"No tears? Oh, come, I expected a little more than silence from a devoted daughter," Henry said.

"I wasn't close to him," she whispered, still searching for an explanation of the terrible truth and not finding one. Her mind was in turmoil. "How did he die?" she asked at last when the silence grew uncomfortably long.

"Of his wounds after Mortimer's Cross."

Rosamund gasped as she recognized the name of the place where the big battle was fought.

"You already knew?" he asked in surprise.

"Not about him. I heard about the battle. I worried you'd been wounded there."

"No, thank God. How did you hear about it?"

"Because I was captured by soldiers."

"What!" Henry leaned forward, his composure slipping. "Whose soldiers?"

"The same men who took us prisoner at York."

"How? Did they come here to Ravenscrag?"

"No, it was later, on the road to Burnham Manor."

Henry gasped. "Burnham? You were coming to me?"

"Your letter was so loving. I believed you loved me."

"I still do. Dear God, that you should ever doubt it."

"Your actions sometimes make it hard to believe," she said, knowing she must get out of the water soon. Cold seeped into her limbs and her sodden hair lay like an icy hand on her back.

"Oh, Rosamund, to think you took such a chance to come to me," he said, his face softening. "They told me how you ingeniously defeated old John of Thurlston. Thank you for your bravery in saving Ravenscrag."

"I did what I could to save your castle."

"I thank you from the bottom of my heart." He smiled at

313

her; then he leaned forward to say, "Come, sweetheart. Get out of that freezing water."

Stubbornly she sat there, knowing she would soon have to capitulate. After the rift between them she would be uncomfortable standing naked before him. It was as if Blanche laughed at her from the shadows. And there were still those lies between them.

"Why did you call me Sir Ismay's get from a tanner's daughter?" she asked, wondering if Blanche could have told him, yet she did not think even Blanche would have discovered such a close-held secret.

"There's no need to pretend any longer. Sir Ismay confessed his . . . your . . . deception on his deathbed. I have to admit I was stunned at first. Only later, I realized it didn't matter. I love you, not the person I believed you to be."

Rosamund's eyes widened and her heart pounded in shock. "Who else knows?" she whispered, afraid that the entire castle was aware she was not noble and that all would return to their former contemptuous manner. She could not endure such treatment.

"No one. Oh, love, I swear, it doesn't matter to me. In fact, now I know you come from Whitton village, I'm amazed by you. You can read and write. You have a sharp wit. You've learned every skill demanded of you, not to mention being the most beautiful woman in the land. To me you're a miracle."

Rosamund smiled at his extravagant praise. "I'm no miracle. Sir Ismay paid for my board with the Sisters at Thorpe. They taught me to read and write. They even tried to make a gentlewoman out of me. At one time Sir Ismay thought to marry me to one of his household, but he decided he had not the money to waste on educating a bastard daughter. So I was sent home."

"And then you lived in that pigsty village with whom?"

"My mother and her husband and children. Only then I didn't know Sir Ismay was my father. In the village they always said my father was a nobleman, but I thought it was just my mother's tale."

"I'm surprised at your age you weren't already wed."

Rosamund decided she could stand the water no longer. She stepped from the icy bath and looked away shyly from Henry's admiring gaze as he held out a warm towel and wrapped her in its generous folds. Rosamund shuddered with cold as he dried her gently, swathing her wet hair in a separate towel before he drew her into the protective circle of his arms, where she stood warming herself before the blazing fire.

"Henry, there's something else I must tell you. There's no need to keep this secret now."

His hand stopped rubbing as he braced for an earth-shattering revelation. "What is it? By God, don't tell me you already have a husband!"

"No, but I was betrothed to the blacksmith's son."

Rosamund breathed a sigh of relief since she had told him her final secret, feeling the weight lift from her shoulders. She relinquished herself to his strength, sinking against him as he drew her on his knee.

"The man is Steven, the leader of those men."

"That yellow-haired giant? That explains a lot. Why didn't you tell me this before?"

"I couldn't tell you that without telling you everything. Sir Ismay threatened to punish me if I ever gave him away. Besides, I thought you wouldn't want me if you knew I wasn't really a noblewoman."

Henry pulled her close and softly kissed her cheek. "I'll always want you," he said, his breath fanning her face and sending a delicious shiver down her spine.

"In the beginning I'd no idea what he planned. Sir Ismay told me I could be his daughter's maid. I thought it was a godsend to get away from Whitton and my stepfather. Later I learned his real reason, but by then it was too late. His daughter, Rosamund from France, died and he buried her at Whitton with my name on the stone. All the villagers think it's me."

Henry whistled in surprise, understanding the extent of the old man's scheme. Matters had been so cleverly arranged that Rosamund could never go back. "But if Steven thinks you're dead, none of this makes sense.''

"He's not been right in the head since the funeral. He was camped in the forest the day we went out riding. When he saw us and realized it was me, he thought you had stolen me from him, bought me as your mistress. I suppose he thinks the funeral was meant to trick him alone.''

"So he only thinks he's reclaiming what's rightly his. That explains why he hates me so. He didn't really want to ransom me.''

"He was going to kill you after it was paid. Oh, love, as long as he lives, Steven's a threat to you. He'll make you pay for taking me.''

"Doesn't he understand you're my wife?''

"He thinks of little beyond getting me back and making you pay. We're both to be punished because I love you.''

Her words pleased Henry and he kissed her neck. "So you really do love me?''

"From the first time I set eyes on you.''

"At the wedding?''

"Long before that. I saw you first at Appleton Fair, but then I didn't know who you were. I thought maybe you were a prince. I had such romantic dreams about you. When I learned it was you I was going to marry, I thought all my dreams had come true.'' Rosamund dipped her head, suddenly feeling uncomfortable to be telling him her secret fantasies.

"You're all my dreams come true as well,'' he whispered sincerely, his hand stealing inside her towel to stroke her damp flesh.

"Oh, Harry Ravenscrag,'' she whispered, swallowing a lump in her throat. "Were you the King of England, I couldn't love you more, though I do resent having to share you with Blanche . . . or with any woman.''

"You don't have to share me. You'd be proud of me if you knew how faithful to you I've been of late.''

"Really?''

"Really. I've been saving all my passion just for you, lady.

So you'd best be well-rested,'' he said, tracing his tongue down the column of her throat.

Rosamund arched her head back, delighting in the feel of Henry's mouth. When he finally kissed her lips, she eagerly kissed him back. She could feel the heavy swell of his passion, grown long and full, pressing against her towel-wrapped thigh. Henry throbbed and ached to make love to her. She could feel the mounting tension in his arms, and his thighs grew taut beneath her buttocks. She had waited so long for that moment.

"My dreams of you weren't modest," she said with a giggle as she rested her head against his. "I imagined that you made passionate love to me, that you touched me here."

Rosamund took his hand and she molded it around her full breast, imprisoning him inside her towel.

Henry's breathing quickened and his kisses grew hotter. Then she took his other hand and slid it high between her thighs, shivering with passion as his fingers sought the sensitive folds between her legs.

"You see, I wasn't a very modest maiden, even then," she said.

"A fault only to be commended," he whispered, his mouth buried in her neck.

With his tongue, he traced a passage over her chest, finally circling her breasts. He flicked her nipple gently with his tongue before molding his lips about the rising bud. "What other delights did I share with you on those cold, lonely nights?"

Rosamund smiled with pleasure, aware he was entering her love game. "We always made such wonderful love together. Our passion could not be matched," she whispered, moving her soft lips along his hard jawline. Resisting the urge no longer, she finally ran her hands over his chest, across his belly, and down along his thigh until he grunted impatiently.

"Wrong thigh, sweet fool," he said, his voice hoarse with longing as he nudged her hand over.

Trembling expectantly, Rosamund slid her hand over the throbbing heat that threatened to burst his clothing apart. How hot he was for her. She knew other women envied her his lovemaking because he had a lusty reputation. All her carnal instincts were aroused by her knowledge of his great need. Fire blazed between her legs, tugging in the pit of her belly before circling back through her thighs until they throbbed and ached with longing for him.

"Only then I didn't know about your famous attribute," she whispered wickedly, lightly running her forefinger the length of him inside his hose, her touch tantalizing, arousing him even further.

"And when you found out?" Henry said, grasping her face in his hands. His eyes were black with passion, glinting in the fireglow.

"I was thrilled beyond measure," she said softly, "because you fill me to the brim."

Her words were inviting, her smile desirous. As she flicked the tip of her tongue over her lips, her eyes glowed in the reflection from the fire.

"Oh, sweet Jesus." He gasped, unable to endure much more. "Then, come. Let me fill you now."

They slid down together on the rushes, rolling toward the hearth. The logs in the fireplace hissed and spit, sending showers of sparks up the black chimney. Rosamund's damp towels made a bed on the herb-sweetened rushes when she stretched languorously, lazily moving her limbs, her movements belying the raging heat thundering through her veins. Henry gazed down at her as he fumbled with his clothing. He found her so beautiful that she seemed unreal. He was desperate to take her.

Rosamund reached up to stroke his shoulders, his smooth flesh golden in the firelight. From chest to belly the ladder of his ridged muscles rippled as he moved this way and that, desperate to be free of his constricting garments. She smiled at his haste, knowing it sprang from his eagerness to blend his flesh with hers. She traced her fingertips over his hard body, her gentle caresses not making his task any easier.

His boots were kicked aside. His velvet doublet fell against the copper tub; his cambric shirt followed. Then his hose, his

drawers. She did not help him undress; she merely lay there
watching him, throbbing with desire as she renewed her acquaintance with his muscular body and longed to kiss his firm
golden flesh.

In the orange-hued light his handsome face was tense, his
nose strong and proud. His shadowed profile cast across the
hearthstone reminded her of his heraldic Ravenscrag crest. But
her dark bird of prey could be tender too.

"Henry, come. Show me you love me."

"Oh, sweetheart, that you would ever doubt it," he murmured, dropping to his knees before her.

"I don't doubt it anymore," she said, stretching out to touch
the throbbing, moist tip of his organ, which was darkly engorged with blood and quivering to claim her. He was on fire.
She moaned low in her throat at the wonderful promise of this
coupling.

"Love me now, don't torment me any longer," she said,
kissing his flesh and laving him gently with her tongue.

Henry groaned as he seized her head, threading his strong
fingers in her hair, which curled damply about his hands. He
could only keep her there for a moment before he had to move
her away. They fell together, his hot mouth covering hers.
Rosamund shuddered with desire, finding his kisses so passionately demanding that they drained the life from her. Their
tongues plunged searing hot as they plundered each other's
mouths. Panting, they rolled together on the rushes, oblivious
to the spiky reeds. With a deep sob of passion, Rosamund
spread her legs wide in invitation, urging Henry to take her.

Henry positioned her beneath him. His kiss was like fire as
he covered her mouth with his own. His throbbing flesh
brushed her tender portals, which were open and eager to receive him. Seizing her, Henry lifted Rosamund off the rushes
as he drove home, filling her with heat. His hands slid to her
buttocks and he gripped her, impaling her deep on the shaft
of his desire.

Rosamund felt so hot, so full, that every nerve ending was
bathed in molten fire. She cried out in delight as she clutched

his back, gripping tight as he rode her, faster and faster, until she could no longer hold on to consciousness, until she soared with him into space, relinquishing her will to their mutual desire.

Henry possessed her completely. Rosamund's intense climax reached a crescendo of delight until she cried out. Henry did not absorb her cries with his mouth, he wanted to hear her raw passion, to know she had surrendered wholly to his will.

They stayed in their room all day. Their meals were sent up, and except for mending the fire and taking away the copper bath, the servants quickly departed, leaving them alone. The lovers talked and made love; they dozed and woke to love again. They bared their souls to each other during those passionate hours, locked away in the firelit tower room while the cold wind moaned around the stonework and rattled the wooden shutters. Their emotions were heightened by the knowledge that Henry would soon be back on the road. His impending departure made them aware of how few hours of their precious time together remained.

At dawn Henry left Rosamund sleeping while he made final arrangements with Benton, the captain of his guard, to take the men on the road, intending to catch up to them the following day. That plan gave him one more night with Rosamund. Men and wagons traveled slowly and he was sure Diablo could easily overtake them. Capt. Benton was agreeable to the arrangement, suggesting if the troops left that morning they could rendezvous with the Ireton men at the crossroads.

With a great clanking and clattering, the castle soldiers assembled in the courtyard. Horses whinnied and stamped their feet, jingling bridles and harness. Traces of frost iced the battlements and both horses and men breathed clouds of vapor as they waited in the pale sunshine.

These unmistakable sounds of an army preparing to move roused Rosamund from sleep. Alarmed, she leapt out of bed and ran to the window. Her heart lurched in dismay as she saw columns of armed men ready to depart. Surely Henry was not leaving this morning without saying goodbye. He had said he must soon be on the road, but she had not thought he meant that morning! Bright silken banners and pennants fluttered in the sharp breeze as the column clopped toward the gate. Father John stood there in his vestments, accompanied by a lad with a censer. He must have been blessing the troops. Rosamund's stomach lurched and she fought a wave of nausea as she searched the assembly for Henry astride his big black horse. There was no sign of him, though the familiar bobbing standards assured her the men were from Ravenscrag.

Just then the door creaked open and she spun around to find Henry framed by the light shining through an arrow slit across the stair. He wore a fir-green velvet doublet and hose, a glinting medallion dangling about his neck. His boots were red suede, their tops only reaching to his ankles. Such garments were not his usual dress for riding to battle.

He laughed at her shocked expression when he came inside the room and closed the door. "Aha. Thought I was leaving without saying good-bye to repay you for last time," he said. Then seeing the pain in her face at his jest, he promptly regretted making it. Henry drew her protectively into his arms and kissed the top of her head. "Here, I've something to show you," he said, going to the bed.

"Are you leaving with them?" Rosamund asked, ignoring the rolled parchment he dropped on the covers.

"I'll join them later."

A wave of relief washed over her and she let out an audible sigh. "I was so afraid. Oh, sweet, you're staying for me."

"Who else?"

Henry slipped his arm about Rosamund's waist as she came to stand beside him, where she rested her head against his shoulder. He spread out the parchment on the bed and she looked down at the colorful depiction of a blue shield with white and gold embellishments.

"How lovely. Is this a manuscript?"

"In a way. One of the brothers drew this for me at the abbey where we rested after the battle. This, my love, is your very own coat of arms."

Rosamund gasped in surprise before leaning closer to study the picture as Henry held a candle to show the details of the shield. "A rose—for Rosamund?"

He smiled and nodded. "Yes. The predatory raven of Ravenscrag will carry you gently in his beak and keep you from all harm. You'll become known the length and breadth of the land as the Rose of Ravenscrag."

"The Rose of Ravenscrag," she said softly, her eyes shining. "I like that."

"I hoped you would."

Then a painful thought struck her. "Did you have this drawn up before you knew about me?" she asked suddenly, her heart sinking at the thought.

"No, after." Henry pulled Rosamund close to kiss her cheek. "When I knew the truth, it seemed even more important to show that you belonged with me. I'd been thinking about this device for some time, but I was never in one place long enough to commission it. A seamstress is making the first banner in silk for you to carry as your standard."

"Oh, sweetheart, thank you. I never dreamed I'd ever have a banner of my own."

"Eventually we'll make a device with the quartered arms of De Gere and Ravenscrag with your special insignia in the center," Henry said, aware that such an arrangement would not delight the college of heralds, but in Yorkshire he was a law unto himself.

Rosamund's smile faded when he mentioned the De Gere arms. She was about to protest her claim to them when she realized as Sir Ismay's heir she had every right to display the De Gere gold leopard rampant. At least Henry was sensitive enough not to have added the bar sinister of illegitimacy to her crest.

"Will the banner be ready soon?"

"Today, I hope. You can fly it before you when next you travel."

"Which will be in a couple of days."

"What?" Henry had been rolling up the parchment and her

words caught him off guard. "A couple of days? Where are you going?"

"Wherever you're going."

"Oh, no, Rosamund. No, it's too dangerous for you to come with me."

She stubbornly set her mouth, and her chin went up in that defiant manner he knew so well. "You can't frighten me with danger. I've known plenty of it lately."

"But it's impossible, love. Men just don't take their wives with them to battle."

"Some men do."

Henry had to agree that some nobles traveled with their households, who were usually billeted in a nearby town or at a neighboring friend's or relative's manor. But where they were headed, he had no relatives.

"There's nowhere for you to stay. You can't sleep in a tent on the field among thousands of men."

"Where does the queen stay? She travels with the army along with the little prince, doesn't she?"

Henry reluctantly agreed. "She does, but bringing the lad with her is not a popular move among the men. Children don't belong on battlefields."

"I agree. But I'm not bringing a child, just myself. Where the queen and her women lodge, I'll stay too. Surely you're important enough to be granted that right. No one can have made any more effort to recruit her troops surely?"

Again Henry had to agree. Damn, she kept making good points. "But I'll worry about you on the road. Far better to stay here, love, where you're safe."

They looked at each other and suddenly burst out laughing at his foolish assumption.

"Safe? I don't think my recent experiences bear that out," she said tartly, squeezing his arm. "I'll be able to see you every day—and night. If you need nursing"—she paused and they both grimaced, aware such care might very well be needed—"I've seen other women caring for their men in the field. I promise to take good care of you, sweet, especially to keep you from all those cold and lonely nights. Now where is it we're headed?''

"The rendezvous is south of York.''

"Ah, well, though it's spring already, York will still be cold. You'll definitely need someone to warm your bed and make passionate love to you.''

Much later, as they lay sated and drowsy before the hearth, Henry still could not believe he had allowed Rosamund to talk him into agreeing to her plan. It was ridiculous, yet the idea of having her close, of not needing to endure all that lonely time apart, pleased him. He also realized the campaign could very well be his last. Though they had not discussed the prospect of death, she knew so too. The sobering reminder made the idea of having Rosamund with him all the more precious. It was a reckless plan and he must be insane to have agreed, but by agreeing Henry found he no longer dreaded his departure. They would travel together across Yorkshire in the chilly spring, enjoying each day of grace they were allowed.

A messenger came to Enderly that morning, sent by Hoke to inform Blanche of a change of plans. Annoyed, she read and reread his brief note. Change of plans—what change of plans? When questioned, the messenger told her Lord Henry's troops were preparing for the road. She had been waiting for that message. Hoke must have meant that Henry was to leave earlier than expected.

Excited by the idea of being with Henry again, Blanche ordered her maids to pack for the journey, ignoring the practical needs of travel in favor of her most alluring gowns and most flattering colors. Billowing silks in lavender, purple, and sea green, mist blue and deepest gold were packed inside her trunks. Blanche was not sure how many trunks Henry would allow her to bring. Men could be most annoying where baggage was concerned. But it was likely she would meet the queen and she would have to dress appropriately for that important event. With that in mind she would insist on bringing all her trunks. Surely Henry had wagons enough to carry them.

He had always been more indulgent with her whims than Walter.

Walter! She paused on the stairs, gazing out at the gray blue sky as she considered her late husband. She must convince Henry that Walter was dead before she had any real hope of a lasting commitment.

Blanche hurried up the stair. She alone knew Walter was not in a French, or Saracen, prison, rotting with the passing years. She paused, her fair brow drawn into a frown. He rotted all right, but he was at Northcot. Possessing that knowledge often made her uneasy. Though she could command the dark elements, sometimes the superstition of her age bled through. Uneasily she wondered if Walter's ghost would haunt her. When she passed that part of the paneling she always quickened her steps and clutched her amulet while muttering a quick incantation for her protection. Walter lay behind a hidden panel that they had discovered some years back. After treacherously luring him there, she had closed the panel, aware there was no opening on the inside. When he had cried for help, she had ignored his cries, having cleverly planned the deed to coincide with their hour of departure for London. Most of the servants had already gone outside, and they'd heard nothing. She had told them that Sir Walter would join her after his business in York was finished.

She had had to stay away from Northcot for months until she was sure it would be safe to return. The only way to prove to Henry that Walter was dead would condemn her. To that day, she had never opened the panel, not having the courage to do so. A colorful tapestry hung over the place. It was she who was the source of the rumors placing her husband either in the Holy land or in France, imprisoned while about the king's business. Once Walter was gone, her way lay clear to capture Harry Ravenscrag. She had not counted on his stubborn insistence that as long as Walter lived they could not wed. She always wanted to shout at Henry that Walter was as dead as a mackerel, but she was forced to hold her tongue. She had not dared press Henry further, afraid he might guess she had a part in Walter's disappearance.

Blanche continued to climb the narrow stairs to the secret attic room where she practiced the black arts. She was dressed appropriately in flowing black silk with silver trimmings; her bright hair was hidden by a turban decorated with silver symbols of the zodiac. Whatever force was unleashed when she called on the powers of darkness to aid her, she needed its full cooperation that day. Sometimes she even frightened herself with the moanings and voices echoing from the cobwebby corners of the room. At first, guilt had driven her to think it was Walter's ghost who tormented her, but she had learned it was the combined forces of earthly and satanic elements. The more she delved into the ancient grimoire she had inherited from her grandmother, the deeper she was lured by the promise of power as yet untapped. She did not ask much: All she wanted was the body and soul of Henry Ravenscrag. And she would begin that possession by traveling with him to whatever place he chose, in the hope of convincing him how much he needed her. With the aid of potions and spells, she would persuade him he could not function without her.

Blanche collected some last-minute ingredients from the bottles and jugs lining the shelves at the far end of the room. Bunches of drying herbs and embalmed rabbits' feet swung from the exposed beams overhead, brushing against her face as she moved along the shelves. Bottles of adders, frogs legs, and mice were there; a preserved human embryo, all shriveled and brownish, floated in a dish; labeled boxes containing hair, blood, and nail clippings gathered for future use were crowded into the drawers. Even Blanche found some ingredients repulsive, but they were necessary to complete the more powerful spells in the grimoire. Though she used many of her powders in love potions for gullible wenches, there were some whose potency was as yet untried. It was to those she would turn to further enslave her lover and permanently turn him away from the hated Rosamund.

Before Blanche stepped inside the pentagram painted on the floor, she murmured a protective incantation. Then she lit a single candle to light the gloomy room, whose only source of light was the unglazed window overlooking the moor. It was cold in there and she shivered as she set down the candle before the divining pool. She looked into the vessel on the floor, where the water appeared murky. She had to have the water clear enough to see Henry's face.

Blanche sat cross-legged before the divining pool and cleared her mind of all but Henry's image. Slowly the waters began to churn until finally she saw his face in the water, distorted but unmistakable. Again she concentrated on a picture of the high table in the great hall, where at that time he would probably be supping. There was the table, but no Henry. Surprised, Blanche craned forward, trying to see the image she had visualized. The table stayed empty. Where could he be? Perchance in his bedchamber? Alarmed, she shut her eyes, concentrating so hard that her arms and legs began to vibrate. When next she opened her eyes the vision of his bedchamber, on which she had concentrated, was imprinted on the calm surface of the water. Ah, there he was, lounging before the hearth. Then she scowled, cursing beneath her breath. It was as she feared: He was not alone in the firelit bedchamber. Damn him! He dallied with a castle whore! By the shadowy softness of the image, she could tell it was a woman. But the image was too vague for her to tell who the woman was. In anger she threw a handful of powder in the water instantly destroying the picture in a sizzling curl of smoke.

Her temper flaring, Blanche snuffed the candle and picked up her basket of ingredients. She must get to Ravenscrag before her hold over Henry waned further. She had imagined him pensive and longing for her, not whoring the day away. Her mouth tight, Blanche locked the door, putting the only key inside her chatelaine.

It was already gloomy outside. It would be dark when she arrived at Ravenscrag, but that could not be helped. At least for that night she would be there early enough to forestall his randy dalliance. The buxom castle strumpet would be sent packing with either a slap on the cheek or a kick in the rump, whichever Blanche found most convenient.

Chapter Fifteen

Henry moved along the silent corridor, his suede soles hissing over the stone floor. He had been making final preparations with his squire and body servants for an early morning departure. The wagons of supplies had gone on ahead. A lady and gentleman traveling with their servants should not arouse suspicion if they met Yorkist troops. Though his journey would not be as unencumbered and swift as he had expected, the added benefit of having Rosamund at his side far exceeded the drawbacks.

It was chilly in the stone-walled passage and he clasped the front of his bedgown, glad of the fur-lined velvet. He was alerted to a movement in the shadows and his hand went to the dagger at his waist. Henry never stirred without arming himself; there were too many ambitious men in the world for that, even inside the comparative safety of his own castle.

"Henry," a woman's voice said.

His hand hovered about the dagger hilt as he backed against the wall. "Who is it?"

"It's me."

Startled, he gasped in surprise as Blanche materialized from the shadows, clad in flowing purple velvet, her red hair loose about her shoulders. "What in God's name—" he said, but she put her slender hand over his mouth to quiet him.

"We need to talk alone."

"About what?"

"Our journey. I've already ordered my trunks packed, but I thought, why wait?"

He took her arm, bringing her into the pool of flickering

The Rose of Ravenscrag

light shed from a sconce burning overhead. He had no idea what she was talking about. "What journey?"

"You know well enough. I'm traveling with you. We discussed it."

"But I don't remember giving you an answer. So I'll give it now: no! You're not coming on any journey with me. You'd best go home to Enderly. I don't know how you got inside the castle at this hour—"

She smiled strangely, her green slanting eyes glittering in the torchlight. "Don't you? Since when do I need open gates and doors to come to you, my love?"

Henry's heart thumped uncomfortably and a chill ran down his spine at the implication behind her words. He had heard much gossip about Blanche's supernatural powers. Sweat beaded on his brow as he considered the possibility that the rumors might be true.

"Don't fear danger on my behalf, love. I've power enough to protect us both," she whispered, her hands stealing into his hair as she bent his head toward her.

Henry pulled away. "You don't belong on the road with the troops. You should stay home with your children."

"And yours," she said softly, pressing her breasts and hips against him in a most provocative manner. "They'll want for nothing. They're well cared for by the servants. Now, no further excuses, my lord. You can't rid yourself of me that easy."

"I'm beginning to find that out," he muttered as he pushed her away and held her at arm's length. "What we shared is over, Blanche. What must I do to convince you?"

Her eyes narrowed as jealousy got the better of her. "Just because you tumble some castle whore doesn't change our relationship. You didn't think I'd find out about her, did you? Well, let me tell you, Harry Ravenscrag: There's little you do that I don't either see or hear."

"A castle whore?" he said, exerting even more force to hold Blanche away as she thumped about in anger, struggling to embrace him.

"The woman whose been in your chamber these hours

past,'' she cried, finally breaking away to slip under his out-stretched arms. Blanche took hold of his shoulders and bent his head toward her, but her kiss only glanced off his cheek before Henry extricated himself from her embrace.

"The only woman in my chamber these past hours has been my wife.''

Utter silence met his astounding statement before Blanche erupted in rage, hissing like a cat as she tried to claw his face. "How can she be here?''

"Your power must be weaker than you think," he said, gripping her wrists to prevent her from scratching him. "Now go home before I call the guards.''

"That's why you won't take me with you. She's going in my place! Don't you dare tell me a woman doesn't belong with the army when you're taking her.''

"Rosamund's my wife. It's her right," he said coldly, grasping Blanche's arm and moving her ahead of him. "Come. I'll see you to your horse.''

Blanche turned on him, spitting in fury. "You can't get rid of me that easily. Surely you've not forgotten the way I make you feel. No other woman can do that because no other shares my secrets.''

Though he did not consciously do so, Henry suddenly found his hand cupped about her breast, where Blanche clasped it. He pulled away as if she was on fire. Blanche tore open her flowing purple gown to reveal her nudity: milky, curving flesh aglow as if lit by an inner light. Henry closed his eyes because the unexpected sight of her voluptuous body stirred his lust, as well she knew it would.

"Now, can you honestly say I don't arouse you?'' she asked him triumphantly as she pressed against him.

Henry leaned back against the stonework, his head buzzing as if he had drunk too much wine. His legs felt heavy, lacking the power to move, almost as if he was rooted beside this woman for all eternity. Sweat trickled down his neck as she softly caressed him, her hands slipping inside his bedrobe, kneading and stroking his body. He was drowning; the strange words she repeated made a rhythmic drumbeat in his ears. Almost too late, as her chanting grew louder, he realized she was casting a spell to ensnare him, filling his mind with the strange words of her evil incantation.

Henry made a supreme effort to rouse himself from the hypnotic state into which he was sinking. "No, get out, you foul woman," he cried, feeling as if he forced his way through thick, enveloping mists, his heart beating wildly and his legs shaking. A sudden gust of cold, invigorating air blowing through a nearby arrow slit awakened him from his lethargy as he finally overcame her powerful hold.

Blanche's face was contorted evilly through the swirling mist until all he could see was her mouth, with those white animallike teeth. She mouthed the same wicked words over and over.

"Get out," Henry cried again, making a superhuman effort to stay free of Blanche's power. He leapt at her, his hand raised to strike. When his fist came down, he sliced empty air. Shaken, his heart pounding, Henry reeled back against the stonework, crossing himself as he desperately tried to master his senses. Blanche was gone. He looked in both directions, seeing nothing but empty corridor. She had disappeared without a trace. He might even have thought she had never been there, were it not for the perfume lingering in the air mingled with a less pleasant odor, something faintly like brimstone.

Henry steadied himself against the cold wall, his legs weak and shaking. How could it have happened? Surely he had been dreaming. But he knew he had been wide awake and standing alone in the cold, dark passage. Dark. To his surprise he glanced up to see the overhead sconce had been extinguished. The only light came from strips of moonlight shining through the arrow slits.

Stumbling on unsteady legs, Henry headed toward the tower, still not sure what had happened. But whatever it was, he knew he never wanted to repeat the experience. He decided not to tell Rosamund; it would be far better that she not have her worst suspicions about Blanche confirmed.

He was chilled to the bone; his head buzzed as he stumbled up the tower stairs. What had just taken place affirmed all those foul rumors about Blanche's satanic powers. It also made something unpleasantly clear, something he had always dismissed as peasant fantasy: His former mistress was a witch!

Still shaking with rage, Blanche wrenched open the door to her secret room. Voices seemed to call to her from the corners. She had been completely humiliated. Why had she not known Rosamund had returned to Ravenscrag? She admitted it was her own fault for not focusing on the woman's identity earlier, but she had been far too eager to see Henry again.

Tears of rage ran down her cheeks, yet in her heart she knew they were not only from rage, but from heartache as well. Though at first her intention had been to possess Henry Ravenscrag, she discovered she also loved him. Her heart ached for him, making her just like those silly wenches who begged for love potions to recapture their sweethearts whose attentions had wandered. How she had scoffed at those women, cursing their stupidity.

Blanche leaned against the door, fighting to master her tears. She must not cry over a man. She had more power than any-one thereabouts. How dared that bitch Rosamund supplant her? What had gone wrong? Rosamund should have been dead. Blanche had seen her bound and captive in the charge of some ragged lout. How had she escaped?

For a few minutes longer Blanche bowed her head and wept. Her conscience—she assumed that was what her weakness was called—pricked when she considered all she had done for Henry. She had cheated, lied, and even murdered for him, yet still he was not hers. At the last meeting, she had seen such loathing in his face. She had become repugnant to him.

Finally Blanche straightened her shoulders and smoothed her purple gown. She had not even bothered to change into her black-and-silver gown. She felt so much power flooding through her that she had no need of assistance. If Henry would not love her, then he would love no one. The mighty Lord of Ravenscrag must be made to realize that his power was nothing compared to hers.

Still shaking with anger, Blanche stepped inside the pentagram, her hands clasped and her head bowed. How could she have allowed that wench to steal her lover? She had put too much trust in others: in foolish Hoke, who'd been shamefully demoted by his lord for his treachery, and in all those sly castle wenches who had begged her for potions, then turned against her. But Blanche would have the last word because she had something the others did not.

Blanche took the ancient grimoire from its hiding place and opened it to the marked place. Just in case she needed the special spell in a hurry, she had already started it, doing the preliminary steps of steeping and grinding the magic powder. To invoke the most deadly of charms the two must be combined. For a moment she hesitated, fresh anguish over her lost love making her pause. Could Henry be turned away from Rosamund? Was there any chance he could be made to love her again?

Those insistent voices from the shadows urged her on. Grimly she tipped the horrid concoction made from ground larks' tongues, adders' dried blood, and a dozen other hideous ingredients into the murky green liquid. The dark powder made it smoke.

Staring fixedly at the thick smoke, she uttered the verse written in a spidery hand at the foot of the page. Rosamund would have no joy of Henry, nor he of her for as long as Blanche lived. The power coursed through her limbs, taking hold of her heart and head.

In the curling smoke Blanche saw their worried, stricken faces, already aware some great calamity was to befall them. Blanche took great comfort from the knowledge it was she who had engineered their downfall. Rosamund would pay for stealing Henry from her, Henry for loving another. As Blanche stared mesmerized at the thick, slow curling smoke, other disturbing visions beyond her control came to life, showing many soldiers screaming and dying until she recoiled from the horrid pictures. Then a face she had seen before appeared in the smoke. It was the tall blond man she had seen with Rosamund, the one she had believed would keep Rosamund away from Ravenscrag forever. Steven, a voice in her head said. He would be the instrument of death. Blanche was aware of a new surge of power that she tried to master and direct to enforce the curse to hold firm for as long as she lived.

More images appeared in the smoke: a road choked with troops, signposts going by so fast she could barely see the names, a bridge, a river in which men bobbed like so many bundles of rags, snow, wind. The last name she saw before the images faded was the name Towton. Wanting to discover more, she tried to stir the liquid to produce more smoke, but it only bubbled. Exhausted, Blanche sank to the floor, where she rocked herself back and forth, weeping from exertion and pain at what she had done, aware that she had just condemned to death the man she loved!

Within an hour, a servant was dispatched to find the man Steven, whom Blanche had seen camped on a place called Bingley Heath. The messenger was to tell him the hated Lord of Ravenscrag rode forth unprotected, coming to join his men. Instinctively Blanche knew she and the blond peasant were kindred spirits. He too had been robbed of his prized possession. She also knew that Rosamund and Henry's fates were strangely intertwined with that of Steven. She did not care to learn more. She had already suffered enough. She longed to run freely over the moor, to hunt and forget she had ever known a man named Henry Ravenscrag.

Sometime later, while the moon still shone brightly over the moor, a large white cat sprang upon a rocky outcropping and crouched, licking its paws. From there could be seen the great castle of Ravenscrag looming darkly against the horizon, its massive towers and battlements filling the sky.

"Cursed be the house of Ravenscrag, its lord, its lady." The white cat stopped licking, stiffening as something stirred under the nearby gorse bushes.

It was time to hunt.

PART III

PART III

Chapter Sixteen

Rosamund waited in the shelter of the inn door for Henry to finish the preparations for their journey. Her heart lurched with love as she watched him, lithe and broad-shouldered, striding across the innyard. She still found it hard to believe he was really her husband. She had dreamed of holding him in her arms for so long that sometimes when they were together she wanted to pinch herself just to make sure she was not just having one of her dreams.

They had learned the day before that the bulk of their troops were less than a day's ride away. That news heralded the end of their idyll since Henry had to join his men. They were headed for Tadcaster, where the army made camp. The last night they had spent in York at the same inn where they had stayed in December. Recalling the frightening events of that time still made Rosamund uneasy, and she kept glancing behind her as if she expected to find Steven lurking in the shadows. Though Henry laughed at her fears, she suspected he did not as confidently dismiss them as once he had done.

Henry set his red velvet feathered cap at a jaunty angle and fastened his cloak. "Ready, love?" he asked, smiling down at her.

Rosamund smiled in reply, and reaching up to kiss him, she found his lips chilled by the blustering wind. "Yes, but reluctantly so. I don't want to give you up."

"It's only for a little while. Queen Margaret's staying at Gupsill Manor while she reviews the troops. I've arranged for you to stay there also."

"With the queen?" Rosamund gasped in awe, clutching his arm.

Henry laughed at her shocked expression. "Well, not with her exactly, though I'm sure she'll want to meet you."

"Will the little prince be there too?"

"Yes, his mother's afraid to let him out of her sight."

When Rosamund mounted her horse, her mind was awhirl with the news. She was ill-prepared to meet royalty. Though she had made vast adjustments in her life the past year, it had not yet included meeting the queen. She smiled at her own foolishness. Then a startling thought shot through her mind with such clarity that it made her gasp. That gypsy fortune-teller had told her she wold stand close to the Crown. How much closer could she come than Queen Margaret and the Prince of Wales?

As they rode along the rough moorland track, Rosamund considered the rest of that prediction, including the warning to watch her back at all times. So far everything foretold had come true, especially the part about the handsome lover—and the danger. Something told Rosamund she was not yet finished with danger. She constantly glanced behind her as they rode because the wild land revived unpleasant memories of Steven and his ragged men. Henry seemed unconcerned with her fears, but he did not have a gypsy woman's prophecy to fulfill.

As the hours passed, they saw many small bands of soldiers crossing the moor. Some were probably not Lancastrians. Henry thought he recognized banners belonging to supporters of Edward, Earl of March.

Henry wore a velvet doublet and cap without armor, though he carried a sword and dagger. By his dress, he hoped not to arouse attention, continuing their ploy of country squire and his lady accompanied by their household servants. Going against the usual custom, they displayed neither banner nor pennant as they rode; however, on closer inspection, his suit of plate armor and the arsenal of weapons he had hidden under the blankets in the wagon would betray him. Henry gambled they would not arouse enough interest to make such a search necessary.

The day was heavily overcast. The moorland appeared desolate and windblown, populated only by sheep. A few isolated huts sheltered behind stands of trees or in the lee of rocky outcroppings. In the distance campfires flickered in the gloom. Rosamund looked about at the forbidding landscape and wondered where Gupsill Manor was since she could see nothing grander than a stone barn.

"What's this place called?" she asked Henry as they rode side by side over a rugged stone bridge spanning a swollen stream.

"They tell me it's Bingley Heath. We ought to see Tadcaster from the high ground, though surely we'll find the army long before that."

The narrow road ran downhill, and it was edged with gorse thickets. Rough heather and tangled undergrowth spread to the horizon, where huge boulders were heaped as if cast down by a giant hand. In fact, the Giant of Bingley Heath had supposedly thrown them there in rage when his captive sweetheart had escaped to rejoin her mortal family. Rosamund could see why the locals firmly believed in giants, witches, and fairies in that lonely place. The riders were forced into single file as they traveled along a sunken road between stands of trees. Small thickets of woodland blackened the landscape as the ground gradually sloped downhill from the high moor.

Suddenly, as they slowed to bypass an icy puddle straddling the track, an arrow whistled past their heads and lodged in the canvas wagon cover. That warning of danger sent the riders desperately maneuvering for shelter. It was too late. From both sides parties of men rode out of the woods. Behind the riders ran a ragged band of men who fanned out purposely over the scrubby ground. Their leaders looked ungainly in the saddle, as if unused to riding.

As the terrible nightmare began to unfold, Rosamund looked closely at the advancing ruffians and her stomach lurched. The foremost rider was a huge man wrapped in sacking, but even at that, there was no mistaking his broad branching shoulders or deep yellow hair.

"Oh, Mother of God," she groaned, the words strangling in her throat. The man was Steven.

"You're my captive, Ravenscrag," Steven bellowed, jogging forward to cut off their escape. A score of men with staffs and bills surrounded them.

"We're peaceable travelers. What right have you to take us prisoner?" Henry shouted, still trying to be affable, yet at the same time bearing the authority of his rank. As yet he had not recognized his captor, thinking the men were straggling deserters from the enemy ranks.

"By divine right. A messenger came from God to warn me you rode this way," Steven said, reaching for Henry's reins. He jerked Henry toward him.

Henry had vacillated a fraction too long, still hoping to play the innocent traveler by not taking up arms. His actions were to no avail. In fact, the men seemed to have been waiting for him. When he finally resisted, it was too little, too late. Henry was quickly overpowered and dragged from the saddle, though not before curses and cries of pain echoed from his captors as his dagger found its mark.

Rosamund did not wait to be pulled out of the saddle. She dismounted and stood there, her legs trembling as she looked at Steven. He appeared even wilder than the last time she had seen him with his straggling hair and a growth of beard stubbling his cheeks. Several of his front teeth were missing, probably lost in some recent skirmish. Yet for all his forbidding appearance, Steven smiled at her, trusting as a child.

"Oh, Rosamund, love, I knew you'd come back to me," he said softly, stroking her hair with his filthy hand, tidying the bright mass which escaped her hood. "I allus knew we was meant to be together. The Lord led me to you."

His connection to the Almighty was a startling new aspect of Steven's delusions. Rosamund saw Henry had recognized Steven, but when she tried to go to him, they held her back.

"What do you want with us?" Henry said, trying to maintain his balance as he was pushed and shoved up the incline toward the trees. "We've no money or jewels." But he knew the precious jewel Steven sought was already in his possession.

The men tried to control Diablo, who thrashed and whickered, his eyes rolling wildly. Despite Steven's barked orders to capture the stallion, the men were afraid to get too close.

"Let me bring him," Henry said, not wanting harm to come to his beloved horse.

Though Steven hated to allow his lordship anywhere near a horse for fear he'd bolt, he also hated to let such good horseflesh stray. "Right, then, but she's coming with me," he said, reaching down to yank Rosamund onto his horse.

Rosamund trembled as a cold knife was pressed against her throat. Could she gamble Steven cared enough for her not to harm her? She did not know.

Nor did Henry. He knew he could not risk having Rosamund hurt. Abandoning all thoughts of escape, he calmed Diablo and led the big horse up the incline to the men's camp, keeping watch on Rosamund out of the corner of his eye to make sure she was safe.

"I've been waiting a long time for this, Henry Ravenscrag," Steven said after he had dismounted on the fringe of scrubby trees, where they had crude tents and a cookfire.

"What do you propose to do with us?" Henry said.

Steven chuckled at Henry's naive question. "Do with 'e?" he said, picking up a cup of ale and downing it. "I'll kill thee and bed her."

The other men laughed uproariously at his succinct reply.

"You'll have to kill me first," Henry said.

"Aye, I intend to. None of you touch him. He's all mine," Steven said, his face set in a murderous scowl. "I'll slit the throat of any who interferes."

The other men agreed, wondering at Steven's command. Those who had been with Steven for some time recalled taking the same captives before. No one knew why Steven continually sought out the nobleman and his lady or what plan lay behind their latest encounter.

"Do you intend to fight me to the death?" Henry asked, all the while trying to maneuver closer to the wagon and his weapons. Warily he signaled to his young squire not to try any heroics.

"If tha likes. Or I can slit tha throat now and save us all a lot of trouble," Steven said with a grin, encouraged in his newfound wit by the guffaws of his supporters. "Outcom'll be the same. You'll die. This was all arranged for me, see, by a heavenly messenger. I'm blessed, Henry Ravenscrag. I, Steven of the Forge, was chosen to end your evil life."

His last statement was met by silence and his men shifted uncomfortably. The messenger they had met on the moor seemed like a mortal man to them, though Steven had kept insisting he was an angel sent from God. Since that day nearly a week earlier, they'd been combing all roads leading to and from York and Tadcaster, searching for their prey. The whole time Steven had hardly eaten or slept, so driven was he to complete his mission.

"Mayhap I'll torture thee first," Steven said, crouching down to stir the fire's embers with a stick. "Brand you, just to show who's in charge now."

Rosamund cried out in alarm at his suggestion and she was cuffed into silence. Steven's attention shifted immediately and he cursed the man, grabbing him and flinging him down, reminding all not to lay a finger on the woman or they would answer to him.

"Brand me if you want, but it won't prove you're the better man," Henry said. "You do want to show me you're stronger and more worthy of Rosamund's love, don't you?"

Puzzled by his question, Steven turned to his captive. "Aye, I reckon I do. I've got divine help now—just like David when he fought Goliath."

Henry smiled sarcastically. "You forget: David won that contest. Give me a fair chance. Fight with weapons. If you're ordained to win, it'll make no difference," Henry said

342

shrewdly, aware that the other man was bigger and stronger, but knowing he was far more skilled with a sword.

Puzzled by the nobleman's suggestion, Steven tried to reason it out in his muddled mind. His own men kept urging him to be quick because their lookout reported armed men heading that way. If those were Lancastrian troops, they would be cut off from the main Yorkist force camped near Ferrybridge.

In the foggy twilight of his mind Steven envisioned Rosamund still as fair as an angel, unsullied by the evil man who had used his wealth to enslave her. The black-haired, dark-skinned man who stood mocking him suddenly assumed a strange humpbacked appearance, like some fiend from hell.

Steven dashed his hand across his eyes. He could hear heavenly music in his head . . . probably harps, but he was not sure what a harp sounded like. And he also heard trumpets, as if heralding a second heavenly messenger.

Almost able to guess the thoughts passing through Steven's deranged mind, Rosamund started to go to Henry to warn him, but she was grabbed from behind. The men thrust her against the side of the wagon, loosely binding her ankles to keep her from running. Two men held here there at knife point.

Steven slowly withdrew a broad-bladed knife from his belt as he sized up his opponent. The frightened men traveling with Ravenscrag were likely only unarmed servants. After Steven had killed their master, he would let them go; his newly acquired divine aid made him feel unusually generous and he was sure he would be expected to do the Christian thing. Yes, somewhere in the distance he could hear those heavenly trumpets growing louder, as if applauding his decision. His own men were glancing apprehensively at each other and they shielded their eyes to scan the undulating moor for approaching troops. Fools. They didn't understand. His messengers were not of their world. Steven smiled, feeling the hand of God on him. He told his men to give the nobleman back his sword and dagger.

The opponents circled each other. Henry was quicker than Steven, his sword extending Steven's reach, but the big man's superior strength and skill with the knife would even the odds. Suddenly Henry lunged forward, slicing down Steven's forearm with the point of his sword. The fight had begun.

With an animallike cry, Steven leapt. Henry dodged out of the way, but he failed to see a heap of stones, and when Steven drove him back towards the tree, he stumbled over them and his sword was snatched from his hand. In an instant the big man was on top of him and they rolled together, grappling in the dirt. Steven's superior strength was an advantage at such close quarters. Henry finally managed to draw his dagger and stab upward. At the same time he kicked Steven's hand aside, deflecting a knife thrust into his belly. Startled, Steven fell back before quickly regaining control, but it was time enough for Henry to spring back to his feet. His fallen sword lay close by in the dirt since, after Steven's warning, none of the men dared interfere.

As Henry grasped his sword, his confidence returned. The familiar feel of the weapon reminded him of the power behind his blade. He sliced an arc, catching Steven's forearm a glancing blow that flicked away his knife, sending it sailing harmlessly through the air. With a cry of rage Steven sprang forward, ignoring the blood trickling down his arm. He was freshly encouraged when he saw that his enemy fared worse then he. Henry's doublet sleeve was already soaked with blood. The battle would soon be over.

"Now, my pretty, if'n they'm both killed, you can be my woman," one of Rosamund's captors said as he watched the two men rolling about the ground, desperately trying to strangle each other.

The man's suggestion made Rosamund shudder. She turned away from his toothless grin, praying that hideous fate would never come to pass.

A blare of trumpets and galloping hooves startled the band of ragged men. Shouts of alarm echoed through the trees and those who had horses leapt into the saddle. Even Henry's servants' nags were ridden away. The men on foot scattered through the trees in a mad dash for freedom.

344

Rosamund turned to see a mounted party bearing down on them. The soldiers had a portcullis on their banner. She blinked, staring in disbelief at the fluttering silk, hardly able to comprehend she was looking at the Ireton banner. Oh, God be praised! The tide of fortune had miraculously turned.

Grunts and screams of pain, followed by heavy breathing, riveted her attention to the two men on the ground grappling for control. The mounted soldiers were busy rounding up the rabble fleeing on foot, though they did not pursue the riders.

Henry struggled to rise, his wounded arm crimson; his face was also splattered with blood. Steven sprawled on the ground, dead. Henry's jeweled dagger protruded from his chest.

Rosamund was so eager to go to Henry and help him that she forgot her feet had been hobbled. She fell, then struggled up again as she fought free of her bonds. Though Henry was hurt, he smiled in triumph, aware he had finally vanquished Steven of the Forge. Rosamund wept out of relief. Their luck had shifted indeed. Even the sky was lighter, and behind the clouds, she could see the rim of the sun peering out, its pale light creating halos about their rescuers' helmets.

Rosamund crouched beside Henry, helping his squire and body servants pull away his sodden doublet to examine his wounds. She gasped in dismay as she saw the flesh neatly divided into flaps, but the men all assured her the deep wound would knit cleanly.

When the Ireton troops came forward, they were amazed to discover they had rescued their neighbor. A wineskin was quickly offered and Henry drank deep while his servants cleansed his wounds and bound his arm with Rosamund's silk scarf.

Rosamund rocked back on her heels and looked up at the promising sky. Their terrible ordeal was finally over. The torment of Steven's insane pursuit had died with him; she was free at last. Rosamund's newfound freedom brought with it sweetly relieving tears and she knelt on the ground sobbing. Henry comforted her, not sure if she cried out of fear or relief.

"Come. Ride with us, my lord. Our master's just up the

road,'' the leader of the Ireton men said. ''But what of the lady?''

''She's to join Queen Margaret at Gupsill Manor,'' Henry said, fondling Diablo's head, glad the stallion was so fierce that none of the fleeing rabble had dared try to mount him.

''Then we can escort you there,'' the man said. ''It's on the way.''

Rosamund mounted before Henry on the big black horse, and when she rested against his comforting body, she was careful not to jostle his wounded arm.

Henry had suggested that they first should bury the dead man, but the others thought it not wise to tarry so late in the day. They chose to leave Steven for the crows.

Rosamund did not look back. She fixed her sight firmly into the misty distance, aware that a new chapter in her life had just begun.

The misty afternoon sky suddenly parted to reveal the sun and a glorious blaze of sunlight spread across the battlements of Ravenscrag Castle. Chrysty Dane rubbed his eyes, hardly able to believe that sudden change had taken place. Up till then, the cold, forbidding day had been locked in mist. In fact, of late, every day had been the same, the weather matching the prevailing feeling of gloom inside the castle.

Almost to the hour of their lord's departure, ill fortune had beset Ravenscrag's inhabitants. First, a servingwoman had been crushed by a shifting barrel; then several of Chrysty's men had been struck down by a mysterious malady. Fire had all but destroyed the blacksmith's hovel, and strange, wiggling black worms had been found in the well. When one calamity after another struck, all had begun to wonder if the castle was bewitched.

Chrysty tied their misfortunes to the appearance of that blasted white cat. It had been seen everywhere—on the battlements, in the bailey, even in his lord's bedchamber. So sure was Chrysty that the cat had brought their ill fortune, he offered a reward to the man who killed it.

Eager to earn a bonus, the castle soldiers began to shoot at anything that moved until Chrysty had to caution them not to be so reckless. Though countless arrows winged their way toward the elusive cat, none had harmed it. The night before, Chrysty himself had shot at the creature, positive he had hit it because he had heard it squawk. Yet when he had sent men down in search of the cat, they found neither the cat nor his spent arrow.

"Captain, captain, come quick," one of his men at the gate shouted.

Distracted from his gloomy thoughts, Chrysty Dane strode out into the bailey. "What is it?"

"The Lady Blanche," the man replied in hushed tones, his face seemed with worry as they stood back to admit a wagon.

"In the wagon? Is she hurt?"

"Dead. Shot by an arrow," the man said quietly.

"Blessed Mother! What next? We'll surely pay for this. I told the lads to stop firing at anything that moved. Where did they find her?"

"At the bottom of the outer wall."

Grimly Chrysty Dane approached the wagon, where he carefully turned over the body to see Blanche's face. Pale as a ghost, her tangled red hair sodden with frost and mist, Blanche Pomeroy looked as perfect as a marble statue. She was dead; there was no doubt about that. An arrow protruded from her chest, its barbed point exiting through her back.

"Send a messenger to her people at Enderly. Then get Hoke to take her to the chapel and tell Father John."

What next? he thought gloomily, running his hands over his brow as he sat brooding in the keep. Surely his lord would punish them harshly for the terrible accident. Though Lady Blanche was no longer in Lord Henry's favor, she was still a noblewoman. He knew he should try to find the culprit, but he realized the search would be futile.

As he sat there thinking about the dead woman, he recalled the rumors surrounding her and he wondered if any of them were true. The people in the nearby villages called her the Red

Witch. Some of the castle wenches bought love potions and beauty preparations from her, yet she could not have been a real witch. A real witch would not be dead. Real witches had ways of protecting themselves from harm by changing into animals who could escape over the moor. He'd heard tell that in a blink of an eye they could become stoats or hares—or cats!

Chrysty Dane sat upright, startled by that thought. When he considered it, the arrow in her chest had looked suspiciously like his own. The castle's fletcher made them a special way and it would not be hard to confirm ownership. Chrysty's heart pounded anew in shock. What if he had killed her? She might have been out there below the walls when he had shot at that damned cat. Dear God, surely that was not what had happened. His earthy lord would punish him in one life, his heavenly Lord in the next.

Chrysty paced nervously, reviewing the events of the previous misty night. It was strange that, though it had been sodden outside, the cat had shone through the mist as plain as a summer's day. After he had shot at it, he knew he had heard the thing squeal, yet he had found no trace of a wounded cat.

No wounded cat, but a dead woman! Alarmed by the awful conclusion he was making, Chrysty Dane sat heavily on the bench inside the door. Had he perhaps shot at the cat and killed it, but since it was no ordinary cat, they could find no corpse? The hair on the back of his neck stood up as a chill crept along his spine. Had that mysterious cat really been the Red Witch?

The weather change, so sudden and marked; the lifting of that mist and the castle being bathed in golden sunshine, almost as if released from a spell—could that cat have taken so long to die? Had those changes occurred when the witch died?

As Chrysty thought about it, he began to know beyond any doubt that, if he went to the infirmary, he would find his men miraculously healed. If he enquired about the state of the well, it likely would be restored to purity again.

Sweat trickled down his neck. He reached for a cup of wine,

his hands shaking. With a muttered prayer of thanks for their deliverance, aware that the witch's evil power had died with her, Chrysty Dane realized he was a hero. He was the savior of Ravenscrag Castle!

Rosamund felt nervous. She was virtually tongue-tied when she was finally ushered into the presence of the Queen of England. She had not expected Queen Margaret to be so young and attractive. The queen wore rose damask trimmed with sable; precious jewels glinted on the headdress covering her dark gold hair. Though young, there was little soft or vulnerable about the queen, who fairly bristled with determination when she discussed the Lancastrian cause. The boy prince looked thin and wan, eclipsed by the shadow of his ambitious mother. Though once Rosamund had considered the name insulting, she understood why the queen was sometimes referred to as the She-wolf of Anjou.

Rosamund managed a passable curtsy before the queen, though her knees were shaking. She was introduced as the wife of the Lord of Ravenscrag, and Rosamund found to her relief little was required of her beyond a smile. Queen Margaret spoke to Rosamund in French, as did her ladies, since they all assumed she spoke the language. Feeling very foolish, Rosamund murmured what she hoped were appropriate responses, saying *oui* and *non*, just as Henry had rehearsed with her when he had wisely anticipated the embarrassing lack.

Rosamund heaved a great sigh of relief when she finally left the royal presence, convinced the queen and her ladies must think her a half-wit because of the monosyllabic answers that she hoped had been the appropriate responses to the royal questions.

The queen was soon to depart for York and it was suggested that Rosamund travel with her party, but she declined, wanting to stay close to Henry. There was a battle imminent. The enemy had already drawn up his ranks north of Ferrybridge, while the large Lancastrian army was virtually camped on the grounds of Gupsill Manor.

Rosamund's chamber inside the old manor house was small and made gloomy by dark paneling. The welcome blaze in the hearth was her only source of light. To Rosamund's surprise she only discovered the next day was Palm Sunday when she was invited to attend Mass. At that rate she would probably spend Holy Week at Gupsill Manor, still waiting for word of Henry. No one had said how imminent the battle was, but Henry thought it close enough to stay with his men. Rosamund was disappointed by the decision since she had envisioned sharing a passionate rendezvous with him inside the firelit bedchamber, with the wind howling outside and them snuggling in each other's arms.

The servants said it had started to snow, but when Rosamund peered around the shutters, all she could see was dense blackness. It seemed impossible that somewhere out there in the dark were camped thousands of soldiers, commanded by the most powerful men in the realm, all gathered on that bleak Yorkshire heath to decide England's fate. Uneasily Rosamund realized such a decisive battle could well determine the outcome of the civil war. Though she knew he would not turn coats in battle as some nobles had done, Rosamund also knew Henry had seriously begun to doubt the future of the Lancastrian cause. Though he supported the Crown, it was becoming apparent that the most worthy contender for the throne was not poor, befuddled King Henry, or his sickly prince, but young Edward, Earl of March, whose blood was undeniably royal and who had emerged as a true leader of men.

Rosamund considered the facts as she drowsed in her soft featherbed, watching flames leaping up the sooty chimney. Her poor Henry would have to sleep rough on the cold heath in the snow. If only he could have spent just one more night with her. She chose not to dwell on the possibility of his being wounded or, worse still, of his not surviving the conflict, thinking instead about Ravenscrag and the future. Henry had ignored her pleas to stay out of the fight to give his arm time to heal. Instead she had applied salve and bound the wound tight, finding Henry was most eager to show her he could still wield a sword.

She smiled as she pictured his boyish eagerness to get at the enemy. Men were all alike. Even Meade Ireton, despite his wounds, couldn't wait to enter the fray. They seemed unstoppable, these men who had been trained for warfare almost from the cradle. She liked to dream of a time when the fighting would be over and Henry could stay home to teach his sons to care for their estates without the necessity of training them for battle.

Their sons. She smiled at the thought. Again she felt her stomach where there was a definite, solid mound. Was she with child? Since her monthly courses had never been regular, Rosamund was not sure how long it had been since her last flux. She was also ignorant of the time when a child stirred in the womb. Though she laced her hands across her stomach, trying to feel the swell of arms and legs or the beat of a tiny heart, she could not. It was in that position that she finally drifted off to sleep, unusually peaceful in the firelit room as she thought about the happy future when she and Henry need never be apart again.

The ground was cold and hard. Henry huddled in his cloak, with a blanket thrown over him to ward off the cold. On the morrow, Edward, Earl of March, would make his move. The Lancastrians had chosen their position well, situating their troops on the higher ground of Towton Heath outside Tadcaster. To their right flowed Cock Beck, a narrow, rain-swollen river between steep banks. Northumberland's forces were positioned closest to the beck and the Ravenscrag and De Gere troops stood beside their powerful ally.

Snowflakes blew intermittently in the icy wind, which crept inside every chink of Henry's clothing. Gupsill Manor was so close Henry could have seen Rosamund's room had she not been on the side facing away from the camp. He had wisely arranged with some of his men to warn her to flee if the outcome of the battle looked ominous. Those men would escort her to friends in York, where he intended to join her when, or if, he were able. Henry was also aware of Queen Margaret's contingency plan for her escape to Scotland if things did not go well for the Lancastrians. The ever practical queen would regard such an eventuality as a temporary setback, nothing more. Since Henry owned land north of Berwick, where he had spent several summers as a lad, the queen had chosen him as a reliable guide if they were forced to retreat.

To fulfill that obligation, he must live and remain unscathed. Henry smiled grimly in the darkness; those were both tall orders given the thousands of men facing each other across Towton Heath.

Rolling himself tighter in his blanket, he cleared his mind of thoughts about the queen and the coming conflict, thinking instead about Rosamund. He was relieved to be able to put dangerous Steven of the Forge in the past. Had he known the truth about Rosamund earlier, he would not have underestimated the blacksmith's tenacity in seeking his lost love. Though he wished Rosamund was safe inside Ravenscrag, it was too late to worry about that; instead he had made arrangements for her safety in case of a Lancastrian defeat. On the morrow, when he concentrated on staying alive, he would not be thinking about the French queen and her weak-minded husband, but about his beloved Rosamund.

The bitter cold night seemed endless. The two large armies were spread for miles over the heath and the surrounding countryside. Men huddled close to each other for warmth, trying to sleep on the cold ground wrapped in blankets. When they awoke on Palm Sunday, many men also wore a light covering of snow. Parish church bells clanged loudly to herald the holy day, summoning the villagers to Mass. The sound was blown to them on the icy wind as thousands of soldiers took up their positions for the bloody fight.

On Palm Sunday, March 29, 1461, the massive armies of York and Lancaster faced each other across bleak, windswept Towton Heath with snow blowing in their faces and the clanging bells to remind them of the holy day. As the challengers, the Yorkists made the advance, led by Edward, Earl of March,

Fauconberg, and Warwick. Northumberland, Somerset and Exeter commanded the defending Lancastrians.

Though the advancing force was blinded by swirling snow, the great noise they made told Henry they were a formidable foe. Reputedly the enemy numbered 30,000. Despite that fact that the Lancastrians outnumbered their enemies, Henry was not sure how the Scots and Burgundians recruited by Queen Margaret would handle themselves in the fight. From what he had heard, the undisciplined hordes were more skilled at pillaging than at standing their ground in a pitched battle.

Suddenly, out of the white blanket of snow driven into their faces by the buffeting wind, came a deadly hail of arrows. Men screamed as they tried to ward off the onslaught with their shields. When their own archers retaliated, their range fell short. Much to their chagrin, the Yorkists returned their spent arrows, sending them whistling out of the blinding snow. Once their arrows were spent, archers on both sides became lightly armored infantry and when the opposing armies clashed those men usually suffered high casualties.

With a great, deafening crash, the ranks finally engaged and there was no longer time to contemplate the latest move. There was time only to try to keep from being killed and in the process to take out as many of the enemy as possible.

All around Henry, men fought furiously in hand-to-hand combat. Henry's sword arm soon tired and he tried to compensate for his weakness by using his left arm. He was not as skilled with the left and he finally resorted to fighting with his mace and battle-ax. As he fought in the midst of hundreds of struggling men, he concentrated on destroying helm and plate. His feet continually slipped in the bloody snow as the deafening slaughter continued.

After hours of fierce engagement, Henry felt almost too weary to stand, yet the fighting continued without any abatement. Though Henry's throat and mouth were parched, he dared not take off his helm to drink. His squire offered him a skin of watered wine. Henry lifted his visor, trying to squirt the liquid in his mouth, but much of it ran down his chin. He had heard tell of men's thirst leading to their deaths since vigilant enemies watched for such carelessness. Without their helms armored men were vulnerable. Henry wondered how much longer his own helm could protect him, dented and battered as it was after being severely damaged by a spiked morning star. His head ached and his ears still rang from the assault.

Sometime in the late afternoon the enemy received reinforcements and gradually the tide of battle shifted. The Lancastrian right was slowly being driven toward the fast flowing river where they scrambled madly for a foothold on its steep, muddy bank.

Shouts to flee the field suddenly went up as Henry maneuvered around heaps of the slain, trying to find a sheltered place to lay down Meade Ireton, who had been mortally wounded. Henry's first intention had been to carry Ireton to his horse, but the wounded man had begged Henry to let him die there, saying his own men could take care of him for the short time he had left. Henry knelt beside Ireton and eased off his friend's broken helm, laying him down out of the bitter wind in the shelter of a mound of bodies. Ireton urged Henry to go while he still had the chance.

Henry's own men were also urging him to flee. The Yorkists had begun to exact bloody payment from their defeated enemy. Northumberland had been badly wounded and had already left the field. Hours earlier, Henry had sent his men to take Rosamund to safety, because, while the battle raged all day in the bitter weather, his hopes for victory had dwindled. Though Henry was reluctant to quit the field, he had many obligations to fulfill, and for them, he must live. It would serve no purpose to continue to fight only to be murdered by the victorious Yorkist troops.

Henry was soon up in the saddle and seeking a clear way. Diablo's hooves slipped on icy patches and the horse floundered in the churned mire of blood, snow, and mud. Henry finally found a clear space, and commanding his men to follow, he threaded his way through the opening. On every side the carnage was terrible. Narrow Cock Beck was choked with bodies. Dead men formed a bridge for their fellows to cross and the swift flowing water ran red with blood.

Encountering sporadic pursuit, Henry galloped flat out to elude his enemies. To his relief, the opposing forces soon fell back. There was far easier prey, and for the moment, the Yorkists had sport enough around Towton. It would be later when they pursued their escaping foes to York.

Chapter Seventeen

At first Rosamund resisted the men's efforts to make her leave
Gupsill Manor, begging them to let her stay there to wait for
Henry. Only when she learned that they had come at his order
did she finally give in. The Lancastrians must be close to defeat for Henry to have put his urgent plan in place. Fear for
his safety consumed Rosamund's mind as she hastily stuffed
her possessions into her saddlebags.

With tears pouring down her cheeks, Rosamund set out on
that gloomy afternoon. Her escort either couldn't or wouldn't
give her news about Henry, saying only her husband had been
well when last they saw him. The air was heavy with the smell
of battle. Shouts and the clang of weapons echoed from all
sides until Rosamund began to wonder if she and the others
would be able to escape the fight. By following a route
mapped out for them by their lord, the two young soldiers
skillfully wove their way past cottage and shippen, eluding
scavenging parties robbing the dead and dying. In between
looting, these men often pursued stragglers for sport, and Rosamund was relieved when her party had left the looters far
behind.

The icy wind seared Rosamund's face, which soon felt
numb; even her fur-lined cloak was not enough protection
from the cold. The fleeing party rode for their lives. All the
roads heading north were choked with fleeing men, many sup-
porting wounded comrades. The reek of burning wagons and
horseflesh blew in the wind and the air was filled with the
cries of the wounded and the din of battle.

Rosamund was never more relieved than when the party

finally reached York and she saw the great gates standing open to admit the battered remnants of Queen Margaret's army. Henry's men took her to a house in the north part of the city, where his friends, the Marstons, had promised to hide her if necessary. Though Rosamund wanted to stay awake in case Henry reached York with the others, Mistress Marston insisted she at least lie down and rest while she was waiting for her husband.

By their worried expressions, Rosamund could tell the Marstons were not sure Henry would ever come for her. Fiercely clinging to her hope, Rosamund prayed for his life, promising more faithful attendance at Mass, even promising to found charities for the poor if only her prayer could be granted. Huddled inside her cloak with blankets thrown over her, Rosamund was still cold after her numbing ride; even the heat of the fire was not enough to thaw her icy limbs.

The Marstons generously fed Rosamund's escorts, though she herself did not eat; the family also rubbed down and fed the horses. The Marstons did all they could to make Rosamund comfortable and she was grateful for their kindness. Yet the only thing that would make her truly comfortable was to see Henry walk through the door unscathed.

Sometime during that black, cold night, a thundering racket on the street door woke the household. The streets of York swarmed with wounded. Everywhere men sought shelter. It was rumored that the triumphant Yorkists were killing all Lancastrians in their path.

"Lady, wake up. It's time to leave," Mistress Marston said, shaking Rosamund by the shoulder to rouse her from a deep sleep.

Rosamund looked up at the strange woman's face, wondering at first where she was. When she remembered, her stomach lurched in fear. "Have you news of Henry?" she asked, her hands shaking as she fumbled for her boots under the bed.

"News! What news would you have, Lady?" a familiar deep voice said from the doorway.

Rosamund looked up and she saw him, battered and blood

splashed, his face lined with weariness. The miracle she had prayed for had finally come to pass: Her beloved had been returned to her safe and sound!

With a shriek of delight, Rosamund flew across the rushes, stumbling with one boot on, one boot off. She fell weeping into Henry's arms, but her tears were of joy. Henry's clothes were wet and cold, and he stank of battle. But she did not care. All that mattered was that he was alive!

Despite the iciness of his cheeks, his mouth was hot against hers. "Are you hurt, love?" she asked him anxiously.

"A little, but I'll live. Now, come. I intend us all to live and we haven't much time. Even now they're inside the city taking prisoners."

Quickly they hugged each other. Then Rosamund pulled on her other boot and stumbled after Henry down the narrow stair as he took the treads two at a time. Much commotion in the courtyard told her there were many others in their party.

"Come on, love. Hurry. We don't want to give those bastards any more sport," Henry said.

"Where are we going?"

"Scotland."

"Tonight?"

"This minute, if we're able," he said, laughing at her shocked expression. He stooped to kiss her face before quickly hoisting her into the saddle.

In a whirlwind of icy darkness amid the noisy, jostling strangers, their party spilled out of the Marstons' courtyard onto York's cobbled streets. There was a growing buzz to the south, giving truth to the rumors of Yorkist reprisals. Fortunately the Marstons' house lay north of the city, close to Monk Gate. Henry had chosen that location since it was far from the Micklegate, through which any pursuit from the south would come. Henry had gambled that the enemy would hack and murder their way across York before they reached Monk Gate, giving his followers precious time to escape.

Soon the travelers had left the city and ridden through black countryside, where patches of snow glistened in the light from the lead riders' lanterns. They did not slacken their frantic pace until York was left far behind. Rosamund guessed Queen Margaret and her son rode with them since that had been the plan. But because their party straggled so far and everyone was swathed in dark cloaks, she could not tell which rider was the young queen. Following far to the rear was a litter for the queen when she tired of the saddle. Rosamund guessed the boy prince was asleep inside.

They did not really reduce their pace to normal traveling speed until they were safe across the Tweed. Fortunately, the weather held. But it was very cold and Rosamund kept wondering how much farther they had to go. Henry laughingly told her a whole nation lay to the north, yet they had traveled so far already that it seemed to her as if they had already ridden across several nations. The county of Northumberland was friendly to their cause and farther north Scottish allies waited to receive Queen Margaret.

On a crisp morning, with the sun peeking out from behind silver-edged banks of cloud, they finally bid farewell to the queen's party. Queen Margaret presented Henry with a purse of gold and a medal bearing her likeness in payment for his bravery in bringing her safely into Scotland. The queen headed for Berwick. She hoped to set up headquarters there to direct her continued fight to regain England's throne for her son.

Rosamund curtsied to the queen and smiled when the monarch spoke to her in French, not knowing if she should say yes or no in answer to her question. It no longer mattered if the French queen thought Rosamund a half-wit. Their paths might never cross again.

Rosamund leaned back against the comforting warmth of Henry's body as they watched the royal party riding away into the distance. Henry breathed a great sigh of relief as he swept Rosamund into his arms and swung her joyously about.

"Good riddance," he said, his breath hot against her ear as he covered her face with kisses. "Now we're free to do what we want."

"Are we staying here?" she asked, looking back at a poor

hovel that called itself an inn. "Or are we going home to Ravenscrag?"

Henry sighed, his face clouding at her question. "We can't return yet. We're going into the Lammermuir Hills. I've a small fortress there. We'll have to lie low till all the furor dies down."

"Just the two of us?" Rosamund asked in disbelief, her eyes shining in delight at the prospect of their being alone at long last.

"Yes, and them," Henry said, sweeping his hand to include his squire and body servant and the handful of men-at-arms who formed his personal bodyguard. The bulk of the Ravenscrag troops had already headed home, taking with them the maid, Margery, and the men-at-arms Rosamund had left stranded in Cheshire after she was captured.

"They're looking for you, aren't they?" Rosamund asked suddenly when Henry fell silent. She was frightened by his grim expression. She should have guessed when she had asked him if they were going to Ravenscrag that it would not be safe there. "Will there be reprisals?"

"Yes, in answer to your first question," he said finally, "but I hope I've taken measures to stop the reprisals."

"What measures are those?" she asked as he helped her into the saddle, cupping his hands for her to mount.

"Drastic measures, banking on the fact that men say Edward is a fair man. If he is, then I've a chance to come out of this with most of my lands intact."

"Edward? The Yorkist prince?"

"Aye, that's the one. I offered him my backing. You didn't know, did you, love, that soon you'd become a Yorkist wife?" He threw back his head and his laughter rang out when he saw her rounded eyes and shocked expression.

"Queen Margaret just gave you her medal. She honored you."

"So she did, and rightly so. I've always fulfilled my duty to the crown with the greatest loyalty. None of that's changed. I intend to do so in the future. Only it's Edward who'll be

England's next king, not her little bastard. Trust me, Rosamund. This is so."

"Is the war over then?"

"Let's say it's enjoying a temporary lull."

As they rode across the undulating terrain, the sun glowed like a huge orange ball shimmering through mist. Finally breaking through the cloud, the sunlight glistened on the snowcapped hills rising in the distance. Henry reined in to show Rosamund where they were headed.

"I thought Scotland was all towering mountains and wild clansmen," Rosamund said in surprise, standing with Henry on the edge of the track to survey the bare winter landscape spread out before them.

"They're farther north, love. These are just lowlands, like the borders we've already crossed. But it's good country and we can stay safe here for a while. What's most important is that we're together," he said, slipping his arm round her shoulders. "We'll live like a country lad and lass, because, I warn you, this is a poor border stronghold, nothing grand like Ravenscrag."

"How long are we to stay?" she asked, laying her face in the warm hollow of his neck, where she traced the tip of her tongue across his skin until he shuddered in arousal at her touch.

"For as long as you promise to make love to me," he whispered ardently as he pulled her against him to kiss her mouth.

Rosamund laughed in pleasure as she hugged him back, rejoicing in the strength of his body, reveling in the firm substance of his arms and shoulders, finally having something tangible to hold in place of all her impassioned dreams.

"First you'll have to bathe, my lord," she said, wrinkling her nose at his soiled clothing.

"Done. In fact, I thought a shared bath before the fire would be most pleasant," he said, holding Rosamund protectively against him. "Sweet, I'm sorry we have to go into exile. I promise it's only for a little while, just until its safe to go home."

"I don't mind as long as we're together," she said sincerely, looking deep into his blue eyes and seeing them soften with love for her. "I just wanted to know how long we'd stay in Scotland in case you minded your son being born a Scot."

"What?" Henry's expression changed and he held her out at arm's length, not sure he had heard correctly. "You said . . . Rosamund are you . . . we . . . having a babe?"

"Yes."

"You're sure?"

"Positive."

Her eyes filled with tears as she saw his delight. Henry very carefully put her aside, newly conscious of her delicate condition. "There'll be none of that, Harry Ravenscrag," she said tartly, putting her arms around his neck and pulling his face down to hers to kiss. "I want to enjoy our exile; so you're going to have to make some promises of your own."

Henry showered her face with kisses, his heart filled with love for the woman in his arms. "I promise to love you forever, my beautiful Rose of Ravenscrag."

And she was content with that.

SWEET CHANCE

CAROLE HOWEY

Bestselling Author Of *Sheik's Promise*

Paris Delany is out to make his fortune, and he figures cattle ranching is as good a way as any. But the former Texas Ranger hasn't even set foot in Chance, Wyoming, before his partner becomes smitten with the local schoolmarm. Determined to discourage the match, he enlists the help of a sharp-tongued widow—and finds himself her reluctant suitor.

Pretty, reserved, and thoroughly independent, Cressida Harding has loved and lost one husband, and that is enough for her. She doesn't need a man to stand up for her rights or protect her from harm, even if dumb luck has brought virile Paris Delany to her doorstep. But the longer he is in town, the more Cress finds herself savoring the joys of sweet chance.

_3733-5 $4.99 US/$5.99 CAN

Hunters of the Ice Age Theresa Scott

At the dawn of time, a proud people battle for survival, at one with the harsh beauty of the land and its primal rhythms.

Broken Promise. Her people destroyed, her promised husband enslaved, Star finds herself at the mercy of a fierce warrior. And even though she is separated from everything she loves, the tall, proud Badger woman will not give up hope. With courage and cunning, the beautiful maiden will survive in a rugged new land, win the heart of her captor, and make a glorious future from the shell of a broken promise.

_3723-8 $4.99 US/$5.99 CAN

Dark Renegade. Talon has stalked the great beasts of the plain, but he has never found prey more elusive than Summer, the woman he has stolen from his enemies. But only a bond stronger than love itself can subdue the captor and make him surrender to Summer's sweet, gentle fury.

_51952-6 $4.99 US/$5.99 CAN

Yesterday's Dawn. Mamut has proven his strength and courage time and again. But when it comes to subduing one helpless female captive, he finds himself at a distinct disadvantage. He claims he will make the stolen woman his slave, but he soon learns he will never enjoy her alluring body unless he can first win her elusive heart.

_51920-8 $4.99 US/$5.99 CAN

Dorchester Publishing Co., Inc.
65 Commerce Road
Stamford, CT 06902

Please add $1.75 for shipping and handling for the first book and $.50 for each book thereafter. NY, NYC, PA and CT residents, please add appropriate sales tax. No cash, stamps, or C.O.D.s. All orders shipped within 6 weeks via postal service book rate. Canadian orders require $2.00 extra postage and must be paid in U.S. dollars through a U.S. banking facility.

Name _____
Address _____
City _____ State _____ Zip _____
I have enclosed $_____ in payment for the checked book(s).
Payment <u>must</u> accompany all orders. ☐ Please send a free catalog.

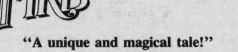